ONE WEEK IN AUGUST

August, 1955. Janice Butler is working as a waitress at her mother's Blackpool boarding house before she heads off to university. When Val and Cissie, both from Walker's woollen mill in Halifax, come to stay for a week, the three young women form an instant friendship. They attend a local dance at the Winter Gardens, which changes all their lives, both for better and for worse. Romance beckons for all three girls but can a holiday fling ever lead to something deeper? As autumn approaches, the three friends discover that life doesn't always turn out as one would expect and the course of true love never did run smooth...

ONE WEEK IN AUGUST

ONE WEEK IN AUGUST

by

Margaret Thornton

Magna Large Print Books
Long Preston, North Yorkshire,
BD23 4ND, England.

British Library Cataloguing in Publication Data.

A catalogue record of this book is
available from the British Library

ISBN   978-0-7505-4444-3

First published in Great Britain 2015 by
Severn House Publishers Ltd.

Cover illustration © Elisabeth Ansley/Arcangel by arrangement with
Arcangel Images Ltd.

Published in Large Print 2017 by arrangement with
Severn House Publishers Limited

Magna Large Print is an imprint of Library Magna Books Ltd.

Printed and bound in Great Britain by
T.J. (International) Ltd., Cornwall, PL28 8RW

ONE

'Are we fully booked for August, Mum? I know it's been a good season so far, hasn't it?'

Lilian Butler looked questioningly at her daughter, Janice, as she answered her. 'Yes, it's been very good, love, and I'm pleased to say we're fully booked for August...'

Janice had very little to do with the running of the small hotel. Lilian liked to refer to her business as a hotel rather than a boarding house, which was what her late mother had always called it. Lilian had made sure that her daughter would never be involved in the business as she had been forced to be from an early age. No, Janice had been encouraged to work hard at school and concentrate on her studies. And she had done so. She was now awaiting the results of her A level exams, and in September she would be going off to university.

'Why do you want to know?' Lilian asked her now. 'I'm not going to ask you to give up your bedroom, if that's what you're thinking.'

'Of course I'm not thinking that, Mum, you've never done that. No, I was wondering if I could help in some way. I'd love to be a waitress. I've never minded washing up – you know that – but I'd like to do something else as well.'

'Oh, there's no need, love, really there isn't,' replied Lilian. 'Olive and Nancy are very capable waitresses, and they help out in other ways as

9

well. No, you enjoy your holiday while you can. You'll be off to college soon, so you might as well make the most of your freedom.'

'But I'm bored, Mum! Some of my friends have got jobs for the season. Susan's working at Marks and Spencer's, and Jean and Kath have got jobs in big hotels on the prom, so I don't see them very much. But you didn't want me to get a job, did you? So why don't you let me help out here? I know Olive and Nancy are rushed off their feel sometimes. I've heard Olive complaining about her swollen ankles and–'

'Oh, all right then!' Lilian sighed, but she smiled at her daughter. 'I'll think about it. But we've enough people working for us, in one way or another. That's why I've never wanted you to be part of it, nor your dad...'

This conversation was taking place one evening towards the end of July of 1955, in the large kitchen at the rear of the hotel. The washing-up – a mammoth task – following the evening meal had been done, with Janice helping as she did nearly every evening, along with Olive and Nancy. This was one job that Lilian allowed her daughter to do. And the waitresses were worth their weight in gold, as Lilian often remarked. Not only did they serve the guests at meal times; they came in each Saturday, which was known as 'change-over day', when the beds were changed in readiness for the next lot of visitors. And they arrived early each morning to serve the breakfasts, and had never been late. Both of them were in their forties, with husbands and children who were in their late teens or married. They were glad to earn some money to help with the household expenses, and to give them a bit of independence, without having to travel far to their place of work.

Lilian reflected now, though, that it might not be a bad idea to have a younger person helping them. They were both attractive enough and were always clean and tidy, but Janice ... well, her mother had to admit that she was a lovely-looking girl and was always so bright and cheerful. So Lilian told her that she really would consider it. She was rewarded by a quick hug and a kiss on the cheek.

'Thanks, Mum. I'll work hard, and I'll get up early for the breakfasts. I'll go up and read for a while now, and leave you to watch *Emergency Ward Ten*.'

Lilian joined her husband, Alec, in the family living room where he was hidden behind the *Blackpool Evening Gazette*. He put down his paper and smiled at her. 'All done and dusted, love?'

'Yes, thank goodness! I really think washing up is the worst chore of all. I've been thinking, Alec, we should get one of those dish-washing machines. It would be a real godsend, I'm sure.'

'Then why don't you?' said her husband. 'We can afford it, can't we? You've said we've been nearly fully booked all season, so you might as well get all the mod cons you need.' He laughed. 'Just listen to me, "We're fully booked!" As though I had anything to do with it! It's your business, Lilian, and you make a damned good job of it an' all.'

'I couldn't do it without your support, Alec. You're always there when I need you. You do all the odd jobs, and move the furniture around,

11

things that women can't do very well. And you know that I made it quite clear to Mother when you first came here that you were to have no part in the running of the boarding house. That's one place where I did put my foot down. You'd already given up your job and moved here so that we could get married. And I made sure we had our own rooms as well; a bedroom for us and one each for our Janice and Ian when they came along. I never knew where I'd be sleeping next when I was a kiddie, and our Len as well. We shared a room until ... well, until long after the age when we should have had our own rooms. And many a time at the height of the season we had to sleep on the floor; well, on a mattress, in any odd corner where there was room.'

'Never mind, love,' said Alec. 'Those days are over now. I know you still work jolly hard, but you're no longer the slave that you used to be for your mother, are you? You're able to please yourself and do things the way you want to. So you go ahead and get that dishwasher and anything else you want.'

Lilian nodded. 'Yes I think I will... Janice has just asked me if she can help out as a waitress; and I've more or less said that she can. What do you think?'

'I think that's a great idea, love. Good for her! These school holidays are so long and the kids get bored... Where's our Ian, by the way?'

'He's off playing football with his mates. You can't really say he gets bored; he's always out and about somewhere. But Janice says she's a bit fed up at the moment with her friends working, and

12

she's no need to do any more studying, not yet.'

'Well, you let her be a waitress then. You can be sure she'll go down well with the visitors. But make sure you pay her a reasonable wage. She'll need a bit of extra cash when she goes off to college.'

'Yes, you can be sure I'll do that. I was working for peanuts when I was her age. Mother seemed to imagine I didn't need paying when I was getting my bed and board.'

Alec chuckled. 'Yes, but I made her change her tune when I came to live here, didn't I? She wasn't such a bad old girl, your mother, all things considered. I managed to get on the right side of her, though God knows how I did it!'

'She was relieved that you weren't carrying me off to live in Burnley, wasn't she pleased that you'd decided to come and live here? Of course, I could have defied her and left home; I was well turned twenty-one. But it was hard – well, impossible – to say no to my mother...'

Florence Cartwright, always known as Florrie, had moved to Blackpool from Wigan in the spring of 1919 with her two children, Lilian, then aged nine, and Leonard, aged seven. She had been widowed in the Great War, like so many of her generation. But Florrie had never been one to give way and feel sorry for herself, or let the grass grow under her feet. She had a little money put by, earned during the long hours she had worked at the cotton mill, and with a little help from her parents she was able to scrape together enough money to put down a deposit on a boarding house

13

in Blackpool. She had enjoyed a couple of holidays and day trips to the seaside town, as had many of her friends at the mill.

In 1919, in the aftermath of the dreadful war, Blackpool was the place to be to recapture some of the fun and gaiety of the prewar days. The introduction of cheap railway excursions meant that ordinary working folk were able to afford a few days' holiday, and motor charabancs, too, were becoming a popular means of travel.

The boarding house where the Cartwright family came to live was in Blackpool's North Shore, in a long street of similar three-storeyed buildings, adjacent to the promenade. There were fifteen bedrooms, including the attic rooms, one of which was assigned to Lilian and Leonard. It was a mid-Victorian dwelling with none of the facilities that the owners and the visitors now took for granted in the mid-fifties. There was no bathroom and only one indoor toilet, known as the WC, on the first landing; plus another lavatory outside at the bottom of the backyard.

There was no running water in the bedrooms, only a large jug and bowl on a washstand in each room (with a chamber pot, known as a 'guzzunder', on the bottom shelf of the stand). Hot water had to be carried up to each room every morning, and then, later, the slops had to be emptied. There was running water downstairs, of course, heated by a coal fire in the kitchen range, then, later, by a geyser.

Victorian families had been visiting Blackpool throughout the nineteenth century and even before that time, often returning year after year to

14

the same house. In those days they were usually referred to as lodging houses. The landladies – they were invariably women who were in charge of the houses – worked long hours from early dawn till dusk. Not only did they take care of their visitors' ablutions, they also cleaned their shoes and cooked a vast variety of food stuffs brought in each day by the separate families. There was a nominal charge each day for milk and potatoes, and some landladies even charged extra for the use of a cruet. This was something that Florrie Cartwright had never done. By the time she took over the boarding house the rule of charging for the cruet had come to be regarded as a music hall joke.

There were many of the old Victorian ways, though, that were still being adhered to. Every available bed was filled during the summer season, visitors sometimes sleeping three to a bed, but no one ever complained. Lilian, nine years old at the time, remembered those days very well, more so than her brother, Leonard. It was taken for granted that Lilian, on leaving school, would work full time in the boarding house, but Florrie had had no such plans for Leonard. She had agreed that he should do as he wished and start work as an apprentice at a local garage. He had been fascinated by this newish form of transport ever since he was a tiny boy. Now, in 1955, he had his own business, a thriving garage on the outskirts of Blackpool, on the road leading to Poulton-le-Fylde.

Lilian had enjoyed going to school. She was a clever girl, always near to the top of the class, and she had not wanted to leave. But she had been given no choice in the matter, there was a ready-made 'career' waiting for her. Some of her friends were in the same position, many of them were the daughters of landladies. Other girls were going to work in shops or offices in the town, to learn the skills of typing and shorthand, and some were going on to further study, maybe to train eventually as teachers or nurses. Lilian had never really considered what her chosen career might have been, had she been given the choice. She was catapulted at fourteen into boarding-house work: cooking, cleaning, mending, shopping, washing, ironing... She was paid little more than the spending money she had been given as a child, although her mother did still buy – and usually chose – the clothes she wore.

During this period, until the early 1930s, the boarding houses were run largely on the old lodging house system, with visitors bringing, then buying their own food each day. But this was gradually phased out until, by the late 1930s, the visitors were enjoying 'Bed and full board'. This tariff consisted of a cooked breakfast, a midday dinner, and a meal at around five thirty known as 'high tea'.

It must be said, in all fairness, that Florrie did employ extra help to assist with the many and varied chores. There were two full-time chamber maids and a cleaning woman who came once a week to do the rough housework.

Florrie did all the cooking, following the skills she had learnt from her mother. The job came naturally to her and she did not find it arduous, although it was tricky, to say the least, juggling

16

with the various foods that the visitors brought in to be cooked to their special requirements. A young girl who had just left school was employed as a scullery maid to help with the menial tasks: peeling potatoes, preparing vegetables and coping with the endless round of washing up.

So when Lilian left school there were three of them working in the kitchen. Lilian was trained, by her mother, in the art of cooking. Florrie, though largely self-taught, conjured up palatable meals from the most basic ingredients. Lilian was a quick learner and, on the whole, she enjoyed the work. It was best not to think of the lost opportunities, the various paths that she might have followed if she had been allowed to please herself.

Her mother did allow her a certain amount of freedom. She had a half-day off each week when she could look round the shops and treat herself to something to wear from the small allowance she was paid; or she could walk along the promenade or the North Pier, which was near to the boarding house, enjoying the fresh sea air and the bracing Blackpool breezes. She had a few friends from her school days and they occasionally visited the cinema or went dancing at the Winter Gardens or the Tower Ballroom. But visiting the dance halls was something that Lilian was not allowed to do until she had reached the age of eighteen.

It was in 1930, when she was twenty years of age, that Lilian met Alec Butler. He came, with two friends, as a visitor to the boarding house. The three young men were from the Lancashire town of Burnley where they were all employed in a cotton mill. Alec had progressed from his first

17

job as a weaver and was now an overlooker – often referred to as a tackler – in charge of a weaving shed.

The twenty-two-year-old Alec was immediately attracted to the pretty dark-haired young woman who served their meals. In addition to her work in the kitchen Lilian also waited on the guests at meal times along with the current scullery maid. They quickly discarded their working overalls and donned white aprons. Alec soon discovered that she was the daughter of Mrs Cartwright the proprietor, and he lost no time in asking her to accompany him to the cinema.

Florrie had no objection to this. She soon summed up Alec as a nice, well-brought-up young man, and she watched with interest as the two of them became friendlier over the week that the lads were staying there. He had certainly brought a sparkle to Lilian's eyes and a rosy glow to her cheeks. That would be the end of it, though, she surmised, when the trio returned to Burnley.

But that was not the case. Alec returned to Blackpool in the autumn to see the famous Illuminations and, of course, to renew his friendship with Lilian. They had been writing to one another at least once a fortnight. Their relationship progressed as Alec continued to visit Blackpool each year, and Lilian was allowed, when the season ended, to visit Alec and his family in Burnley.

Florrie was not surprised – in fact she was quite pleased – when they became engaged when Lilian was twenty-two. He was a grand lad, she told her neighbours, she couldn't have wished for a nicer young man for her only daughter. She had not given much thought to where the young couple would live after their marriage. At all events Lilian's work was there, in the boarding house, and she could not be spared. Her daughter tentatively explained that Alec had a very good job in the mill with every chance of promotion. But Florrie was deaf to her daughter's words and refused to even discuss the matter. Alec realized, eventually, that if he wanted to marry the girl he loved he would have to give up his responsible job and come to live in Blackpool.

They were married in 1934 and, after a spell of casual labour, Alec was employed by the local electricity company as a maintenance engineer, his work with the machinery in the mill having given him the experience he needed.

Their first child, Janice, was born in 1937, and their son, Ian, six years later in 1943, in the middle of the Second World War.

TWO

Although Janice had been brought up in a Blackpool boarding house she had had little to do with the work involved. She knew that her mother worked long hours and was often tired, but she always had time to spend with her and her brother, Ian.

Janice knew, intuitively, that her grandmother, Florrie Cartwright, was the one in charge of the business, but as time went on her mother, Lilian, assumed more and more responsibility.

Janice had been distressed when her grandma had died two years ago, in 1953. It had been a great shock to them all as she had very rarely been ill, but the years of hard work had taken their toll and she did not recover from a massive heart attack.

Her granddaughter remembered her as a short, stout woman with iron grey hair which she wore in a roll, often covered with a hairnet, and shrewd all-seeing eyes behind her steel-rimmed glasses. She was invariably clad in a voluminous cross-over floral apron, edged with red bias binding. There were jokes made about seaside landladies, reputed to be veritable battle axes – their caricature was pictured on hundreds of comic postcards – and Florrie fitted the image very well. But she was nowhere as forbidding as she looked. The same visitors returned year after year to the boarding house, which had a good reputation. She had treated Janice and Ian with love and kindness, although Janice had sometimes heard her mother grumbling to their father about Grandma's stubbornness and unwillingness to move with the times.

It was in the early fifties that Mrs Sanderson, who owned the boarding house next door, started referring to it as a private hotel. She had even given it a name, 'Sandylands', to the contempt and amusement of Florrie Cartwright.

'Did you ever hear the like?' she said to anyone who would listen. 'Who does she think she is? "Sandylands" indeed! It's nowt but a boarding house, same as this. I reckon nowt to these jumped-up ideas.'

'I think it sounds rather good, Mother,' Lilian had dared to answer. 'It's a nice play on their name, the same as a lot of people are doing nowadays.' There was a 'Kenwyn' across the road and a 'Dorabella' a few doors away.

'Well, we don't want any such nonsense here!' she had declared.

Last year, however, Lilian had given their house a name as well and had begun to refer to it in the adverts as a private hotel. Janice wondered whether her mother had done this to 'thumb her nose', so to speak, at Grandma. In fact their father, Alec, had said more or less the same thing.

'Your mother would turn in her grave!' he said.

'Not at all,' replied Lilian. 'Why should she? I've tried to think of a name that is a tribute to Mother and all the hard work she did.'

The name she had decided on was 'Florabunda'. 'It's using her name – well, a part of it – and Florabunda is the name of a rose, a rambling rose with lots of blooms; and Mother loved roses, didn't she? She liked to go and see the rose garden in Stanley Park, if she ever had the time. I thought of "Floravilla" at first, but I think the other is better.'

And as it was now Lilian's business they all agreed that it sounded nice and was quite original. Janice could not help but feel, though, that her mother had her tongue in her cheek and was having a quiet laugh to herself.

Lilian had also decided, now that her mother was no longer there to protest, that it was high time to change their tariff to bed, breakfast and

21

evening meal, instead of full board. Many of the smaller hotels were doing the same, giving the visitors the whole day to themselves, instead of returning at midday for a meal. Three full meals a day was quite an undertaking.

Janice scarcely remembered her early years in the boarding house. When she was two years old the Second World War had started. She could not remember that, of course, but she remembered it ending, in 1945. They had been given a day off school, and Pablo's, the famous ice-cream parlour in the town, had been giving out free ice cream.

She recalled little of her father, too, from those early war years. Alec was in his early thirties, far older than the majority of the army and airforce recruits, but he had joined the army, anxious to do his bit to beat Hitler. He had been stationed in Britain, though, the whole time, with the Royal Engineers, which was a great relief to his wife. Janice remembered him coming home on leave, probably from about 1941, and in 1943 Ian had been born. Only in 1945 were they able to settle down as a proper family unit.

Janice had enjoyed hearing stories of the war years from her mother. In the September of 1939, immediately after war had been declared, they had been obliged to fill the house with evacuees. Their quota had consisted of mothers – including expectant mothers – with children under school age. They were from Liverpool, where it had been anticipated that bombing would soon take place. But this did not happen and by the end of the year the evacuees had all gone back home, having had a nice holiday at the seaside, and leaving in their

22

wake, in many cases, soiled bedclothes, torn and scribbled-on wallpaper and cigarette burns on the furniture.

Following hard on the heels of the evacuees, RAF recruits doing their initial training had filled Florrie's boarding house to the brim, one batch following another throughout the war years. Janice had no recollection of the evacuees, but she did remember the RAF lads. Cheerful, noisy young men, forever laughing and joking as though they hadn't a care in the world. She knew now, of course, that many of them would not have lived to see the end of the war. Several of them, though, who had come through it unscathed, now visited their former billet as holidaymakers, with their wives and young families.

At the end of the war Florrie had agreed that certain changes had to be made to bring the boarding house more up to date, to suit the requirements of visitors returning for a holiday after almost six years of war.

A toilet was installed on each landing and washbasins in each bedroom. There were still no bathrooms for the visitors, just as there had been none for the RAF recruits. They had used the facilities at the nearby Derby Baths, and the visitors had to be content with the luxury of running water in the bedrooms, which was a vast improvement on the bowl and jug system, not only for them but for the landladies and their helpers as well.

Florrie had also agreed, after much persuasion, to have a bathroom put in for the use of the family. No rooms upstairs could be spared, so it was installed in an annexe, an extension to the kitchen at the rear of the house.

Janice recalled what a novelty it had been to soak in a porcelain bath with water running from the hot and cold taps. They had formerly used a huge zinc bath which hung in the wash house when not in use. It had to be placed on the hearth in the living room and filled with buckets of hot water heated by the coal fire. She had not been able to linger too long as the bath water had to be left for Ian when she had finished.

She had never thought about what her parents and her grandmother had done about their weekly baths before the installation of the bathroom. It was considered, especially by Grandma, that one bath a week was sufficient. But Janice had now managed to persuade her mother that a bath each day, or at least every other day, was necessary for personal hygiene and cleanliness.

Blackpool had soon got into its stride again at the end of the war, as the leading holiday resort in the north of England. Visitors returned in their hundreds and thousands. Some, indeed, had continued to holiday there even in wartime, despite the warnings on the propaganda posters, 'Is your journey really necessary?'

Blackpool had been one of the resorts where there was no threat of invasion. On the south and east coasts, nearer to the mainland of Europe, the beaches had been covered with stretches of barbed wire and made inaccessible to the public. There were no such restrictions in Blackpool, and wartime visitors cheerfully accepted the shortages of food and fuel. The town had lost little of its gaiety,

24

the dance halls and the many cinemas remaining open throughout the conflict.

The famous Illuminations were switched on again in 1949, on a much larger scale than before. The landladies and hotel proprietors rejoiced at the lengthening of their holiday season. They were now able to open from Easter until the beginning of November. Some of the larger hotels were open all year round, and many of the others opened up again for a Christmas break.

Nineteen fifty-five was proving to be a memorable year for Blackpool. What would long be remembered as the highlight of the year had taken place on the 23rd of April, when the Queen and the Duke of Edinburgh had visited the town to attend a Royal Variety Performance at the Opera House. It was the first time that such an event had taken place outside of London, and it was regarded as a feather in the cap for the northern seaside resort, so often the subject of jokes by those who lived in the south.

Janice had stood with her friends in the centre of the town amongst a vast crowd of excited people, cheering and waving flags as the black limousine drove slowly along the road. There where gasps of delight and whispers of 'Isn't she lovely!' as they set eyes on the young queen. She was, indeed, beautiful; as lovely as any film star in her ermine stole and dazzling coronet, with her handsome husband at her side.

And what a lavish entertainment was in store for them once they arrived at the Opera House. It had been widely advertised in the local paper, telling which stars had been chosen to perform for Her Majesty. Among them were many who were already well known in Blackpool from their appearances year after year in the season shows. Morecambe and Wise, Arthur Askey, George Formby, Alma Cogan, the Tiller Girls, and children from the Tower Ballet, a show that was put on each year in the Tower Ballroom by children from the local dancing schools.

Then the crowds of folk had turned away to go back home, Janice and her friends to a coffee bar in the town. The special performance was not for the hoi polloi, but for an audience of VIPs and for the lucky few who had been able to procure a ticket. The event had been talked about for long afterwards, throughout the glorious summer. The sun had shone all through June and July, and now, in August, there was no sign of an end to the brilliant weather.

Janice was looking forward to starting work as a waitress on the first Saturday in August. This was the Bank Holiday weekend, when most of the hotels and boarding houses in the town would be filled to capacity. She had persuaded her mother that she must be dressed just as the other waitresses were dressed, in a black skirt and white blouse, and a white waist apron with a frill of broderie anglais.

She was giving far more thought to, and feeling far more excited about, this, her first foray into a job of any kind, than she was about going to university in September. It had been taken for granted by her parents and her schoolteachers that this was what she would do, and Janice had fallen in with their plans for her. She was a clever girl and had always done well in the school exams. Studying came easily to her, and she was able to retain facts in her head, a very necessary skill for the A levels she had taken a couple of months ago. But she was by no means a 'swot' – such serious-minded girls were often ridiculed by less able pupils – and she had always been a popular member of her peer group.

Janice knew that her parents were very proud of her, and ambitious for her as well. She knew that her mother had been obliged to leave school at fourteen to work with Grandma in the boarding house, and that her father, too, had left behind a job with prospects to marry the girl he loved.

This was the main reason that Janice had gone along with her parents' wishes. She had been accepted at Leeds University, depending on her A level results, but they were more or less a foregone conclusion. She would be reading English Literature, which had always been her favourite subject, but she had given little thought what her eventual career might be. She had an idea that she might like to be a librarian, or to go into publishing … but that was a long time in the future. Only three years, in point of fact, but Janice's thoughts were very much in the present.

She started work, full of enthusiasm, on the first Saturday in August. Her first appearance as a waitress would be at the evening meal, serving the new visitors who had arrived that day. Those who were leaving – apart from a retired couple who were staying for a fortnight – would be departing after breakfast. Janice was not serving at that meal, but she was up bright and early ready to help her mother, and Nancy and Olive, with the other jobs that awaited their attention.

It being 'change over day' all the beds had to be stripped and made up again with clean sheets and pillow cases. Fresh towels were required as well, and a new tablet of soap on each washbasin, which would be made sparkling clean again with a touch of Vim. The dusting and polishing, and the 'hoovering' of the rooms was done on a different day by two cleaning ladies. Another necessary boon was that all the bed linen and towels were collected each week by the laundry van and returned a few days later in pristine condition.

When the bedrooms were finished Nancy and Olive went home for the rest of the morning and the afternoon, and would return to set the tables ready for the evening meal at six o'clock. It was an early meal each evening to enable the visitors, if they so wished, to attend the second house – there were two performances each evening – at one of the many theatres in the town, or to go to the cinema.

Janice went into the kitchen in the middle of the afternoon. 'What are they having tonight, Mum?' she asked, 'and can I help?'

'We're doing chicken tonight,' Lilian replied. 'A nice traditional roast meal to start the week, and it'll be a roast again tomorrow, seeing that it's Sunday – roast beef and Yorkshire pudding; a lot of our guests are from Yorkshire – and roast potatoes and two veg, like your grandma always used to insist on. I shall do some of my more fancy meals, as your gran might have called them, later in the

28

week. And no ... I don't want you to help with the cooking, love. You've done your stint for the moment. You can help Nancy and Olive to set the tables when they come back. We're alright here, aren't we, Freda?'

'Yes, perfectly alright, Mrs Butler,' answered Freda, the woman who came in each day to help with the preparation of the evening meal. 'You go and get your feet up, Janice love, while you can. You'll be rushed off those little feet of yours when you're waiting on all those folk.'

'I'm looking forward to it,' said Janice cheerfully. 'OK, Mum, I'll see you later, if you're sure there's nothing I can do...'

'No; I've already said so. Go on with you! Like Freda says, you'll be glad of a rest once you start waitressing.'

Janice went up to her bedroom and made herself comfortable on the bed. She picked up the book she was currently reading, *A Pair of Blue Eyes* by Thomas Hardy. It was one she had not read before although she had read most of his well-known books. He was one of her favourite authors. They had studied his works for the A level exam, and he was on the reading list for uni. She would be reading the whole range of English literature during the three years, from the pre-Victorian era up to the present day.

She knew, when the time came, that she would enjoy the studying, although she was not too sure how she would feel about leaving and then living away from home. Some of her friends were looking forward to this, they couldn't wait to cut loose the apron strings and have a taste of freedom. Or so they said. They complained about their parents and all the dos and don'ts they had to endure. Janice considered that she was lucky with her own mum and dad and her home life. They allowed her all the freedom she wanted, although she probably didn't ask for very much. She had never wanted to disobey them or to stage a minor rebellion, as some of her friends said they had done.

If she went into town, to one of the dance halls, which was very rarely, or to the cinema, she was expected to be home by eleven o'clock. The youth club she attended at the local church finished at ten, and she always came straight home. The activities there, though, had begun to pall recently; playing table tennis, listening to records, and lessons in ballroom dancing in which only the girls seemed to be interested. She had been going there since she was fourteen, and most of the teenagers now were much younger than she was. Yes, maybe she was ready for a more mature way of life. At the moment, though, she had a job of work to start, and she was determined to work just as hard as the other women and to be as proficient and helpful as they were.

She spent much of the afternoon wool-gathering rather than reading, her mind all over the place. Her friends who were working in hotels on the prom didn't appear to be enjoying it very much; they were just doing it for the money and they were treated as minions by the permanent staff. Janice had the advantage of familiarity with her surroundings and her workmates, but she would try to make sure that they looked on her as a co-worker and not someone who was just playing at the job.

Olive and Nancy, whom she had known for several years, did seem to take her seriously right from the start and were glad of her help. There were thirty-two guests that week, which was as many as the house could comfortably hold. The larger rooms were occupied by families and, where necessary, extra camp beds were used.

The first task was to set the tables for two, three, four or five. Lilian tried to give each group a separate table, as far as possible. Each table was covered with a white damask cloth, which was supposed to last for the week. This, alas, was not always possible, depending on the eating habits, especially of the children, but the tablecloths could be turned over to use the other side. Each guest had a white napkin in a silver ring, which they were supposed to put back at the end of the meal, a nicety that was often ignored. The silver cutlery had been in use for years but, fortunately, stayed shiny and clean for quite a while. The table mats depicted fruit and flowers and added a bright and colourful touch to the room as did the floor-length red curtains, a new addition since Lilian was in charge. It was a large and airy dining room with enough room to move about between the tables, and a partition separated it from the smaller lounge at the back. The view from the windows was not as interesting as that from the sea-front hotels – a row of identical houses on the other side of the road – but the guests were usually too busy talking or eating to notice.

Janice had, until now, only popped into the dining room from time to time. She almost – but not quite – gasped on entering the room full of people, all looking forward to the first meal of their stay. She took a deep breath and stepped forward, smiling brightly, to greet her first guests. She and the other two waitresses had their own row of tables to serve. Olive and Nancy had said how much easier it would be now, with an extra pair of hands.

The evening meal consisted of three courses. This was another of Lilian's innovations. When her mother was in charge there had been only two, but that was in the days when lunch – always known as midday dinner – was served, with high tea in the early evening. They were not given a choice of menu, such as was usual in the more prestigious hotels, but they were very rarely disappointed in the fare and there were few complaints. Children who were fussy eaters could generally be catered for, Lilian did her best to satisfy everyone's needs.

The first course that evening was tomato soup. Janice was soon to discover that soup was the trickiest of the starters to serve without mishap. It was piping hot, in a large tureen which was wheeled into the dining room on a trolley together with the soup bowls. The waitresses ladled it out then carried it very carefully to each guest, serving each one from behind their right shoulder, as Janice had been informed. Her heart was in her mouth, but she managed to do her first serving without any spills. They waited until everyone had finished before removing the bowls. In the meantime they stacked the trolley again with the items for the main course.

Several of the guests remarked on how tasty the

soup was. Janice did not inform them, of course, that it was not home-made. This was one instance in which Lilian, in company with many of her fellow hotel owners, cheated a little. The soup was a powdered substance which was made in several varieties – tomato, chicken, mushroom, oxtail – and was delivered in large tins. All that was required was the addition of boiling water but it was really very palatable.

The main course, the chicken, was served on hot plates. Lilian always made sure that the plates were warm – there was nothing worse than eating your meal from a cold plate. Slices of white breast meat were served, with a little brown from the legs and thighs for each person with rather smaller portions for the children. There were a couple of roast potatoes on each plate as well, but there were more for those with larger appetites in a tureen, which also held carrots and brussels sprouts. The tureen was placed in the centre of the table for the guests to help themselves. When Florrie had been in charge the whole meal had been dished out on to the plates, but Lilian had decided that this was a far more genteel way of serving – it was what one should do in a private hotel! In the posher hotels, of course, everything was served out by the waitresses – or waiters – from a large silver salver, but there was certainly no time to do that. Janice, Olive and Nancy did, however, go round with dishes of bread sauce, apple sauce and gravy for those who required the extra touches.

This course would take longer to eat and Janice sat down, to take a breather, on a kitchen stool.

'Come on now, don't say you're tired already,

33

are you, luv?' said Nancy jokingly.

'No, I'm not tired,' replied Janice, smiling back at her. It was true, she wasn't tired. 'Just a bit ... bewildered. But I'm enjoying it.'

'You're doing splendidly!' said Olive.

But there was little time to rest. The dinner plates had to be collected and the refuse – although there wasn't much – disposed of before the dessert course was served. It was apple crumble that evening – home-made – although Lilian had used Bird's custard from a tin. Who didn't?

Tea was served following the meal, in the adjoining lounge, most guests, being from the north of England, preferred tea to coffee. They served themselves to this from a side table, whilst the workers started on the mountain of pots to be washed. Not for much longer, though. Lilian had already chosen and ordered the dishwasher, which would be delivered and installed towards the end of the week.

Not all the guests stayed for the cup of tea. Many of them preferred to go out again and make the most of the sunshine, if there was any, or to take a stroll along the nearby promenade before the daylight faded. Some may have booked for a second house at one of the theatres and would have to walk the mile or so into the town.

After they had helped with the washing-up Nancy and Olive went home. They saw little enough of their husbands and families at the height of the season and took advantage of the leisure time they had. Lilian's family dined as and when they were able, sometimes before the visitors had eaten, sometimes afterwards, depending on the meal and the circumstances. Lilian made sure that they did not go short themselves and ate the same choice food as their guests.

Janice now, of course, was part of the staff, but Lilian had always made time for her husband and children to eat their meal in a civilized and un-hurried manner. Alec did a full-time job outside of the home, and Janice and Ian were ready for a good meal after a day at school.

It was turned half past eight that evening before Lilian and Janice had cleared away. Alec and Ian were not expected to help with the chores. Lilian thanked her daughter for the hard work she had done that day.

'It isn't really what I wanted you to do, love,' she told her. 'I would rather you made the most of your holiday instead of working here every hour that God sends. You must make sure you have time to see your friends. You will have a day off, of course, same as the others. And if you want to go out one evening...'

'We'll see, Mum,' replied Janice. 'Kath and Jean said they were going to the Winter Gardens to-night. I said I might meet them there if we'd finished in time. But it's too late now, and I'm not bothered anyway.'

'There you are you see! It means you can't go out...'

'But what about you, Mum? And you and Dad? You hardly ever go out, do you?'

'Oh, it's different for us, and we're used to it. We get out more in the winter. But I want you to be able to enjoy yourself.'

'I am enjoying myself, honestly. And when I

want to go out somewhere, I'll tell you. But just now I'm quite happy here, and I'm earning some money, aren't I?'

'Very well, dear. If you say so...' But Lilian wondered how long Janice would continue to look upon her job as a novelty, which was what she appeared to be doing at the moment?

THREE

'Only a few more days and we'll be on the train to Blackpool,' said Valerie Horrocks to her friend, Cissie. They were walking home together at the end of their day's work at Walker's woollen mill. 'Are you looking forward to it?'

'I'll say I am,' replied Cissie Foster, 'after the carry-on I had persuading Mam and Dad to let me go. Anyone'd think I was a kid of fourteen, not nineteen going on twenty. It's alright for you, your parents let you do as you like.'

'I wouldn't say that. They like to know where I'm going and who I'm going with, but they're not so bad, all things considered...'

Cissie and Valerie lived in the same street in the west Yorkshire town of Halifax, and were both employed at one of the smaller woollen mills there, owned by Joshua Walker and Sons. The two girls had long been friends, attending the same schools and leaving at the same time at the age of fifteen. Valerie was undoubtedly the brainier of the two, as they were both aware, but it had never made any difference to their friendship. It did mean, though, that they were employed in different capacities at the mill. Valerie worked in the office having started as a junior who made the tea and ran errands, but she was now an accounts clerk, dealing with invoices and letters to clients. She had gone to night school to learn the necessary skills of shorthand and typing.

Cissie worked in the 'burling and mending' room, having progressed to this after a time in the weaving shed. This job, dealing with the imperfections in the finished cloth – pulling knots and slubs through to the back of the cloth and mending broken threads and loose ends – was much more to her liking than the noisy clatter of the looms in the weaving shed.

Both of the girls' families had been employed at the mill for generations, the women as well as the men, fitting their working hours around caring for the needs of their families. Children had been destined to enter the mill on leaving school, just as their forefathers had done. Boys occasionally acquired scholarships and went on to further their education, but this was unheard of for girls of working-class families. A word from a relative who already worked there was enough to procure a relation a steady job. This was particularly so in smaller mills such as Walker's. It was a close-knit community and the workers were treated well.

There remained a distinction, however, between the bosses and the workforce, and, to a lesser degree, between the mill girls and the office girls. The latter were often regarded as being toffee-nosed, whether this was true or not; and the dero-

gatory comment, 'She's only a mill girl,' was sometimes heard. But after the Second World War there
was more of a feeling of equality, and Val and
Cissie were both contented in their allotted places.

'And what about your Walter?' Val asked now.
'You're lucky he's letting you off the leash next
week, aren't you?'

'He's not my Walter!' retorted Cissie. 'We're not
engaged or owt like that, much as our parents
would like us to be. I've not made up my mind,
and I'm not going to be influenced by Mam and
Dad. I know he's got a good job and he's steady
and reliable. And trustworthy, they think, if only
they knew! He's OK about me going away with
you, though, because he's off cycling in the Dales
with some of his mates.'

Walter Clarkson was in his mid-twenties, a few
years older than Cissie. He worked as an overlooker in the same mill, in charge of several looms,
and was looked upon by the girls as a 'sobersides'.
They all assumed that he would marry Cissie
Foster, as they'd been going together for a couple
of years.

'Mam and Dad and Walter's mam and dad,
they're all off to Bridlington next week. They
wanted Walter and me to go with them, same as
we did last year, but both of us had other ideas.
Like I said, he's going cycling.'

'What did you mean, Cissie, when you said "If
only they knew"? Isn't Walter the model of virtue
that your parents think he is?'

'Is he heck as like!' replied Cissie. 'I've had many
a tussle with him. He wants me to, you know ... go
the whole way,' she added in a whisper. 'But I

won't! Mam and Dad would have a fit, and so would his parents. I've been brought up to believe that you don't do that till you're married. Well, we all have, haven't we? Anyway, I don't want to. I don't feel like that about him.'

Val was surprised, to say the least. Walter Clarkson of all people! 'No, you're right, Cissie,' she said indignantly. 'I wouldn't either, not with anybody. Not that I've been tempted.' Val had had one or two casual boyfriends, but she had not met anyone whom she felt might be the right one for her.

They had reached the street where they both lived, a row of terraced houses sloping up from the bottom of the valley. 'Ta-ra, Val,' said Cissie, arriving at her door and taking out her key. 'See you tomorrer... At teatime, I mean. I've an early start in the morning.'

'Yes, see you Cissie,' said Val. She hurried along to her home at the other end of the street. Her mother would be preparing their meal, which they always called their tea, although it was more like a dinner.

Sally Horrocks, Val's mother, no longer worked at the mill, although she had done so at one time, since being a young girl. Her two sons were married and had moved away to other parts of Yorkshire. Her husband, Bert, worked at Walker's mill as a supervisor in the packing department. There were only the three of them at home now. Valerie, as the youngest child and the only daughter had always been especially loved and cherished, but never spoilt.

Val opened the door, calling out, 'Hello, Mum,

I'm back. There's a good smell, and I'm starving!'

'Aye, it's steak and kidney pie,' said her mother, appearing from the kitchen. She was a short plump woman and her round rosy-cheeked face was always cheerful. 'Sit yerself down, luv, and we'll have a cup of tea while we're waiting for yer dad.' Bert finished work at six o'clock and would be home in half an hour or so. 'Now then, what sort of a day have you had...?'

Cissie's welcome when she arrived home was not as warm as Valerie's.

'Is that you, our Cissie?' called her mother Hannah, when she heard the door open and close again. 'Get yerself in here and peel these spuds for me. I'm all behind what with one thing and another, an' yer dad'll be wanting his tea as soon as he gets in.'

'Give us a minute, Mam,' said Cissie. 'I'll just have to go to the lav and wash me hands. I've been working all day you know.'

'An' I've not exactly been idle either,' retorted her mother. 'You seem to think I do nowt because I'm at home all day. I work just as hard as I did in t'mill, washing and cleaning and cooking and tidying up after you. Get a move on now. We're havin' chips tonight with a nice bit of lamb's liver I got from t'butchers.'

Cissie sighed as she went upstairs to the bathroom. These houses, though small, did have a tiny bathroom and toilet combined, as well as an outside WC in the yard at the back. They were mostly privately owned, both the Horrocks family and the Fosters owned their own property,

40

which put them a cut above their neighbours, who still paid rent – according to Hannah Foster at any rate, who was rather a snob despite her humble upbringing. Cissie, in truth, couldn't wait to get away from home, but she was damned if she was going to settle for Walter Clarkson despite her parents' wishes.

Her mother turned round from the stove when Cissie entered the kitchen. She was a small sharp-featured woman with an almost permanently disgruntled expression on her face, at least when she was at home. She smiled, though, when she was in the company of friends, especially the Clarksons, whom they had met at the church they all attended. Millie Clarkson had persuaded Hannah to join the Mothers' Union, and Hannah's husband, Joseph, was a sidesman along with Archie Clarkson. The four of them were what might be termed pillars of the church. Walter sang in the choir, and Cissie went along most Sundays because she really had no choice in the matter.

'Have you seen Walter today?' asked Hannah.

'No, Mam, I haven't,' replied Cissie. 'Is there any reason why I should?'

'Don't take that tone with me, young lady! Every reason, I would say, when you're gadding off to Blackpool next week without him.'

'And what is he doing, eh? He's going away with his mates. I need a change, Mam, and no doubt he feels the same. It's our business any road; it's got nowt to do with you and Dad.'

'Don't you be so cheeky! You're not too big to get a good hiding!'

I'd like to see her try! seethed Cissie, her hands

41

in water, scrubbing the mud off the potatoes. There was silence for a few minutes, then her mother started up again.

'I'm still not happy about you going off to Blackpool with Valerie...'

'Why? What's wrong with Val?'

'Nothing really, I suppose,' said her mother grudgingly. 'She's a nice enough lass, but she never sets foot inside a church, does she?'

Cissie didn't answer that. If she did she would be tempted to say too much about hypocrites and people who pretended to be 'holier than thou'.

'Val's a good friend,' was all she said. 'You don't need to worry about us. And there's nothing wrong with Blackpool neither. It's no different from Scarborough or Filey.' She didn't mention Bridlington where her parents were going. Cissie thought it was a deadly place.

'You'd be better going to Brid with your dad and me and the Clarksons. But we've said you can go to Blackpool, so that's that, I suppose. It's all them dance halls, the Winter Gardens and t'Tower Ballroom. And all them bars and pubs. I've heard of such goings-on in Blackpool.'

'Have you ever been?'

'Aye, once, and that was enough for me. I prefer to stick to Yorkshire. You know where you are wi' Yorkshire folk...'

Cissie gave an inward sigh. Her mother had such a cock-eyed way of looking at things. Cissie couldn't wait to go dancing at the famous Tower or the Winter Gardens. And then there was the Pleasure Beach, and three piers, and all those cinemas and theatres. She and Val would have a

42

whale of a time...

Janice had enjoyed her first week's work as a waitress. Her mother wondered if it was just a novelty to her at the moment and that she might tire of the routine before long. But Janice felt sure she would not do so. At the end of the first week she had received a nice amount in tips from the guests. They had appreciated her friendliness towards them and her courtesy as she served them. Some of them knew she was the daughter of the proprietor, Mrs Butler, but Janice did not tell them unless they asked. She wanted to be regarded in the same way as Olive and Nancy.

In the middle of that week the dishwasher was installed, and when Lilian had got accustomed to its workings it was found to be a great boon, cutting down considerably on their work load.

'You must take your time off, same as the others,' Lilian told her daughter. 'Get out and spend some of that money you're earning. It won't be long before you're away at college, so make the most of your freedom while you can.'

Janice knew, though, that students did have a certain amount of freedom as well as the time spent in lectures. She had spoken to a few who seemed to spend a good deal of their time drinking and partying, but she did not tell her mother that.

'Yes, OK, Mum,' she said. 'I've said I'll meet some of the girls at the Winter Gardens on Saturday. We finish earlier, now that we've got the dishwasher, don't we? I bet you wonder how you managed without it.'

'Yes, so I do,' agreed Lilian. 'It has to be stacked properly, of course, and I like to wash the mucky pans in the sink, like I always did. But it's certainly money well spent.'

Janice had learnt a good deal more about the running of the hotel that week. Although her mother had not expected her to do so she had popped into the kitchen most afternoons to see what was being prepared for the evening meal. She helped with some of the work involved as she was at a loose end with her friends working, and tired of taking solitary walks along the prom. Besides, she wanted to learn more about the art of cooking. She knew that her mother had always been more lenient with her than were some mothers. She had not been expected to help very much in the house, except for keeping her own room tidy. When she was away at uni she would have to fend for herself more than she been used to doing.

Janice found that the menu her mother had planned was varied and interesting. She had always known that the family, by and large, ate the same food as the guests, but she had not paid much attention to the preparation. Meat was more plentiful now. It was incredible to think that food rationing had only ended the previous year in 1954, nine years after the end of the war. Food stuffs had gradually become more accessible over the last few years, and meat was no longer the luxury it had once been.

Whilst her grandmother was in charge of the boarding house the food had been well cooked, plentiful and wholesome. Lancashire hot-pot, shepherd's pie, liver and onions, sausage and

44

mash, and fish and chips. Meals such as these had been the standard fare, and they had always been well received. It had been a two-course meal, the main course followed by a pudding such as spotted dick, jam roly-poly, rice or sago pudding, apple pie and custard, tinned fruit and ice cream.

Lilian now served three courses, with a different starter each evening. She had attended night-school classes during the last two winters to learn about more adventurous and popular dishes of the present time. She watched cookery programmes, too, on the television, where chefs such as Philip Harben and Marguerite Patten entertained viewers with their skill and dexterity of hand.

Lilian's starters included pâté with fingers of toast, prawn cocktail, melon, grapefruit segments or a half grapefruit decorated with a maraschino cherry, or the ever popular soup. Some of Jessie's traditional meals were still served; Lancashire hot-pot or fish and chips, for instance. It was always fish on a Friday, to appease any guests who might be Catholics. The fish man called in his van once a week with cod or haddock fresh from the docks at Fleetwood, further up the Fylde coast, which Lilian served battered or coated in breadcrumbs. Then there was Coronation chicken – breasts of chicken in a white sauce, with mushrooms and onions, and a touch of curry powder, a dish made popular at the time of the Coronation two years before as a tribute to Britain's links with the commonwealth countries, scampi and chips, quiche Lorraine, steak Diane... And her gran would never have dreamt of serving baked ham with pineapple, of all things! Frozen peas, too, were a great time saver, instead of the laborious shelling of pea pods, and a crinkly cutter made ordinary chips look very professional.

Lilian had done away with the more stodgy puddings beloved of her mother. Her home-made fruit pies were served with cream instead of custard. She served lemon meringue pie (admittedly from a packet!), sherry trifle, fresh strawberries with ice-cream, meringue nests with fruit and piped cream, and cheese and biscuits as an alternative to the sweet dishes.

Janice was full of admiration for her mother's expertise, especially as she was largely self-taught. A thought passed through her mind...Who needed a degree from a university when one had a talent such as this?

FOUR

Walker's mill closed down during the second week in August each year, when all the workforce took their annual holiday. Many of them went to the popular seaside resorts in Yorkshire like Scarborough, Filey, Bridlington or Whitby, whilst others travelled further afield across the Pennines into Lancashire, to Blackpool, Southport or Morecambe.

It was not unusual to come across a neighbour from the same street, or someone who worked in the same weaving shed, when walking along the promenade. Many of the workers were creatures of habit, returning to the same resort year after year.

For Valerie and Cissie, though, it was quite an adventure to be going to Blackpool. Cissie had never been there, and Val had been taken there as a little girl with her parents and had only dim recollections of the place. They were both up at the crack of dawn on the Saturday morning, and their cases, packed and ready the night before, stood in the hallway whilst they waited for a taxi to take them to the railway station. A luxury for both the girls but a necessary one as neither of the families owned a car, and the buses would be crowded.

Cissie's parents were taking little notice of her; they were busy preparing for their holiday with their friends, the Clarksons. That family did own a car, and Hannah and Joe Foster were waiting for the large black Hillman to arrive at their door. Cissie's taxi arrived first, and whilst her father carried her suitcase out her mother placed a perfunctory kiss, more of a peck, on her cheek.

'Now remember what I've told you,' she said. 'Behave yerself in Blackpool and don't go getting up to any mischief.'

'No, Mam,' answered Cissie. She couldn't wait to get away. Her father wasn't too bad, but he usually took the line of least resistance and went along with whatever his wife dictated.

'Have a nice time, lass,' said Joe Foster. He pushed a ten shilling note into her hand, after making sure that his wife had gone back inside.

'Here's a bit of extra spending money for you. Don't say owt to yer mam, mind.'

'Thanks, Dad,' she said, quite touched by his gesture. She kissed his cheek, then they were off up the street to collect Valerie.

Val came out of the house with her parents when she saw the taxi arrive. Sally and Bert Horrocks were splashing out this year and going on a coach tour to the Cotswolds, which would be a complete change for them after their usual seaside holidays, and for which they had been saving up all year. They both gave Val a hug and said 'Have a good time', without any warnings about behaving herself.

'Well, we're off, Cissie,' she said, sitting down next to her friend. 'Isn't it exciting? Mum and Dad are getting excited, too about their trip. They set off tomorrow. I hope they have a great time, 'cause they deserve it.'

'At least mine have shut up about me not going away with them,' said Cissie. 'I'm jolly glad to see the back of them for a week, and Walter an' all ... although Dad's not so bad,' she added. 'Anyway, I'm going to forget about 'em all.'

They arrived at the station with plenty of time to spare for the midmorning train. It was a good job they had done so as there was a long queue at the ticket office stretching quite a way out of the station and along the cobbled street. There were young people such as themselves, and they spotted one or two familiar faces from the mill. There were families with excited children running around with buckets and spades, and more sedate couples waiting patiently.

The queue was quickly dealt with, and it wasn't too long before the train, which had started off in Bradford, arrived. The platform was crowded, but fortunately not everyone was waiting for that train. Val and Cissie managed to find a seat together, although many of the seats were already occupied. An obliging man heaved their cases on to the rack above their heads, then they settled down to enjoy the journey.

It was a through train bound for Blackpool North Station. As it was almost a three-hour journey both girls had brought sandwiches. Cissie had made her own with cheese and some left-over corned beef. Val's mother had bought boiled ham from the market to make sure her daughter had a tasty packed lunch, and she had added a packet of crisps and two wrapped chocolate biscuits which Val would share later with her friend.

The journey did not seem to take long as they chatted about their plans for the week ahead and, from time to time, looked out of the window at the passing scenery. When away from the crowded houses and mill chimneys of their native town they were soon travelling through the Pennine hills. There was a dramatic change in the landscape. Sheep grazed on the lonely stretches of moorland, and here and there was a greystone farm tucked away in the valley. Streams flowed down the hills, the water from which had once supplied the cottage industry which was the start of the woollen trade. This home industry, the livelihood of families working in their own little houses, had come to an end with the introduction of machinery and the building of the huge mills. The streams, flowing into the rivers and reservoirs, now served the vast urban population of the towns and cities.

Val and Cissie were leaving all that behind them for a week. The train crossed the border into Lancashire, the home of the cotton industry. They ate their packed lunch as they travelled through the mill towns of Burnley and Accrington, where the mill chimneys were just as prolific as they had been in Yorkshire. When they had passed though Preston they knew it would not be long before their journey came to an end.

'We must look out for Blackpool Tower,' said Val, as the train left Kirkham station. Luckily their seats were on the side of the train from where they would have a good view of the famous landmark. They could hear other people near to them talking about it, especially the children, who were having a game to see who could be the first to spot the tower.

When they had passed the next range of low hills there was a cry of 'There it is!' Just at the same time Val had spotted the structure of ironwork, looking no larger than a tall finger at that distance, pointing up into the sky.

'Hurrah! Hurrah!' the children were calling, jumping up and down on their seats, despite the remonstrations from their parents.

They alighted from the train at North station, the end of the line.

'Gosh! I don't want to carry this very far,' said Cissie as they struggled along the platform with their heavy cases. 'We'd best get a taxi, hadn't we?'

'I don't think we've any choice,' agreed Val.

On the station forecourt there were young lads touting for custom for their parents' boarding houses. But Val and Cissie had already booked their holiday at the Florabunda Private Hotel, proprietor, Mrs Lilian Butler. They had seen the advert in the holiday guide, and it seemed to be just what they required, promising a homely welcome to young and old, and the price was reasonable, too. There was a line of taxis waiting and a long queue of people as well. But in a few moments they had scrambled aboard a black cab and were on their way.

'I'll give you a hand with the bedrooms today,' said Janice to her mother on Saturday morning. 'I'm going out tonight, you know, so I'll do what I can to help out now.'

'There's really no need, love,' Lilian replied. 'It's time you went out; you haven't had a night out for ages. I'm glad you're going to meet your friends. And we're getting through in record time, aren't we, with this magic dishwasher? You don't need to help out this morning. Olive and Nancy are here, and we always manage.'

'But an extra pair of hands makes all the difference,' said Janice. 'Anyway, what else would I be doing? I'm tired of walking to the pier and back, and I don't intend to do any studying when I've no need to. No, I'll get my pinny on, same as you. Let's get cracking, Mum.'

Janice knew that it was jolly hard work on a Saturday morning, no matter what her mother said. All the beds to be stripped and made up again, and the rooms to be left ship shape. Most guests were considerate, but others left the room in a chaotic state. Towels flung around, grimy washbasins, dressing tables with spillages of face powder and lotions, and messy tissues all over the place.

The majority of the visitors would arrive in the afternoon. Lilian's husband, Alec, would help out then as well – he did not go out to work on a Saturday – giving the arrivals a hand with their suitcases; and Janice, at her own request, was given the job of showing some of them to their rooms.

The family snatched a quick lunch of soup and sandwiches at midday, and planned to have an early evening meal before the visitors were served. Lilian, Alec and Janice had started their meal at the kitchen table when Ian came dashing in.

'Am I late, Mum? Soree...' This was his usual cry, but Lilian was very tolerant.

'Yes, but never mind. Just wash your hands and come and join us. Had a good time, have you?'

'Yeah, great,' he replied, turning on the tap at the kitchen sink. He had been on the beach playing five-a-side football with his pals. 'There's more room on the sands on Saturday, with the visitors going home. And nobody to shout at us for getting in their way.' The beach at Blackpool was never referred to as such but was always called 'the sands'.

'Come on then, Morty,' called Alec to his son. 'Come and grab a butty before we've eaten 'em all. And I think there's a drop of soup left, isn't there, Lil?'

Ian was football mad, like most of the lads – and some of the girls, too – in Blackpool. Morty was the name given to the player Stan Mortensen, Ian's idol, renowned for his lightning speed and superb heading of the ball. Then there was the one and only Stanley Matthews, the international wizard. The Blackpool team had won the FA Cup in 1953 and this had been a talking point in the town ever since. Ian couldn't wait for the football season to start again at the Bloomfield Road ground. He had gone along most Saturdays with his dad, but would soon be old enough to go with his mates.

Lilian was proud of her two children. She watched them quietly now as they sat at the table chatting to one another. There was six years difference in their ages but Janice was always interested in listening to her young brother. Lilian knew that Ian would miss her when she went off to university, as would they all. They were not very much alike in looks, apart from a certain family resemblance. Ian was dark-haired, like his father, whereas Janice was fair, like her mother, although Lilian's hair was now grey at the temples. They both had brown eyes, though, like Alec. Lilian's were blue, but the brown strain was so often dominant in the children of such couples.

She considered she was a very fortunate woman. A good husband, two lovely children, attractive-looking – although that didn't matter too much – as well as being clever. Ian had passed his eleven plus exam and would be starting at the grammar school in September. And as well as all that she had a job that she enjoyed very much. What else could a woman wish for?

The taxi drew up in the middle of a street at a three-storeyed building with a small attic window, one amongst similar-looking houses on either side. But to Val and Cissie this house appeared very welcoming, more so than some of the others. The stone window sills were edged in white with what they had heard their mothers refer to as a donkey stone, a finishing touch that many housewives did not bother with nowadays. There was a gaily striped red and white awning above the window to keep the sun off the wooden bench below, although there was no one sitting there at the moment. Above the door was a brightly painted sign which read 'Florabunda Private Hotel', decorated with a border of roses.

The driver carried their cases up the short path to the door, which opened immediately. 'Ta-ra, you two,' said the taxi driver. 'Enjoy yourselves now. P'raps I'll see you again next week, you've got my number.'

A pleasant-looking woman, whom they guessed was Mrs Butler, stood on the threshold. She was a middle-aged person, though young-looking, with short fairish hair just turning grey, bright blue eyes and a welcoming smile.

'Hello,' she said. 'I think you must be Miss Horrocks and Miss Foster, though I'm only guessing?'

'So we are,' replied Val, 'but that sounds very formal. I'm Val and this is my friend Cissie. We're from Halifax.'

'Come along in then. I'm Lilian Butler, and this is my husband, Alec. He'll carry your cases up for you. And this is my daughter, Janice. She'll show you to your room.'

The husband was a slim dark-haired man who smiled cheerfully as he said hello to them. 'Second floor, is it, Lilian?' he said. 'Righty-ho then, off we go.'

The girl called Janice smiled at them too and said, 'Hello, nice to meet you,' in a gentle voice that sounded rather posh to their ears. She was similar in looks to her mother, though a little taller and a little slimmer, and her fair hair was longer, waving softly around her neck.

'Come on then,' she said. 'I'll show you where you'll be sleeping.'

There were three flights of steepish steps up to the second floor. The carpet looked new. It was dark red with a gold leaf pattern, toning well with the cream and gold embossed wallpaper. The dark oak bannister rail and the spindles were highly polished, and there was a pleasant aroma of furniture polish and a very faint smell of cooking, but not the cabbagey smell such as there might be in some guest houses.

'Here we are,' said Janice, pushing open the door for them to enter the room. Mr Butler had already deposited their cases, one on each of the two single beds. 'It's quite a nice room, and it's at the front. Not that that makes a lot of difference, but it's a better view than you get at the back, of dustbins and backyards. Further up on the third floor and the attic you can get a glimpse of the sea and Blackpool Tower, if you crane your neck!' She laughed. 'But I think you'll be comfortable in here.'

'Thanks very much,' said Val, and Cissie echoed, 'Yes, thanks. It's nice in here, isn't it, Val?'

Janice seemed to be a very friendly sort of girl, around their own age, Val guessed.

'Do you work here?' she asked her, 'I mean, is this your job, helping your mother in the hotel?'

'Well, not exactly,' answered Janice. 'I'm helping out at the moment, during the holiday. I'm going to university next month, you see.'

'Ooh, clever you!' said Cissie. 'You must be real brainy.'

Janice laughed. 'Not really,' she replied, a little embarrassed. 'It's just something that I'm doing, that's all. It's what my parents always wanted me to do, so they're very pleased about it.'

'And aren't you pleased?' asked Val.

'Well, yes, I suppose I am. I haven't thought about it very much. I'm happy at home, you see, and it'll be a big change for me. But I expect I'll be OK once I get there... Where do you two work?' she asked.

'Oh, we work at the mill; well, at one of 'em, don't we, Val?' replied Cissie. 'No, let me get this right. Val works in the office, but me, I'm just a mill girl. I started as a weaver.'

'Don't run yourself down, Cissie,' said her friend. 'She's got a responsible job,' she told Janice. 'She works in the mending room, putting right all the mistakes that the weavers have made in the cloth. It's an important job, and they only let the experienced girls do it.'

'OK, if you say so,' said Cissie, laughing. 'But we've always been friends, haven't we, Val? Ever since we were four years old and started school together.'

'That's lovely,' said Janice. 'I still have some

friends that I was at school with... Well, I'd better leave you to do your unpacking and get on with my job. I'll see you later at the evening meal. One of my jobs is waitressing, so I'll make sure that I'm serving your table. 'Bye for now...'

'She's a nice sort of girl,' said Cissie, when she was out of earshot. 'I thought she was a bit – you know – lah-di-dah, at first, but she's quite normal, isn't she, even though she's going to university.'

'Yes, why shouldn't she be?' answered Val. 'It takes all sorts, as they say. Rather her than me, though. I wouldn't fancy all that studying, would you?'

'Chance would be a fine thing!' said Cissie. 'No, I wouldn't swap places with her, though her mam and dad seem very nice. I'm glad to see the back of mine for a week. Now then, which bed do you want?'

'I'll have this one, where Mr Butler's put my case,' said Val. 'There's nothing to choose between them. Yours is nearer the window, but like Janice said, there's not much of a view.'

There was a row of similar houses across the road, and further along, a row of small shops. They were well suited with their room. The beds were covered with pink candlewick bedspreads, and the pink theme was echoed in the floral curtains, the carpet, and the towels on the rail by the wash-basin. Most probably there would not be a bath-room – they would have to be content with a good 'up and down' wash for a week – but there was a WC at the end of the landing.

There was ample room to move around without

bumping into one another. The furniture was plain light oak, the standard items that were produced when the war ended, plain and functional: a large wardrobe with a full-length mirror, dressing table, and a handy little cupboard between the beds.

'Come on, let's get sorted out,' said Cissie, 'then we can have a walk along the prom. I can't wait to see the sea.'

They hung up their summer dresses in the wardrobe, hoping that the creases would drop out. They had both treated themselves to a new dress from C&A in Bradford, when they had been on a spending spree there, something they did only a couple of times a year. Their clothes had to last a long time as neither of them, especially Cissie, had a great deal of money to splash around. They each had an accordion pleated skirt, and a fuller one in a dirndl style to wear with white or pastel shaded blouses. The new synthetic materials such as nylon and terylene were a godsend as they were shrink-proof and easy to wash, as well as being light-weight.

It was the same with their underwear which they put away in the dressing table drawers: nylon panties, bras and suspender belts, and nylon stockings which were now known just as 'nylons'. They hoped, though, that the weather would be warm enough for them to go without stockings. They each had a short nylon nightdress, and a can-can petticoat – which took up most of the room in the drawer – with frills of nylon net to make a skirt stand out.

After a quick wash to get rid of the grime of the

journey they were ready to sample the delights of Blackpool.

'Ready?' said Val. 'Let's go...' They giggled and hugged one another excitedly, then they set off for the promenade which was just at the end of the street, past the impressive hotel on the corner.

'That's where the posh folk'll be staying,' remarked Cissie. 'But never mind, eh? We're going to have a smashing time.'

There was invariably a breeze blowing along the prom no matter how brightly the sun was shining. It was not cold, though, just fresh and bracing, a change from the smokey pall that often hung over their native town. The salty smell of the ozone drifted from the sea, and seagulls wheeled around, screeching raucously above their heads.

The tide was in, lapping against the sea wall, so there was no chance of a stroll along the sands that day. Although it was not the sea and sands that the girls were particularly interested in. They had both – hopefully – brought a bathing costume in case it might be warm enough to lounge in a deckchair in the sunshine, but neither of them were swimmers. Besides, they had been told that the sea at Blackpool was always cold and not very clean either. But it would be lovely to see the endless sweep of golden sand when the tide went out. Seven miles of sand, it was said, stretching from Lytham St Anne's to the south of the town up to Fleetwood to the north.

'Shall we go on the pier?' said Cissie. They were approaching North Pier – there were three piers in Blackpool, North, Central and South – which was only a ten-minute walk from their hotel.

'Yes, let's!' replied Val, giggling like a child at the novelty of it. They pushed their way through the iron turnstile and walked along the wooden planking, their feet making a clip-clopping sound on the boards. Through the cracks between the planks they could see the waves splashing, and the breeze was stronger here, ruffling their hair and blowing their skirts around their knees.

At the end of the pier there was a theatre where, every year, there was a variety show called 'On with the Show'. It had been running for many years starring a comedian, Dave Morris, who had made his name in Blackpool. But that was only one of the many season shows in the town. The girls intended to go to at least one, provided they could get the tickets. They walked almost to the end, deciding not to venture along the jetty which reached further out to sea, where fishermen waited hopefully for a catch of whiting, the most common fish in that part of the Irish Sea.

They leaned against the railings, looking back at the miles and miles of promenade. To their right, to the south, they could see the other two piers, and on the opposite side of the tramtrack the Palace Theatre, and a little further along the Tower building with the massive structure reaching up into the sky. There was a lift making its ascent to the top.

'Shall we go up the Tower?' said Cissie. 'Another day, I mean. Ooh, there's so much to do, Val. We could do with a month, or at least a fortnight, not just a week.'

'Well, a week's all we'll get,' said Val with a laugh.

'Our money wouldn't last that long anyway. Just be content with what you've got, Cissie.'

'Oh, I am, really I am,' Cissie replied. 'I can still hardly believe I'm here. Gosh! What a lot of hotels. D'you think they'll all be full?'

The hotels stretched in a long line southwards as far as the Pleasure Beach, where they could just make out the undulations of the Big Dipper.

'Most of them are probably full during August,' replied Val. 'It makes you wonder, doesn't it? All these folks on holiday. I wonder if we'll meet anybody we know?'

'I hope not,' said Cissie. 'I've come away to forget all that lot at home. It'd be nice to meet a millionaire, though, wouldn't it?'

'What, in Blackpool!' Val laughed. 'They all hang out in Nice or Monte Carlo.'

'You don't know. There'll be some rich blokes staying at those big fancy hotels – like that one over yonder. Can you see it?'

It was the Imperial Hotel with a flag flying from a turret on the roof. On their left, to the north, there were many such impressive hotels. From their vantage point they could see the red sandstone cliffs on the lower promenade, reaching up to the tramtrack. They were man-made cliffs, in fact, Blackpool was entirely constructed by the efforts of man. It did not have the natural beauty of landscape such as could be found in Scarborough or Whitby. But Blackpool had grown and thrived, glorying in its popularity as the leading seaside resort in the north, if not in the whole, of England.

'Who's bothered about rich blokes?' said Val.

61

'I'm not! It would be nice, though, to meet some-body ... well, you know ... somebody that I really liked, and who meant what he said.'

'You're not still upset about Neil, are you?' asked Cissie. 'You deserve somebody better than him, Val. Just forget him.'

'No, I'm not still thinking about Neil. He's welcome to his little Fräulein, if that's what he wants. At least he told me, didn't he?'

'I never liked him. You're better off without him.'

'Just let it drop, Cissie. I've come here to enjoy myself. I know now that he wasn't right for me...'

Val's friendship with Neil Parker, a young man who was also employed at Walker's mill as an over-seer, had come to an end when he was in the army doing his national service. He had promised to write to Val, which he had done, spasmodically. Then he had been posted to Germany and had met a German girl. He had written to tell Val what had happened. He was sorry, but it was all over between the two of them. She had been shocked and hurt for a while, but consoled by the know-ledge that her parents had never trusted him. They had never tried to interfere, but she had known, deep down, that they were right.

'Sorry; won't mention him again,' said Cissie, tucking her arm through Val's in a matey fashion. 'Come on; let's treat ourselves to an ice cream from that kiosk, then p'raps we'd better be getting back. We're going dancing tonight, aren't we?'

'So we are. There's the Tower and the Winter Gardens. I believe they've both got super-duper dance floors...'

They bought their huge cornets then strolled back along the prom, looking forward to the delights of the evening ahead.

FIVE

'Hello again, you two...' Janice appeared at their table for two, dressed as a waitress in black and white with a frilly apron. 'Here's your soup. Hope you enjoy it, it's mushroom. Now be careful, it's hot.'

The soup was delicious, as was the tender chicken that followed. The potatoes and vegetables were served in a separate dish, a nice touch which made them feel like special guests in a posh hotel. After they had eaten the pudding, lemon meringue pie, they felt they couldn't eat another mouthful.

'That was super!' said Cissie, when Janice came to collect the plates.

'Yes, tell your mum how much we enjoyed it,' added Val. 'She's the cook, isn't she?'

'Yes, she does most of it,' said Janice, 'I know she's a smashing cook. I'm trying to learn, but it'll take ages before I'm as good as Mum... What are you two doing tonight? Going dancing? That's what most of the girls do.'

'Yes, that's what we were thinking of,' said Val. 'We can't decide, though. The Tower or the Winter Gardens. What would you say? I expect you've been to both, haven't you?'

'Yes, I go occasionally. I prefer the Winter Gardens; the Tower can get a bit rowdy on a Saturday night, so they say. As a matter of fact, I'm going to the Gardens tonight. I'm meeting some friends there ... but you can come along with me if you like. I'll be going on the bus. It stops just across the road, so I can show you the way ... that is if you want me to?'

'Yes, course we do, thanks,' said Val. 'Don't we, Cissie?'

'Yeah, that'd be great. What time are you going?'

'Well, when I've helped to clear away here, and got myself ready, I should say about a quarter to eight. Is that OK with you?'

'Yes, sure it is.'

'I'll meet you in the hallway then. Mum'll give you a front door key in case you're late back. She's not fussy about visitors coming in late, so long as they're not drunk. Oh, sorry! I'm not suggesting...'

Val laughed. 'No, we know you're not. We're well behaved young ladies, aren't we Cissie?'

'We don't get much chance to be any other,' added Cissie. 'No, we promise to be good.'

'OK, I'll see you later then.'

They met as arranged at just before quarter to eight, the three of them 'dolled up to the nines', as Janice's mum might say in their colourful summer dresses.

Janice looked appraisingly at her two new friends. The two girls were unalike in looks. Valerie was dark-haired with warm brown eyes, and slim with a small face and elfin features. Her friend, Cissie, was just the opposite; fair and fluffy would

64

be a good way to describe her. Wispy blonde hair framed a roundish face with big innocent-looking blue eyes. She was pleasantly plump, in contrast to her friend. Both of them, though, were very attractive girls.

Val was clearly the more sensible and steady of the two, the one who would take the lead, if Cissie would listen to her! Those blue eyes were probably not as guileless as they seemed. Their dresses were similar in style with full skirts held out by can-can petticoats. Val's dress was pink and white check with a large white collar, pretty and demure, such as the film star Debbie Reynolds might wear. Cissie's, also, was a full-skirted style in a bright floral design with a tight-fitting bodice which showed off her ample curves, and a halter neckline.

Janice felt that she looked just as good in her blue-and-white polka dot dress with the sweetheart neckline. She guessed that the other two girls, like herself, did not get the opportunity to dress up very often.

'Ready?' she said. 'You look very nice, you two.'

'So do you,' they answered.

They were all carrying white cardigans. 'I think I'll wear my cardy,' said Val. 'It might not be quite as warm now.'

'Good idea,' said Janice, and they all donned their knitted cardigans. 'We can leave them in the cloakroom. Handbags are a nuisance, though, aren't they? And you daren't leave them anywhere.' They all had a smallish bag, just big enough to hold loose change, a hanky, a lipstick, comb and powder compact.

'Off we go then,' said Janice, leading the way

out of the door then across the road to the bus stop.

Mrs Butler had given the girls a key each – Janice, of course, had her own – in case they did not return together. She knew young girls only too well and trusted they would be careful, but she did not have the authority to put herself 'in loco parentis'. She trusted Janice, and knew that she did not need to tell her to behave herself.

Janice found herself walking with Val, whilst Cissie came along behind, teetering a little on her higher heels. 'I always feel a little bit nervous, going dancing,' she admitted to Val. 'I don't often go, you see, and I'm afraid I'll be stuck there at the side of the ballroom like a wallflower. Girls dance together sometimes, but I always think it looks rather daft.'

'I feel just the same,' said Val, 'though I don't say so to Cissie. She's always raring to go.'

'Quite a live wire, is she?'

'When she gets the chance.' They were talking quietly, and Cissie seemed oblivious. 'She's got a steady boyfriend, at least he thinks so, but she isn't so keen.'

'And what about you, Val?'

'Me? No, not at the moment.' She laughed. 'What about you, Janice?'

'No. I went to an all-girls school, so there wasn't any chance there to meet anybody. There was a lad at youth club, but it fizzled out. He's away now, doing his national service, so that was that.'

'Yes, that's what happened to me, too,' said Val.

'What happened to you?' asked Cissie, catching

up with them.

'I was just saying that when Neil joined the army, that was that.'

'Good riddance!' said Cissie. 'Never mind. P'raps we'll all get lucky tonight.'

The cream and green bus soon arrived and they all got on. In less than ten minutes they were at the impressive entrance to the Winter Gardens. They paid their entrance money and entered the building through the Floral Hall which led to the various venues in the complex: the ballroom, the theatres, bars, cafes and amusement arcade.

'Gosh! It's like a park,' exclaimed Cissie, gazing at the palms in large pots, the ferns and foliage which adorned the hall beneath the glass roof.

Janice led them down a flight of stairs to the cloakroom where they stood in a queue to leave their cardigans in exchange for a little pink ticket, then went into the ladies' to powder their noses, refresh their lipstick and tidy their hair.

'Ready, girls?' said Janice. She led the way through the ornate Indian lounge, up a flight of steps to the Empress ballroom. Both Cissie and Val gasped with astonishment when they set eyes on the rich red carpet, the red velvet chairs and settees against the walls, the marble pillars leading up to the balcony, where more rows of plush seats overlooked the ballroom floor, an intricate design of highly polished wooden blocks in mahogany, oak and walnut.

Janice caught sight of her friends, Jean and Kath, at the pillar on the right-hand side of the dance floor facing the stage where she had arranged to meet them.

'Hi there,' she greeted them. 'I've brought two of our guests with me. Cissie ... Val, this is Jean ... and Kath.' They all said hello and smiled at one another.

'We've not been here very long,' said Jean. 'In fact, we've not had a dance yet.'

'Seems as though there's a lot of competition,' remarked Val. 'Gosh! I've never seen so many folk.'

'It'll get even more crowded later,' said Janice.

There were, it seemed, hundreds of girls and older ladies – though not quite so many of those – similarly clad in bright colourful dresses, many of them standing in groups around the ballroom floor, just as their little group was doing. There were lots of men there, too, young men in the main, although the females outnumbered them.

Janice remembered, during the war years, that Blackpool had often been described as a 'sea of air force blue'. The town had been a training ground for the RAF recruits. She vaguely remembered them being billeted at the boarding house. And now, ten years later, it could be described in a similar way. There were two large RAF camps in the outlying villages of Weeton and Warton, only a few miles from Blackpool, and this was where the national servicemen spent much of their leisure time. Indeed, they considered themselves lucky to be sent to such a place as the Fylde Coast with all the nearby attractions.

Many of the RAF lads were dancing and some were standing in groups. There were other young men, too, some dressed in conventional suits and ties, and others in more casual gear of sports coat and grey flannel trousers. There were also a few

Teddy Boys, standing quietly and not making a nuisance of themselves. The majority of them, in fact, were well behaved on the whole, although they had a reputation for being rebellious. They wore long single-breasted jackets with padded shoulders and velvet trimming on the collars, narrow 'drainpipe' trousers, and white shirts with a shoe-string tie. There was a group of them standing not far away from the girls.

'Don't stare!' Val admonished Cissie. 'You don't know what they might do.'

'They're harmless,' said Cissie with a shrug.

'How do you know? Look, there's one coming over. Now look what you've done.'

The lad with the carefully coiffed hairstyle, known as a DA, was sauntering across, making a beeline for Cissie.

'Care to dance?' he asked in a casual voice, and she took to the floor with him. The band was playing Bill Haley's 'Rock Around the Clock', and the other girls watched as Cissie tried to follow the rhythm in time with the lad's feet, which were clad in shoes with thick crepe soles.

'Trust Cissie!' said Val. 'I might've known she'd be the first one to dance. I hope we're not going to stand here all night like a row of wallflowers.'

'It's early yet,' said Janice. 'I know what you mean, though. We should try and look as though we're not bothered.'

They agreed that they would come back to this spot, provided they didn't get a better offer! Although they didn't put it in those exact words.

Cissie flounced back, not very taken with her partner. 'I kept falling over his feet,' she said. 'Is it any wonder, in those brothel creepers!' That was the name given to the heavy suede shoes.

Janice was feeling a little ill at ease, all of them standing around as though they were keen to get a fellow. Kath and Jean had decided to dance together. She was almost beginning to wish she hadn't come when she heard a quiet voice at her side.

'Would you like to dance with me?' It was an RAF lad, smiling at her a little shyly and uncertainly. He had a friendly face, glossy mid-brown hair – short, of course, in the usual military style – and grey eyes that were looking at her questioningly. Janice felt at once that he was a nice, conventional sort of young man. She said yes to him without any hesitation.

She wasn't an expert dancer but she could cope quite well with a waltz, and so, it seemed, could he. He put an arm around her and they started to dance to the strains of the 'Tennessee Waltz'.

He spoke after a brief moment. 'I'd better introduce myself. I'm Phil ... Philip Grundy. And you are...?'

'I'm Janice,' she replied. 'Janice Butler.'

'Hello, Janice, Nice to meet you.'

'Hello, Phil. Nice to meet you as well. You're doing your national service, I suppose?'

'Yes, that's right. I'm stationed at Weeton camp. Not for much longer, though. I finish in September, then I'll be going home.'

'And that is ... where?'

'I'm from Yorkshire, just outside Ilkley. I'll be going back to work with my father. He runs a guest house there; a sort of country pub.'

Janice smiled. 'That's interesting; quite a coincidence, really. My mother runs a boarding house – well, a small hotel, really – here in Blackpool. I'm working there at the moment, waitressing and helping out generally. And in September I shall be in Yorkshire. I'm off to university there, in Leeds.'

'I'm impressed,' he replied. 'What are you reading?'

'English Literature ... but I don't know what I shall do afterwards when I've got my degree. My parents are keen for me to go to uni, to have the chances they never had, Mum says, but I haven't made my mind up yet about a career.'

'I was training to be a chef,' said Phil, 'but then National Service broke into all that. I shall resume my studies, I suppose – just night school classes, you know – to bring me up to scratch.'

They were quiet for a little while, then Phil said, 'I'm glad I plucked up courage to ask you to dance. I had noticed you, and I thought you looked just like I was feeling. A bit unsure, and wondering what on earth you were doing here.'

Janice laughed. 'That's exactly how I was feeling. I don't often come here, not as often as some of my friends do, and I've come tonight with two girls who are staying at our hotel. So there were five of us standing around, trying to look nonchalant.'

'Yes, I know what you mean. I sometimes come here on a Saturday night with my mates, or else to the Tower – I like to listen to Reginald Dixon on the organ – but I'm not as eager for the bright lights as some of my mates are. Oh dear! I sound dreadfully dull, don't I?'

'Not at all,' she answered truthfully.

A discordant note brought the dance to an end. Phil smiled tentatively at Janice. 'Shall we ... er... I'd like to go on talking to you. And I don't want to dance all the time. Shall we ... would you like to go for a drink?'

'Yes, thank you. That would be very nice,' she replied.

They walked together to the corner where Janice had left her friends. Cissie was standing there looking rather cross, and Jean and Kath were just returning from their dance together. Val was nowhere to be seen.

'I'm just going to ... this is Phil ... and we're just going to have a drink together,' said Janice, feeling a little embarrassed. 'I'll see you later,' she added to Cissie. 'We'll go home together, the three of us.'

Cissie shrugged. 'Don't worry about me. I'll be OK.' She sounded rather peeved, probably because all the others had been dancing, but Janice felt sure she would not be standing there much longer without a partner.

Just after Janice went off to dance with the RAF lad, another young man came and asked Val if she would dance with him. She recognized him at once, but decided not to say so, not straight away. Better to see how it turned out. She was pretty sure, though, that he did not know who she was.

'Hello,' he said in a friendly way, as they started to move around the dance floor. 'I'm Sam ... Samuel Walker, but most people call me Sam.'

'Hello,' she said, rather wary of calling him Sam,

although there was no reason why she should not do so. 'I'm Val, short for Valerie, of course ... Val Horrocks.'

'Are you on holiday, Val?' he asked her.

'Yes, we only arrived today, me and my friend. We're here for a week.'

'The same as I am then,' he replied. 'I'm here just for the week... And unless I'm very much mistaken, we are both from the same neck of the woods. Am I right in assuming you're a Yorkshire lass?'

'Yes, dyed-in-the-wool Yorkshire, same as all my family.' She laughed. 'I can't really disguise it, can I? Not that I would want to.'

'No, why should you? There's nowt wrong wi' a Yorkshire accent,' he said, in a rather exaggerated way, although his voice, though somewhat more refined than her own, did have a trace of the northern harshness and flattened vowel sounds. 'I'm from Halifax, actually, and you can't get much more Yorkshire than that.'

Val decided that she must dissemble no longer. 'Yes ... I know you are,' she said, 'I'm from Halifax as well. I work at Walker's mill. I'm in the office there, but I realize that you don't know me. There's no reason why you should.'

He gasped. 'Oh dear! I'm so sorry. How dreadful... Of course I should know you; do forgive me.' He looked down at her – he was several inches taller than Val's five foot three – with a concerned look in his hazel brown eyes.

'Don't be silly,' she said, although she was aware that it was not the way to speak to one of the bosses. 'You don't come into our office, do

73

you? Only occasionally, maybe. It's your brother who sometimes deals with the correspondence. I've met him because he dictates letters for me to take down.'

'Yes, that's Jonathan's job, he has far more to do with the administration and the dispatching of orders. I'm more involved with the wool buying, and I'm out of the mill quite a lot. Anyway, I'm very pleased to meet you now, Val.' He sounded as though he meant it. He had a lovely smile and his eyes glowed with warmth. He was a good-looking young man – she had always thought so when she had seen him, briefly, and on rare occasions – with golden brown hair, almost the same colour as his eyes.

Val knew that there were two brothers, the sons of Joshua Walker who owned the mill. Jonathan was the elder, and the one who would take over the reins when his father retired, or so the employees assumed. Walker's was a smallish mill compared with many in the area, but it had a good reputation for high-quality cloth. It had been started by Joshua's grandfather, and handed down from father to son. The owners had always been renowned for their fairness and honesty; the workers were treated well and there were rarely any complaints. But the fact remained that Samuel Walker was one of Val's bosses, and she was conscious of that as she danced with him.

'Where are you staying?' he asked. 'I'm in the part they call North Shore.'

'Yes, so am I,' replied Val. 'It's a small hotel called Florabunda in a street just off the prom. Where is your hotel?'

'It's called the Carlton. It's on a corner of the promenade and Dickson Road. Very comfortable and homely; not too lah-di-dah, if you know what I mean.'

She laughed. 'Yes, I think I do. The Carlton ... that's the cream painted one we passed on our way to the pier this afternoon. So you're only just round the corner.' She stopped talking suddenly, in case he was thinking she was being too familiar, dropping a hint, maybe, about them meeting again. That, of course, would be out of the question.

He smiled at her. 'Well, that's handy, isn't it?'

She looked down, feeling a little embarrassed. Then she asked. 'Are you staying there with your brother?'

'Oh, goodness me, no!' he answered. 'My brother and I...' The music stopped at that moment and all the couples stood there clapping, wondering if the band would start up again. But it seemed that it was time for a short break. 'Let's go on talking,' said Sam Walker. 'I'm so pleased to have met you. Shall we go and have a drink?'

'Are you sure?' she asked, hesitantly.

'Of course I'm sure,' he replied with a chuckle. 'I wouldn't ask you if I wasn't sure. That is, if you would like to?'

'Yes ... yes, I would. Thank you.'

'That's great then.' To her surprise he took hold of her hand as they left the dance floor and they walked to the bar area in the adjoining lounge. 'Now, what would you like?' he asked as they sat down on the red velvet bench at the back of the room.

Val was nonplussed for a moment. She didn't often drink and was not sure what to ask for. 'Oh ... a shandy, I think,' she replied. 'Just a small one. Lager with lemonade ... no, lager and lime, that's what I'll have, thank you.' She had heard people ask for that, and it sounded as though she knew what was what.

He smiled. 'OK then, coming up. You stay right there, Val. I won't be long.'

Val glanced around at the others in the bar area, mostly couples, several of the men in RAF uniform. In a far corner she noticed Janice with the RAF lad who had asked her to dance. They were deep in conversation. Val wondered if she had known him before or if they had only just met. However it was, they looked very matey together. And what about herself, Valerie Horrocks, hobnobbing with one of the bosses from the mill? Who would have thought it?

Sam was soon back with her greenish-yellow drink in a small glass, and a pint of light ale for himself, brimming over at the top. 'There we are,' he said, sitting down next to her. 'Cheers, Val...' He lifted his glass and she did the same.

'Yes ... cheers,' she replied.

He looked at her quizzically. 'My name's Sam,' he said. 'Please call me Sam!'

'Oh, alright then. Cheers, Sam,' she said.

He smiled and nodded. 'That's better. As I said, I'm really pleased to have met you, and I'd like to know more about you.'

'There's not very much to know,' she replied. 'I've worked at Walker's mill since I was fifteen, that's four years ago. My father works there, too,

76

he's a supervisor in the packing department. And my mother worked there at one time. That's probably why I got the office job. I know it helps if you have relatives there.'

'Yes, my father believes in rewarding loyal service. But you must have given a good impression at your interview, and I'm sure you're very good at your job... Do you enjoy it? You can tell the truth, you don't have to pretend!'

'Yes, I do enjoy it,' she replied. 'Well, maybe enjoy is not the right word. It's rather repetitive; just facts and figures, but I know I'm good at it, though I say it myself, and I'm lucky to have a steady job with a good firm. I wouldn't like to think I'd be doing it forever, though.'

'No, I know what you mean, but I'm sure you won't be. Tell me other things though, not about work. Who did you come here with this week? You said you're with a friend.'

'Yes, Cissie, she works in the burling and mending room. She started at the same time as me. She tries to pretend she's a bit dim, you know, because I work in the office, but she's not at all; just a bit scatterbrained. We're good friends and we've known one another since we were in infant school.'

Janice, at the other end of the room caught sight of Val, and they waved to one another.

'Is that Cissie?' asked Sam.

'Oh no, that's Janice. She works at the hotel. Cissie and I only met her today, and she came along with us tonight. When I say she works there, I mean it's only just for now. She's going to university in September.'

'It seems as though she's got friendly with one of the RAF lads, unless she knew him already.'

'I don't think so. She said that she had a boyfriend, but it fizzled out when he went to do his national service. That often happens...'

'It happened to you, did it, Val?' Sam looked at her questioningly.

'Well, sort of...'

'And ... there's no one that you're seeing at the moment?'

'No. No one at all.'

Sam nodded, as though he was pleased at her answer. 'Yes, national service can cause havoc sometimes, getting in the way of relationships, and interrupting your training.'

'Did you do national service ... Sam?'

'Yes, I was called up when I was eighteen, in 1950.' A quick calculation told Val that he must be twenty-three now, four years older than herself. 'I'd started working at the mill. My father insisted that I must have experience in all the procedures before I was ready to be ... well, one of the management.'

'I would have thought you'd be exempt from the army, working at the mill?'

'No, not anymore. It was considered a reserved occupation for some, during the war, but not now. I must admit I enjoyed it. I served in Germany for a while. It was quite an experience, and I'm glad I didn't miss it. My brother, Jonathan, he didn't have to go. He's five years older than me, so he didn't fit into the age group. A pity really... It might have done him some good, knocked a few corners off him! He's not very good at mixing with the … er … ordinary folk.'

Val looked at him inquiringly.

'My brother and I don't get on too well. I was just about to tell you when you asked if I was with him this week. No, definitely not! He's in Scarborough with his fiancée and her parents. They're getting married next spring.'

'Oh … I see. And what about your father? You get on well with him, do you?' Val wondered if she should be asking such a personal question, but Sam was so easy to talk to, and he seemed to want to tell her.

'Oh yes, my father's OK. There's nothing pretentious about Dad, even though he's the head of the business. He's very much a man of the world. Well, you probably know that, don't you? He likes to be fair with his employees and treat them as though he really cares about them.'

Val nodded. 'Yes, he's always very pleasant when you see him.' Not that she saw much of Joshua Walker. He was a very busy man, but he made time to have a word now and then, to make his workers feel as though they mattered. She knew what Sam meant about his brother, Jonathan. She had never liked him. He was brusque and stand-offish. She felt much more at ease when he sent one of his underlings to dictate a letter rather than do it himself. She would not tell Sam, though, that she had no time for his elder brother. He had probably divulged too much already.

'So you've come away with a friend, have you?' she asked.

'Yes, two friends. Lads I was at school with; nothing to do with the mill, but we've always kept

79

in touch. We were at the grammar school to-gether.'

'Oh ... I thought you might have gone away to school?'

'To public school, you mean? No, as I said, my father's a pretty ordinary sort of chap, and he's not a great believer in social climbing. I think Mother might have liked it, but Dad put his foot down. Anyway ... that's more than enough about me. I know very little about you. What do you do when you're not at work?'

She laughed. 'What is there to do in Halifax?'

She realized as she chatted with Sam that her horizons were very limited. She had hardly ever travelled beyond the boundaries of Yorkshire. She had visited Blackpool before but that was the furthest she had been. She didn't doubt that Sam had travelled far and wide. He had been to Germany with the army, but she was sure he would have visited many parts of the British Isles and even further afield during his twenty-three years. She knew that the Walker family lived in a large house on the outskirts of Halifax, as befitted their status as mill owners. Her home, in one of the streets of terraced houses in the centre of the town, could not be more of a contrast.

She did not try to pretend that her life was wildly exciting, because it wasn't, but she was contented enough in her own way. She hoped, though, that she was not giving the impression that she was totally boring and unimaginative. This trip to Blackpool, she told him, was the highlight of the year, as well as Christmas, which was always a happy family time.

'Cissie and I go to the pictures now and again,' she said, 'and we sometimes go to a dance and social evening at the church she attends. I don't go to church very often,' she added, 'but Cissie's parents insist that she goes.'

Sam laughed. 'She has to toe the line, does she?'

'Her mother would like her to, but at least she was allowed to come away with me this week. That reminds me ... I'm neglecting her, aren't I?'

'I'm sure she'll be alright,' said Sam. 'She's big enough to look after herself, isn't she? Don't worry, though, I'll make sure you get back safely to your place, you and Cissie and ... Janice, isn't it, the girl from the hotel? Although she might have other arrangements.' Janice was still talking animatedly to the RAF lad. 'We'll get a taxi back to North Shore.'

'Oh no, you mustn't,' said Val. 'We'll be OK, honestly...'

'But I insist. Anyway, the night's still young. Come along, Val. Let's go and trip the light fantastic again. That is, if you would like to keep me company a little longer?'

'Yes,' she replied. 'Of course I would.'

'OK then, let's go.' He took hold of her hand as they walked back to the ballroom.

SIX

By the end of the evening Janice felt as though she had known Philip Grundy for ages. He wasn't pushy or flirtatious, just nice and normal and so easy to talk to. He asked if he could see her again – apparently they were allowed a fair amount of time to themselves – and she agreed that she would like that very much.

They spoke, too, about the time when he would be back at home, near Ilkley, and she would be at university in Leeds. Even after such a short acquaintance it seemed perfectly right for him to suggest that they should meet again in Yorkshire; and Janice did not feel she was being too forward in going along with the idea.

Sam Walker was as good as his word. At eleven o'clock he hailed a taxi outside the Winter Gardens building. His two friends who had been with him earlier obviously had 'other fish to fry', as he put it. Janice's new friend Phil, was very apologetic about not seeing her home. He would have to catch the bus back to camp or else it would involve a ten-mile or so hike!

When Val went to find Cissie she could see her friend was rather cross and disgruntled.

'What d'you think you're playing at?' she demanded of Val. 'You know who that is, don't you? It's Samuel Walker!'

'Yes, of course I know. Actually, he's very nice.'

'He won't want to be bothered with the likes of us. Haven't you told him where you work?'

'Yes, I've told him,' replied Val, feeling more than a little irritated. 'He's a very nice young man, and he's not snobbish at all. Anyway, I'm glad of a ride back in a taxi even if you're not.'

'Of course I'm glad, but I wouldn't trust him if I were you.'

Val guessed that Cissie was a little peeved because all the partners she had danced with had not asked her a second time. At least, she assumed that this was the problem.

Sam sat at the front of the taxi and the three girls sat at the back. Janice directed the driver to the 'Florabunda' hotel, then he would drive back to the Carlton on the corner where Sam was staying.

'Thank you for a pleasant evening,' said Sam, as the girls left the taxi, although his remark was really addressed to Val. He gave a slow smile and a suggestion of a wink in her direction, which the other two noticed. 'See you soon,' he said quietly.

'Yes ... see you,' repeated Val in a whisper.

'So you're seeing him again, are you?' asked Cissie, as Janice opened the door with her key and they all entered the house.

'Yes, why not?' asked Val, a trifle belligerently.

'You know why not!' retorted Cissie. 'You're asking for trouble and you can't say I haven't warned you.'

Janice looked at the two of them in bewilderment. 'What's all this about?' she asked. 'He seems very nice...'

'Yes, so he is.' Val nodded in agreement.

'He's only one of the big bosses from the mill!'

Cissie's face was pink with indignation. 'Samuel Walker. His father's Joshua Walker, the owner. She's playing with fire ... and she'll get burnt!'

'Oh, I see,' said Janice. 'You'll just have to wait and see how it goes on, won't you?' she said to Val, smiling at her understandingly. She guessed that Cissie was being awkward and argumentative because she hadn't met anyone 'special' as she and Val had done. 'It's been a good evening, hasn't it?' she added. 'Thanks for your company, both of you. See you in the morning.'

'It's alright for some,' grumbled Cissie, as Janice left them. 'I felt like little orphan Annie, standing there on my own.'

'Oh, come on, Cissie! You were dancing a lot of the time. I saw you with lots of different partners.'

'How would you know? You were gadding off with Lord Samuel! Nobody asked me to go for a drink with them, did they?'

'Well, don't blame me. It's not my fault!' Val looked at her friend's crestfallen face and put an arm round her. 'Oh, Cissie, love, we mustn't fall out about it! It's only our first evening. I didn't know I was going to meet ... him, did I? But it won't make any difference to you and me. You know that, don't you?'

'S'pose so,' said Cissie, with a shrug. 'I was really looking forward to this holiday.'

'And it'll be great, you'll see. Come on now, let's get off to bed. You'll feel better in the morning.'

Cissie said very little as they got ready for bed, and Val decided it would be better not to chatter. 'Goodnight, God bless...' she said, switching off the bedside light.

'Goodnight, Val,' Cissie replied. 'God bless... Sorry if I've been grumpy.'

'It's OK, forget it,' said Val. She would tell Cissie in the morning about her next meeting with Sam Walker.

Cissie seemed much more agreeable the next morning, more like her old self. They both tucked into their breakfast of porridge, followed by bacon, egg, sausage and fried bread, as though they hadn't eaten for a month.

'I couldn't eat this at home,' Cissie remarked, 'not that I get the chance, only once in a blue moon. I've hardly time for a piece of toast before I'm dashing off to work.'

'Well, we've all the time in the world now,' said Val, 'so let's enjoy it.'

'So, when are you seeing lover boy again?' asked Cissie in a cheerful voice, as though she really couldn't care less.

'If you mean Sam, then I'm seeing him on Tuesday,' replied Val.

'Oh, not till Tuesday? What's wrong with today?'

'He's playing golf today.'

'Oh ... I say!' mimicked Cissie.

'With his two friends,' Val continued. 'There's a golf course near Stanley Park. That's one of the reasons they've come on this holiday, to play golf.'

'So where are you going on Tuesday – do you know?'

'Sam wants to go to the Tower Ballroom in the evening instead of the Winter Gardens. But I told him that you'd be coming with us. I've no intention of leaving you on your own, Cissie. I shall only see him when it's convenient. It's our holiday, yours and mine. What would you like to do today?'

'It's Sunday,' said Cissie. 'I ought to go to church, but I think I'll give it a miss. A nice long walk along the prom, I suppose. I wonder if Janice will be seeing her RAF bloke? Let's ask her.'

Janice stopped for a chat when she came to clear the table. 'Yes!' she answered with a delighted smile when they asked her about her new friend. She told them he was called Phil. 'He's coming here to call for me this afternoon, then we'll go for a walk on the cliffs, up to Norbreck. I want Mum and Dad to meet him.'

'So soon?' said Val, rather surprised.

'Yes; why not? I don't keep secrets from my parents. Not that I've had any worth keeping so far!' she added with a smile. 'I have the feeling, somehow, that we'll carry on seeing one another, Phil and me. Especially as he lives in Yorkshire, not too far from where I'll be at uni, and he's being demobbed next month. I don't know, of course – I've only just met him – but it seems promising.'

'Lucky you!' remarked Cissie.

'It'll be your turn next, you'll see,' said Janice brightly, as she piled the pots on to a tray. 'What are your plans for today?'

'We haven't really decided,' said Val. 'We'll just walk around and do a recce of the place, I suppose. We were thinking of going to a show one night, if we can get tickets. Would you like to come with us?' Val and Cissie had already talked about this and decided it would be a good idea to ask Janice to accompany them.

'That's nice of you,' said Janice. 'Thanks very much. I haven't seen any of them this year. It will

86

have to be the second house, because of the meal time. We have the evening meal early so that visitors have the chance to go to the theatre or the cinema. The show at the Opera House is usually the most spectacular. So count me in, please. Which night are you thinking of?'

'Not Tuesday,' said Cissie, with a sly grin in Val's direction. 'She's got a date!'

'Oh ... that's nice. Any night's OK with me, Wednesday, Thursday... I'll probably be seeing Phil again on Saturday. Oh, you'll have gone by then, won't you?' The two girls would be leaving after breakfast on Saturday. 'It's such a short time, isn't it?'

'Don't remind us!' said Cissie. 'I'm dreading going back already. We'll have to make the most of it while we're here.'

'OK. I'll see you this evening then,' said Janice. 'Have a lovely day.'

'Thank you ... and you too,' said Val.

They walked in a northerly direction, past the large Imperial Hotel, to Gynn Square. Beyond there were the so-called cliffs. They did not have the scenic beauty of the cliffs in their native Yorkshire, near Filey and Flamborough Head; but the sun was shining, a gentle breeze was blowing, and the sea was ebbing, revealing a rippled stretch of golden sand. On the top of the cliffs the tableaux for the Illuminations, due to be switched on at the beginning of September, were already being erected, and strings of coloured light bulbs – unlit of course – were strung along the promenade.

Below them was the walled-in area known as the Boating Pool, most popular with the children.

There you could have an automated ride on the back of an elephant or a giraffe, take to the water in a paddle boat or rowing boat, or buy ice cream and pop from a stall with a striped awning. When they had walked as far as the Norbreck Hotel, a grey and rather forbidding-looking building, turreted like a castle, they decided to take a tram ride back to the town. Boarding the cream and green tram was quite a novelty for them. The driver tooted on the horn as it rattled along the track, swaying from side to side. They alighted at the North Pier, then crossed the tramtrack into the centre of the town.

All the usual shops were there – Woolworths, Marks and Spencer, Littlewoods, British Home Stores – and jewellers and fancy goods shops, all with tempting window displays, the majority of them closed, of course. The box office was open at the Opera House, however, so they booked seats for the three of them in the back stalls for Wednesday evening.

After a light lunch at a snack bar they walked back to the promenade, walking south this time to sample the dubious delights of the Golden Mile. There were stalls selling Blackpool rock, ice cream, candyfloss, 'Kiss me Quick' hats and cheap souvenirs, and hot dogs, oozing with fried onions, their odour lingering on the air all around. There were games and sideshows where you could win a horse race, throw balls at a pile of cans, play darts to win a teddy bear, or have your fortune told. Cissie was tempted by the amusement arcades where countless pennies were lost when the little silver ball failed to enter the hole, and sixpences, too, when the hand failed to grasp hold of a plastic toy or a useless trinket.

'Never mind, it's good fun, isn't it?' said Cissie, with her bulging purse now a good deal lighter.

They bought some Blackpool rock – bright pink mint rock, and pineapple flavoured in a lurid shade of yellow – from the most reputable-looking of the stallholders, although they had the whole week ahead in which to do so. Then they made their way back to the hotel to flake out on their beds until it was time for the evening meal.

Janice was bright and cheerful. She told them that she had enjoyed her afternoon with Phil, and was meeting him again later in the week. He had said he would phone her to arrange the time and place.

'Mum and Dad liked him,' she told them, 'so that's a good start. But it's too soon to be asking him to come for a meal. We're very busy here, any-way... Now, it's roast beef and Yorkshire pudding tonight,' she said with a smile as she brought their main course, 'just to make you feel at home!'

It was another delicious meal, and both girls felt 'full to bursting', as Cissie put it.

'Shall we have a stroll down to the prom and walk it off?' suggested Val. 'We should do, really, after such a big meal.'

'No, I'm knackered,' said Cissie, 'after all that walking we've done today. We can sit in the lounge and read, or just talk. There's nothing else to do, is there, with it being Sunday?'

The cinemas would be open, but both girls had been brought up to regard Sunday as a special day. Even if you didn't go to church regularly you had to observe the Sabbath day. After a trip upstairs to get their books – Cissie's was a film magazine and Val's the latest Agatha Christie – they took a peep into the lounge, but decided not to stay.

Two middle-aged couples were avidly watching a variety show on the television set provided for the use of the guests. They looked up, not exactly crossly, but the girls got the impression that they did not want to be disturbed. Television was still quite a luxury for many people. Some, the more go-ahead or affluent ones, had bought a set especially for the Queen's Coronation two years ago. On that occasion neighbours and friends had gathered together in the homes of the fortunate ones who owned a set to watch the great occasion.

'Oh, come on, we'll be frowned on if we do so much as whisper,' said Cissie. 'Let's go for a walk, like you said. It's just like that at Walter's house,' she told Val as they strolled along the promenade. 'Well, worse than that. When they've finished their tea his mam and dad close the curtains and light the standard lamp, then they sit there glued to the bloomin' television all night. You daren't speak or you get told to "Shush!" We go out, Walter and me, and we usually end up at our house. Mam makes a fuss of him and gets us some supper. She'll do anything for Walter. She thinks the sun shines out of his ... you know what! Anyway, let's not talk about him. I'm trying to forget about him this week. Time enough to decide what to do about Walter when I get back.'

When they returned to the hotel the TV watchers had disappeared. There was a group of four visitors playing cards and a few more sitting around reading or chatting. Cissie and Val sat in a corner and talked about their plans for the week.

'What about the Pleasure Beach tomorrow?' said Cissie. 'I'm dying to have a ride on the Big Dipper.'

'Yes, a good idea,' agreed Val. 'We'd better go there while we've still got a good bit of money left. Goodness knows what it'll cost on all those rides.'

'And what about Tuesday and Wednesday? There's lots to see in the Tower, apart from the ballroom. There's an aquarium and a zoo, and we said we'd go to the top of the tower, didn't we?'

'Let's not plan too far ahead until we see how things go,' said Val.

'Oh no... You're seeing His Lordship on Tuesday, aren't you?'

'Tuesday night, yes. But that's not what I meant. I don't suppose I'll be seeing him again after that...' Although Val was secretly hoping that she might do so. 'He's with his friends, isn't he, just like I'm with you?'

'OK then, we'll take a day at a time and make sure we do everything we want to do. We've only got a week.'

Mrs Butler came into the lounge in a little while to see if anyone would like a suppertime drink. Tea, coffee, hot chocolate and biscuits were available at a nominal charge. The girls both requested chocolate, and Janice brought them their drinks with custard cream biscuits a few moments later. They chatted together for a while about the films and records they liked, and the latest fashions – all sorts of 'girly' things that they found they had in common.

'She's nice, isn't she?' Cissie commented to Val when they returned to their bedroom. 'Quite normal. You'd never think she was such a brain-box – university an' all that.'

'I get the impression she's not really bothered about going,' said Val. 'It's her parents who want her to go. Of course she's got this new boyfriend now, and he lives in Yorkshire. So that might make a difference to how she feels.'

'If it lasts,' commented Cissie.

'She seems to think it will...' But what about herself and Sam Walker? thought Val. They had liked one another straight away and had got on famously, but she knew she must not get her hopes up too much. How could there possibly be a future for the two of them when they returned home?

The following morning they rode on a tram to the Pleasure Beach at the far southern end of the promenade. The fine sunny weather was continuing, and there was already, by midmorning, a good crowd of holidaymakers strolling around, some eating ice cream and candyfloss, and all enjoying the fun of the fairground. Val and Cissie mingled with them, savouring the sights and sounds, and the scents that lingered on the air; the odour of fried onions from the hotdog stalls, the sickly sweet scent of candyfloss and the smell of the diesel oil from the mechanical rides.

'What shall we do first?' said Cissie. 'Shall we see if we can knock that chap into the water?'

'No, we'd never do it,' replied Val. 'We'd only waste our money, but we can stop and watch for a while if you like.' A man was seated on a plank above a bath of water whilst eager folk, mainly men, threw balls at a target above his head. They watched for a few minutes until, at last, a ball hit the target and the poor chap fell into the water, to the cheers of the onlookers. There was a nominal prize for the winner, and the stooge, dressed in waterproof clothing and none the worse for his dipping, climbed back on to his seat.

There were easier feats of skill. Cissie won a miniature model of Blackpool Tower by rolling balls into holes. She seemed pleased with her prize, but Val was more discerning and careful with her money.

'Let's go in the River Caves,' she suggested, anxious to lure Cissie away from the money wasting sideshows.

They sat together in a boat which glided through the water, propelled by an unseen source, through scenes of exotic delight – eastern temples, snow-capped mountains, verdant forests and jungles – if you didn't look too closely at the plasterwork and the paintwork. The last scene was the Blue Grotto, which shone with an eery blue light, illuminating the glaciers and the shimmering ice all around them.

They came out blinking in the brilliant sunshine, as their eyes adjusted to the light. They dined at midday, sitting on a bench in the shade, on ham rolls and a bag of chips, and bottles of fizzy lemonade.

Cissie wanted to ride on the Big Dipper, but Val said that it would not be a good idea until their lunch had settled. Outside the Fun House they stood with a small crowd watching the Laughing

Man. A huge figure of a clown was seated inside a glass booth, rocking from side to side with laughter, his eyes rolling and a fixed grin on his face. His cries of 'Ho, ho, ho!' could be heard from far away, and you could not help but smile, too, at his merriment. He was an advert for the Fun House, and they decided to see what was inside.

There were draughty corridors where a gust of wind blew your skirt up around your waist, wobbly walkways, ghosts and ghouls lurking in dark corners, and halls of mirrors which distorted your figure, making you appear short and fat or tall and thin.

The climax of the day was the Big Dipper. Cissie was raring to go, Val rather more timorous as they sat, strapped firmly into their seats and grasping tightly to the bar in front of them. Then they were off, slowly up the first incline, then rushing downwards with the wind blowing their hair and their stomachs turning somersaults as shrieks of delighted laughter burst uncontrollably from their mouths. They were used to the sensation after the first descent and entered wholeheartedly into the thrill of the ride.

They came off feeling shaky and light-headed, laughing with the sheer delight of being on holiday in such an exciting place. They drank a cup of strong tea to settle their stomachs and their nerves before boarding the tram back to North Shore.

'We've had a great time,' they told Janice, as she served their meal of haddock and chips.

'Have you ever been on the Big Dipper?' asked Cissie.

Janice admitted that she hadn't, that residents

didn't always sample all the attractions of their own town. 'What are you doing tonight?' she asked.

'We thought we might go to the pictures,' said Val. 'There are lots of cinemas, aren't there?'

'Dozens,' said Janice, 'and there's the Imperial round the corner, only a few minutes' walk away. I think there's a Doris Day film on this week.'

'Smashing!' said Val. 'Would you like to come with us, if you're not too busy?'

'I'd love to,' said Janice, 'but it'll be a little while before I'm ready.'

'It's OK, we'll wait,' said Cissie.

It was a continuous programme, so they managed to see the Gaumont British News and the second showing of *On Moonlight Bay*.

'Thanks for your company, once again,' said Janice. 'It's ages since I was out so often in the evening. Saturday and Monday, and Phil has rung to ask me to meet him on Thursday. Things are certainly looking up for me!' She had believed she was contented with her lot, but life was beginning to be much more exciting.

SEVEN

Tuesday morning dawned bright and sunny. It was amazing how the fine weather was continuing. Val and Cissie had no definite plans for the day. Val was trying to hide her excitement and a certain amount of trepidation as she looked forward to seeing Sam again that evening. Would he be pleased to see her again, or might he have changed his mind and decided that it was not quite right to be associating with a girl who was one of his father's employees?

They decided to have a good mooch around the Blackpool shops which were far larger and more exciting than the ones at home. They walked into the town as they had all the time in the world to please themselves; and what a relief that was, to be free, if only for a week, from the strictures of a job and, in Cissie's case, the petty grievances of living at home.

The small shops along Dickson Road, leading to the town, were such as you might find in any sea-side resort. Local hairdressers, newsagents, green-grocers, confectioners and souvenir shops selling comic postcards and views of the area, buckets and spades, sun hats and suncream, and all the requisites for a day on the beach. They passed the cream-coloured Art Deco-style Odeon cinema near to North Station before turning into Talbot Road and the town centre.

The town seemed large to them, but they knew they could not get lost because ahead of them was the promenade and a view of the sands and the sea. There were shops such as Sally Mae's, Diana Warren's, and the American Dress Shop where girls like Val and Cissie could only window shop and walk away again. There were two large Marks and Spencer stores, though, and a Littlewoods where the clothes on sale were more within their budget.

Val didn't really need any more blouses, but she

was tempted by a bright pink one with a wide neckline almost, but not quite, off the shoulder; it would tone very nicely with the pink flowers on her full skirt that she intended to wear that evening.

'That's just your colour. It'll go lovely with your dark hair,' said Cissie. Not to be outdone she bought a sleeveless blue blouse with wide shoulder straps which Val said would match exactly the colour of her eyes.

'I've nobody to dress up for, like you,' she commented, 'but you never know your luck, do you?'

The large department store, RHO Hills, situated opposite the back entrance to the Tower was a delight to all the senses. There was an exquisite fragrance, as you entered, from the counters selling perfumes, powder and all manner of beauty products. In the basement were the more mundane household goods, and sales persons demonstrating the latest in vegetable cutters, knives and magic liquid to remove stains from clothing. On the first floor there were stylish coats, dresses and hats. Assistants lurked at every corner asking, 'Can I help you, madam?', so they did not spend any time or money there. On the floor above was the carpet and furniture department and, over that, the restaurant. It was a store in which they could only look and linger for a while.

The snack bar in Woolworths suited their pockets for a midday meal of sausage rolls and iced buns. And the merchandise, too, was affordable. The impressive cream and red store on a corner by the Tower was huge compared with their tiny little Woolies at home and they were amazed at the vast variety of goods on sale. They both treated themselves to a lipstick, eyeshadow and mascara.

They walked back along the prom instead of through the town. There was plenty of time before the evening meal to get ready for their visit to the Tower. All they would need to do after their meal was put the finishing touches to their hair and make-up.

'Enjoy yourselves tonight,' said Janice as she cleared the table. She was having a quiet evening at home, looking forward to seeing Phil again in a day or two.

Sam had arranged to meet Val at the front entrance to the Tower at eight o'clock. She and Cissie took a tram along the promenade, then crossed the tramtrack and the busy road to the meeting place. Val was feeling slightly apprehensive, butterflies fluttering away in her tummy as she wondered whether Sam might have changed his mind about seeing her again. Supposing it had been an impulsive, spur of the moment idea and he had thought better of it? What a fool she would feel if he didn't turn up! She knew that Cissie, too, was feeling anxious. Val had not voiced her own fears, and neither had her friend, but Cissie had gone very quiet and appeared ill at ease.

'You won't want me tagging along,' she had said at first when Val told her about the proposed meeting.

'Don't be silly,' Val had protested. 'I told him that you would be with me, that I didn't intend leaving you on your own, and he said of course I mustn't do that. He said he'd bring his friends along with him, so there'll be quite a few of us.'

When they arrived at the Tower entrance Val saw, to her relief, that Sam had meant what he said. He was there, lifting his hand to her in greeting, and with him were two other young men.

'Hello again, Val,' he said cheerfully. 'I was hoping you wouldn't stand me up!' Val just smiled, she couldn't think of a reply. 'This is my friend, Cissie,' she said.

'Hello, Cissie,' said Sam. 'I'm Sam Walker.'

'Yes ... I know,' answered Cissie, almost in a whisper, not at all like her usual self.

'And these are my mates, Jeff and Colin,' said Sam. They all smiled and said 'Hello' but did not shake hands.

'OK then, let's go in,' said Sam.

Val took out her purse to pay her entrance fee, but Sam stopped her. 'No, I'm paying for you and for Cissie. I asked you to come, didn't I?'

Val might have expected her friend to say that she could pay for herself, but Cissie just said, 'Thank you,' in a quiet voice.

The girls left their jackets in the cloakroom then went to join the men.

'There you are, you see,' Val said to her. 'I told you it'd be OK. Those two, Jeff and Colin, they seem nice and friendly.'

Cissie shrugged. 'They're alright, I suppose.'

Her air of nonchalance seemed to subside, however, when Jeff and Colin walked one on each side of her, chatting in a friendly way. And she and Val both stopped in their tracks, staring in awe and wonder when they entered the ballroom.

'Gosh! I thought the Winter Gardens ballroom was amazing,' exclaimed Val, 'but this, it's just ... magical!'

The ballroom was, indeed, breathtaking, especially if you were seeing it for the first time. The vastly proportioned room had been designed in the French Renaissance style. At the end of the room was a large stage with words from Shakespeare inscribed on the proscenium arch above, 'Bid me discourse, I will enchant thine ear.' Above the lettering was a classical painting, and other similar paintings of idyllic Arcadian scenes – shepherds and shepherdesses, frock-coated gentlemen and crinolined ladies – decorated the ceiling. The two gilded balconies above the dance floor were supported by massive pillars. The ballroom floor was a work of art in itself, composed of highly polished wooden blocks of varying shades in an intricate design; and shining down on the scene was the light cast by huge crystal chandeliers suspended from the ceiling. Truly a scene from fairyland.

The focal point on the stage was the Wonder Wurlitzer organ. Seated at the keyboard – four keyboards to be exact – was the resident organist, Reginald Dixon, the man who was known as Mr Blackpool. An unassuming-looking man, slightly built and wearing a light-coloured lounge suit, he was half turned, smiling at the dancers on the floor as they stood there applauding. Then he struck up with his famous signature tune, 'Oh, I do like to be beside the seaside', following that with the popular, 'Mister Sandman'.

'Shall we dance?' said Sam to Val, and they took

to the floor.

'Now, which of us is going to have the pleasure of dancing with this lovely young lady?' said Colin, the taller, dark-haired one.

'I don't mind if I do,' answered Jeff, who was fair-haired and shorter than his friend. 'Shall we dance, Cissie?'

'Don't feel you've got to dance with me, just because I've come along with Val,' she told him, as they stepped out to the rhythm of the quickstep. 'She'd got this date with Sam, y'see. It seems funny calling him Sam – well, I don't think I dare, actually. He's Mr Walker to us 'cause he's one of the bosses at the mill. He must've told you how he met Val, but he didn't know she worked there, not at first. I'm a bit worried about it actually. I've told her not to get carried away, like.'

'You don't need to worry about Sam,' said Jeff. 'He's as honest as the day is long. He won't lead her up the garden path, if that's what you're afraid of. If he's with Val it's because he genuinely likes her.'

'Oh ... well, I'm glad about that.'

'There's nothing snobbish about Sam, nor his dad for that matter. It's his snooty brother, Jonathan, that I can't stand. He looks down his nose at us lesser mortals, just because his dad's a mill owner. Maybe I'm speaking out of turn, he's one of your bosses, isn't he?'

'Yes, but we don't know any of 'em really. Val knows Mr Jonathan a bit better 'cause she works in the office. Me, I just work in t'mill, in the mending room, tidying up the mistakes in the cloth. How do you know ... er ... Sam then?'

'We were at school together, the three of us were always good pals. I left, though, when I was sixteen. I didn't get very good results in my School Certificate, not like the other two. Anyway, I got a job at the Co-op in town; I'm one of the under-managers now, so I can't complain. And Colin works for an insurance company. We've stayed together, us three, through thick and thin.'

'Like Val and me, we've known each other since we were four years old. She's cleverer than me, but it makes no difference. Anyway, thanks for dancing with me,' she said, as the music came to an end and the dancers left the floor.

'It's been a pleasure, Cissie,' he replied courteously. He might not have the social standing of his friend, Sam, but he was polite and well spoken.

The five of them stayed together for a while. Colin asked Cissie to dance next, and when they all returned to the spot where they had been standing Sam suggested that they might go and have a drink. Cissie was beginning to feel a little ill at ease with the situation. The two young men were being very attentive. Jeff had insisted on buying the shandy she was drinking, but she felt that they might be there only because they were being polite. She had an idea that they would rather go off together and see what the talent was like elsewhere.

They all returned to the ballroom, to a different spot near to the stage. Val and Sam appeared to be getting along famously, chatting together as though they had known one another for ages. Jeff and Colin, too, were deep in conversation, about football from what she could hear, and the chances for Halifax Town in the coming season. So, for a little while she was standing on her own feeling a little lost and wishing she were somewhere else, but she wasn't quite sure where.

'Would you care to dance?' said a voice at her side.

'Yes, I don't mind,' she replied before she had even looked at him closely. She was only too relieved that someone – anyone – had noticed her and asked her to dance.

When she looked more closely she saw that he was a young man with very fair tousled hair, blue eyes that were looking at her keenly, and a cheerful grin. 'You were looking all lost and on your owny-own,' he said. 'I just had to come and rescue you.'

'I'm quite alright,' she answered pertly, although she was, in fact, very grateful to him. 'I don't need rescuing. I was just enjoying the music.'

'Aye, Reginald Dixon. He's jolly good, isn't he?' said the young man. The organist was playing a catchy tune dating back to the wartime era, 'Yes, My Darling Daughter'. 'I must say this place has got our local dance halls beat to a cocked hat.'

'And that would be in Yorkshire, I take it?' said Cissie. She had recognized his accent immediately.

'Aye, it takes one to know one, doesn't it?' he replied with a chuckle. 'I'm from Bradford, and I reckon you're from my neck of the woods an' all, aren't you?'

'Yes, not so far away. I'm from Halifax. We're almost neighbours, aren't we? And I suppose you're on holiday here, same as me?'

'Aye, that's right. Nice little boarding house in Regent Road, not so far from here. So where are you staying?'

'A small hotel in North Shore.'

'Ooh! That's the posh part, isn't it?'

'I don't know about that, but it's very nice. We came on Saturday, me and my friend.'

'Aye, so did we, me and Charlie. Anyroad, we'd better introduce ourselves, hadn't we? I'm Jack ... Jack Broadbent.'

'And I'm Cissie,' she told him. 'Cissie Foster.'

'How do, Cissie?' he said, smiling down at her. He was just a few inches taller than her five feet two. 'Pleased to meet yer.'

'Same here,' she replied, and they danced in silence for a few moments.

Then, 'What have you been doing so far?' he asked.

'Walked on the prom, went on North Pier, been to the Pleasure Beach and had a ride on the Big Dipper. Went to the Winter Gardens on Saturday night. That's a smashing ballroom an' all, but I think this is even better.'

'Aye, I've got to agree there,' said Jack, 'and there's lots more to see in here as well as the ballroom... Shall we go and have a drink?' he suggested, as the dance came to an end.

'That would be nice,' replied Cissie, 'but I've just had a drink. When you asked me to dance we'd just come back from the bar, me and Val – that's my friend I came on holiday with – and the three fellers.'

'Well, we can do summat else, can't we? Let's have a stroll around, that's if you would like to,

104

Cissie? Like you said, we're almost neighbours, an' I'm sure we'll find we've a lot to talk about.'

'Yes, I'd like to,' said Cissie, trying not to sound too eager. But she had decided she liked Jack Broadbent, from what little she knew of him at any rate. He seemed a jolly, carefree sort of young man – a few years older than herself, maybe – and fun to be with. Not like Walter, her 'intended', as her mother might say. He could be a real sobersides despite his eagerness to get Cissie to do things that she didn't want to do.

'Just a minute, I'd best tell Val where I'm going,' she said. She went over to where her friend was standing with Sam. 'I'm just going for a stroll around with ... Jack,' she said. 'He's from Bradford, and ... he seems OK,' she added in a whisper.

'That's OK,' said Val, and Cissie got the impression that she was somewhat relieved. She grinned at her. 'Go and have fun then!'

'I hope so,' said Cissie.

'You weren't with one of those chaps, were you?' asked Jack as they walked off together.

'Oh, no, nowt like that. Actually I was feeling like a spare part...' She explained to him that her friend, Val, had got friendly with Sam Walker who was nothing less than one of the bosses from the mill where they worked. 'I hope she's not heading for trouble,' she said. 'I've warned her, but she seems real taken with him. And the other two are pals of his.'

'Well then, good luck to her,' said Jack. 'If she's got herself fixed up for the week it leaves you free, doesn't it? Come on, let's go and explore.'

They went up the stairs to the second floor

where the zoo, or menagerie, as it was once called, was situated.

'Pooh! It pongs a bit, doesn't it,' observed Jack as they entered the long room with wire cages on either side and an observation platform with seating in the centre. 'Ne'er mind, we'll p'raps get used to it.'

They sat on the bench observing the animals from a distance. Cissie didn't want to get too close although there were braver people venturing much nearer to the cages. There was a cage with long-tailed monkeys leaping around, and another with almost human-looking chimpanzees. There was a table and stools in the cage because, each afternoon, a tea party was held there for the amusement of the visitors, who were in danger of being drenched with tea or pelted with bread and cakes. There was a lonely-looking giraffe, a rhinoceros and a fierce-looking lion pacing back and forth in his cage.

'I wonder if that's the lion that ate Albert Ramsbottom?' said Cissie.

'What?' enquired Jack, looking puzzled.

'You know; that poem, "Albert and the Lion". I've heard a chap recite it at our church concerts. Haven't you heard it?'

'Oh aye, mebbe I have,' said Jack. 'I wouldn't like to get too near to that chap, I can tell you.'

'No... It seems cruel, though, having 'em caged up like that. They don't look very happy.'

'Happen safer, though, than they would be in the jungle,' said Jack.

They stayed a little while, chatting together, and Cissie learnt that Jack, also, worked in a woollen mill in Bradford. He had started at fifteen, as she had done, and he was now an overseer in charge of a weaving shed; the same job that Walter did, but Cissie didn't mention him. She also learnt that he was twenty-two. He had done national service, then returned to the job that was waiting for him.

'Now, what else shall we do?' he said when they left the zoo. 'What about a trip to the top of the Tower?'

'Er ... no, I don't think so, not tonight,' said Cissie. 'That's one of the things I've said I'll do with Val. Anyway, we wouldn't be able to see much at night, would we?'

'Fair enough,' agreed Jack. 'Well then, what about the Aquarium? Not that I'm right interested in fish, unless they're on a plate wi' some chips. But it's happen worth a look.'

The Aquarium was on the ground floor, a mysterious cave-like place illuminated with a faint greenish light. There were stone pillars covered with crustaceans – lifelike in appearance although they were man-made – holding up the low ceiling. Around the side were fish tanks with fish of many colours, shapes and varieties swimming around. There were turtles, too, and other sea creatures. The eerie silence in the room made you feel you must talk in a whisper.

They sat on a circular bench surrounding one of the pillars. There were just a few other people wandering around. Jack put an arm around Cissie's shoulders drawing her closer to him.

'This is nice and cosy, isn't it?' he said. 'I'm glad I've met you, Cissie. You're my kind of lass.'

'That's nice to know,' she replied. 'I'm glad I've

met you an' all.'

He turned her face towards him and gently kissed her lips. It felt good, but she did not respond too readily because she hardly knew him, and he drew away.

'Come on,' he said getting hold of her hand and pulling her to her feet. 'Let's go and have a drink now.'

They went to the bar nearest to the ballroom which was quite crowded now. Cissie drank her second shandy of the evening and Jack had a pint of bitter. In a few moments Val and Sam came in, his arm around her and their heads close together. Jack was asking Cissie if, or when, they could meet again.

'Tomorrow?' he suggested. 'P'raps we could go somewhere together. Anywhere you like, I'm not fussy. I'd like to get to know you better, Cissie. We're getting along OK, aren't we? More than just OK, I'd say.' He put an arm round her and pulled her closer to him.

'Oh, I'm not sure about tomorrow,' Cissie demurred. 'We're going to the show at the Opera House tomorrow night, and I think we'll be spending the day together as well.'

Jack Broadbent's a fast worker, she thought to herself. She'd only known him five minutes! In fact she didn't really know him at all. He seemed alright, a down-to-earth Yorkshire lad, the same sort of background as herself, she guessed. And he was already an overseer at the mill. She was not reluctant to get to know him better, but she had come away with Val and they had planned to spend most of their time together. But Val, of course, might now have other plans...

She was relieved when she saw her friend and Sam come into the bar. 'That's Val, over there,' she said. 'I'll go and ask her, shall I, if she'd mind if I spent some time with you?'

'The dark-haired girl?' said Jack, looking towards where she was pointing. 'She's quite a looker an' all, isn't she? I bet the pair of you have turned a few heads! It looks to me as though she'll not object, they seem to be getting along like a house on fire.'

'OK, I'll go and ask her then,' said Cissie. 'D'you want to come with me?'

'No, I'll stay and keep our seats, or we might lose 'em. How about us meeting on Thursday? And tell yer friend that I'll see you back safely to yer digs tonight. Sam'll be taking her back, won't he?'

'Yes, I expect he will. Thursday's OK with me, so I'll go and tell her. Shan't be long...'

'Hello there, Cissie,' said Sam in a friendly way when she appeared at their table. 'Enjoying yourself, are you?'

'Er ... yes, thank you,' she replied. 'I've met this chap, Jack he's called. He's from Bradford and he wants to see me again. He said tomorrow, but I told him we're going to a show tomorrow night. I thought it was a bit too soon, seeing as we've only just met. So I've said I'll see him on Thursday, that's if it's OK with you, Val?'

Val and Sam looked at one another, and she could tell that they were relieved at her remark. She guessed that they, too, had been making plans.

'That's great, Cissie,' said Sam. 'I've asked Val

109

if she'll spend some time with me on Thursday. I'm playing golf with Jeff and Colin tomorrow.'

'So I've said I will,' added Val, 'provided it's alright with you. I didn't want to go off and leave you on your own. But now you're all fixed up, aren't you?'

'Yes, it seems like it,' said Cissie. 'I'll have to see how it goes. And Jack says he'll see I get back to the hotel safely, so I'll see you back there, shall I?'

'Yes,' said Val, a trifle uncertainly. 'You'll be OK with this Jack, will you? You don't really know him very well...'

Cissie was tempted to tell her friend that she didn't know Sam very well either, but she couldn't do so. She knew what Val meant only too well. 'Oh yes,' she answered. 'I'm a big girl now, I can look after meself. See you later then, Val. 'Bye for now ... Sam.'

'That's all sorted out,' she told Jack. 'They've made plans for Thursday an' all.'

'There you are, you see. I told you so. What shall we do on Thursday then?'

'Oh, I don't know... P'raps a long ride some-where on a tram? I think they're such fun.'

'Fleetwood's not far away, we could go there. Now, I'd best get you back safe and sound. Come on then, let's go.'

Cissie collected her jacket from the cloakroom, then they set off walking back along the prom. 'We'll walk back shall we?' said Jack, 'seeing as it's a warmish sort o' night. Can you walk in them shoes?'

'Yes, they're OK,' said Cissie. 'They're quite comfy.' He obviously wasn't going to suggest a taxi, as Sam would no doubt be doing. It was a fair stretch, though, back to North Shore. 'We could get a tram, though. I know where to get off, near the Carlton Hotel.' She remembered that Sam was staying there.

'OK then, a tram it is.' One came along almost at once, and they alighted a few stops further along the promenade. It didn't seem far but it would have been a good distance to walk.

They crossed the road to the Carlton Hotel, then walked along the street to where the hotel was situated. Jack put his arm around her, as she had expected he would, then he drew her into the shelter of a shop doorway and started to kiss her. Gently at first, then more urgently, and she found herself responding. Why not? she thought. He was a friendly lad and there was no harm in it. She knew that any red-blooded young man such as he would have done the same. But when his hands strayed beneath her jacket and started to fondle her she drew away.

'No ... I don't think so, Jack,' she said, and to her relief he backed away. That was somewhat to her surprise as well, but he appeared contrite.

'Sorry, Cissie,' he muttered, 'but I do like you a lot, you know.'

'But we've only just met, Jack...'

'OK then ... let's go...'

The hotel was on the next block, and they stopped outside the gate. 'You still want to see me on Thursday, do you?' he asked, a little pensively.

'Yes, of course I do,' she answered.

'That's alright then. Shall we say ten o'clock, at North Pier? That's not too far away from your

111

digs and mine. Then we can decide what we want to do.'

'Yes, that's fine, Jack. See you on Thursday then...'

He kissed her lightly on the lips. 'Ta-ra then, see you soon.' He blew her a kiss as he strolled away along the street.

Bemused, she entered the hotel using the door key that Mrs Butler had given her. Val had not yet returned, but she came into the room when Cissie had washed and was in her nightdress.

'I've had a smashing time,' she said, her eyes glowing with delight as she started to undress. 'Sam's really nice, you know ... and he says he would like to go on seeing me – when we get back home, I mean. Don't look like that, Cissie! I'm sure he means what he says.'

'I hope so,' said Cissie. 'I know he seems very nice, but...'

'But nothing! What about you and that Jack?'

'Oh, Jack's OK,' said Cissie off-handedly. 'At least he's more our sort, isn't he? You know – one of the workers.'

'Maybe... You must watch him, though, Cissie.'

'I've told you, I can look after meself. Anyway, it's time for beddy-byes. Goodnight, Val, God bless.'

'Goodnight, Cissie. Sleep tight.'

EIGHT

'Another sunny day,' said Val as she drew back the curtains on Wednesday morning. 'Come on, Cissie, wakey-wakey!'

There was a grunt from Cissie's bed, then she sat up, rubbing the sleep from her eyes. 'What d'you say?'

'Another lovely day. We've been really lucky with the weather, haven't we? What shall we do today?'

Cissie was soon wide awake. 'Oh ... I don't know. We're going to that show tonight. What would you like to do first?'

'P'raps we could go up the Tower,' suggested Val, 'while the weather's fine. We'll be able to see for miles.'

Cissie hesitated. She remembered that Jack had suggested a trip to the top of the Tower, but it was something she had said she would do with Val, and Val was her best friend.

'OK,' she replied. 'Let's do that. An' we can see all the rest of the Tower an' all, once we've paid to get in.'

'Don't forget the show tonight!' said Janice as she served their breakfast.

'As if we would!' they both answered.

'I'm really looking forward to it,' said Janice. 'We'll set off as soon as you've had your meal. Enjoy your day – what have you got in mind?'

'We're going up the Tower!' said Cissie.

'Lucky you! Wish I was coming... Never mind. See you later.'

They decided to do the Tower ascent first before there was a long queue for the lift. There were several others waiting to make the journey to the top of the Tower, but not right to the top. The Tower itself was 518 feet, 9 inches in height but the lift ascended only to a height of 380 feet.

There were, in fact, two lifts, working simultaneously, one ascending and the other one descending. It took less than one minute to arrive at the landing platform. The girls stepped out somewhat timorously, never before having been so far above ground level. It was perfectly safe, though, and anyone who had a fear of heights did not need to feel at all threatened. There was ample room for a goodly crowd, but so early in the morning there were no more than thirty or so up there. Each cabin could hold twenty-five people but there was only a dozen in the cabin with Val and Cissie.

The viewing platform was not open to the elements as the girls might have expected. The scenes all around were viewed through glass windows. There was, however, an iron staircase leading to a higher level. Some more intrepid folk were climbing up, but Val and Cissie decided to stay where they were.

It was truly amazing what they could see as they walked around the circuit of the viewing area. Looking west was the Irish Sea stretching away into the distance, as far as the Isle of Man and beyond, but that was not quite visible. The tide was out and there were people on the sands or paddling in the sea, looking like miniature dolls from that distance. And there were the three piers, North, Central and South, reaching out over the ocean. Looking north, beyond the long line of hotels – the Metropole, the Imperial and the Norbreck hotels recognizable from their distinctive shapes – were the hills of Barrow, the most southerly of the Lake District hills.

Walking around and looking inland, to the east, were the thousand upon thousand houses of residential Blackpool. Val and Cissie tried to locate their hotel.

'Look,' said Val. 'That's the railway station, so that must be Dickson Road, and the Odeon cinema, so we're just along there. Look a bit further; see, over there...'

Then, to the south, another long vista of hotels on the promenade, the Golden Mile, and the outline of the Big Dipper at the Pleasure Beach. Across the estuary of the River Ribble that entered the sea at Lytham St Anne's they could see the seaside resort of Southport.

'That was terrific!' said Cissie when they had completed the circuit. 'What shall we do now? It's all free, isn't it? So we might as well make the most of it.'

The half-crown entrance fee entitled them to visit all the attractions of the Tower building, apart from the circus. This performance took place in the circus ring at the very bottom of the building, the ring being between the four legs of the Tower itself. That was an entertainment that the girls might have to forgo; a week was such a short time to see all the delights that Blackpool had to offer.

Cissie had already seen the zoo and the aquarium with Jack, but she visited them again with Val. She and Sam had spent their time dancing and talking together without any need for other diversions. They ate a snack lunch in a cafe near to the roof gardens where exotic plants, trees and ferns flourished beneath the glass canopy. It would be a pleasant place to shelter when the rain was pelting down on the glass roof, but the day was sunny and it became rather too warm up there.

Another 'free' attraction was the Childrens' Ballet which was performed every afternoon and early evening in the ballroom.

'Shall we give it a try?' said Val. There was already quite a crowd of people sitting on seats, with eager children sitting on the floor at the front, waiting for the performance to start.

'If you like,' said Cissie. 'I suppose we might as well. They'll all be posh kids, though, won't they, prancing about? Not the likes of you and me.'

Neither Val nor Cissie had been to dancing lessons – tap or ballet – such as just a few of their school friends had done. Neither family had been able to afford such a luxury. Cissie had always scoffed that it was showing off, 'prancing about like that', but Val, secretly, would like to have had the chance.

They watched the performance by local children, mainly girls, from dancing schools in the area as they went through their routines of tap, ballet and ballroom dancing. There seemed to be as many as a hundred of them in a highly polished show, and the appreciative audience applauded and cheered with enthusiasm.

'It was OK, I suppose,' said Cissie as they made their way back to the hotel. 'Rather them than me, though. It looks like jolly hard work for kids. But happen it's better than being at school, eh? It's a school holiday now, but I wonder what happens when they go back?'

'Perhaps it finishes then,' said Val. 'We've another show to look forward to tonight, and that should be even better.'

The show at Blackpool's Opera House prided itself on being the biggest and best that the town had to offer. The 'Big Show of 1955', as it was called, was indeed the most sparkling and scintillating performance that Val and Cissie had ever seen. Janice had seen it in previous years, but she, too, said that this one surpassed many of the others.

It was presented by George and Alfred Black, well-known impresarios, with the comedians Jewel and Warriss, well-known Blackpool comedians, topping the bill. The singer Alma Cogan was another popular star in the town; then there were the John Tiller girls, familiar to many from their television performances, dancing and high-kicking in perfect precision; and the Flying de Pauls, making the audience gasp in fright and admiration at their daredevil manoeuvres on the high wire and trapeze.

'Gosh! That was fantastic,' said Val as they stepped out into the darkness of the night. They decided to walk back as it was still a warm evening.

'Only two days left of our holiday,' said Cissie. 'It's flying past, isn't it? But in some ways it feels as if we've been here for ages.'

'Yes, a lot has happened,' said Val, thinking of her meeting with Sam.

'I'll say it has,' agreed Cissie.

'And for me, too,' added Janice. 'I feel as though I've known you two for ages. I'll be sorry when you have to leave on Saturday. We'll keep in touch, won't we? I'll write to you both.'

'I'm not much of a letter writer,' admitted Cissie, 'but Val will write, won't you, Val?'

'Yes, of course. And there's always next year. We might come again...' Val was wondering, though, what the next year would have in store for them, especially in the near future when they returned home.

'And we all have something to look forward to tomorrow,' said Janice. 'I'm not seeing Phil until the evening, but you two have plans for the day, haven't you?'

'Yes, not sure what, though,' said Cissie. 'What about you, Val?'

'No, I don't know either; but we'll meet up for our evening meals, you and me, won't we, Cissie?'

'Of course we will! I'm not going to miss one of Mrs Butler's slap-up meals for any bloke!' said her friend.

Janice laughed. 'I'll tell my mum what you said. She'll be real pleased. Anyway ... here we are, back home.' She opened the door for them. 'Goodnight, you two. Thanks for asking me to go with you. We've had a great evening, and I've enjoyed your company.'

'And yours, too,' said Val. 'Goodnight, Janice...'

'She's nice, isn't she?' said Cissie as they went up the stairs. 'A bit posh, like, but I'm glad we met her.'

Cissie met Jack, as arranged, outside the North Pier at ten o'clock. She had wondered if he might have decided not to come after she had put a stop to his advances the night before. But she was relieved to see that he was already there, waving to her as she approached, the sun glinting on his mop of fair hair.

'Hi there, Cissie,' he called. 'I'm glad you've come. I thought you might have changed your mind.'

'No, why should I?' she retorted.

'Dunno ... but I'm glad you're here. There's a tram coming, an' it's going to Fleetwood. It's a double-decker an' all. Let's go up to the top, then we can see more.'

It was a pleasant ride along the coast to the fishing port of Fleetwood, some four miles or so away. On their left the tide was receding and holidaymakers were already putting up deckchairs on the rippled sand, children were making sand pies and some were paddling in rock pools left by the ebbing tide.

A little way beyond the Norbreck Hotel the tram went inland towards the resort of Cleveleys, a pleasant place to shop and where some visitors stayed rather than in Blackpool itself.

They alighted in Fleetwood, near to the light-house which was a little way inland. The town, away from the sea front, did not have the enticing

119

shops or the busy holiday feeling that Blackpool had. They passed by the railway station and the pier and on to the dock area.

'Pooh! It's a bit niffy, isn't it?' said Cissie, wrinkling her nose.

'What d'you expect?' said Jack, laughing. 'It's a fishing port.'

Fishing boats were being unloaded, and on the promenade were stalls selling white fish as well as shrimps, cockles and mussels. Further along the sea front, a little way away from the town, there was a pleasant park area with a lake, but the place did not have the bustle or the excitement that Blackpool had.

'There's nowt much here,' Jack observed, when they had strolled around for a while. 'An' I'm feeling hungry. At least we should be able to find a decent fish and chip shop here. Come on, let's go back to t' town.'

They did find such a place, fish and chips to take out or to eat in the small cafe at the back. 'Let's be posh and go inside,' said Jack. 'I don't want to get me hands all greasy.'

They dined handsomely on battered cod which almost overhung the plates, chips and mushy peas, with bread and butter and tea included in the price of two shillings.

Ships left from the dock at Fleetwood bound for the Isle of Man, a popular day trip if you had the time, or for a longer holiday. There was also a ferryboat which crossed the estuary of the River Wyre to the small village of Knott End. There were a few people waiting for the boat, and as it seemed to be 'the thing to do' when you came to

Fleetwood Jack and Cissie joined the queue.

It was a five-minute journey across the water, and the ferryboat landed them near a long stretch of featureless promenade. 'There's nowt much here,' Jack remarked, as he had done earlier.

The shops behind the prom had little to offer either. 'Must be the last place God made...' he muttered. 'Ne'er mind, eh?' He put an arm round Cissie as they strolled back to catch the ferry. 'We're enjoying ourselves, aren't we? Can I see you again tonight?'

She hesitated for a moment. 'I'm not sure. It depends what Val's doing.'

'She's got herself fixed up with that posh chap, hasn't she?' said Jack. 'He's sure to want to see her tonight.'

'Well, yes, probably he will...'

'You'll see me then? Please say you will, Cissie.'

'Alright then. It'll be half past seven, though, by the time I'm ready.'

'That's OK. We could go to the pictures. There's a little cinema called the Tivoli, not far from North Pier. Shall I meet you there, at the pier, at eight o'clock? Then we can go and see what's showing.'

Cissie agreed, and they made their return journey on the tram. They parted at North Pier. Jack kissed her cheek, then he pulled her towards him and kissed her lips. 'You're a smashing girl, Cissie,' he said. 'See you later, then.'

He walked off along the prom in a southerly direction, and she crossed the tramtrack and the road to Talbot Square. She noticed the Tivoli that Jack had mentioned, a tiny cinema tucked away in an arcade. She guessed that the films they showed there would not be the up-to-date ones. She was right. The poster outside portrayed Marilyn Monroe in *Gentlemen Prefer Blondes*, which was at least two years old. Cissie had already seen it, but she wouldn't mind seeing it again.

She had decided that she liked Jack. She had enjoyed herself today, and Jack, who was fun to be with, had certainly given an added spice to the holiday. He had said that they must see one another when they got back home. Bradford was not very far from Halifax. But that remained to be seen. She, of course, had made no mention of Walter. She would worry about that when the time came.

Val was already back at the hotel, sitting on the bed, reading. 'Hi there, Cissie,' she greeted her. 'Had a good day?'

'Yes, smashing, thanks. We went to Fleetwood and had fish and chips, and went on a funny little ferryboat across the river. It was good fun, thanks to Jack. We get on real well, Val, an' he makes me laugh. We didn't reckon much to Fleetwood, but it doesn't matter, does it, when you're with somebody you like? What about you? How did you get on with Sam?'

'We've had a lovely time,' replied Val, looking very starry-eyed. 'Like I told you before, Cissie, he's really nice, not at all stuck-up like his brother. He says he doesn't get on with Jonathan. I'm not surprised. I always thought he was high and mighty, looking down his nose at the likes of us. Sam's so different. He wants to see me tonight,' she added, a trifle anxiously, 'and I've said I will. I hope that's OK with you?'

Cissie laughed. 'Course it is. I'm seeing Jack an' all. We'll probably go to the pictures. I thought you'd have made other plans. So ... what have you been doing all day?'

'We went to Stanley Park,' said Val. 'I know it might not sound very exciting. It's quiet up there, and rather more refined, I suppose, than the rest of Blackpool.'

'More suited to folk like your Sam, you mean?'

'No, that's not what I meant at all. It's quieter, though, more peaceful. It's good to get away from the crowds for a while. It's like being in the countryside. We had a lovely day.'

Sam had suggested Stanley Park which was in a residential area not too far from the town centre, in a part of Blackpool that Val recognized as being more middle-class. Sam played golf on the course there, and wanted to have a look round the park to which it belonged.

'We'll have to go on the bus, I'm afraid,' he said to Val. 'I left my car at home this week. It's only a small car, a Morris Minor, and we all had so much luggage with the golf clubs and everything, so we decided to come on the train.'

'Don't worry about that,' said Val. 'I'm used to travelling on buses, when I need to. But that's not very often. I live near to town, and Cissie and I walk to work'

They alighted from the bus near to Blackpool's Victoria Hospital. Sam knew there was a side entrance to the park further up the road, which was one of the tree-lined drives surrounding the park. The path led them through an area of parkland with overhanging trees and stretches of well-tended grassy areas, with park benches where one could rest awhile in the peaceful countrified surroundings. It was quite early in the morning, so they encountered no one else on their walk. Sam put his arm around her, drawing her close to him.

'I meant what I said, you know,' he told her, 'about us seeing one another when we get back home.'

He had mentioned it on Tuesday evening when they were at the Tower Ballroom, and that night he had kissed her when they parted. 'I know you feel rather ... what shall I say? ... unsure about it, but it will be OK, I assure you.'

'But what about your parents,' she had asked, 'and ... your brother? They won't like it, will they, you being friendly with one of your employees?'

'Leave them to me,' said Sam. 'I've told you; my father's all right. Mother is inclined to be ... well, she has rather grand ideas. But I can manage Jonathan. Don't you worry.'

Now, as they walked through the park, he stopped and gently turned her face towards him. He kissed her lips tenderly, then gave her a hug. 'Don't worry, Val,' he told her again. 'Everything will be fine.'

'I hope so.' She smiled at him. 'But we don't really know one another very well yet, do we?'

'Then we'll look forward to finding out more, won't we?' He smiled back at her. 'Come along, I think the lake's just round this corner.'

Sam knew that he was getting fonder of this lovely girl each time he saw her. As she said, they did not know one another well, but he had been attracted to Valerie Horrocks in a way he had not been with any of his former girlfriends. He had been out with a few girls, usually the daughters of family friends, but he had never wanted to do anything but kiss them in a friendly fashion. Sam was a circumspect young man, he knew that some of his friends might consider him old-fashioned. Admittedly, he had sown his wild oats, to a certain extent, whilst he was in the army, but that was all behind him now.

He now had respect for the girls he met. That was something that his mother had drummed into him, although he knew that, in many ways, she was a snob. She had managed to influence Jonathan with her way of thinking, but her patronizing and often unfriendly attitude to those she considered inferior to herself had cut no ice with Sam.

Val was quieter by nature than her friend Cissie, but he liked Cissie's down-to-earth honesty and how she called 'a spade a spade'. Val was lovely; her softly waving brown hair and her brown eyes that lit up with warmth when she smiled. Her elfin features and slim build made her look delicate, but he guessed that she was really quite a strong girl, physically as well as mentally. Sam feared, yet also rejoiced, that he was falling in love with her. He hoped, despite her misgivings, that she felt the same way about him.

When they turned the corner they crossed a bridge that spanned the end of the lake. It was a large lake, man-made, and already there were a few rowing boats on the water. Skirting the edge of the lake they came to a part where there were children's paddle boats for hire, and the landing stage for the pleasure boat which would operate when more customers arrived. There were water fowl there; ducks, geese, and a couple of swans scrambling for the tit-bits being thrown to them by excited children, and their parents, too.

'D'you fancy a trip in a rowing boat?' asked Sam. 'I'll row, of course, that is if you can trust me?'

'I'm sure I can, but ... later, perhaps. Let's have a wander round first, shall we?'

'Fine, let's get our bearings.'

Leaving the lakeside they came to the restaurant, a largish building that served light refreshments and also more substantial meals.

'We'll come back here for lunch,' decided Sam. 'Probably a darned sight cheaper than the Carlton,' he commented, clearly a true Yorkshireman at heart. 'Mustn't complain, though, the food's great... Let's see what else Stanley Park has to offer.'

There was a rose garden tucked away down a winding path, with well-tended beds, the roses, in mid-August, being at the height of their flowering period. There were all types of rose bushes in every colour, ranging from pure white to a deep purplish red, scenting the air all around with their fragrance.

'There's a Florabunda,' said Val, pointing to a bush with copious blooms. 'That's what our hotel is called. Janice says it's named, partly, after her grandma. She was called Florrie, and she was in charge before Mrs Butler took over. She ruled the roost, according to what Janice told us.'

Sam laughed. 'A typical seaside landlady, eh? They were the subject of music hall jokes for

126

years, but I think they might be a dying breed now.'

Down a flight of stone steps they came to an Italian garden with a pond, statues of classical figures and symmetrical flower beds. A path led to a tall clock known as the Cocker clock, commemorating a well-known Blackpool man. They retraced their steps to the lake and Sam persuaded Val to take a trip in a rowing boat.

The boat wobbled as she got in and a sneaky breeze blew her skirt up almost to her waist. She pulled it down and sat demurely on the seat opposite Sam, straightening her skirt and keeping her knees close together. He took his jacket off before he started to row. Val watched him thoughtfully as he concentrated on his rowing. She liked what she saw. She was beginning to feel very attracted indeed to Sam Walker. He was a sturdily built young man, but by no means plump. His arm muscles in his short-sleeved shirt stood out as he pulled on the oars. His golden-brown hair flopped over his brow. He brushed it away then smiled at her, his brown eyes lighting up with warmth.

'Hope you're enjoying yourself,' he said. 'How am I doing?'

'You're doing fine, Sam,' she replied, smiling happily.

When they had had their allotted time on the lakes it was time for lunch. Despite their large breakfasts they were rather peckish by that time. They opted for one of the three-course meals that were on offer, tomato soup, roast lamb, and ice cream for dessert, in preference to steamed pudding with custard.

'We need to walk that off,' said Sam, 'How about a round on the putting green?'

'What? With an expert golfer like you?' she protested. 'You've got to be kidding!'

'I'm not expert at all,' he told her. 'Come on, Val, it's just a bit of fun.'

She gave in, and she managed reasonably well. It was not the first time she had played, so she had some idea how to proceed, and Sam gave her a few hints. 'In case you ever decide to take up golf,' he said with a grin.

They went back to Blackpool a different way. After walking along the broad driveway to the park gates they went down a tree-lined avenue and boarded a tram back to the town centre. Sam said he would wait for her outside her hotel at eight o'clock, then they would spend the evening together.

Val was relieved that Cissie, also, had made plans with Jack.

'So we've all got dates tonight,' said Cissie. 'Janice an' all. She's seeing that RAF lad, isn't she? Where are you and Sam going then?'

'We haven't decided,' said Val, 'but it doesn't matter. It's just nice getting to know one another.' She smiled, remembering the happy day they had spent together.

'You're falling for him, aren't you?' said Cissie.

'Yes, maybe I am.'

'Just watch yourself, Val. I don't want to see you getting hurt.' Cissie really did seem quite concerned.

'I'm sure I won't,' replied Val. 'But the same applies to you. Just be careful, Cissie.' Personally, she wouldn't trust Jack as far as she could throw him.

'I'm OK,' answered Cissie, with an exaggerated sigh. 'I've told you before, I can take care of meself. There's no need to worry about me.'

Val feared that there might be every need. But what could she do? She was not responsible for her friend.

NINE

Sam was waiting outside when Val left the hotel at eight o'clock. Cissie had already left to meet Jack at North Pier.

'Hello again,' said Sam. 'Have you had a good meal?'

'Yes, lovely, thanks,' she replied. 'We seem to do nothing but eat this holiday. It was steak and kidney pie – homemade, I'm sure – and sherry trifle.'

'I've had a hearty meal, too,' said Sam. 'What about a walk along the prom? You're not too exhausted by the exertions of the day, are you? The putting and all the walking?'

'No, not at all. I'm as fit as a flea. This Blackpool air is really bracing, isn't it? I can't remember when I felt so well.'

'Let's make the most of it then. Unless ... would you rather go to the pictures?'

'No, certainly not. Not on a lovely evening like this.'

'My feelings exactly.' He took hold of her hand

as they walked towards the prom. They crossed the road to the sea side of the promenade, then down a slope to the lower prom. This was where the waves dashed over the sea wall in stormy weather, drenching the intrepid folk who liked to play games with the tide. But the sea was calm tonight, gradually creeping towards the land. A few people were still walking on the remaining stretch of sand, no doubt keeping an eye on the incoming tide. There were danger signs and life-belts at intervals along the prom, warning of the danger of swimming in the treacherous sea. There had been several fatalities over the years.

Sam put his arm around her as they walked to-wards Gynn Square, then ascended a slope back to the higher level. He suggested that they should spent the rest of the evening in the comfort of the Carlton Hotel. When they arrived back Val's feet were telling her that she had done enough walk-ing for that day.

The lounge was roomy and comfortable with large settees and easy chairs, subdued lighting and little tables dotted here and there. There was a homely, welcoming feel to the place. They chose a seat near the window overlooking the prom. Dusk was falling, and the trams rattling along the track were lit up inside. Their clanging sound was always there in the background, but one grew accus-tomed to it. It was part of the Blackpool experi-ence.

Val admitted to Sam that she wasn't all that used to social drinking, so what should she choose? At first she had not wanted to look foolish, but now that she knew him better she realized that it didn't matter, that he would never make her feel inferior. He suggested that she should try a Snowball, a cocktail of lemonade and creamy advocaat, which he said was a liqueur made from eggs, sugar and brandy. She found it delicious and had to resist the temptation to drink it all at once. During the evening she drank two of them, refusing a third for fear of being lightheaded. Sam ordered coffee before he saw her back to her hotel. It was served with cream and brown sugar lumps, with dark chocolate mints.

They sat close together on the settee, with Sam's arm around her. 'It's been a wonderful week,' he told her, 'more especially so because I've met you. You do want to go on seeing me, don't you, after we get back home?'

'Yes, I would like to, very much,' she replied. She knew now that he was serious about what he said, that he would not 'lead her up the garden path', as the saying went. 'But people will talk, won't they? The girls at work, I mean. They'll say I'm getting big ideas, hobnobbing with the boss, that sort of thing. And what about your family? I'm sure they'll have a lot to say about it ... that is if you intend to tell them?'

'Of course I shall tell them! Why shouldn't I? It's none of their business who I choose to have as a friend. I won't be dictated to by my mother or by Jonathan. Fortunately my father is a pretty understanding sort of chap.'

'Yes, I've always thought so...'

'And surely you can hold your own with the girls in the office? They might be surprised, but so what? We met on holiday and discovered that we like one another. It would have been just the same if I'd got to know you back home, but I didn't, did I?' He smiled at her. 'This had to happen, Valerie, love. You and me. Don't you think so?'

'Yes, I hope so, Sam,' she replied,

He leaned forward and kissed her gently. 'Now, I'd better see you back to your hotel.'

As they walked the short distance to where Val was staying Sam explained that the next time he would see her was when they were back home.

'I'm spending tomorrow with Jeff and Colin,' he told her. 'I'm sorry. I didn't know I was going to meet you, and we'd planned to have a golfing holiday.'

'You don't need to explain,' said Val. 'You came away with your friends, and I came away with Cissie. I don't know what plans she might have made for tomorrow with this Jack she's met, but I should think she'll want to spend the last day with me.'

'And tomorrow night we're going to the Opera House show,' said Sam. 'We've heard such good reports of it, and it's a must when you're in Blackpool, to see one of the shows. We don't get anything like that back home.'

'All the same, that's where we live, isn't it?' said Val. 'It's great to come away, but it's always nice to go back home.'

'Even more so, now I know I'll be seeing you again,' replied Sam. He put his arms round her when they stopped at the gate, then he kissed her, more deeply and longingly than before. 'I'm afraid it's goodbye for now, but I'll see you next week, as soon as I can. Don't worry, now, it's all going to be fine. Enjoy your last day here... And

I'll see you soon.'

'Yes ... see you, Sam.' She kissed his cheek. 'It's all been lovely. Thank you ... for everything.'

'The pleasure is all mine. Thank you ... for saying you'll go on seeing me. You're a wonderful girl, Valerie.' He held her close for a moment, then reluctantly drew away.

She watched him as he walked back along the street. She could scarcely believe all that had happened over the last few days. It had been like a dream, but going home would be a return to reality. She would think about that, though, only when it was time to do so. She still had her last day in Blackpool to enjoy with Cissie, and to look forward to seeing Sam again.

Janice and Phil spent an enjoyable evening together, doing not very much apart from getting to know one another and discovering what else they had in common.

Her mother had told her she must have the afternoon and evening off, and Nancy and Olive had agreed that they could cope with the evening meal.

'Off you go and enjoy yourself,' they told her. 'You're only young once so you make the most of it.'

Lilian had taken a liking to Philip Grundy as soon as she met him. He was very polite to her and Alec, without being ingratiating or too effusive. He was just nice and friendly and she felt she could trust him with her daughter. He had certainly put a smile on her face. Janice had cheered up considerably these last couple of weeks. She was enjoying her job of waitressing and was very popular with the guests. She had also made friends with the two Yorkshire girls who were staying there; Val and Cissie, a lively pair who had invited her to share in some of their outings. Lilian had been concerned that she was spending too much time on her own and was pleased that she had some new friends. The two girls would be returning home on Saturday, but Janice had said that they intended to keep in touch. And the lasses were already talking about staying at Florabunda again next summer. But who could tell what another year might bring?

Phil called for Janice soon after six thirty. 'What would you like to do?' he asked as they walked towards the promenade. 'We could go to the pictures, but I'd have to make sure to catch the last bus back to camp or else it'd be a long walk.'

'Oh, I'm not bothered about the pictures,' said Janice, 'It's a nice evening, why don't we just walk on the prom?' She had complained recently that she was tired of solitary walks to the pier and back, but it was different now she had met Phil.

'That's the best idea of all,' said Phil, 'but I didn't want you to think I was too mean to pay for the cinema.'

She laughed. 'Of course I don't! Actually, my mum suggested you might come back and have some supper at our place, if you like. I'll make sure you don't miss your bus.'

'That would be great,' he agreed. 'It's a damned nuisance always having to keep an eye on the time. There's a later bus on a Saturday, so I thought we could go to the Tower, if you would like to?'

'I'd love to,' she said. 'It's not a place I'd go to on my own or with the girls, it can get a bit rowdy sometimes. I remember you saying that you like Reginald Dixon, and I'd like to hear him play again.'

'That's settled then,' he said with a satisfied smile. 'Let's walk north, shall we, to the cliffs? Then we can get the full benefit of the Blackpool breeze – if it's not too windy, of course.'

It was certainly breezy when they got to the cliffs; the air was hardly ever still in Blackpool. Janice told him about the popular meeting place, Uncle Tom's Cabin, which had stood on the cliffs near that point during the last century. It had been no more than a wooden hut with the figures of Uncle Tom, Topsy and little Eva, from the story of the same name, up on the roof. It had been a favourite place for refreshments and for dancing until the sea had done its worst. The cliff side had eroded and the building had eventually fallen into the sea.

'Long before our time, but I'd love to have seen it,' said Janice.

'Not so sophisticated as the Winter Gardens or the Tower,' commented Phil, 'but I guess it was jolly good fun. Shall we head back now?'

He took hold of her hand as they strolled back along the cliff top. The sun was setting and soon it would disappear at the point where the sea met the sky. The clouds were tinged with orange and red, golden-rimmed where the sun caught their edge. Dusk was falling by the time they arrived back. It was already two months past the longest day with autumn approaching far more quickly than Janice could wish. At the end of September she would be off to Leeds University. It would mean sharing 'digs' with two other students, about which she had mixed feelings. Unlike many girls she was not looking forward to this as a great adventure. She was happy at home and had no desire to leave. But she got on well with most people, so maybe it would not be so bad. Just lately she had been making sure that she knew how to cook, simple dishes at least, so she would not be completely helpless in the kitchen.

Besides, Phil would be there, not far away in Ilkley. They talked on the way back about her move to Yorkshire. He was due to be demobbed early in September, a couple of weeks before she went to college

'You'll be able to spend some time with us,' he told her. 'My parents will be pleased to meet you. You won't have lectures on a Sunday, will you? And there are the evenings as well. There's a good bus service from Ilkley, and the uni's not far from the city centre, is it?'

'No, just a short tram ride. And I expect my digs will be near the college.'

They enjoyed a light supper when they returned to the hotel. Lilian had made some ham sandwiches for them, as well as the usual coffee and biscuits for the visitors. She left them on their own for a while. There were no other people in the lounge as there would be later, when the visitors returned from a show or the cinema.

Phil did not attempt to be any more intimate with her. They sat side by side on a settee but without any contact. Janice guessed he was being circumspect because he was in her home, with her mother not far away. But she was quite content with the situation at the moment. She and Phil were becoming good friends. They chatted together easily and never ran out of things to say, just as though they had known one another for ages. It was, in fact, still less than a week.

Lilian came in after a while to see if any of the guests wanted supper drinks. There were two couples there, and when she had served them with tea and biscuits she sat down to chat with Phil and Janice.

Lilian and Phil compared their respective guest houses. 'My parents' place is more of a country pub,' he said. 'We can't accommodate as many guests as you have here – there are only five bedrooms apart from the family ones – but we stay open all year. No high season as you have in Blackpool.'

'We're lucky here,' Lilian told him, 'because the season is extended with the Illuminations trade, and that goes on till the end of October. It tails off then, but we open again at Easter if we get any bookings, and the real season starts round about Whitsuntide.'

Phil said that he had been training to be a chef, so he would continue with that and help his parents, for the time being. 'Dad's still quite young, though,' he said, 'and he's no thoughts of retiring. So I might consider a move if something interesting turns up. Who knows?'

'We'll bear you in mind then,' said Lilian with a smile.

Phil looked at Janice and grinned. She smiled

back at him a little unsurely, not knowing what to make of her mother's remark. Most likely it was made in jest, but Mum had certainly taken to the young man,

He looked at his watch. 'Well, I'm sorry to break up the party, but it's time I was on my way. Thank you for the supper, Mrs Butler, and for making me feel so much at home.'

'It's a pleasure, Phil,' she replied. 'You're always welcome. We'll see you soon, I dare say? 'Bye for now...'

Janice walked to the gate with him. 'You've made quite a hit with my mum,' she said. 'She really likes you.'

'And I like her, too,' said Phil. 'She's a lovely lady ... and so are you.' He put his arms round her then, the first time he had done so, apart from when they were dancing, then he kissed her firmly on the lips.

'I'll see you on Saturday then. I'll call for you at – what time shall we say – half past seven?' He kissed her cheek then hurried away.

Janice smiled to herself. So far, so good. He certainly knew the correct way to behave, and her mother liked him, too.

Cissie met Jack outside the pier as arranged, and they crossed the road to Talbot Square and the Tivoli cinema. It was small compared with many of the cinemas in the town and felt stuffy inside.

'Gentlemen prefer blondes!' said Jack as they made their way up the stairs. 'And so do I!' He squeezed Cissie's arm as he led her towards the seats on the back row.

She might have known what to expect, but she was quite agreeable to a kiss and a cuddle, so long as he did not attempt anything else. The news was showing as they sat down. He put his arm round her straight away, then after a moment he kissed her and carried on doing so until the news ended. When the big picture started she told him she would like to watch it if he didn't mind. He shrugged and took his arm away, but after a moment he took hold of her hand. They watched the picture for most of the time, with an occasional kiss which, despite her misgivings, she was starting to enjoy.

'That Marilyn Monroe, she's quite a corker, isn't she?' he whispered, 'but no more than you, Cissie.' He fondled her hand in an intimate way. 'I'll bet she's pretty hot stuff an' all.'

Cissie didn't answer, but as the film went on she felt herself getting closer and closer to Jack. When the film ended they pushed and jostled their way with the crowd, down the narrow stairs and into the street.

'The night's still young,' he said, although it was after half past ten. 'You don't want to go back yet, do you?'

'No, not really. I've got a door key,' she told him.

'Let's make the most of our last evening, then... Our last one for now, I mean. I won't be seeing you tomorrow, Cissie. I'll be spending the day with the lads. You don't mind, do you?'

'No, of course not. I'm going to spend tomorrow with Val. Sam's playing golf with his mates.' She grinned. 'Don't suppose you're doing that, are you?'

'What, me? Not on your Nellie! We'll most likely go to t' Pleasure Beach. We've not been there yet. And tomorrer night, well, a pub crawl, I reckon.'

Jack was heading towards Yates's Wine Lodge which was on the corner near to the cinema. 'Come on, let's go and have a drink ... or two,' he said.

The bar room was crowded but Jack found a table for two tucked away in a corner.

'What are you havin' then?' he asked. She decided to have a short drink, not lager or shandy, or she would be wanting the loo before long.

'I'll have a gin, please,' she said. 'A gin and lime.'

'Okey-doke. Coming up right away.' Jack pushed his way to the bar, and it didn't take him long to get served.

One gin and lime led to two, then to three as they talked together. Jack knocked back his pints without showing any ill effects. Cissie was beginning to feel light-headed, but pleasantly so as she felt Jack's arm around her and listened to him telling her how much he liked her and wanted to go on seeing her after they got back home.

'I'll get in touch very soon,' he said. 'Don't suppose you've got a phone, have you?'

'No, we haven't ... but I'll give you my address.' She scribbled it down on a page from the notebook in her bag. He grinned and tucked it away in his wallet.

'We've got a phone,' he said. 'Not 'cause we're posh or owt like that. Me dad's got his own business, y'see. He's a sort of odd job man and does all sorts of odds and sods for folk. A bit of painting and decorating, and joinery and plastering. Here y' are; that's the number. But make it early evening if you call me, then I'll be back from work. But I'll get in touch with you before you ring, that's for sure.'

Cissie put the paper with the Bradford number written on it into the back of her purse.

'Come on, let's have a stroll on the prom, shall we?' He stood up and pulled her to her feet. She felt rather wobbly and dizzy. It was hot and stuffy in the pub but the fresh air brought her round, to some extent.

They crossed the tramtrack to North Pier, then went down an incline that led to the middle promenade, to the part known as the Colonnades, a series of shelters looking out on the sea with stone pillars supporting the roof. They passed a couple sitting on a seat, closely entwined, but apart from that the place was deserted.

Jack led her to a bench and when they sat down he started to kiss her. She responded eagerly to his touch and to his further advances. She found that she did not mind anymore, she was willing to go along wherever he led her. He was gentle with her, surprisingly so she realized, as she looked back on it later. At the time it seemed inevitable that it should happen, and she offered no resistance. She was vaguely aware that Jack was not inexperienced, and if he gathered that it was, for her, the first time, he made no comment.

She said very little afterwards as she straightened her clothing and rose, rather unsteadily, to her feet.

'I'd better get back,' she murmured. 'It's late,

141

isn't it?'

'Don't worry, I'll make sure you get back safely,' he said.

There was a taxi cab parked in Talbot Square. Jack opened the door and helped her to get inside. 'Make sure this young lady gets back alright,' he said to the driver as he handed him some coins. 'I won't come with you,' he said to her. 'My digs are quite near, so there's no point. This man'll take care of you.' He kissed her cheek. 'I'll be seeing you soon, Cissie. 'Bye for now. Look after yerself...'

''Bye, Jack,' she answered dazedly. 'Yes ... see you soon.'

'Where are we going, luv?' asked the driver.

She told him the street. 'The Florabunda Hotel, it's just off the prom, near the Carlton.'

'Oh aye; I know it. I'll have you back in a jiffy.'

He helped her out of the cab and up the path, then waited while she found her key.

'Quite a night, was it?' he asked.

'Yes ... you could say so,' she replied bemusedly.

'Well, you take care then, luv. You'll feel better in the morning.'

She made sure the door was locked, then staggered up the stairs to the bedroom. She guessed that Val would be back, and so she was, fast asleep it seemed, so Cissie did not put on the light. Val stirred as she undressed quietly in the dark.

'I tried to wait up for you, but I was too tired,' she said. 'What time is it?'

'I don't know. Go back to sleep, Val. I'll see you in the morning.'

'It's late, isn't it? Where've you been till now?'

142

'It doesn't matter. I'm ... OK. I don't want to talk now, I'm tired.'

'Alright, then, night-night...'

'G'night, Val... Sleep tight.'

TEN

Cissie woke up the following morning feeling slightly dizzy and with the sense of something there at the back of her mind, something that was troubling her. She lay still for a few moments, gathering her thoughts together. She knew she must have had too much to drink and it didn't take much for her to start to lose control of her senses.

She recalled the pub near to the cinema, Yates's Wine Lodge, and Jack plying her with gin and limes in quick succession. She remembered the walk on the prom, the secluded shelter behind the stone pillars... She gave an audible gasp of horror as it all came back to her. Jack kissing her and fondling her in such a persuasive way, and she had been like putty in his hands, not protesting at all, just going along with him. She sat bolt upright in bed. Oh, dear God in heaven, whatever had she done! The thoughts in her mind were not really blasphemous. Cissie just felt that she was badly in need of some sort of help right now.

Val, in the next bed, sat up too, awakened from her sleep by Cissie's cry.

'Whatever's the matter, Cissie?' she asked.

'I don't know,' answered her friend. 'I'm ... not sure. I must have been having a bad dream.' She couldn't tell her friend what had happened, she would be so shocked. They had talked about such matters, and they had both agreed that they would never go so far. She shook her head in bewilderment.

'I'm not feeling too well,' she said. She gave a shaky laugh. 'Too much to drink last night, I'm afraid, and I'm not used to it, am I? Silly me, it's my own fault.'

'Yes, you were rather late back, weren't you?'

'We went for a drink after we'd been to the pictures. I had three gin and limes, so no wonder I'm feeling woozy. I'll happen feel better when I've had some breakfast, though I don't think I can face bacon and egg.'

Val gave her an odd look, hoping that that was all that had happened. Cissie had been out so late, and she didn't really know that Jack. You don't know Sam all that well either, whispered a little voice inside her, yet she did feel certain that he meant every word he said. Whereas that Jack, he was a real wide boy, unless she had got it all wrong. There was something about the fellow that Val did not trust.

Cissie tried to pull herself together and act normally. She didn't want Val to suspect that anything was wrong. She could not face the cooked breakfast, but after a bowl of cereal and a slice of buttered toast with marmalade she began to feel much better, in body if not in mind.

She answered Val's questions regarding Jack. Yes, she had said goodbye to him for now, because he was spending today with his friend. 'But I've got his phone number,' she said, 'an' he wants me to ring him. It's his dad's number, actually, 'cause he's got his own business. Jack's got my address, an' he's going to get in touch soon after we get home. He's really nice, Val,' she added, a shade defiantly. 'I really like him ... a lot. What about you and Sam? Will you be seeing him again?'

'Yes, of course.' Val smiled serenely. 'I like him a lot, just as you said about Jack. It might be complicated with Sam's family and everything, but he's sure it will work out alright. Now, the important thing is what we're going to do today, our last day.'

'Nothing too strenuous,' said Cissie. 'I mean, we don't want to walk miles along the prom, do we?' She could not tell Val that she was feeling rather achy and sore, but she did need a breath of fresh air to make her head feel clear again.

'The sun's still shining,' said Val. 'And, d'you know what? We've never worn our bathing costumes, have we?'

'We can't swim,' said Cissie. 'I can't think why we brought them.'

'To sunbathe, that's why. It'll be a waste of money if we don't wear them. What about getting deckchairs and sitting on the sands for an hour or two? We can have a paddle in the sea if we feel like it, or just sit and read and soak up the sun.'

'That suits me,' replied Cissie. 'Then p'raps we could have a last look at the shops after we've had some lunch. I want to get a present for me mam and dad. She's so hard to please, though, is Mam. And Walter an' all. I suppose I'll have to get something for him.'

'What are you going to do about Walter ... if you're going to see Jack again?'

'I've promised I'll see Jack,' said Cissie, sounding quite definite about it. 'An' I'm going to, an' all! I don't know what I'm going to tell Walter... But it was never really an engagement or owt like that. He might've thought so, but it wasn't.'

Val thought that her friend sounded very anxious about it all. 'Well, never mind all that now,' she said. 'Let's get ready and go to the beach.'

They put on their bathing costumes with their clothes on top, then put one of their own towels in a bag, just in case they decided to dip their toes at the edge of the ocean. They walked along to North Pier, then hired a couple of deckchairs which they had to carry down the slope to the sands. The tide was well out so they should be able to sunbathe for a while, provided the sun kept it's early promise.

Cissie put on her sun glasses and tried to read her *Woman* magazine, but found that she could not concentrate. The happenings of the previous night were looming large in her mind. The problem page and the replies of the Agony Aunt only served to make things worse. There was, as usual, a girl who was pregnant and did now know what to do, and a woman whose husband was unfaithful. It seemed that everyone had problems one way or another. She cast a glance at Val who looked very contented, reading her *True Romance* magazine and smiling to herself. But things didn't always work out the way they did in romantic stories.

The sun disappeared behind a cloud and Cissie gave a shudder. She put on her cardigan, which was not the thing to wear with a bathing costume, but it was turning rather chilly. Val looked across at her, then up at the sky.

'Oh dear! What's happened to the sun? It looks as though we might be unlucky with our sunbathing. I'd better put my cardy on as well... That feels better,' she said, pulling the woolly garment round her shoulders. 'Maybe it wasn't such a good idea after all... Cissie, what's the matter?'

Cissie had taken off her sunglasses and Val could see the blank expression in her eyes, so unlike her normal cheerful self. She looked distraught, and as Val regarded her in concern she gave an intake of breath, a sort of sob, then she began to cry.

'Oh, Val ... I've done something dreadful. I wasn't going to tell you 'cause I knew you'd be shocked, but I can't keep it to meself any longer.'

'Cissie ... whatever is it?' Val went over and knelt on the sand beside her friend. She put an arm round her. 'Come on now, you can tell me. I'm your friend, and we share everything, don't we?' She did have an inkling as to what might be troubling Cissie. After all, what else could it be? She had been very strange when she woke up, and she had admitted that she'd had too much to drink.

'It's Jack ... Jack and me,' said Cissie, her voice shaky and indistinct between her sobs. 'What we did... Oh, Val. I know it's awful, an' I shouldn't have done it, but I let him ... you know ... we've done that!'

'Oh, Cissie...' She held her friend close to her,

not knowing what to say. There was no point in being shocked and horrified, as that would only make her feel worse. 'Don't get upset about it. It's not the end of the world. I expect he ... well, he knew you'd had too much to drink, and he made the most of it, didn't he?' She, Val, had had the feeling all along that Jack was not to be trusted.

'No ... no, it wasn't like that,' Cissie protested. 'He didn't force me. I did it because I wanted to, and now ... I feel so dreadful. I know I shouldn't have done it.'

'But you did, and that's that,' said Val, possibly more bluntly than she intended. But to think that Cissie could have been so stupid as to let it happen after all she had said, after the way they had both talked about it and said that they never would. But then she, Val, had never been tempted, had she? If it had been herself and Sam... She knew that she was falling in love with him. Who could tell how she might behave if ever...?

She put an end to her rambling thoughts. 'I can see why you're worried,' she said, 'but it was the first time, wasn't it? And I don't think it can happen the first time ... that you could ... be having a baby. But time will tell, won't it?'

Cissie had stopped crying now, but she looked fearfully at her friend. 'But I won't know, will I? It might be ages before I know...'

'What do you mean?' asked Val. Then she remembered. 'Oh yes, you told me once, didn't you, that you have problems with ... all that?'

'I never know when I'm going to start,' said Cissie. Like most girls of their time, Cissie and Val had been brought up to keep such matters as monthly periods to themselves. It was considered unseemly to talk about such private things. Cissie's periods were irregular, but her doctor had said there was nothing to worry about. She was perfectly healthy, and it would probably sort itself out in time.

'I can go six weeks or even longer,' she said now. 'I just never know when it'll happen. I had one the week before we came away, so it'll probably be ages before... Oh, Val, what am I going to do?'

'It won't have happened, not the first time,' said Val, with more conviction than she was feeling. 'Anyway, you'll be seeing Jack next week, won't you? You must tell him that it mustn't happen again. And if he really likes you, as you say he does, then he'll listen to you, won't he?'

Cissie nodded numbly. 'Yes, I hope so. And then there's Walter...'

'Don't think about it now,' said Val. 'It won't do any good to keep talking about it. Come on, it's turning really chilly now. Let's go and have some lunch, then we'll have a look round the shops.'

Cissie stood up. 'OK, I'll try to forget about it for now. But I'm glad I've told you. It was driving me mad, keeping it to meself.'

When they had put their clothes on they decided to go back to the hotel to get changed. Their bathing costumes were proving to be impractical as well as unnecessary now that the sun had disappeared.

They took a bus back into the town and had lunch at the cafeteria in Marks and Spencer's, before looking round at all the tempting merchandise that the store had to offer.

'I think I'll get a headscarf for my mum,' said Val. 'There are some really colourful ones here, see. Do you think your mum would like one?'

'Goodness knows,' said Cissie. 'She might or she might not, there's no pleasing her sometimes. Yes, I suppose it's as good as anything. She usually wears one when she goes shopping.'

Val chose one with a pattern of autumn leaves and Cissie one striped in red, white and blue. It was rather bold in design, but she thought her mother might like it as she had been a staunch royalist since the young Queen Elizabeth had come to the throne. They chose ties for their dads, discreetly patterned, to be worn with their best suits on a Sunday.

'I'd better get a present for Walter,' said Cissie. 'A tie, do you think, or a scarf? It gets cold when he's out cycling.'

'Do you really think it's a good idea?' said Val. 'I mean if you're going to start seeing Jack, perhaps it might be better not to bother. If you give him something he might think that everything's alright.'

'But he'll probably bring summat back for me,' said Cissie. 'I can't say Walter's not generous. He's always buying me chocolates. I don't know what to do, honest I don't. I know I'll have to tell him, 'cause I do want to see Jack again. Oh heck! Why does it have to be so bloomin' complicated? I'd better get him a present anyway, then I'll just see how it goes when I get back.'

She chose a plaid scarf for Walter; then they window-shopped and wandered round RHO Hills department store until it was time to go back to the hotel. The good weather they had enjoyed all week had come to an abrupt end. There was a chilly breeze blowing and a feeling of autumn in the air.

They decided not to go out after their evening meal. As was the custom in many hotels, Mrs Butler had prepared fish for the main course because it was Friday. Today it was freshly caught haddock in bread crumbs, with chips and garden peas, with her special sherry trifle to follow.

They packed their suitcases, apart from the items they would need the following morning.

'It's rather sad, isn't it?' said Val. 'But we've had a great time. And we've met all sorts of people.'

'Yeah...' said Cissie doubtfully. Then, 'Yes, 'course we have,' she agreed. 'Who'd have thought we'd each get a new boyfriend?' There was a touch of bravado in her statement.

Val knew that her friend was worried, as well she might be, but she was trying to put a brave face on things after unburdening herself of her feelings of guilt.

Janice joined them in the lounge later that evening. She wrote down their addresses, promising that she would keep in touch.

'You've got my address here,' she said, 'and I'll write to you when I get settled in my digs in Leeds. Not that I expect us to exchange letters every week, or even every month, but we mustn't lose contact with one another now that we've met and got on so well. I've had a lovely time with the two of you.'

'And now there's Phil, isn't there?' said Val.

'Yes...' Janice smiled happily. 'He'll be de-mobbed before I go to college. He's only here for another three weeks or so, but it's nice to know we can meet up again when I go to Yorkshire. And you'll be seeing your new friends again, Sam and Jack, won't you?' she added.

'Yes, I hope so,' replied Cissie, sounding not all that sure.

'She's got the problem of Walter to sort out first,' said Val. 'That's what she's worried about ... isn't it, Cissie?' She didn't want her friend to go blurting out the full extent of her problem. 'But she's bought him a nice present to soften the blow.' Val was trying to make light of the situation.

'Oh yes, you told me about Walter,' said Janice. 'Life's complicated sometimes, isn't it?'

'You can say that again!' Cissie answered glumly. Then she laughed. 'Ne'er mind, eh? There are worse troubles at sea, as my mam sometimes says, whatever that means.'

'Yes, it'll all come out in the wash,' added Val. 'That's one of my mum's favourites. Don't worry, Cissie. It'll all sort itself out,' she said, with a meaningful look at her friend.

The taxi, driven by the same man who had brought them the week before, was at the door of Florabunda at nine o'clock, in good time for them to catch their train back to Halifax. Janice's parents seemed sorry to see them leave although they were, in reality, only two visitors among the many who had stayed there that summer. Mr Butler carried their cases to the car, and Mrs Butler kissed both of them on the cheek.

'It's been nice to meet the pair of you,' she said,

'and we hope we'll see you again. Take care now. Janice will give me news of you, I'm sure.'

Janice hugged them both, and their goodbyes to one another were a little tearful.

'You've had a good time, have you?' asked the taxi driver as they set off. 'It sounds as though you have.'

'Yes, smashing, thanks,' replied Val.

'And you've behaved yerselves, have you?' he said, grinning. 'I've got a lass about the same age as you two.'

'Yes, of course!' said Cissie primly. 'We're good girls, aren't we, Val?'

'Most definitely,' said her friend.

'That's alright then,' said the driver. 'I can tell who are well-brought-up lasses when I see them... Look after yourselves,' he added as Val paid the fare. 'I might see you again next year, who knows?'

The station was crowded with returning holidaymakers, but there was no problem in finding their train as Blackpool was the end of the line. It was ready and waiting to depart.

The train was crowded but they managed to get a seat opposite a middle-aged couple at a table for four. The man obligingly heaved their cases on to the rack above their seats, but once they had thanked him they did not enter into conversation. Val and Cissie tried to read, but each of them was wrapped up in their own thoughts about what had happened that week, and what might be to come.

Not all the passengers were travelling as far as Yorkshire. The couple opposite them left at Blackburn, and by the time they reached the Pennine hills the train was far less crowded. They found, though, that they still had very little to say to one another. The silence was companionable, however, such was their closeness and understanding of one another.

They had to take yet another taxi when they arrived at their destination. It would be the last time for some while, though, that they would avail themselves of such an extravagance.

Val knew that her parents would already have arrived back from their holiday as the coach tour to the Cotswolds was from Sunday to Friday. Cissie did not know what time to expect her parents to be back from their holiday with their friends, the Clarksons, but she guessed it would be later in the day.

'Come in and have a bite to eat with us,' said Val when the taxi pulled up at her house. Both girls were feeling rather hungry as they had not taken sandwiches to eat on the train this time. 'My dad will carry your case home for you later – it's only just up the street.'

But Cissie refused. 'No, ta,' she said. 'I'd best get home. I don't suppose there'll be anything much to eat in the house, so I'll have to nip out to the corner shop and get some milk and bread, and maybe some boiled ham. I expect Mam'll bring some meat back for our Sunday dinner. Don't worry about me. I'll be OK.'

'Alright then, if you're sure?' Val was concerned for her friend. She would not get the warm welcome at home such as she, Val, would receive. She kissed Cissie's cheek. 'Here's my share of the taxi fare, you settle up with the driver. And I'll see you on Monday.'

'Yes, see you...' said Cissie, giving her friend a quick hug.

Val's dad was already coming out of the door to carry his daughter's case, with her mother close behind. They both waved cheerily to Cissie as the taxi drove away. She could not help but feel slightly envious, knowing how Val was cared for and cherished.

The driver carried her case to the door, and she let herself into the house. It felt cheerless and empty, and chilly, too, although it was still summer, but a far colder summer day than it had been at the start of their holiday. The place was very tidy, however. Her mother would never go away and leave the house without everything being in its proper place.

She flopped down in the nearest chair feeling forlorn and miserable. It had been such a wonderful holiday ... apart from one little episode, one foolish mistake she had made. But that had happened because she and Jack cared about one another ... hadn't it? Now the lovely time had all come to an end so suddenly, and she felt dreadfully alone, and lonely. And whatever was she to do about Walter?

Cissie put her head in her hands and burst into tears.

ELEVEN

Val and Cissie did not meet again until they finished work on Monday. Cissie's shift had started earlier in the morning but they finished at roughly the same time. Val waited for her friend outside the main entrance.

She was pleased to see that Cissie looked quite cheerful. She had seemed really down-in-the-dumps when they had parted on Saturday. As for herself, Val had every reason to feel on top of the world, but she knew better than to blurt out her exciting news until she saw how things were with Cissie.

'So, how's it going?' she asked. 'Did your parents get back alright?'

'Yes, middle of the afternoon. I'd been out to the corner shop to get some things we needed, so I was able to make 'em some ham sandwiches, and that put Mam in a better mood than usual. As you might know, they'd had a wonderful time with the Clarksons. I don't suppose I'll ever hear the last of it.'

'And did she like her scarf?'

'I think so, you can never tell with Mam. She said, "By heck! They'll see me coming in this, but at least it's patriotic – red, white and blue." Anyroad, she wore it when she went to church, so I think she was quite pleased. What about your mam and dad? Did they enjoy the coach trip?'

'Oh yes, they were thrilled to bits with it. They're already planning the next one, probably to Devon, next year.'

They were quiet for a moment before Cissie said, 'And Walter came round last night, you might know!'

'Oh ... and what happened? Did you say ... anything?'

'About the holiday? About ... Jack, you mean? No, I couldn't very well, could I? He was real nice and friendly. Me mam pushed Dad out of the room so as we could be alone, an' he said how much he'd missed me. He gave me some Kendal mint cake an' a big box of fudge. So I gave him his scarf, an' he said he really liked it, then he started getting all lovey-dovey. I told him to stop it 'cause Mam might come in. Anyroad, I've said I'll see him on Wednesday night. What else could I do? But I 'spect I'll have heard from Jack by then, so I shall have to tell him.'

'He won't like it, Cissie...'

'Then he'll have to lump it, won't he? I've been trying not to think about that other little problem. Val, you don't really think I could be ... pregnant, do you?'

'It's highly unlikely, but if you keep worrying it might make it worse. Worry can play havoc with the way your body works, you know.'

Cissie nodded. 'I'll try not to worry then. But I shall keep me legs crossed in future, I'm telling you! Anyway, what about you? I don't suppose you've seen Sam yet, have you?'

'Actually, I have,' said Val, trying to curb her feeling of elation.

She told Cissie how he had come into the office midmorning and asked the supervisor if he could have a word with Miss Horrocks. The other girls had stared as she went out into the corridor with him, and had been all agog when she went back, wanting to know what it was all about. She hadn't told them anything much, just said it was a query his brother had about a letter she had written. But he had really come, as he had promised he would, to assure her that he wanted to see her again.

'So he's calling for me on Wednesday night, and we'll go for a drive in the country and have a drink somewhere,' she said casually, but it was hard to quell the excitement she was feeling at the prospect.

'You mean ... calling for you at your house?' Cissie sounded surprised.

'Yes. He says he wants to say hello to my parents and make it all above board.'

'And have you told your mam and dad about him?'

'Yes. I told them on Saturday. They were rather wary about it, and Mum said the usual things about not wanting me to get hurt, and what about his family and all that.'

'So what about them then, Sam's family? All the Walker clan. Is he going to take you to meet them?'

'I don't know,' Val replied doubtfully. She didn't know the answer to that. 'But first things first,' she added. 'I trust Sam, and that's the most important thing.'

They had arrived at Cissie's house now, so they said goodbye and 'See you on Wednesday.' Their

158

shifts did not coincide the next day.

When they met on Wednesday to walk home from work together Cissie appeared a little worried.

'What's the matter?' asked Val, although she had an idea as to what it might be. 'Aren't you happy about seeing Walter tonight?'

'No, you're dead right I'm not,' snapped Cissie. 'I've told you how I feel about him. But it's not just that ... I haven't heard from Jack yet, and he said he'd get in touch with me. I thought I'd have heard from him by now.'

'It's only Wednesday,' said Val. 'We've only been home four days, and he'll have to write, won't he? He can't contact you by phone. It's early days yet.' But she understood why her friend was worried.

'I won't be able to tell Walter, though, that I don't want to go on seeing him, not till I've heard from Jack. It wouldn't be right if I was to go out with both of them, would it? I wouldn't like it if anybody did that to me... I don't know what to do.'

'Just go out with Walter tonight and be nice and friendly. There's no point in upsetting him, not until you know how things are with Jack.' Val had her doubts about that young man as she had had all along, but it would only upset Cissie even more if she voiced her misgivings.

'Yes, I suppose I'll have to,' said Cissie. 'But I shall make sure there's no ... you know what! I've learnt my lesson there.'

'Well, try to enjoy your evening,' said Val as they parted. 'Walter's not so bad, and at least you know him and everything about him.'

'S'pose so,' agreed Cissie, looking as though

she understood what her friend meant. 'You enjoy yourself an' all. See you soon...'

When Walter called for Cissie that evening she was surprised to see that he was in his father's car. He had passed his test, but his father very rarely lent him the car and he could not yet afford one of his own. So despite her ambivalent feelings about Walter Cissie found it quite pleasant to be chauffered around instead of walking as they usually did, especially as the evening was chilly. The weather had changed since their return from holiday and was feeling far more autumnal.

'Where d'you want to go then?' he asked. 'I thought we'd go and have a drink somewhere.'

'Oh, I don't know,' said Cissie, 'You decide; you know these places better than me.' He often cycled out into the countryside with his friends; whereas she seldom went far from the town, apart from an occasional trip to Bradford or Leeds.

'We'll go to Hebden Bridge, then,' he said, turning to smile at her. 'There's one or two decent pubs there.'

She smiled back cautiously. She had decided that she must make the best of the evening and try to be friendly towards Walter and, for the moment, put all thoughts of Jack to the back of her mind.

Walter was quite a good-looking young man, in a dark, swarthy sort of way, she thought now. His hair was very dark brown, almost black, dead straight and always sleek and well groomed. His eyes were dark brown, too, with well-defined eyebrows. His nose was very slightly aquiline, and he had a haughty look except when he smiled, which he did only when he was very pleased about something.

Cissie could not help her thoughts turning to Jack as she compared the two of them. Jack could not be more different, with his tousled mop of fair hair, and his blue eyes that twinkled mischievously as he laughed. He was continually finding something to amuse him or to make a joke about.

'What's the matter?' asked Walter. 'Don't you fancy that?'

'Yes, of course I do,' she replied hastily, realizing that she had been wool-gathering instead of answering him. 'That's fine. I was just thinking that it's ages since I was in Hebden Bridge,' she said, in an effort to excuse her rambling thoughts.

Walter did not say much as he drove, carefully, as he always did, the short distance, to the nearby small town. Hebden Bridge was a picturesque place, though somewhat stark and forbidding-looking in the sunless evening. A hump-backed bridge spanned the River Calder between rows of dark greystone houses. Numerous mills were crowded together in the valley bottom, with the wild moorland towering above.

They found a parking place without much trouble, and went into a pub on the main street which Walter said served good ale. Cissie was glad of the warmth from the fire burning in the grate. There was a homely feel to the inn. A golden spaniel was sleeping on the hearth and there were dark oak tables, spindle-backed chairs, and wooden beams on the ceiling.

'What are you having then?' asked Walter, when they had found a quiet table in an alcove.

Cissie shuddered inwardly as she remembered the gin and limes that had been her downfall. 'Something that'll warm me up a bit,' she said. 'It's real parky tonight.'

'OK. What about a drop of whisky, then? Whisky and ginger. How about that?'

'That's fine, thanks,' she replied. 'Not too much whisky, though...'

'It'll do you good,' said Walter.

He returned in a few moments with her drink and his own glass of strong Yorkshire ale. 'Cheers,' he said, raising his glass.

She did the same. 'Yes ... cheers, Walter,' she said. 'This is a nice change. I've not been here before.'

'So ... tell me about your holiday,' he said, looking at her keenly. 'How was Blackpool? You've not told me anything about it, and what you got up to.'

'That's because I haven't seen you,' she replied, a little flustered. 'Not on our own, I mean. And you haven't told me about your holiday neither.'

'Oh, we cycled till our legs nearly dropped off. We enjoyed the scenery and the good weather, then we had a slap-up meal every night and a good night's kip. Nothing all that exciting, but it was good being with the lads... I missed you, though, Cissie. I want to go away with you next time. Did you miss me?'

'Course I did,' she replied hastily. 'But I was busy with Val. We did all sorts of things. There's so much to do in Blackpool – the Pleasure Beach, an' the prom, an' the piers, an' the Winter Gardens, an' the Tower. We went dancing there... Everybody does,' she added, possibly a shade defiantly, knowing what he would say.

He picked up on her remark straight away. 'Oh, so you went dancing, did you? And who did you dance with?'

'Oh, just a few chaps, that's all. There's an RAF camp near Blackpool, and the lads go there on Saturday night, so there's no shortage of partners.

'I see. So you danced with some RAF blokes, did you?'

Cissie shrugged. 'One or two. But we really went to see the ballrooms at the Winter Gardens and the Tower. Both of 'em are fantastic. There's nowt like that round here.'

'So I've heard.' He was looking at her questioningly, waiting, it seemed, for her to tell him more.

She had wondered whether or not to tell him about Val and her encounter with Samuel Walker. She decided now that she would do so, if only to take his attention away from herself.

'Oh ... and I must tell you,' she said eagerly. 'You'll never guess what happened!'

'Go on then. Surprise me. What have you been up to?'

'Not me,' she answered hurriedly. 'It was Val. She got friendly with Mr Samuel from the mill. He asked her to dance, but he didn't know who she was. She knew him, of course, right away. Anyroad, she told him where she worked and they've got real pally. She's calling him Sam as though she's known him for ages. In fact she's seeing him tonight. I don't know where they're going, but she's getting real keen on him, I can tell you.'

'Well, good for Valerie, but I'm glad it was her he took fancy to and not you.'

'She works in the office, though, a cut above what I do. Don't suppose he'd want owt to do with a mill girl such as me. But he's quite nice when you get to know him, not all stuck-up and superior. I thought he might be havin' her on, like, and that he'd drop her after the holiday, but it seems that he wants to go on seeing her.'

'Yes. I've always found Mr Samuel much easier to get on with than his brother,' said Walter. 'But never mind about him. What did you do while Valerie was off hobnobbing with the boss? Were you on your own, eh?'

'Oh no, she only saw him a time or two. We all went to the Tower together, him and his mates and Val and me, an' he paid for both of us. But we got friendly with a girl who works at the hotel. Well, she doesn't really work there all the time, she's the landlady's daughter. So I wasn't on me own. I went out with her. Janice she's called. I went to the pictures with her, and we all went to see the show at the Opera House, Janice and Val and me.' What Cissie was telling him was mostly the truth, but she was not telling him all of it. Now was not the time. She was sure to hear from Jack soon, then it would be time enough to face up to reality.

'So a good time was had by all,' said Walter. 'But the next time you visit Blackpool it will be with me; you can be sure of that.' He put his arm around her in a proprietorial way. She was trying not to encourage him but it seemed that he was determined, tonight, to make it clear to her that she was his girl.

This became more obvious as they drove home. She knew now why he had borrowed his father's car. He drove to a secluded spot down a narrow lane. He stopped the car and drew her close to him.

'Cissie...' he whispered. 'What must I do to show you how much I care for you? You must know that I want you. I want us to be close ... real close, but you always push me away. I won't force you, it wouldn't be right and I would never do that, but why don't you feel the same way as I do? We've been going together for ages, and I thought that by now...'

'But it wouldn't be right, Walter,' she interrupted him. 'I don't care what other girls do. I've always believed that it's something you don't do, not until... And just think what my mam and dad would say, and yours an' all. They'd go mad! My mam's always going on about girls who are no better than they ought to be.'

'It's got nothing to do with them,' said Walter. 'Cissie ... I do love you, you know.'

She was somewhat taken aback. It was the first time he had said the word 'love'. Did that mean that he was really committed to her ... or was he just trying to have his way with her? She had carried on seeing him because she had nothing else to do. No other boyfriends had come on the scene until Jack. She did not know how to answer Walter. It would not be right to say that she loved him, too, because she didn't. In fact she was waiting for the right moment to tell him that she did not want to go on seeing him, that she had met someone else.

But just supposing Jack didn't...? She had felt sure she would have heard from him by now.

There would probably be a letter tomorrow. But supposing there wasn't? And what if...? There was a vague idea forming at the back of her mind...

'Cissie, what's the matter?' said Walter, shaking her a little. 'You're miles away, and I'm telling you that I love you. And it's not because I want you to do something you're not sure about.'

'No, I know that, Walter,' she replied. She responded to his kisses and more intimate embraces for a while, then she put a stop to it. 'No, Walter, I can't. Not now. Anyway, it's getting late, an' you know what my mam's like if I'm not back by eleven. She'll be pacing the floor.'

'I thought she didn't mind if you were with me? Your mam seems to like me. I can't think why.'

'Because she's pally with yer mam and dad, and she wants to keep on the right side of them.' She likes you because you toady up to her, she thought. 'But I've told you she'd have a fit if she knew what you wanted me to do.'

'I doubt it,' said Walter. 'They've been young once, haven't they? Though it's hard to imagine it sometimes.'

'Come on, Walter, we'd better get going,' she said, pulling her jumper down and straightening her skirt. 'You don't want to get in her bad books, do you?'

'OK then...' Reluctantly he started the car. 'But you'll see me again on Saturday, won't you? That's the night we usually go out.'

'Alright then...'

Walter felt like laughing out loud. He had an idea that, finally, her resolve was weakening.

The next day was Thursday and there was still

no word from Jack, nor again on the Friday. On Saturday morning Cissie walked into town and found a phone box. It was time she tried to get in touch with him. He had told her to ring in the early evening when he would be home from work, but maybe, like herself he would not be working on Saturday. Or there might be someone she could leave a message with – his mother, maybe?

She took out the paper that Jack had given her, put her pennies in and dialed the number. The phone at the other end did not ring; there was a continuous buzzing noise indicating that the number was wrong. She must have dialled a wrong digit, so she tried again. Once again, though, she got the sound that meant that the number was unobtainable, and her money was returned. Cissie felt a chill run right through her, but she could not face up to what her mind was trying to tell her.

She found a newsagent's and bought a local paper, then she went into the town market and bought a cup of tea and a scone. Sitting down at a table she opened the paper, perusing the list of adverts for odd job men. Jack's name was Broadbent, at least that was what he had told her, although she was starting to wonder if even that was true. She did not know his father's first name, but it was worth a try. There were adverts galore for plumbers, electricians, joiners, decorators and, unfortunately, several Broadbents. Jack had said that his dad did a bit of everything, a sort of Jack of all trades. Perhaps he was called Jack as well? There was a J Broadbent, a Mike and a Peter.

But what would be the point of it all? How could she ring up and ask these men if they had a son called Jack? A son who clearly did not want to be traced. Unwilling though she was to face up to it Cissie was realizing that Jack had no intention of seeing her again. She had been, to him, just a holiday flirtation.

She buttered her scone which was surprisingly moist and full of fruit. She had had only a small piece of toast for breakfast; with so much on her mind she had not felt like eating. She decided now that there was no point in shedding tears about Jack, she had to face facts. She had 'gone the whole way' with a fellow she hardly knew, and it was possible that she might be pregnant. But, as she had told Val, she might not know for ages, and by then it would be too late. It was only three weeks since she had what her mother called her 'monthlies' and it was unlikely that she would have another one soon.

Cissie knew that it was time for her to go along with what Walter wanted. Then, if the worst happened she could say that it was Walter's baby. No one would have any reason to think otherwise except for Val, and she knew that her best friend would never split on her. Her mother would be shocked and ashamed and, more than likely, so would Walter's mother. Of course she might not be pregnant. She might be worrying unnecessarily, but she could not afford to take the risk. She didn't like deceiving Walter but she had no choice. At least he would be a willing scapegoat.

When he called for her that evening he was not in his father's car as she had thought he might be. He explained that his parents had gone to a whist drive at his dad's bowling club a little way out of town, and that they needed the car.

'So there will be no one at home,' he said. He raised his eyebrows, looking at her meaningfully.

Cissie nodded, but did not respond immediately to his suggestive smile. It would not do to appear too eager after she had been spurning his advances for so long.

'I thought we could go and have a drink some-where,' he went on, 'and then we will have the house to ourselves. Mum and Dad won't be back for ages. It's always after eleven when they've been to a whist drive.'

'Alright then,' she said, still a shade reluctantly, 'but you know how I feel about ... things.'

'And I've told you how I feel about you,' he said, putting his arm around her and drawing her close.

There was a pub a little way out of town which did not get as crowded on a Saturday night as those in the town centre. It was near to the estate of semi-detached houses where Walter's family lived.

'What are you having then?' he asked as they sat down in comfortable chairs in the lounge bar. 'Whisky and ginger, like you had the other night?'

'I think I'll have brandy with ginger,' she replied. She was not feeling chilly as she had done the last time they were together, but rather shaky and churned up inside. Maybe the brandy would help to settle her stomach. The first drink and the second did just that and also calmed her mind, in-ducing a sense of detachment from her problems. The chatted in a casual way, and Cissie knew that Walter did not want to stay there too long.

His home was a few minutes' walk away in one of the newer suburbs of the town, in a tree-lined avenue facing a small area of parkland. He took her coat and hung it on the hallstand, then they sat together on the settee in the living room. There was a small fire still burning in the grate with a fireguard round it for safety. Cissie responded to his eager kisses, but demurred a little when he suggested they would be more comfortable upstairs.

'Do you really think we should...?'

'Why not? I got the impression that you were changing your mind, that you wanted this just as much as I do?'

'I'm not sure, Walter. Supposing your parents come back?'

'I've told you, they won't, not for ages. And ... afterwards, we can watch the television. They won't mind you being here. I told them we might come back here. You know that they like you, Cissie.'

She let him believe that she was still a little unsure as he led her upstairs and into his bedroom. It was, of course, the first time she had been into Walter's room, she had been upstairs only to use the bathroom. She scarcely noticed her surroundings. Her thoughts were a confused jumble – part anxiety, part relief that this would solve her problem, and, to her surprise, part desire brought about by Walter's embraces. He undressed and encouraged her to do the same. She did so, feeling embarrassed, then he removed the last of her underwear.

He made love to her in a gentle and considerate way, unlike his more usual curt and bossy manner.

She wondered, fleetingly, if he would know that it was not the first time for her, and she had the presence of mind to behave as though it was. She knew, as she had known with Jack, that it was not the first time for Walter. He had had other girlfriends before herself, so maybe she should not be surprised.

He held her close afterwards and kissed her tenderly. 'There,' he said. 'You didn't mind too much, did you? I do love you, Cissie.'

She felt that he spoke the truth, but she could not say in honesty that she felt the same way about him. She was grateful, though, that he had got her out of a dreadful predicament, but that was something he must never know.

They dressed quickly and went downstairs. Obviously Walter, also, was a teeny bit anxious lest his parents should return, despite what he had said. He made a pot of tea, then switched on the television set. They settled down to watch – or to make a pretence of watching – the variety show, as though that was what they had been doing all evening.

'You're very quiet,' said Walter. 'You're not having second thoughts, are you?'

'No...' Cissie answered a little unsurely. 'But ... supposing something has happened? You know... What if I'm having a baby?'

Walter laughed, but rather nervously. 'You can't be, not the first time. It can't happen ... not the first time.' So he had obviously been none the wiser about her former experience. But he was sounding a shade doubtful.

'I think it could happen,' she replied. 'It's not

very likely, but it might. I know a girl that it happened to.'

'Well ... we'd get married then,' he said, without any hesitation.

'But what would our parents say?'

'I've told you before, it's nothing to do with them. I love you, Cissie. And it's what I've always wanted; well, for quite some time. But I had to know that you felt the same. Cissie ... will you marry me?'

She stared at him for a moment, surprised and bewildered. She had not been expecting that. On the other hand, was it really all that much of a surprise? And what else could she say but... 'Yes, I'll marry you, Walter,' she said quietly. She couldn't very well say, Let's wait and see. She knew that he really did love her, and maybe she would come to love him, in time.

'Oh ... you don't know how happy you've made me,' he said, hugging her tightly. 'My parents will be pleased as well. Shall we tell them when they get back?'

'Yes, if you like,' said Cissie. It was all happening very quickly, far too quickly for her liking. One moment of holiday madness, and now she had said she would marry the man she had decided, only a few days ago, to send packing.

'You don't sound very sure about it,' said Walter. 'We must tell them. I know they'll be thrilled to bits.'

'Yes ... happen they will. But we mustn't do that again, Walter, what we've done tonight. Not until...'

'Until after we're married?'

172

'Yes, that's what I mean.'

'Alright, if you insist. But that's going to be very hard, Cissie, now that I know you feel the same way as I do.'

She was totally confused. She had only done 'that' with Walter so that she could blame him if the worst happened. But if it didn't happen and she was not pregnant after all, then she would be forced to go along with a marriage that she did not want. What a complete mess it all was!

'I think it would be better, though,' she said quietly, 'if we don't.'

'OK then, we'll see...' He nodded. 'Now, we must get you an engagement ring, and we'll put it in the paper so that everybody will know. Have you got any time off next week?'

'Yes ... Wednesday afternoon.'

'That's my half day as well. So we'll go into town and get you a really nice ring. What sort would you like?'

'I don't know. I've never thought about it.' Nor had she. She was only nineteen. Lots of girls got married young, but she had believed it would be ages before it happened to her. On the other hand, she would not be sorry to get away from home.

'You must have a diamond ring. P'raps with a ruby or sapphire, but you've got to have a diamond.'

'Let's just wait and see what they've got. And diamonds are expensive, aren't they?'

'That doesn't matter. I've got a bob or two saved up, just in case you said yes. And now you have.'

He kissed her again, but she was pleased, then, to hear the front door open as Walter's parents returned. They were delighted when he told them the news. Archie Clarkson insisted on opening a bottle of sherry to have a toast to the happy couple.

'And now you'd better take your bride-to-be home,' said Walter's mother. 'We're real pleased, love,' she said, kissing Cissie's cheek. 'And we know your parents will be an' all.'

TWELVE

'I've got some news for you,' Cissie said to Val when they met outside the mill gates on Monday. They hadn't seen one another for several days as their shifts had not coincided.

'What?' asked Val. 'Have you heard from Jack?'

'No... It's nowt like that. It's me and Walter. We're getting engaged.'

'But ... why?' Her friend stared at her in astonishment. 'After all you've said about him.'

'I know, but I've no choice, have I? I've got to do it.'

She explained to Val what had happened; how Jack had failed to get in touch, and she had realized that he wasn't going to do so. And Walter was there, so ready and willing.

'So you've tricked him?' said Val, a mite disapprovingly.

'Well, I suppose I have. Oh, don't look at me like that, Val. What else could I do? It would be a disaster if I found out I was having a baby.'

'But you might not be.'

'I know, but I couldn't risk it. Anyway, we're going to choose a ring on Wednesday. Walter's not so bad, you know, and he really does love me.'

'But do you love him?'

Cissie shrugged. 'I think I might...'

'I expect your parents were pleased, weren't they?'

'Oh yes, Mam was over the moon, you might know. She thinks Walter's the bee's knees. I reckon she thinks he's too good for me really. She said to me, "Well, you've seen sense at last, girl. Let's hope you make him a good wife, like he deserves." Dad was OK though. Walter did things proper, like. He asked Dad if it was alright if we got married, even though he'd already asked me an' I'd said yes. An' Dad said he hoped we'd be very happy... But that's enough about me. What about you and Sam? Did you have a good time on Wednesday?'

'Yes, thanks,' said Val. 'And on Saturday as well. I've seen him twice.' She could not help smiling happily at the memory of it all. 'We had a lovely drive out into the countryside, to a little village called Heptonstall, just beyond Hebden Bridge.'

'Well, fancy that! Walter and me, we had a drink there an' all, at Hebden Bridge.'

'The countryside's lovely round here,' said Val. 'I don't think I've ever really appreciated it before. Heptonstall's right up at the top of the moor. There are some old weaver's cottages and a ruined church... So picturesque,' she added dreamily.

Cissie sniffed. 'Depends on who you're with, doesn't it? Have you met his parents yet?'

175

'No ... not yet. But he's said he'll take me to meet them soon. He's met my parents, though, and he was really friendly and chatty with them. Mum was quite charmed.'

'Well, she would be, wouldn't she? He'd know how to get round her.'

'She kept calling him Mr Samuel, but he said he was just Sam. Dad wasn't quite so much in awe of him, though. He's met Sam in the warehouse and he finds him easy to get along with.'

'So he'll be invited round for Sunday tea soon, will he?'

Val smiled. 'Maybe ... in a little while.' To be invited for tea on a Sunday was a sign that the couple were serious about one another. She changed the subject. 'So ... when are you and Walter getting married then?'

'Oh, we haven't got that far yet. Give us a chance! Anyroad, it depends, doesn't it?'

'Yes, I see what you mean... I really do hope you'll be happy, though, Cissie. Walter's got a good steady job, and I know he thinks a lot about you. He's been very patient, hasn't he, waiting for you to make up your mind?'

'Yes, I suppose he has... Anyroad, it'll be nice to have a diamond ring...'

Val wondered, too, when she might meet Sam's parents. She already knew his father, of course, from their occasional meetings at work, but his mother had nothing to do with the mill and no one seemed to know much about her. Sam had hardly mentioned her, but from the little that he had said she had formed the impression that his mother and his brother were two of a kind, regarding themselves as somewhat superior to the ordinary workforce. His father, on the other hand, liked to get to know and befriend his employees.

But it was early days yet, she told herself. She and Sam had known one another only a short while, too soon, maybe, to be formally introduced to the family. She felt sure, though, that Sam wanted to go on seeing her, that he was already regarding her as his steady girlfriend.

They continued to enjoy their outings together as the weeks went by, and by mid-September Val felt as though she had known Sam for ages. As she had told Cissie, she had not realized how lovely the countryside was around Halifax, once you got away from the smoke and grime of the mill chimneys.

One Saturday afternoon they drove to Shipley Glen, then walked along by the canal and the River Aire. They saw the huge mill at Saltaire, and the village that Sir Titus Salt had had built for his workforce, all the streets named after the children in his large family.

'A Victorian philanthropist,' said Sam. 'He really cared about his workers, like my father tries to do, but his scheme was on a much larger scale.'

One Sunday he told her to put on her strongest walking shoes. They drove to Haworth, the home of the Brontë family and, after viewing the Parsonage, they walked across the moors to High Withens, the setting for Emily Brontë's novel, *Wuthering Heights*. Val had to admit that she had never read the book, but decided that she would do so now that she had seen the bleak ruin and the wild moorland landscape. They ended the day with a meal at the Black Bull Inn, the haunt of Branwell Brontë.

As he said goodnight to her later that evening Sam told her, for the first time, that he loved her. His kisses and embraces thrilled her, but apart from the physical aspect their minds were well attuned, and despite the difference in their backgrounds they found they had much in common.

Her parents liked him very much, and after a few weeks they were quite used to the idea of their daughter keeping company with one of the bosses.

'Does his father know about it?' asked Bert Horrocks. 'He hasn't mentioned it to me when I've seen him around, but then I wouldn't expect him to.'

'I'm not sure, Dad,' said Val. 'Perhaps it's rather soon for me to be introduced to the family.'

'I'm sure he'll do what's right,' said her mother. 'He's a decent young man, and I can see he's real fond of you. I reckon it'll be his mother, though, that'll be the difficult one. I've heard she's a bit of a tartar. Puts on airs and graces, but she's no need to, considering where she came from.'

'How do you know all this, Mum?' asked Val. She hadn't realized her mother was acquainted with the woman.

'They lived not far from us. Her and me, we're about the same age, though I can't really say I knew her, not to speak to. Beattie Halliwell, that was her name. She was one of a big family; an ordinary family, same as ours. There was some sort of trouble...' Sally Horrocks looked puzzled for a moment, deep in thought. 'No ... I'm blessed if I can remember. It's a good while ago. Anyroad, she went up in the world when she married Joshua Walker. And now she doesn't want to know the likes of us.'

Val didn't like the sound of Sam's mother at all and dreaded the time when she would have to meet her. But all she could do was bide her time and try to make a good impression when she was eventually introduced to the family.

The Walker family lived at Queensbury which was a few miles out of Halifax on the moorland road leading to Bradford. It was a stately mansion standing in its own grounds with a carriage drive where, at one time, horses and carriages drew up to the front door. It had been in the family since the time of Sam's great-grandfather who had started the mill, and had been handed down from father to son.

Sam's paternal grandparents were still living, both now in their eighties. They had moved from the family home to a bungalow not far away. Jacob Walker still liked to keep an eye on the business and to know what was going on. Sam had always been very fond of his grandfather, Jacob. Being stocky in build and having a beard he resembled pictures that Sam had seen of the old King George the Fifth, who had died a couple of years after Sam was born. His grandmother, too, was a nice old lady, although it was difficult to think of either of them as being old. There were both active, although Jacob had had to stop driving his car due to failing eyesight, and Grandma Isobel walked with a stick, due to arthritis, but was still a keen member of the Women's Institute and the local church.

Sam and his brother Jonathan had only a few close relatives. There was Aunt Phyllis, Joshua's sister, her husband George and their son and daughter. Joshua's elder brother had been killed in the battle of the Somme in the First World War. Joshua had come through it all unscathed, apart from the bad memories which he seldom mentioned.

As far as Sam's mother, Beatrice's, relations were concerned, it was as though she had none at all. Sam seldom met his maternal grandparents. His mother had a sister, Hannah, who lived near Bradford. She and Beatrice met very occasionally, but nothing was ever said about the rest of the family. Sam had once asked his father if he had any more aunts or uncles, but his father had answered, 'Best not to mention them, lad. Your mother doesn't like to talk about them.'

It was during the first week in September that Beatrice reminded Sam that there was an important event that he would be expected to attend in October. Their maid had cleared the table after the evening meal and the family, Joshua, Beatrice, Jonathan and Sam, were taking their ease in the lounge with an after dinner sherry.

'Don't forget it's your father's Masonic dinner on the first Friday of October,' she said, addressing her younger son. 'It's an occasion that we all attend, and one where ladies are invited.'

'Yes, Mother, I hadn't forgotten,' said Sam. He had thought that he might invite Valerie along to that occasion, and now was the perfect opportunity to tell his parents of his intention. He had been plucking up courage to tell them about his friendship with the young lady, the courage he needed being for breaking the news to his mother, rather than his father. And now, here was his chance.

But his mother forestalled him before he had time to go on.

'And of course we have invited Priscilla along to be your partner.'

Sam stared at her in disbelief. 'You've done ... what?'

'You heard what I said, Samuel. I've invited Priscilla along as your partner, as she has been for the last two years. Why are you looking at me like that? You know she always comes to the Ladies' Evening with her parents.'

Sam shook his head. 'I can't believe you would do that, Mother, without asking me first. If you have already invited her I suppose she will have to be there, but not as my partner. As a matter of fact, I had decided to invite someone else.'

'Someone else? But ... who?' His mother's pale grey eyes were like stones and two red spots had appeared on her cheeks. It was not the first time that Sam had seen his mother in a rage. It happened whenever something displeased her.

'I met a young lady when I was on holiday in Blackpool,' he replied, as evenly as he could. He would not exacerbate his mother's anger by losing his temper. 'She's a local girl, she lives here in Halifax, so I've carried on seeing her since we returned. And I decided it would be a good opportunity for you to meet her.'

'But ... who is she? You can't invite a complete stranger to come along to one of our family occasions. And why haven't you told us about her before? I must say I'm very annoyed with you, Samuel. I don't know whatever Mr and Mrs Forbes will think. They've been expecting to hear about some sort of understanding between you and Priscilla, and so have I. The two of you have been friendly for ages. Oh, what on earth are you thinking about, Samuel, spoiling everything like this?'

'Whatever you hoped for, Mother, it is only in your imagination,' replied Sam. 'There has never been anything between Priscilla and me but friendship. And she would say the same if you asked her. We grew up together, more or less, and she's a very nice girl, but she's not the right one for me.' Sam knew, deep down, that Priscilla might have had other ideas about him at one time. She was a shy and insecure girl, the only daughter of rather older parents, who were close friends of his own mother and father. He had taken her out once or twice, but there had been nothing romantic between them. He had tried to let her down gently by behaving in a just a casual, friendly way, and he thought she had got the message.

'The lad's right, Beatrice,' said Joshua Walker. 'I can see that Priscilla is not the right girl for him. I told you, didn't I, that you should have consulted him before inviting the lass to come along. So ... are you going to tell us, Sam, about this young lady you've met in Blackpool? You say she's local. Is she somebody that we know?'

Sam decided it was time to take the bull by the

horns. 'You could say so, Father,' he replied. 'As a matter of fact, she works at our place...'

'What!' Sam thought his mother would explode with rage. 'She's one of our employees? Oh, Samuel, how could you do this to us? Whatever will people think? You'd better put a stop to this right away before it goes any further. You're letting yourself down, consorting with one of the ... mill girls!'

'Actually, Mother, she works in the office. Not that it would make any difference to me if she was one of the "mill girls", as you put it. They are just girls who have to earn their living in the best way they can.' *Just as you had to do at one time, Mother,* he was tempted to say, but knew that he would never dare to mention such a thing. 'She's called Valerie, and she was on holiday with her friend who does work in the mill, in the burling and mending room. Another very nice girl, and we all spent some time together, myself and Jeff and Colin and the two girls. But Valerie and I knew straight away that we ... liked one another.'

Sam's brother, Jonathan, had been quiet until now, listening but saying nothing, an amused and supercilious expression on his face. 'Valerie...' he said now. 'Valerie ... what's she called? Hornby, Hoskins...'

'Valerie Horrocks,' said Sam, looking pointedly at his brother. 'She knows you, of course. She deals with your correspondence sometimes.'

'Yes, a dark-haired girl, slim and ... not bad-looking, I suppose. Competent enough at her job. But, as mother says, it will not do at all, Sam. Whatever are you thinking of? And to suggest that she

183

should be included in one of our family social occasions! You'd be a laughing stock, and so would all of us.'

Joshua Walker spoke again. 'I think you are over-reacting, Jonathan. As your brother says, everyone has to earn a living, somehow, and there are those who are not as fortunate as we are. Bert Horrocks works in the warehouse. He's a supervisor there, and he's one of the best workers you could imagine. Valerie is his daughter. I've heard him mention her. She's the apple of his eye, you might say. I've spoken with her a few times, and my impression is that she's a grand girl, and one that's got her head screwed on the right way, I should imagine.' He nodded approvingly at Sam.

'You could do a lot worse, lad,' he said with a faint smile. 'In fact, I doubt if you could do any better.'

'Thank you, Father,' said Sam quietly.

'Well, I've heard everything now!' Jonathan sprang to his feet. 'I'm meeting Thelma, and I mustn't keep her waiting.' He stopped at the door, glaring at Sam. 'Let's hope you come to your senses, little brother, before our wedding. We don't want any riff-raff there.'

'You take that back! You apologize to your brother, do you hear, Jonathan?' called out their father. But Jonathan had gone.

Beatrice also stood up. 'I have a headache,' she said icily, 'if you will excuse me.' She made a dignified exit, her head held high, but the words caught in her throat. It seemed as though she was about to burst into tears.

Joshua looked at his son, his eyes full of concern, but there was a hint of amusement there as well. 'Well, this is a pretty kettle of fish, isn't it?' he said. 'I wish I could say that your mother will come round, but it's not going to be easy.' Well nigh impossible, he thought to himself, but he would have to try to make her see reason.

THIRTEEN

Janice received a letter from Val in mid-September. She had been feeling a little downcast as Phil had been demobbed and was now back at home in Yorkshire. Although she had known him for only a few weeks their friendship had blossomed, and she was looking forward to seeing him again once she had settled down in her digs in Leeds and got started on her course at the university. She still had very mixed feelings about leaving home, knowing how much she would miss her parents and her younger brother. Janice had always been very much a home girl, never wanting to spread her wings as some other girls did.

She was rather concerned, too, about her mother. Lilian had been complaining about headaches, although complaining was not really the right word. Her mother had never been one to give way and tell others when she was not feeling well, she tried to keep going at all costs. It was clear now, though, that there was something amiss. She was tired and listless and headaches were something quite new to her.

'Don't worry about me,' she said, as she always did. 'I dare say I'm just tired. It's been a busy season – not that I'm grumbling about that – and I suppose it's taken its toll on me. Only a few more weeks, though, and we'll be able to take a breather.' They were almost fully booked until the end of October, when the Illuminations finished.

Janice was interested in Val's letter. She had one or two items of news to relate. It was no surprise to hear that Val was still seeing her new friend, Sam. Val had been quite concerned when she met him that he was one of the bosses at the mill where she worked. It was Janice's opinion that Val could hold her own with anyone, no matter how important they were in the eyes of her work colleagues. She did say, however, that she had not yet been introduced to the family, and that she was not looking forward to meeting his mother who was reputed to be something of a dragon.

The more surprising news was that Cissie was now engaged to her longtime boyfriend, Walter Clarkson. Janice remembered that Cissie had not been at all sure about that friendship and had been trying to find a way out. Then she had met that Jack ... somebody or other, and had seemed to be quite smitten with him. Janice had thought he was rather a fly-by-night sort of lad, not one to be trusted. Reading between the lines Janice suspected that Cissie had heard no more from him and had gone back to the faithful Walter. She hoped her new friend was doing the right thing. She would send her a card of congratulation and wish her well.

It was at the start of the third week in September, on the Monday evening when they were clearing away after the meal that Lilian gave a cry and then collapsed on the kitchen floor. Olive and Nancy, as well as Janice, rushed to her aid. They managed to get her to her feet and sat her down on a chair. Olive found the brandy bottle and added hot water to a few teaspoons full of the liquid. It was considered a cure-all for every ailment. Nancy knelt at her side as Lilian held her head, unable to say anything but that her head was hurting.

Janice dashed to the living room to find her father. 'Dad ... come quick, it's Mum. She's collapsed. We must get an ambulance, right now. I think she's really bad...'

It seemed ages but it was, in fact, not very long before the ambulance arrived. Lilian by that time was almost speechless with the severity of the pain in her head. The ambulance men lifted her on to a stretcher and carried her out to the vehicle. By that time several of the visitors had become aware of the crisis and were standing outside on the pavement.

'I'll go with her, love,' said Alec to his daughter. 'You stay here and see to things and I'll get in touch as soon as I know what's going on. Try not to worry our Ian, tell him that Mum's going to be alright. Oh, Janice love, I hope to God that she will be!' There were tears in his eyes as he got into the ambulance and Janice, equally distressed, went back into the house.

Ian had dashed out straight after his meal to play football, as he always did. Janice hoped they would have some positive news of her mother's condition before he returned. She kept herself busy in the kitchen, trying not to worry, but that was not possible. She found she was praying continually, a silent plea, over and over in her mind; Please God, don't let there be anything seriously wrong with Mum. Olive and Nancy refused to go home, keeping themselves occupied until they heard what was happening at the hospital.

'Whatever happens,' said Janice, 'I should imagine that Mum will be out of action for some time.'

'How are we going to manage?' said Olive. 'We're fully booked this week, and we're pretty nearly full for the rest of the season. Your mother's the mainstay of this place. She's in charge of the meals, she does all the cooking, with only a little help. The rest of us can't hold a candle to her.'

Janice knew that this was true, but she was thinking about what her mother would want them to do. At the very back of her mind was a dreadful thought that she was trying hard to quell... Supposing Mum did not recover? She pushed it away. She must think positively despite the sick feeling of dread inside her.

'Mum would want us to carry on the best way we can,' she said. 'Freda comes in every day to help prepare the evening meal, and I'm sure she'd agree to stay longer under the circumstances. She's not a bad cook herself, you know. Mum has said that she's a great help. And ... I've been picking up a few hints here and there myself. I've been watching Mum and trying to learn how she does things. She's always telling me to go off and enjoy myself while I can. But I really wanted to help, and in the end she let me.'

'But you're off to your college soon, aren't you?' said Nancy. 'Next week, isn't it?'

'It's supposed to be,' said Janice, 'but I'm not going.' The decision had come to her in a flash. Her place was here to hold the fort for as long as her mother was unable to do so, and after that, who could tell what might happen?

'You can't say that, love,' said Nancy. 'You've been looking forward to it for so long, and you're such a clever lass. Your mum and dad want you to go and have the chance that they never had; that's what Lilian says. Or do you mean you'll put it off for a while?'

'I don't know,' said Janice. 'Maybe, maybe not. I'll get in touch with them in Leeds when we've found out how Mum's going on. But it's out of the question for me to go right now. They can give my place to someone else.'

Nancy and Olive looked at one another in consternation. Nancy shook her head. 'I don't know. Maybe we can manage this week, seems like we'll have to. We can't tell all the visitors to go home.' But at the back of her mind was the dreadful thought that if the worst came to the worst they might have to do that. She hurriedly pushed that thought away. 'But what about the rest of the season? We'll need somebody to be in charge of the cooking. I know you mean well and that you'll do your best, Janice, and so will Olive and me. And then there's Freda, of course. But we've not got the same experience as your mum, have we?'

'Let's not look too far ahead,' said Janice. 'Mum might be as right as rain soon, although I think she

189

is due for a rest, whatever it is that is making her ill. We could advertise in the paper to say that we need a qualified chef. There are always people looking for a job in a place like Blackpool.'

'Your mum's not got any proper qualifications, but she's as good as any of those top chefs,' said Olive. 'You learn by experience when all's said and done. But that's not a bad idea, Janice, to advertise for somebody.'

'Let's just wait and see,' said Janice. 'I wish Dad would hurry up and ring. This waiting is awful. You two should go home, your families will be wondering where you are. I'll let you know as soon as we hear anything.'

But the women refused to leave her on her own. 'Let's go and sit in the living room then,' said Janice. 'We'll be more comfortable, and the kitchen's as spick and span as Mum would want it to be.'

There was an oppressive silence as they waited. The three of them made a pretense of reading a magazine. There seemed to be nothing more to say. As soon as dusk began to fall Ian came dashing in. He stopped and stared at them.

'What's up? Where's Mum ... and Dad?'

'I'm afraid Mum's not well,' Janice told him. 'She had a very bad headache, and she's had to go to hospital. Dad's gone with her. Don't worry, Ian. I'm sure she'll be alright. You know what she's like, never out of sorts for very long.'

'Oh ... that's awful.' Ian looked bewildered and rather frightened. 'She'll be coming home, though, won't she, tonight?'

'I should imagine she'll have to stay in hospital overnight,' said Janice gently. 'That's what usually

190

happens. You go and take your mucky things off and have a wash and I'll get you some supper.' She smiled at him. 'I'm glad you remembered to leave your muddy boots in the kitchen. Did you have a good game?'

Ian shrugged. 'It was OK... Mum's going to be alright, isn't she?'

'We hope so, love. We're just waiting for Dad to phone.'

When Ian came downstairs again, scrubbed clean and dressed in his pyjamas, Janice was talking on the phone in the hall. She looked serious as she motioned to him to go into the living room.

'That must be your dad ringing from the hospital,' said Nancy. 'See, your sister's made you some nice hot chocolate, and there's a couple of your favourite chocolate biscuits. Try not to get upset, love,' she said, seeing Ian's troubled face and the threatening tears, which he was trying to fight. Boys, especially footballers, didn't cry. 'We'll find out what's happening in a minute or two. And you know what a strong person your mum is. She doesn't let anything get her down.'

Ian nodded, sipping at the comforting hot drink and quickly demolishing his biscuits, despite his concern.

Janice reappeared in a few moments. 'Mum has to have an operation, straight away,' she said, 'to find out what is wrong. She's had an X-ray, and there's something there that isn't ... quite right. I suppose that it might be–' She stopped, unable to say the words in front of Ian, although he might not know what it meant.

'You mean … a brain tumour?' Nancy mouthed silently. Both the women looked shocked.

'What?' asked Ian. 'What's up with Mum?'

'Something like a lump, sort of, that's causing the headaches,' replied Janice, 'and they're trying to find out what it is. Dad's staying at the hospital tonight. They've been very kind and helpful, and I have every confidence in the doctors and nurses there. Victoria Hospital has a very good reputation... You go home now,' she said to Nancy and Olive. 'There's nothing we can do but wait. Thank you so much for staying with me. You've been a great help.'

'And we'll be back at the crack of dawn to help with the breakfasts,' said Olive. 'We'll come a bit earlier; won't we, Nancy?'

Her friend nodded in agreement. 'And try to get some sleep,' said Nancy. 'Take a couple of aspirins; they're as good as anything. And don't worry; we'll get though somehow, between us.'

'Aye, we'll take a day at a time,' added Olive. 'Your mum's planned the menus for the week, like she always does, so we'll get through if we all pull together, and happen a little bit of help from Him up there.' She glanced heavenwards, and Janice nodded.

Maybe she didn't go to church as often as she ought to – she knew that Olive went whenever she could – but Janice did believe in a greater power somewhere, and now was the time to ask for help. The two women hugged her and told her to 'keep her pecker up'.

Ian went up to bed after they had gone, saying that he would read for a while. Janice didn't tell him not to read for too long. He had to cope with the waiting time the best way he could. She went into the lounge to tell the visitors there what was happening. She insisted that they should have their supper time drinks as usual, and two ladies offered at once to help her.

Thank God for the dishwasher, she thought, as she stacked the cups and saucers. When she went up to bed she looked in at Ian, and he was fast asleep. And she too, despite her worries, slept until the alarm clock woke her at six o'clock.

By the time she had washed and dressed and gone into the kitchen, Nancy and Olive had arrived. Janice had to tell them that there was no news yet. 'But what do they always say? No news is good news. I don't really go along with clichés, but surely we would know by now if there was anything ... really wrong?'

Nancy nodded. 'That's true. Come on then, Olive,' she said briskly. 'Let's get those tables set, then we can make a start on preparing the breakfasts. What about scrambled eggs this morning instead of fried? It'll be easier, and a nice change as well.'

'Just what I was thinking,' said Janice, 'and there's a huge tin of tomatoes; Mum uses them sometimes instead of fresh ones.'

'And we mustn't forget to warm the plates,' said Olive. 'Lilian's very keen on that, there's nothing worse than breakfast on a cold plate.'

They said very little as they set about their tasks. Alec returned from the hospital at about seven thirty. He gave a weak smile, but at least he was smiling, as he hugged Janice, so she guessed that the news was perhaps not so bad.

'Your mum's had an operation,' he said. 'They're very cagey, they don't divulge too much, you know, but the doctor says they've managed to remove … whatever it was that was causing the pain and, from what I can gather, they're hopeful that they've caught it in time.'

'Oh … thank God for that,' breathed Janice. 'So she's going to be alright?'

'We hope so,' replied Alec. 'She hasn't come round yet, but they urged me to come home and get some rest. We can go and see her later today. Now … how's the work going on? You seem to be coping well, and I know that Lilian will be relieved at that. Although she has other things to think about at the moment, and I don't want her to worry about anything.'

'We'll manage, Dad,' said Janice. 'Freda's a very good cook herself, though Mum does most of it, and I'm sure she'll agree to take charge.'

'And what about your university place?' he asked. 'Are you still of the same mind? Your mum will be so disappointed, and she'll feel it's her fault if you don't go.'

'I can't go, Dad, and that's definite, at least … not yet.' Probably not ever, she told herself.

'OK, love. I understand,' he said. 'You may feel differently about it in a little while.'

They coped as well as they could with the breakfasts. Janice told the guests that her mother had undergone an operation and was doing well. They had known Lilian for only a few days but they were clearly relieved to hear the news. Her pleasant personality and friendliness always impressed

194

the visitors.

When breakfast was over, Janice rang the university office telling them not to expect her as there had been a family emergency, and that she might apply again next year.

Freda Jackson, the middle-aged woman who helped Lilian with the meals, agreed readily to do whatever she could, although insisting, 'I'm not as good as your mother.'

'We'll have to pay her more,' Janice said to her father when he had rested for an hour or two. 'Can we afford it? And if we have to employ someone else that will be an added expense. I don't know much about the financial side of things, you see.'

'No, your mother sees to all that,' said Alec. 'The hotel is her business, but I do know that it's doing well and we've got a tidy sum in the bank. So we'll just have to go ahead and never mind the expense. It's a joint account – your mum insisted on that even though she's the one in charge – so there's no problem with the bank. But I've never dealt with the money side of things. Do you think – as you insist that you're not going off to college – that you could deal with it? Until your mother's well again, I mean?'

Janice was a little taken aback. She was realizing just how much her mother had been doing, and what a strain it must have been although she had not complained. 'I'll try, Dad,' she answered. 'I'm not much of a mathematician – English is my subject. But yes, I'll have a go... Now, when can we go and see Mum?'

'Early afternoon,' said Alec. 'She should be

recovering nicely by then. I'm not going in to work today, and I've let them know what has happened. I had a devil of a job to persuade Ian to go to school, but he's far better there, especially as he's not been long at the Grammar. It'll occupy his mind as he's so worried about your mum.'

Janice looked at the menu that her mother had prepared for Tuesday's evening meal. A starter of grapefruit segments, followed by cottage pie with peas and carrots, and apple pie and fresh cream as the dessert. Well, that should not be too difficult. The minced beef would need to be taken out of the freezing cabinet immediately to defrost. The peas and carrots, also, were frozen ones – Bird's Eye did a very good line in vegetables. So there would be only the potatoes to wash, boil and mash and the gravy to be made.

Apple pie... Janice knew that her mother would have been busy that morning making pastry and stewing apples to make several large plate pies. There was, however, a very good bakery not far away that sold their own produce made on the premises. She would go there right away and buy enough fruit tarts – not necessarily apple ones – for the visitors' dessert. And there was always a supply of fresh cream in the fridge.

After they had eaten a snack lunch Janice and her father took a bus to the hospital on the outskirts of the town. After a long walk through endless corridors they found Lilian's ward, and a nurse took them to the single room where she had been since the operation.

'She needs to be on her own to aid her recovery,' the nurse told them. 'We are satisfied with her progress, but please don't stay too long. She will get tired very easily.'

Lilian's eyes were closed when they entered the room. She was propped up against the pillows, and Janice had to choke back a sob as she looked at her. Her head was bandaged and her hair had been shaved off on one side. All the colour had drained away from her face, and at a first glance she looked ten years older.

'Mum,' said Janice quietly, and she opened her eyes. They lit up at the sight of her husband and daughter and she gave a weak smile. 'Alec, Janice... How nice to see you. I wasn't asleep, just resting, as I'm doing most of the time.'

They gently kissed her cheek then sat down on the chairs at the side of the bed.

'How are you feeling, love?' asked Alec. 'You gave us all a scare, but you're going to be OK. The doctor says you're doing well.' It was a slight exaggeration, but it was best to be positive.

Lilian nodded. 'I feel all woozy, as though I'm not quite here, but the awful pain has gone. They haven't told me much, though, about what it was... I must look a bonny sight.' She tried to smile as she touched her bandaged head. Her voice was weak, the anaesthetic and the drugs to ease the pain were affecting her speech.

'Where is Ian?' she asked vaguely.

'At school, Mum,' said Janice. 'He sends his love, and he'll be able to come and see you, one evening, maybe.'

'Oh yes, of course ... school,' said Lilian. 'I was forgetting.'

'And we're managing alright at the hotel,' said

Janice. 'Olive and Nancy are helping all they can, and Freda's taking charge of the meals, so you don't need to worry about anything.'

Lilian nodded. It was becoming obvious that she was really too poorly to worry about what was going on at home, which was very unlike her usual self.

'And Janice is working her socks off an' all,' said Alec, 'so there's nothing for you to think about except getting better.'

'Good girl,' whispered Lilian. She didn't ask about her daughter going to university. It must have gone from her mind along with all the other matters about which she would normally have been concerned.

They observed the nurse's advice and did not stay too long. Lilian's eyes kept closing and they knew she must have all the rest she needed. It was less than twenty-four hours since she had had the operation.

'We'll see you again soon,' promised Janice. 'You'll soon be alright and back home again with us.' She did not tell her not to worry about the hotel. It was clear to them that Lilian was not worrying about anything, and that was a great relief. Janice tactfully withdrew to let her father have a few minutes alone with his wife. They were truly devoted to one another after more than twenty years of marriage.

It occurred to Janice when they arrived home that she had not yet contacted Phil to tell him what had happened. She had not forgotten about it; it was something that she really did not want to do. She was sad at the thought that she would not be seeing him again, at least not yet ... if ever? She had been looking forward to meeting up with him again, and he had assured her that he was eager to continue their friendship. But who could tell what would happen now? Her mother was her first consideration and, after that, the job of keeping the hotel running.

Freda Jackson arrived almost as soon as they had returned from the hospital. She was a competent, no-nonsense sort of person, not given to chatting overmuch or wasting a minute. She donned her apron, ready to start work at once after she had enquired about Lilian.

'We'll do our best to keep the ship afloat for your mum,' she said. 'Cottage pie today, eh? Well, that shouldn't be much of a problem. You go and ring your young man, and I'll get these spuds peeled.'

It was Phil who answered the phone. 'Hi there, Janice. I thought – well, I hoped – that it might be you. So you're all ready for the off, are you? Only a few more days and you'll be here, well, in Leeds at any rate.'

She interrupted him. 'Phil, I'm afraid I won't be coming. Mum's in hospital...' She explained what had happened, about the emergency operation and how she felt she must stay and help to keep things running at the hotel. 'It would be out of the question for me to start my course, Phil. Dad tried to persuade me otherwise, but I think he realizes now that it's what I must do. I'm really sorry, though, that I won't be able to come and see you...'

'Yes, so am I,' Phil replied. 'What a dreadful shock for you all – and your poor mum! I'm so sorry. Do give her my love; I think she is a lovely lady and she was so nice and friendly to me.'

'Yes, she really took to you, Phil. I'm so sorry and disappointed about ... everything.' It was dawning on her now that she might not see Phil again, that it might be the end of what had started as a promising friendship, maybe even more...

'I know you can't come to Leeds, and that's a shame,' said Phil. 'But there's nothing to stop me coming to see you, is there? That is, if you can find room for me? If not, then I can stay somewhere nearby. I must see you again, Janice. I've told my mum and dad all about you, and they've been looking forward to meeting you. I know that might not be possible just yet but I can come and see you, can't I?'

'Yes, of course you can, Phil!' She felt a sudden spurt of happiness. What a comfort it would be to see him again. 'Aren't you busy, though, working with your father? You said he'd be glad to share the workload when you returned. But I'd love to see you.'

'We're not all that busy. It isn't like your place, you know. We're very rarely fully booked. We have people coming just for a couple of nights or for the weekend. Our busiest trade is with the bar and the restaurant, and my dad's got plenty of help without me. I know what he said about me taking my share of the work, but I sometimes feel like a spare part; they've managed so long without me. I'll have a word with my dad. I'm sure he'll agree to me coming to Blackpool.'

'That would be great, Phil. We're fully booked this week, then it slackens off a bit. We'll be able to find you a corner somewhere, no problem at all... I'd better go now. I've left Freda on her own, and there's the evening meal to organize. So I'll see you again soon, Phil. 'Bye for now...'

'Yes, 'bye, Janice. See you very soon. Take care now. Love to your mum ... and to you, of course...'

Janice went back to the kitchen with a smile on her face, the first real smile of the day. She had smiled at her mother, but it had been tinged with worry. The thought of seeing Phil again had suddenly made the future seem brighter.

FOURTEEN

Joshua Walker was well and truly flummoxed by the situation that had arisen. His younger son had fallen for a girl who worked in their office. So what was the problem? It was Joshua's opinion that the lad could not have chosen anyone better. From what he knew of Valerie Horrocks she was a very nice well-brought-up girl, very good at her job and with a pleasing personality. Very pretty, too. He could see why Samuel was so taken with her. In fact the lass reminded him of Beatrice when he had first known her. Dark-haired and seemingly fragile, a fragility which disguised an inner strength.

The problem, of course, was Joshua's wife and his elder son, who was very much influenced by his mother. What was that expression that folk often used? 'More Catholic than the Pope.' This

201

was not a question of religion but the idea was the same. Beatrice, since she had been married to him had become more regal than the Queen! What astounded him was that she should have forgotten, or had pretended to forget – she had put right out of her mind – her own humble start in life and the one or two skeletons in the cupboard. But it was something about which he did not dare to remind her.

Did he still love her? he sometimes asked himself. Yes, he supposed he did. She had been a very good mother to their two sons, looking after them herself when they were young with hardly any extra help. Of course she had had the experience, as, being the eldest of a family of five children, the role of child-minding had often fallen to Beattie, which was the name by which she had once been known. They had not been a feckless family by any means, but had had a struggle to make ends meet, as so many families had done in the years following the Great War. Beattie's father had not worked in a woollen mill as many of his generation had done. He had been a fireman on the railway, and his wife had gone out cleaning to boost the family income. Yes, a hardworking, industrious family, until one of the sons had disgraced them.

George Halliwell, always known as Georgie, had been employed at Walker's mill ever since he left school at fourteen. He was the eldest boy, the nearest in age to his sister, Beattie, and the two of them, surprisingly for a brother and sister, were very good friends. He grew up to be a charming and out-going young man, but not averse to a bit of shady dealing should it come his way.

Joshua, in his early twenties, had been doing his training at the family mill. His father, Jacob, had insisted that he should start at the bottom – as he, Joshua, had insisted on later with his own two sons – gaining experience in all departments of the mill. He had been working in the warehouse when it was discovered that some bales of cloth had gone missing. The operation had been very cleverly managed between the warehouse and the store, so much so that at first the discrepancy was not apparent. But the thieving had been traced eventually to George Halliwell. He was sacked on the spot and Jacob Walker was determined to press charges and make an example of the lad.

Joshua well remembered the day in the summer of 1925 when Beattie Halliwell had come to Walker's mill asking to speak to Mr Joshua who was in charge of the warehouse and who was, so Georgie had told her, a fair and reasonable young man. She wouldn't have dared to approach the owner, Mr Jacob Walker, who had the reputation of being a tyrant.

Beattie had pleaded her brother's case eloquently, saying that he was young and impressionable, had never been in trouble before and had been persuaded to go along with the theft despite his misgivings. Joshua had taken it all with a pinch of salt. He had summed up young Georgie as a wily character whose charm and easy manner of conversing with anyone and everyone could take him far. He had done wrong, but Joshua had a soft spot for the lad and so he promised he would speak to his father and try to persuade him to drop the matter.

Joshua had heard about the young woman, Beattie, from her brother who, it appeared, almost idolized her. Georgie had said that she was employed at Laycock's mill at the other side of the town, a friendly rival of Walker's. She had started in the weaving shed but her employers had soon realized her potential. She now worked in the office dealing with the accounts. She was eighteen years old, a few years younger than Joshua, and a bright and personable young woman. He found himself attracted to her immediately. She was a very pretty girl with dark hair that waved over her ears and her high forehead. Her features were well defined, quite aristocratic-looking, and her dark brown eyes had glowed intensely as she pleaded with him to overlook what her brother had, so thoughtlessly, been persuaded to do, and to try to persuade his father to drop the charges.

'I'll do what I can,' he had promised. 'Everyone needs a second chance, and your brother's a bright lad. He could go far if he got on to the right path, but I don't think my father will keep him on here.'

Joshua's father had refused to listen at first, determined to bring the lad to justice. 'What sort of a fool would I look if I let him get away with it?' he argued. 'It would encourage others to do the same if they think there's no punishment. No, he has to be shown up for what he is, a common thief. It's not all that long since they were hanging folk for sheep stealing. We can't be seen to be turning soft.'

'You can't believe in that sort of treatment, surely, Father?' Joshua was shocked at his father's words. Surely they had moved on a lot since those times? And it had been the lad's first offence. Until then he had appeared to be a conscientious worker.

Eventually Jacob gave way. 'Alright, alright,' he said. 'I suppose I'll have to let the matter drop. Your mother's been having a go at me as well. But I won't change my mind about sacking him; you must realize that. And he'll get no reference from me. I refuse to tell lies, so he'd better clear off and do the best he can. I must admit he's a bright lad and if he learns to keep his nose clean he might have a good chance elsewhere.'

'Thank you, Father,' said Joshua humbly. He had become quite friendly with Georgie, and this petty crime had come as a shock to him. He did not tell his father, of course, about his attraction towards the lad's sister. She appeared to be a bright and sensible girl, as well as being very pretty, but he decided to wait a little while before making any advances in that direction. If he had assessed the situation correctly, however, he guessed that she might be just as attracted to him.

After a few weeks had gone by he approached her at her place of work and asked her if she would consider taking a walk with him in the park on Sunday afternoon. This first meeting led to many more. Much to Joshua's surprise his father raised no objection when he was finally informed of the friendship, Jacob was as susceptible as any man to a pretty face and winning ways. Joshua's mother, Isobel, was also very taken with the girl who was charming and suitably deferential to both herself and Jacob. The episode with George had been forgotten, or put to the back of their minds, and was not referred to again.

The courtship was a longish one as was usual at the time. The couple became engaged and planned to marry in the summer of 1928 when Beatrice – as she now liked to be called instead of Beattie – was twenty-one years of age. It was during the early summer of 1927, however, that Beatrice discovered she was pregnant. Their feelings had got the better of them, with the inevitable outcome.

Both families were shocked and vociferous in their condemnation of the couple for shaming them in that way, but they were all agreed that the matter should be dealt with as quickly as possible. The families did not, as a rule, meet socially, the difference between their social standing and their way of life being too great. But on this occasion they acted in accordance. The marriage took place at the church in Halifax where the Walker family worshipped. Beatrice's family were Methodists, but Beatrice was adapting readily to the change in her status. She was married in white satin, to observe the proprieties – although her mother had castigated her for not being entitled to wear white, which was a sign of purity and virginity – with her sister, Hannah, as her only bridesmaid.

The couple moved into a small house, not far from where Joshua's parents lived. Their first son, Jonathan, was born in October, 1927, five months after their marriage. If their friends and acquaintances noticed the discrepancy in the dates it was never referred to openly, and in time it seemed to have been forgotten. Beatrice, though, had been determined that Jonathan and then Samuel should never discover the truth. She persuaded Joshua to go along with the fallacy that they had been married a year earlier, in 1926, and for the sake of peace and harmony in the family he had done so.

'But why, in heaven's name?' he had asked her. 'Are you ashamed of the way we felt about one another? We were in love, Beattie. We weren't the first to do that, and we certainly won't be the last.'

'I'm Beatrice now,' she had reminded him. 'That's the name I was christened with, and it's far more suitable. No, I'm not ashamed of loving you, Joshua. I still love you ... but we have certain standards to maintain. I just think it would be for the best.'

'What about our silver wedding, then, when it arrives? I'm damned if I'm going to celebrate it on the wrong date.'

'So we don't do anything, Joshua,' his wife replied. 'Least said, soonest mended.'

Joshua had been surprised, and disappointed as well, over the years, that Beatrice had lost contact with her family. It had been a gradual dropping away at first, but now she had distanced herself from them completely. All apart from her sister, Hannah, whom she saw occasionally. Hannah was married to a bank manager which was, of course, a highly respectable occupation.

As for Georgie, who had been dismissed from Walker's without a reference, he had pulled himself up by his bootlaces and had done very well in a totally different sphere. He had found employment as a grocer's errand boy, telling his boss nothing about his previous job except that he was tired of working at the mill and wanted to do something completely different.

He very soon made himself indispensable, serving behind the counter and charming the housewives who visited the corner shop almost every day, or sometimes more than once a day. Sid Bottomley's little shop on the outskirts of the main town was one that opened from early in the morning until late in the evening to catch all the trade. They sold a bit of everything; newspapers, sweets and tobacco as well as household goods and groceries. All the commodities that housewives were continually finding they had run out of or forgotten to buy.

Ten years later the sign on the door had changed to Bottomley and Halliwell as the young assistant had been made a partner. Now, some twenty-five years after he had started as an errand boy, George Halliwell, aged forty-six, had a wife and three children, two grandchildren, and was the owner, not only of the original shop but of two more in other parts of Halifax.

Joshua had hoped that Beatrice might be proud of her brother who had done so well for himself, after all she was the one who had pleaded for him not to be convicted of theft. It would, of course, have been a slur on the family name. Joshua could see now that it might well have been her own reputation she was safeguarding, not just that of her brother.

As for the two younger brothers, Beatrice had heard from Hannah that one of them had joined the Merchant Navy, and the other one, after the war, had emigrated to Australia with his new wife. Beatrice's parents, now in their late seventies, had saved up as much as they could over the years and had now retired to the seaside, which had long been their ambition, after their children had all left home. They had bought a small cottage, just big enough for two, near the sea at Filey where they had spent some happy holidays with the children, on the rare occasions when they had been able to afford the train fares. Hannah was the only one who visited them a few times a year, and Dick, the sailor, occasionally, when he was on leave. Beatrice and George had done well for themselves, in different ways, but it seemed that they now had little time for their elderly parents.

Joshua often brooded about the situation. His wife was very much the Lady Bountiful now, seen to be doing good works in the community. She was on the committee of several charitable organizations and the Chairman of the local Women's Institute. Joshua longed to remind her that charity began at home. What about her parents whom she no longer visited? Her brother George no longer needed a helping hand, but the two of them had once been very close. But Beatrice had dismissed George's wife as being common and flashy, not the sort of woman with whom she wished to associate.

And now her latest bone of contention was regarding the young woman that Samuel wanted them to meet. Her younger son could have done much better for himself than to take up with a girl who worked at their own mill. Joshua was convinced that she had forgotten her own humble beginnings. What had she been but a mill girl, then an office clerk? This was something that was never mentioned, and if Jonathan and Samuel knew, as he suspected they did, they had not heard it from him.

Thelma Young, however, Jonathan's fiancée, passed muster with Beatrice. Her father was a well-known solicitor in the town, and her mother worked along with Beatrice on a few committees. Thelma had been to university and obtained a degree, and she was now a chief librarian at a branch library in Bradford, to where she travelled each day in her own small car. Beatrice understood that it was quite usual for girls of well-off parents to earn their own living now.

Nothing more had been said about the Masonic Ladies' Evening at the end of October. Joshua knew that the invitation to Priscilla Forbes, along with her parents, would have to stand; but he also knew that Sam would remain adamant about his refusal to go along as her partner. The lad had not said whether he had actually invited his new lady friend, Valerie, or whether the matter was in abeyance. Sam was very quiet about his private affairs, but Joshua assumed that he was still seeing the young lady. All told, it was a tricky situation, made worse by his wife's intransigence.

Val was aware that Sam was unusually quiet and withdrawn at times, although they still continued to spend one or two evenings together during the week as well as spending much of the weekend together. He had had Sunday tea with the Horrocks family a couple of times; and there was no indication that he was tiring of her company. He was still as attentive and loving towards her. His kisses, indeed, were more ardent and meaningful, although he did not stray beyond the bounds of propriety. She knew that he respected her, and that was good, although she guessed that he was aware, as she was, that there would come a time when they both wanted more.

She assumed that his preoccupation was due to the attitude of his family towards her. She had still not been invited to meet his mother although they had been friendly for seven weeks or so and it was now the beginning of October. When she plucked up courage to broach the subject Sam admitted that it would take a while for his mother – and his brother – to get used to the idea of his friendship with her.

'My mother has very fixed ideas about how I should behave,' he told her. 'She has had one or two "suitable" girls lined up for me over the years, and refuses to see that her ideas are not mine. And I'm afraid my brother has been influenced by her. Jonathan's girlfriend is considered highly suitable because her father is a solicitor. Yes, abject snobbishness I know, but that's just the way she is. But she will have to change her tune in time. She may have Jonathan right where she wants him, but she won't win with me.'

Val did not tell him what she had discovered about Beatrice and her family. She felt it would serve no purpose and might make her look like a telltale.

It was Val's father, Bert Horrocks, who had recalled what had happened at Walker's mill all those years ago. 'Don't you remember, Sal?' he said to his wife. 'No, happen you don't because it was all

211

hushed up at the time. I'd just started working in the warehouse meself, along with young Georgie Halliwell, and there were some bales of cloth missing. Anyroad, it turned out that it was Georgie who was the culprit and the boss, Mr Jacob, sacked him on the spot. He was going to take him to court, but then he changed his mind. George was never convicted, although he lost his job. And I heard tell that it was George's sister, Beattie, who came and had a word with Mr Joshua, the boss's son, to see if he could persuade his father to change his mind.'

Sally Horrocks nodded. 'Yes, I seem to remember now, but it's all such a long time ago, and folk have forgotten.' She passed the tale on to her daughter. 'I knew there was some sort of bother, but I couldn't quite recall what it was.' She gave a sly grin. 'So Beattie Halliwell – Beatrice Walker, as she is now – doesn't need to act so high and mighty. Her brother was nowt but a common thief, although it was all hushed up. And I'm remembering now that she worked in the mill herself, not Walker's, one on the other side of town, but I reckon she's forgotten all that now.

'I know that Georgie was a real scamp, but he got on well with folks. He could charm the birds off the trees, as they say. And he's done well for himself. I believe he's got three shops now, dotted around Halifax.'

Val kept all this knowledge to herself. If Sam wasn't aware of it – though she guessed he might well be – it was not her place to tell him.

It was one evening at the beginning of October

212

when Sam heard a knock at his bedroom door. He was surprised to see his brother standing there as they very rarely visited one another's rooms. He noticed the serious expression on Jonathan's face as he said, 'Could I have a word with you, Sam?'

'Yes, of course. Come in,' said Sam, very curious now. Jonathan rarely confided in him about anything.

His brother flopped down on the only chair and Sam sat on the bed. 'So ... tell me what's bothering you,' he said. 'You look as though you've lost ten bob and found a penny.'

'Worse than that,' muttered Jonathan. 'It's Thelma. She's pregnant.'

Sam had to control a smile. This was the last thing he had expected to hear. The prim and proper Thelma who looked as though butter wouldn't melt in her mouth. With her blonde hair worn in a page-boy style and her pale blue eyes she appeared the typical ice-maiden. But you never could tell...

'Oh, I see,' he answered. 'And ... are you the father?'

'Of course I'm the father!' said Jonathan irritably. 'But whatever am I going to do about it? However can I tell Mother?'

'You are asking me?' said Sam. 'It's your problem. What do you expect me to do about it?'

'Just ... just be there for me. Support me if you can. There's going to be a hell of a row. I don't know how I'm going to face it.'

'Well, you'll have to, won't you? What about Thelma? Has she told her parents?'

'She's says she's going to tell them tonight. So

I'll have to do the same before the women – her mother and mine – get together in high dudgeon. Listen, Sam ... I'm sorry I said all those things about Valerie. I know she's really a very nice girl.'

'About not wanting any riff-raff at your wedding, you mean?' Sam gave a sardonic smile although it wasn't in his nature as a rule to be vindictive.

'Oh well, I didn't mean it,' said Jonathan, looking a little discomfited. 'It was only meant as a joke.'

'It didn't sound like a joke to me...'

'Well, you know me. I was half joking, then. You know what Mother's like.'

'And you have no more sense than to go along with her. Why do you kowtow to her, Jon, the way you do?'

'I suppose I know which side my bread is buttered,' he replied. 'I admit I've tried to keep on the right side of her. But I'll be in for a real rocket now, you can be sure of that.'

'So what do you have in mind then? A register office do, all hush-hush with nobody knowing till it's all over?'

'I don't know. You can't tell which way Mother will jump. It might be that, because she's ashamed of us, or, on the other hand she might still want a big do with top hats and morning suits and all that, because that's what everyone will expect. But whichever it is ... I'd like you to be my best man ... please, Sam.'

'My goodness. That's a surprise! You do understand, don't you, that Valerie will have to be with me?'

'Of course I understand. I didn't really mean all

that I said. I've been watching her, quietly like, and I must admit that I'm quite impressed with her. She gets on well with her colleagues, and she's bright and efficient. Very pretty, too. I reckon you've done quite well there, little brother. And, as Father says, her dad's a damn good worker.'

'Yes, all very true,' said Sam, biting back any derogative remark about his brother changing his tune, which had come about, he knew, because his brother wanted his support.

'Listen, Sam... You will stick up for me, won't you, in all this? Oh, what a bloody mess we've got ourselves into! But we do love one another, you know. She's the right girl for me. And I promise that I'll support you about Valerie. If you want her to be with you at this damned Ladies Evening, then Mother will have to see sense. Or else I won't go either.'

Sam smiled at his brother. 'You're not such a bad sort, Jon, all told. And there's only the two of us, you and me. We've got to stick together. I suppose I've always stuck close to Father, rather than Mother. I don't know how he puts up with her at times. Anybody would think she's the Queen Mother, the way she behaves.'

'I suppose it's anything for a quiet life, with Father,' said Jonathan. 'Right, are you ready? Shall we go and brave the lion in its den? Lioness, I should say!'

'Yes, why not?' Sam grasped his brother's arm. 'Let's go and face the music.'

Joshua and Beatrice were both in the sitting room watching a documentary on the television. Sam supposed it was better that they were both there. Father could be relied on to keep a clear head and an open mind.

'We'd like to have a word with both of you,' began Jonathan.

'Dear me! That sounds ominous,' said Joshua. 'The two of you together, that's unusual for a start.'

'Unusual circumstances, Father,' said Sam. 'Go on, Jon, it's over to you.' He nudged his brother, and they sat down together, side by side, on the large settee.

'This is all very mysterious,' said Beatrice, smiling at Jonathan rather than at Samuel. 'Come along now, dear. What do you want to tell us?'

'Er ... well ... it's like this, you see, Mother,' Jonathan began. 'Thelma and I, we've decided that we want to get married soon, and not wait till next year. Actually, it's what we'll have to do ... because Thelma's pregnant.' The last few words came out in a rush before he changed his mind.

The expression on Beatrice's face changed in an instant from one of loving interest to one of shock and disbelief. 'Jonathan, did I hear you correctly? You're saying that Thelma is ... expecting a baby?'

'Yes, Mother,' he muttered. 'That is exactly what I said.'

'Oh, Jonathan! How could you? Whatever will people say? Oh, I can't believe that you would do this to us. What a disgrace!'

'I'm sorry, Mother,' said Jonathan. 'I knew you wouldn't be pleased, but that's the way it is. Thelma and I, we love one another, and that's what has happened.'

'And what has it to do with you?' Beatrice

turned angrily to Sam. 'Why are you here, may I ask? Have you some undesirable news to tell us as well?'

'No, Mother,' answered Sam, 'I'm here to support my brother. I can understand it even if you don't. These things happen. And we've decided, Jon and I, that it's about time the two of us stuck together.'

Joshua hadn't said a word until that point, now a slow grin spread all over his face. 'Well, well, well,' he said. 'You might say it's history repeating itself ... eh, Beattie? It's just like you and me twenty-nine years ago. Yes...' he went on as his two sons looked at him in surprise. 'Your mother and me we had to get wed because Jonathan was on the way. But we had to keep it a secret, you see, because of what folks might say.'

Beatrice sprang to her feet. 'Joshua! How could you? You know what you promised. Oh, I can't believe this. You've let me down, all of you.' Her face was white with anger and frustration as she fled from the room, then they heard her strangled sobs as she went upstairs.

The brothers looked at one another, both of them wanting to burst out laughing but not daring to. Their mother was truly upset and they knew that her embarrassment would be acute.

Joshua spoke first. 'Aye, that's what happened to your mother and me. My folks didn't like it, and neither did hers, but we had to go ahead and have a slap-up wedding, and if people did their sums and realized that it didn't add up, well, they said nowt about it. Folks forget in time, you know, it's a nine days' wonder. But your mother

217

insisted on saying that we got wed a year earlier and, fool that I am, I went along with it. But I saw red just now, her being so shocked and self-righteous about it. I really think she'd forgotten what happened to us...' He shook his head. 'I'm blessed if I can understand the way her mind works, but it's you and Thelma that we've got to think about now, isn't it?' He smiled understandingly at Jonathan. 'This is a right mess you've got us into, isn't it?'

'Sorry, Father,' said Jonathan. 'And I'm sorry that I've upset Mother. Actually, I did wonder... She's so secretive about all sorts of things, isn't she? Her family that we never see, for one thing.'

'Yes, I know. This might turn out to be a blessing in disguise. She'll have to come down off her high horse and wake up to reality. I dare say you know, don't you, that she once worked in the mill herself? Not ours, but that was what she was doing when I met her. She worked in the office, same as Sam's young lady does. So ... what about you and Thelma? What have you got in mind? When's the baby due?'

'Not for ages. She's only just found out. But it's definite. She's been to the doctor, and she's starting to feel sick in the morning. She's telling her parents tonight. And Sam here...' He turned to his brother. 'We've decided to support one another.'

'Yes, all for one and one for all,' replied Sam as they grasped one another's hands.

'He's going to be my best man,' said Jonathan, 'and we must start to include Valerie in our family occasions, just the same as Thelma.'

Joshua nodded. 'That's fine with me, and I'll make sure your mother agrees an' all. It's time Beatrice and I had a serious chat.'

FIFTEEN

It was during the second week of October when Cissie realized that what she had feared, had, in fact, happened. She was pregnant, there could be little doubt about it now. She had missed two periods, as she had occasionally done before, but this time it was different. She had started to feel queazy in the mornings, and she had actually been sick that morning following her breakfast. Her breasts felt tight and a little swollen which, so she had heard, was another symptom.

She confided in Val, as she did over most things, as they walked home from work one evening. 'It's a good job we got engaged, Walter and me,' she said. 'What I really mean is it's a good job that I decided to let him – you know – go the whole way because I think I'm having a baby. Well, I don't just think, I'm pretty sure. I've been sick and I'm sort of tight up here.' She fingered her breasts. 'And I'm more than two months overdue.'

'Oh ... well, I can't really say congratulations, can I?' replied Val. 'As you say, it's a good job you and Walter got together. What does he say about it?'

'I haven't told him yet,' said Cissie, 'nor my mam and dad. They'll hit the roof – at least Mam will – but it might have been worse. At least I can say it was Walter, and he doesn't know any different, does he? I know it's awful to make use of him, but what else could I do?'

It didn't seem to have occurred to Cissie that it might well be Walter's baby that she was expecting and not Jack's, but Val didn't remind her of that. 'Then you'd better hurry up and tell him, hadn't you?' she said. 'Walter, and your parents. Perhaps your parents won't say too much. At least you're engaged to him.'

'I know, but I can't see that she'll take it lying down, not me mam. She'll say I'm a disgrace and no better than I ought to be an' all that. I'm dreading telling her.'

'Take Walter with you then. She might not go on so much if he's there. He thinks the world of you, you know, Cissie. You're very lucky in a lot of ways. Like you say, it could have been a lot worse.'

'Yes, I know. He's more possessive than ever now we're engaged. But he's OK.' She shrugged. 'He's got a good job, and he's not afraid of spending a bob or two. He said he was saving up to get a car of his own, but I can't see that happening now. We'll have to think about getting somewhere to live. I don't fancy living with his parents, and certainly not with mine.'

'Just tell him then. Tell him tonight.'

'OK. Yes I will,' Cissie agreed as they said goodbye. 'Think of me, won't you?'

This was the second forthcoming marriage she had heard of in a very short time, thought Val, as she parted from her friend. Sam had told her that his brother and his fiancée, Thelma, would be getting married quite soon. He had said earlier that they would be married next spring. He had not explained the reason for the change of plan, but Val thought she might have an idea why it had been brought forward. Sam had also told her that he was to be his brother's best man.

'He couldn't do any other really,' he said, 'I'm his only brother. Actually we've been getting on a lot better recently.' Sam also said that his mother was proving much easier to get along with now. 'It turns out that she worked in a mill office before she and my father got married,' he told her, 'just like you do, so she can't pretend that she's always been a grand lady. You mustn't worry about meeting her. It will be OK, I assure you.'

Plans were soon going ahead for the marriage of Jonathan and Thelma to take place in mid-December. A Christmas wedding instead of a spring one, but just as lavish as had originally been planned. Sam assured Val that she would be receiving an invitation before long. She had also been invited to something called a Masonic Ladies' Evening in a couple of weeks' time.

She had not yet met Sam's mother, but Jonathan was now much friendlier towards her when they met during working hours. She had been asked to go for afternoon tea on Sunday, an occasion she was anticipating with very mixed feelings.

'You're as good as her any day of the week,' Val's mother had told her. 'Just be yourself, nice and friendly, like, and don't bow and scrape to her. She's not the Queen Mother. Anyroad, Mr Joshua'll be there, won't he? And you get on well with him.'

'Aye, he's a grand chap,' said her father. 'Just

hold your head up high, that's my girl. Young Samuel's a grand lad an' all. You can trust him to stick up for you.'

Cissie knew that she must tell Walter straight away. He called for her that evening. They had intended going to the cinema but she told him she had changed her mind. Could they just go for a walk, she suggested, and maybe stop somewhere for a drink? There was something she needed to tell him.

'Fine with me,' he agreed. It had become something of a ritual, as it was with many couples, to go to the cinema once or twice a week irrespective of what films were being shown. 'There's nothing much on at the moment, and we'll have to start saving up soon, won't we, for the big day?'

Although they were engaged they had not talked about a date for their marriage. Cissie knew that Walter would like it to be soon, whereas she had been content to wait a while. Now the circumstances had changed and she knew it would have to be as soon as possible.

'Yes,' she said, in answer to his remark about saving up. 'We will need to save up. That's partly what I wanted to talk about.'

'Now, that's what I was waiting to hear,' he said, pulling her closer to him as they walked down to the town centre. 'I can't wait for us to get married, Cissie.'

They went into a pub near the Market Hall which was not too busy at that time in the early evening. She asked for a small shandy, and Walter returned to their secluded table with her drink and a pint of bitter for himself,

'Now, what do you want to tell me?' he said. 'Is it that you want us to get married soon? It can't be soon enough for me, Cissie, love.'

'Yes, that's exactly what I want to say, Walter,' she replied. 'Not that I really want to get married soon. Well ... what I mean is, that I want to, but I thought we could wait a while.' She found she was tying herself in knots and decided to come straight to the point. 'The thing is, we'll have to get married soon, because ... I've discovered I'm having a baby.'

'What?' He stared at her in amazement. 'But ... you can't be! It only happened once. You haven't let me get anywhere near you since then. You said we had to wait, and that's driving me mad, Cissie. Are you sure? Is it possible ... the first time?'

'It seems like it,' she said. 'I was surprised an' all, but there it is. I've been feeling sick, and I've missed twice, so I must be ... pregnant.' Cissie had been brought up to believe that it was not seemly to talk about personal matters with other people, certainly not with a man, so she felt rather embarrassed at mentioning periods. 'So now I've got to tell my parents,' she went on. 'I must tell them tonight, but I wanted you to know first.'

He shook his head unbelievingly, then he took hold of her and kissed her. 'So it means we can fix a date straight away? That can't be bad, Cissie. I'd got it into my head that you'd keep putting it off, but now it's the sooner the better, isn't it?'

'Only because we've no choice,' said Cissie. 'I mean ... what will our parents say, mine and yours? They're not going to be over the moon, are

223

they? I'm dreading telling my mam. She'll tear me limb from limb! She'll say I've let her down, she's ashamed of me an' all that.'

Walter smiled at her. 'You didn't do it on your own, Cissie, love. It takes two to tango, as they say. Look ... I'll be there with you. We'll go and tell them now, then perhaps I'll break the news to my parents on my own. Come on now; sup up, and we'll go and face the music.'

'Thank you, Walter,' said Cissie. 'That's what I hoped you'd say.'

'So, the baby's due in June?' he asked as they left the pub.

'Yes...' she replied evasively. 'I haven't been to see a doctor yet. With my ... er ... periods being irregular it's hard to be sure. It could be earlier ... or later.'

Walter had not even hinted or suggested that he might not be the father, such was his trust in her. And for that Cissie was truly thankful.

'You're back early,' said her mother as they walked through the door.

'We decided not to go to the pictures after all,' said Cissie.

'Oh, I see, you'll be wanting some supper then, I suppose,' Mrs Foster said grudgingly, but she smiled at Walter. 'Come on in, Walter lad. Take your coat off and come and get warm. I'll get the kettle on, though it's sooner than I expected.'

'No, it's alright, Mrs Foster,' said Walter. 'We'll happen have a cup of tea later. Cissie and me, we've got something to tell you.'

'Oh ... summat nice, I hope?' said Hannah Foster. She beamed at Walter. 'Here, Joe,' she shouted at her husband. 'Put that damned paper down and take a bit of notice, can't you? They've got summat to tell us, our Cissie and Walter. And I bet I can guess what it is an' all.'

The living room was overcrowded with large items of furniture that the Fosters had had since their marriage, a mish-mash of styles. There was a sturdy oak table which let down when it was not in use, and four chairs to match, a cumbersome three-piece suite in brown velour, worn with age, and an oversize Victorian sideboard with a mirror at the back. Cissie and Walter perched on the edge of the sofa, and Hannah sat in the large easy chair opposite her husband, who meekly put down his newspaper.

Walter gave Cissie a nudge as if to say, 'Go on, you tell them, they're your parents.'

Cissie looked at him and gave a weak smile before beginning. 'Well, Walter and me, we've decided we want to get married quite soon, happen before Christmas.' She saw her mother smile complacently before she went on to say, 'Well ... actually we'll have to get married fairly soon because ... I'm expecting a baby.'

Her mother's smile disappeared and a look of horror took its place. 'You're ... what! Oh, Cissie, how could you? How could you let us down like this? We've brought you up to be a good girl, and you know that you shouldn't...'

'Hang on a minute, Mrs Foster,' Walter interrupted her. He took hold of Cissie's hand. 'I'm responsible as well, you know. And Cissie and me ... we love each other.' He looked adoringly at Cissie and she smiled back at him, so relieved that he was there with her.

'Yes, happen you do,' snapped Hannah, 'but you should control yourselves. I thought better of you, Walter, but I reckon it would be her, egging you on. You're a decent lad, but you've made your own bed, the pair of you, and you'll have to lie on it. But you've brought shame on us, Cissie, on your father and me. How will I ever hold my head up again in front of all the folks at church?'

'Hey, steady on a minute, Hannah,' said her husband. 'It's not the end of the world, is it? It's happened before to all sorts of folks. Like Walter says, they love one another and at least they're engaged to be married.' He turned to the couple. 'What do you want to do, then? Have a quiet do, like, at the registry office? It doesn't make any difference where it is so long as you're wed.'

'Indeed they won't go to no registry office!' retorted Hannah. 'No, they'll get married in church, good and proper. We'll have no hole and corner affair.' She turned to Cissie. 'But you'll not wear white, young lady. No daughter of mine'll go to the altar wearing white when she's no business to be doing so. No, it'll have to be pink or blue, and if folks talk then it'll be your own damned fault. But we'll have a decent wedding in church with a reception and everything. Nobody's going to say that I didn't give my daughter a good send off, even if she didn't deserve it.'

'Hold on a minute,' said Joe Foster, for the second time. 'She's my daughter an' all, you know. I'll be the one that'll be walking her down the aisle, an' I'll be proud to do so. She's always been a good lass, and if she's made a mistake, so what?

She's marrying a decent lad ... and I wish you all the best, the pair of you.'

He went over to Cissie and kissed her on the cheek, then shook hands with Walter. 'Well done, lad ... er ... you know what I mean. I'm sure you'll be very happy.'

Hannah had the grace to look a little shame-faced. 'Well, I reckon we'll have to make the best of it. What's done is done. I'll go and make that cup of tea.'

'I think we can do a bit better than that, can't we?' said her husband. 'Haven't we got a bottle of sherry somewhere? The least we can do is drink a toast to the ... er ... happy couple.'

'Yes, alright, if you say so.' Hannah shot an exasperated look at Joe. She went to the sideboard and took out a bottle, half full, of dark brown sherry which they drank on occasions such as Christmas. She placed four small gold-rimmed glasses on a chromium tray and poured out the sherry.

'I've got some shortbread biscuits,' she said. 'I'll go and get them.' She disappeared into the kitchen.

'She'll come round,' whispered Joe. 'You know your mother. It could be worse. She'll be making plans at church and choosing a new outfit to wear before long, as though everything's hunky-dory.'

'Thanks, Dad,' said Cissie, 'for ... well ... pouring oil on troubled waters.'

'Yes, thank you, Mr Foster,' added Walter. 'Cissie was real worried about what her mother would say.' He stopped talking as Hannah returned carrying a tin with a Scottie dog on the lid.

'Best Highland shortbread,' she said with a

glimmer of a smile. She handed round the sherry then the tin of biscuits. 'Go on, Joe. Propose a toast, if that's what you want,' she said.

'Aye ... well, here goes.' He rose to his feet and lifted his glass. 'Here's to our Cissie, and Walter, soon to be our son-in-law. I know he'll look after her, and I'm sure she'll do her best to be a good wife to him. So ... all the best to the pair of you. Good health and happiness.'

That was a long speech for her father to make and Cissie was touched. She was amazed when her mother also raised her glass and repeated. 'Yes, good health and happiness, both of you.'

Then, putting her glass down, she went over to Cissie and placed a perfunctory kiss on her cheek, then shook hands with Walter. She nodded at them. 'Well, it's up to the two of you now to make a go of it.'

Cissie reflected that her words were less than effusive, but at least she had made an effort.

It was two days later when Cissie and Val next walked home together.

'Well, how did you go on?' asked Val. 'You told your mum, did you, and you're still here to tell the tale?'

'Yes, just about.' Cissie laughed. 'She went mad at first, but then she calmed down a bit, thanks to my dad. So ... we'll be getting married quite soon. We're going to see the vicar, Walter and me – tonight actually – to see when he's got a Saturday free. An' I want to ask you, Val, will you be my bridesmaid?'

'Of course I will; I'll be delighted,' said Val,

putting an arm round her friend. 'Just me, or will there be another one as well?'

'No, just you,' said Cissie, 'seeing as it's what you might call a shotgun wedding! Mam wouldn't hear of us going to the registry office, though. No, it has to be a church do, but she won't let me wear white. I'm not pure, you see ... not a virgin,' she whispered, 'although Mam didn't actually say that. I suppose I'll have to wear something more like a bridesmaid's dress in a pale colour. Will you come with me to choose it? I thought we might go to C&A in Bradford and choose both our dresses. What do you think?'

'That's a great idea,' said Val. 'I can kill two birds with one stone, as they say. I shall need to buy another dress as well for this Ladies' Evening I've been invited to – some Masonic do. Sam's father's a Mason, and they have this posh do every year. Ladies are invited, but they're usually excluded from everything that the men get up to. I never knew much about it before.'

'Yes, I've heard tell of it,' said Cissie. 'It's supposed to be all hush-hush, isn't it? But I've heard that the fellows parade around with one trouser leg rolled up, and they're blindfolded with a rope round their neck. What a daft carry-on, eh?'

Val laughed. 'Yes, it's a secret society. Nobody's supposed to know about it unless they're a member, but stories have been leaking out recently. Anyway this Ladies Evening's a posh do, so I shall need a long dress. And the men wear evening suits. Fancy that, eh? Something my dad's never worn, nor yours.'

'And it's tea with the gentry for you on Sunday,

isn't it?' Cissie reminded her friend.

'Yes; I get collywobbles when I think about it, but Sam says I've not to worry. His mother's getting used to the idea now, of him being friendly with me. But I shall have to watch my Ps and Qs, won't I?'

'You always know how to behave,' said Cissie. 'Not like me! They wouldn't want to entertain the likes of me.'

'Don't run yourself down,' said Val staunchly. 'I think you're great, and you're a good friend, Cissie. Sam likes you as well and I hope he'll get an invitation to your wedding, along with me?'

'Gosh, yes! If you think he'd come. That'd be summat for me mam to brag about; one of the Walkers at my wedding.'

'Well, he'll be there, I can assure you,' said Val.

And so on Saturday afternoon both girls found themselves wandering round the large C&A store in Bradford, mesmerized by all the colours and styles. They had travelled from Halifax by bus and had a snack lunch at Woolworths. It was a treat for both of them to spend a day at the shops in a city that was bigger than their own home town.

C&A was by way of being a budget store, with a range of clothing to suit every pocket. There was, however, a rather more exclusive range for those special occasions, including dresses, coats and suits copied from designs of well-known fashion houses, but at a much more reasonable price.

'Didn't your mother want to come with you to choose your dress?' asked Val, as they searched through the array of dresses on the racks.

'No; I think she's still quite annoyed with me,'

said Cissie, 'though she put a good face on it the other night for Walter. I reckon she thinks it was all my fault... What colour do you fancy, Val. Shall we both have the same colour, or different ones?'

'You're the bride, so I think you should have something rather more stylish than me, and a different colour, too.'

An assistant came to help them, and Cissie explained that she was the bride, but she didn't want to wear white because she had a pale complexion and blonde hair, and it would make her look rather washed out.

The woman nodded understandingly. 'What about pale blue?' she suggested. 'Pink is pretty, but blue is rather more sophisticated for a bride. And your friend is your bridesmaid, is she? This peach pink would suit you beautifully,' she said to Val, 'with your dark hair. A lovely contrast to the bride.'

After they had each tried on a couple of dresses they took the assistant's advice. The dresses were similar in style: full-skirted, mid-calf length with long sleeves and a scooped neckline. Cissie's blue dress of silk taffeta was covered in lace. She also chose a tiny pillbox hat in a matching shade of blue, with a short organdie veil.

Val's peach-coloured dress was of a similar fabric, but without the lace, and was less elaborate. The fitted bodice showed off her slim figure and the warm colour suited her hair and complexion.

The assistant did not disagree when Cissie decided on a size 14, a size larger than her usual 12. 'I mustn't have it too tight,' she said, 'or else I shall look fat. I'm not like Val here, fancy being able to get into a 10! I'm too fond of cakes and puddings.'

'A very wise choice,' said the assistant, diplomatically.

'My dad gave me some money to buy my dress, and yours as well,' said Cissie as they stood at the cash desk. 'He's been really good about it all.'

'I'm quite prepared to pay for my own dress,' said Val, although she knew it was customary for the bride's family to foot the bill. 'You've got enough expense with one thing and another. It's very good of your dad. Your mum will come round in time, I feel sure she will.'

Cissie had already told her that Walter's parents had taken the news quite calmly without a lot of condemnation. And as the two families were on friendly terms there was every chance that Cissie's mother would be forced to smile and play her part as the mother of the bride.

'Now, let's go and buy your evening dress,' said Cissie as they left the bridal department. 'What colour do you fancy?'

'I don't know, but not pink or blue this time. Apparently all the ladies wear long dresses. I've never had an evening dress before, so I'm not sure what to go for.'

'You'll look as posh as anyone there,' said Cissie loyally. 'Gosh! I'd love to be a fly on the wall, 'cause I don't think I'll ever be invited to a do like that.'

There was a variety of styles and colours, but Val insisted that she didn't want anything too fancy or elaborate. Eventually she chose a slim-fitting silk rayon gown in a deep cherry red colour, sleeveless, but with a wide stand-away collar.

'What about shoes?' said Cissie. 'You'll need some high-heeled evening shoes, and we haven't got our wedding shoes neither.'

'Oh, let's think about that another time,' said Val. 'I don't know about you, but I'm ready for a cup of tea. Let's go and have a drink at the Kardomah before we get on the bus.'

'I had a letter from Janice today,' said Val as they sat in the cafe enjoying their tea and a buttered scone. 'I should have told you earlier, but we've had so much else to talk about.'

It had turned out that Val did the corresponding with Janice on behalf of herself and Cissie, her friend admitting that she wasn't much of a letter writer.

'Oh, that's good,' replied Cissie. 'How's her mother going on?'

'Improving ... but slowly, I gather,' said Val. 'She thanks us for the Get Well card, but reading between the lines I get the impression that she's not too well at all.'

'Oh dear, that's a shame,' said Cissie. 'Mrs Butler made us so welcome didn't she? I thought she was a lovely lady. We won't be going back to Blackpool next year, like we said we would. It's all changed now, hasn't it?'

'Yes, it was quite an eventful week for all of us,' replied Val thoughtfully. She reflected that the happenings of that one week in August were having an effect on all their lives, her own as well as those of Cissie and Janice.

SIXTEEN

Phil had told Janice that he would come to Black-pool to spend a few days with her during the first week of October. She was looking forward very much to his arrival, hoping that he would not only add a sparkle to her own life, but would help to cheer up her mother as well.

Lilian was at home now after her two weeks' stay in hospital. They had been told that the operation had been satisfactory, but Lilian was not at all like her former self. She was no longer the cheerful and optimistic person that she used to be. She did not complain, but on the other hand she did not say very much at all. They could tell that she was pleased to be home, but she had retreated into a little world of her own and it was difficult to communicate with her. As her normal self she would have been anxious to know how the hotel was faring, how her assistants were coping during her absence, but she appeared to have no interest at all. In a way that was a good thing. It would not help her recovery if she were to worry, but to ask no questions was unlike her.

Her hair had been shaved off one side, and Janice made her a light turban to wear until her hair grew again, but Lilian seemed unconcerned about her appearance. She still visited the hospital regularly for check-ups. Apparently it would be a while before she was given the 'all-clear', but the doctors were somewhat reticent about just how long it might be. She was not confined to bed, but spent much of her time sitting in an armchair, dozing from time to time or watching the television.

Phil arrived on the Wednesday afternoon in what was proving to be a chaotic week at the hotel. He had travelled by train and taken a taxi from the station. Janice had explained that she would be too busy to meet him at the station, but that they were all looking forward to seeing him. There was a room prepared for him as the hotel was not fully booked that week.

When he appeared on the doorstep in the middle of the afternoon Janice almost burst into tears of joy, but managed to control herself. He put his arms around her, holding her close for a moment then kissing her gently on the lips. Their relationship was, still, more of a friendship than a romance, but they both knew that the potential was there for it to develop.

'Hello, Phil,' she managed to say after a moment, blinking away incipient tears. 'It's great to see you again. But just look at me in my pinny!' She laughed. 'And flour in my hair I shouldn't wonder.'

Phil laughed as well. 'Great to see you, too. You look lovely, even covered in flour! But I can see that you're very busy.'

'You can say that again!' she muttered. 'Anyway, come along in. Mum will be pleased to see you. I told her you were coming.' Lilian had actually shown some interest when Janice had mentioned Phil. 'Dad's at work, of course, and Ian's at school.

235

There's just Freda and myself preparing the meal for tonight. Leave your case there, and I'll show you your room later.' Janice opened the living room door. 'Mum, look who's come to see us.'

Lilian was sitting by the fire with a magazine on her lap. Janice had bought her a *Woman's Own* to see if it would arouse some interest in her. She used to love magazines, when she had time to read them. She had been dozing, but she opened her eyes and looked round. Her face lit up with pleasure, and there was a spark of animation in her eyes which, regrettably, had been all too seldom seen of late.

'Phil, how lovely to see you!' Lilian got up and took hold of his hands, then she kissed his cheek. 'Sit yourself down and talk to me. I've been in the wars, you know, but I think I'm getting better. I know Janice is busy, but perhaps she'll make us a cup of tea, will you, love?'

'In a minute, Mum,' replied Janice. 'I must go and see what Freda's doing, I've left her on her own. Take your coat off, Phil, and make yourself at home. I won't be long, but I must go and see what's happening.' She smiled at him rather apologetically as she hurried out of the room.

Phil could see that she was harassed and he wanted to go and help. It seemed to him as though Mrs Butler was leaving all the work to her daughter and appeared unaware of how very busy she was. He soon realized that the operation had brought about a change in Janice's mother. She was so unlike her former self. She had been so active and ready to cope with anything. He surmised, from what he could see, that her recovery

236

to full health and strength might take a long time.

'It's really good to see you again, Mrs Butler,' he said. 'I was so sorry to hear about your operation, but Janice says that everything's going well. And I must say that you're looking fine. There's some colour in your cheeks, and you're still smiling.' He knew that a white lie or two could be forgiven. The worst thing you could do was tell an invalid how poorly they looked, and Lilian needed cheering up. In truth she looked drawn, with dark shadows beneath her eyes, and she had lost a little weight.

'I'm smiling because you're here,' said Lilian, 'and it'll be the fire that's made my cheeks red. To be honest, Phil, I feel as though I've no energy. I'm quite content to sit here and do nothing, and it all seems so ... far away. I know our Janice is working her socks off. She's a good lass, but she's young and strong and I know she'll cope. And my Alec is very good; they're waiting on me hand and foot. But I'm so listless, and I know that's not like the usual me at all.'

'It's nature's way of helping you to get well again,' said Phil. 'Your body needs a good rest after your operation, and after all the hard work you were doing before you were taken ill. I'm sure you'll be raring to go again before long.'

'Aye, maybe you're right,' she replied complacently. 'And what about you, Phil? Let me see. You live somewhere in Yorkshire, don't you? And your father owns a pub?'

'Yes, I live near Ilkley,' Phil reminded her. 'It's a sort of country inn rather than a pub. It's called "The Coach and Horses", not a very original name, but it used to be a coaching inn. We've modernized it a lot since my father took it over. We're not too busy at the moment, so my dad can spare me for a few days.'

'I see...' said Lilian, smiling and nodding. He was not sure that she had taken in all that he had been saying.

Janice arrived then with the tea and biscuits on a tray. 'Are you having a good chat, you two?' she asked.

'Yes, Phil's been telling me about where he lives in Yorkshire. Now ... where is it?'

'Ilkley, Mrs Butler,' replied Phil.

'Yes, that's right.' Lilian nodded. 'Ilkley, like in that song, "On Ilkley Moor baht 'at."' She laughed. 'His father's got a pub there.'

Phil thought that Janice was looking a little exasperated, but she was trying not to let it show. 'I'm sorry I can't stop and chat,' she said. 'Freda and I are making steak and kidney pies, and we're just putting the crusts on before they go in the oven.'

'Would you like some help?' asked Phil.

Janice felt that she ought to say no, but it was what they really needed so badly at that moment. 'Would you, Phil?' she said. 'Thank you, we'd be ever so grateful. We might have been trying to do too much today.'

'I'll have my cup of tea, then I'll be right with you,' said Phil, smiling at her reassuringly.

Janice gave him a thankful smile as she went out. Phil drank his tea and ate two custard creams. Mrs Butler was enjoying her tea but not saying anything now. He put the cups and saucers together on the tray and stood up.

'I'll go and see how the ladies are getting on in the kitchen,' he said. 'I'll see you later, Mrs Butler.' She smiled at him, and he could see that she had retreated into her own little world again.

'My goodness, are we glad to see you!' said Janice when he appeared. 'We're not having the best of days, are we, Freda?'

'We've had better,' replied the lady in a floral apron. She looked competent and cheerful, and Phil guessed that she was not the sort to get in a panic. He knew that Janice, on the other hand, was somewhat overwrought at the moment.

'We're getting there,' said Freda, 'but we'd be glad of an extra pair of hands. You've not really come to work though, have you, Phil?'

'I've come to see Janice, because her plans have been changed, and to see her mum, of course. But I'm ready, willing and able!' He smiled. 'Now, tell me what you want me to do. I'd better put an apron on first.'

Janice handed him a blue and white striped butcher's apron. 'The carrots and the spuds need peeling, but we can do that. Perhaps you could see to the trifles, give them a professional look? The jelly's ready, and I must admit we use tinned custard. There's a big tin of peaches, and the Swiss rolls need to be soaked in sherry. And you can put the finishing touches to them.'

While Phil set to work quietly and efficiently Janice and Freda got on with the more mundane jobs of peeling the vegetables. 'We'll have mashed potatoes,' said Janice. 'It'll be easier than roast, and the garden peas are frozen ones.'

239

She then explained to Phil why the day was so fraught with problems. 'Olive's got the flu,' she said. 'She wasn't well yesterday, and today she rang to say she was really bad. So there's only Nancy and myself to serve the meals. We advertised for someone to come and help in the kitchen, and a woman came in last week. She said she was an experienced cook, and she did her best, I suppose, but she wasn't all that good. Actually, she was more hindrance than help, then she said on Sunday that she wouldn't be coming again. So there's just Freda and me now, and Nancy to do the waitressing. I'm still learning the job and feeling my way.' Janice sighed. 'I felt so sure I could do it but it's harder than I thought. Freda's been wonderful, though, and she's taught me such a lot.'

'I'm doing what I can,' said Freda, 'but I'm only an ordinary plain sort of cook, I can't attempt anything fancy. And Janice has worked wonders, despite what she says. There's not much gone amiss, and we haven't had any complaints.'

'You seem to be doing OK to me,' said Phil. 'The kitchen's clean and tidy, and that's a good sign.'

'That's my mother's training,' said Janice. 'She always tidies up as she goes along and I'm the same. And so is Freda. We don't like to work with everything in a mess. But today – I don't know – I felt as though everything was getting me down.' She grinned at Phil, 'You're an angel sent from heaven!'

He laughed. 'I've never been called that before. But I'll help as much as I can while I'm here. I don't intend to sit on my backside and watch you work.'

'I'm really grateful, Phil. But I'm hoping we'll be able to spend a bit of time together. The Illuminations are on, you know, and those of us who live here don't always bother to go and see them. I certainly haven't had time this year.'

'I caught glimpses of them when I was stationed at Weeton,' said Phil, 'but I've never seen them all. How long are they on?'

'Till the end of October. That's two more weeks after this one. I can't wait for the season to come to an end. I know now how Mum used to feel.'

'And you've visitors in right till the last week?'

'Yes, but it's tailing off a bit now. I think there are fourteen next week, so that's not too bad.'

'And then you'll be closed ... for how long?'

'Until Easter. We usually have a few visitors then, but the season starts in earnest round about Whitsuntide. Then it's all go for the next five or six months.'

Phil was thoughtful as he worked away at the sherry trifles. 'What are you going to do when this season comes to an end?' he asked. 'It's too late for you to start your university course, isn't it?'

'Yes, much too late. I had to tell them that I couldn't come because there was a crisis at home, and not to keep my place for me. I said that I might apply again next year, but I don't really think I will.'

Phil thought she sounded rather regretful. 'Your mother might be OK again by then,' he said. 'And she was so eager for you to go, wasn't she?'

'She's forgotten all about that now. She seems to have forgotten about most things. It's really heart-breaking to see her like this, Phil.'

241

'I'm sure it must be. It's early days, though, Janice, and the operation's been a shock to her system. But she'll get better in time... Now ... are these trifles up to standard? I've done my best.'

'They're superb, Phil,' she answered. 'Real professional. Obviously the work of an expert hand. It seems a shame to break into them.' The trifles were in three large dishes. The whipped cream stood up in points, decorated with cherries, angelica and flaked nuts. 'We'll take them into the dining room on the trolley, then the visitors can see your work of art before we dish them out.'

'Now, we're almost finished, aren't we, Freda? You go when you're ready. Nancy will be here soon to see to the tables.' Freda usually left in the late afternoon to see to her own family meal, but since Lilian's illness she had been coming in each morning to help with the breakfasts, as well as doing her afternoon stint.

'OK, if you're sure, Janice,' said Freda. 'Don't worry, it'll all be fine. Everything's under control now, and Phil's here to help you. See you in the morning then, bright and early. Cheerio for now, Phil. We're jolly glad of your help.'

The evening meal went ahead without any hitches. Nancy arrived promptly, and the three of them worked together to set the tables. The cloths were still on from breakfast time, and those that had spillages were turned over.

Phil insisted that he would help to serve the meal as well. He was a young man who liked to look smart on occasions, and he put on a dark jacket to match his trousers. Janice wore her black dress and changed her working apron for her frilly waitress one.

It was well turned eight before the family could start their own meal, after the two of them and Nancy had cleared away the visitors' pots and cutlery.

'Thank God for the dishwasher!' said Janice. 'I can't imagine now how we managed without it. When I hear tales of the olden days, when Grandma was in charge, I'm astounded at all they had to do. It's bad enough now, with all our mod cons.'

'What you've never had you never miss, I suppose,' said Phil. 'Fridges and freezers, washing machines, dish-washers, hoovers, television, aeroplanes... What a long way we've come in this century, and we're only halfway through it. Whatever will have happened by the year 2000, I wonder?'

'We might even be flying to the moon, who knows?' said Janice. 'Although I'm quite content down here. I'd like to go up in an aeroplane though, sometime,' she added wistfully.

Alec and Ian, and Lilian as well, were very appreciative of the meal when the family plus Phil, finally sat down to eat. Their meal was the same as the guests', except for the mushroom soup that had been served as the first course. It was normal for the family to eat just the two courses.

'By heck! That was good,' said Alec. 'You've done us proud, Janice, and I believe you had a hand in it an' all, Phil.'

'He saved my life, Dad,' said Janice. 'It was all getting on top of me till Phil came to our rescue. So it all turned out alright, and Phil says he wants to help while he's here.'

Alec nodded seriously. 'It's very good of you, Phil, lad. We'll see you right, of course.' He cast an anxious glance at his wife who seemed oblivious to the conversation. She was carefully spooning up what remained of her trifle. She had eaten her meal with obvious enjoyment, slowly and carefully, leaving only a little of the steak pie. It was a good sign that her appetite was returning.

'I'm only too glad to be here to help,' said Phil. 'Just a bed for the night, that's all I need.'

When they had cleared away, with Alec and Ian helping as well, Janice showed Phil up to his room on the second floor. They had scarcely had a minute to spare until then.

'Very nice,' he said, taking in the single bed covered with a blue candlewick spread, matching the blue patterned curtains at the windows and the blue cushion on the small armchair. There was a washbasin with two blue towels on the rail, and the wardrobe and dressing table were of light oak in the utility style that had been brought in following the war years, plain but practical and functional.

'Very nice, indeed,' said Phil again. 'I can see your guests have all the home comforts they need, if all your rooms are of this standard, and I'm sure they are.'

'Yes, we got rid of all the old-fashioned furniture, bit by bit, at the end of the war,' said Janice, 'although I wasn't really taking much notice of what was going on at that time. That was when the visitors starting coming again. Grandma was one of the old-type seaside landladies, you know, not all that keen on moving with the times. But

Mum's made changes of her own since Gran died two years ago. I miss her though...' She smiled reminiscently. 'She could be a real old battleaxe, I suppose, but she was kind to me and Ian. Anyway, I'll leave you now to put your things away. The toilet's just next door,' she added. 'Sorry there's no bathroom – one of these days, maybe... But if you do want to have a bath you can use our private one downstairs.'

Phil grinned. 'Thanks, it's all just fine. A home from home. Do you fancy going out in a little while? A walk along the prom, perhaps? Or ... are you too tired?'

Janice was bone-weary, but she didn't want to say so. 'I think I'd prefer to stay in and chat tonight,' she said. 'We'll probably have the lounge to ourselves. Most of the visitors stay out quite late with the Illuminations being on. Is that OK with you?'

'Suits me fine,' said Phil. 'I'll see you downstairs then, in a little while.'

Lilian and Alec were watching the television in the living room, the sound turned down to a quiet murmur as Ian was doing his homework at the other end of the room.

'Phil and I will sit in the visitors' lounge,' Janice told them. 'I feel too tired to go out. We'll go and see the Lights another night, but I don't know just how long Phil will be here.'

'He's been a good help today,' said Alec. 'Not that I'm forgetting what you've done, Janice, love. You're doing a grand job keeping things going.'

'Thanks, Dad. I'm glad there are only two more weeks, though. I know now how Mum feels at the end of the season.'

'And then what will you do?' asked Alec. 'I'm concerned about you, Jan, giving up your course, and it's too late now, isn't it?'

'I had no choice, Dad. I had to keep things going, with help of course, Freda and the other two, and now Phil. But what will happen in the future I just don't know.'

'None of us do, love,' said Alec. 'We'll have to take one day at a time.' He looked fondly, but anxiously, at his wife. Lilian was sitting complacently, seemingly unaware of the conversation. Then she looked at Janice and smiled.

'That Phil's a nice lad,' she said, 'I think he's just right for you, Janice, love.'

'We'll see, Mum,' said Janice. 'Yes, he's very nice, but we'll see how things go.'

As she had hoped, there was no one in the lounge. She flopped down in one of the most comfortable armchairs. The furniture in that room dated back to the thirties. This was something they had not changed, as the contemporary styles such as G-plan and Ercol did not suit the homely feel of the room. It felt good to relax at last, the first time she had rested that day apart from at meal times.

Phil soon joined her, dressed casually now in a chunky sweater and grey flannels. He sat opposite her and leaned forward. 'I've been thinking,' he began, looking at her earnestly. 'I've decided to stay here and help out till the end of the season. That is ... if you would like me to?'

'Of course I would, Phil!' she answered eagerly. 'It would be wonderful! But what about your job at home? You're supposed to be helping your father, aren't you, now you're home again?'

'Dad's had to manage for the two years I've been away, and he's still coping very well with the staff he's got. I told you before that I feel like a spare part sometimes. I'm not really needed all that much. And it was always my idea to branch out on my own eventually, not to stay in Ilkley forever.'

'I'm overwhelmed, I really am,' said Janice. 'We'll pay you, of course. I'll sort it out with Dad.'

'Don't worry about it,' said Phil. 'We'll come to some arrangement. I'll ring my father tomorrow and tell him.' He smiled. 'He might even be relieved to see the back of me.'

'I really thought I could do it,' said Janice. 'When Mum was taken ill I didn't hesitate. I said I'd take over and see to the hotel. I knew it wouldn't be easy, but it's been much harder than I imagined. Not only the cooking and organizing – and I've had help with that – but there's the money side of it as well; the visitors' bills, and the wages and everything. Dad never had much to do with the running of the hotel. It was always Gran, and then Mum. How on earth did she do it all, Phil? There are courses now for hotel management, but she never learnt anything like that. And she never had any training in cookery neither, except some classes at night school...'

'But she had years and years of experience at home,' said Phil. 'She watched what her own mother was doing, and that's a very good way of learning. It's the way all those boarding-house women learned their trade. It was handed down from mother to daughter, trial and error some of the time. And you were only just starting to learn, weren't you? You said you hadn't taken much interest until this last summer. And Rome wasn't built in a day, you know!'

'Yes, that's true,' admitted Janice. 'I still have a lot to learn. Do you know, I found myself thinking, sometimes, that I should have gone to uni after all? That I wasn't cut out for all this. Then I knew I had to carry on because of Mum.'

'Only two more weeks, then you'll have to think about what you want to do next. Have you given it any thought?'

Janice shook her head. 'Yes ... and no. Get a job in Blackpool, I suppose. I've got my O levels and A levels; quite good ones actually. But I intended to go to uni to get a degree – it was what Mum really wanted me to do – and then decide later what career I would follow. But now ... who knows?' She smiled at Phil. 'But I'm feeling better about things already. Now, I'm going to make us a drink. What would you like? Tea, coffee, hot chocolate?'

'Chocolate, of course,' said Phil. 'I'll come with you; and we must go and tell your dad what we've decided to do.'

Alec was alone in the living room. Lilian had retired early, as she usually did, and Ian had gone to bed as well. He was surprised but very pleased to hear what Phil had suggested.

'It's all hanging in the balance at the moment,' he said. 'It depends on Lilian. We can't look too far ahead. But we're OK now till the end of the season. It's very good of you, Phil. I appreciate it, and I know Janice does... Make me a cup of tea, please, will you, Jan? Then I'll call it a day.'

Janice and Phil did not stay up late. Her eyes were closing despite her valiant attempt to stay awake and enjoy Phil's company. It was so good to have him there with her. They had picked up the threads of their friendship with perfect ease.

'Bedtime for you,' he said, just after eleven o'clock. 'Come on, Janice love. You can hardly keep awake.'

They walked up the stairs hand in hand, stopping at her bedroom door on the first floor. Phil put his arms round her and kissed her on the lips, tenderly, then a little more eagerly. 'Goodnight, Janice. Don't worry, it's all going to be fine.'

'Yes ... I know that now,' she replied. 'Thanks, Phil ... for everything.'

SEVENTEEN

Sam told Val that she must not worry about her first visit to his home. 'My mother's looking forward to meeting you,' he said.

That was a slight exaggeration. Beatrice Walker had been forced by circumstances to climb down from her pedestal and remember that her own upbringing had not been far removed from that of Sam's new lady friend. She had agreed, although a trifle grudgingly, that Val should come for Sunday tea.

Val was relieved that it would be, as Sam had told her, a very informal occasion. They usually had their main meal of the day, which they called dinner, in the evening. But on Sundays they had a midday dinner. Afternoon tea was then served in the lounge rather than the formal dining room.

Val had not yet seen the house where the Walker family lived. She just knew that it was at Queensbury, at the top of the hill leading out of Halifax.

Sam called for her in his car at four o'clock, staying for a little while to chat to her parents. 'It'll be fine,' he reassured her. 'You already know my father and my brother...' He had told her again that he and Jonathan were now getting along much more peaceably. 'And Thelma has been invited as well.'

Val was not as intimidated by her first sight of Sam's home as she had thought she might be. It was a large house, as she had expected, set well back from the road, with a circular carriage drive and a large garden with laid out lawns surrounded by trees, now shedding their leaves. There was a magnificent copper beech tree, a horse chestnut, and others which, in the spring, would be covered in pink and white blossom. The house itself looked homely, in spite of its size. A typical greystone building with mullioned windows, the small panes of glass glinting in the rays of the setting sun.

The sturdy oak door was opened at Sam's knock by a woman dressed in black, a housekeeper or some such servant, Val assumed. She was cheerful and friendly, not seeming at all subservient. Was she what was known as an old retainer? Val wondered. Someone who had worked for the family for a long time? She was well past middle-age.

Sam introduced her as Mrs Porter. 'This is my

friend, Val,' he said. 'Valerie Horrocks.'

'Very pleased to meet you, Miss Horrocks,' said the woman. 'Mr Samuel told me you were coming. Let me take your coat, my dear. It's a cold day, isn't it? But there's a nice fire in the lounge.'

She hung Val's coat on the mahogany hallstand, then opened a door to the right. 'Here's Miss Horrocks come to visit you, Mrs Walker,' she announced.

Sam took her arm as they entered the lounge. She felt her apprehension returning as a sea of faces turned to look at her. At least it seemed like a lot but there were, in fact, only four: Mr and Mrs Walker, Jonathan and Thelma.

Sam led her forward to where an elegant dark-haired lady was sitting near to the fire. 'Mother, this is Valerie,' he said.

The woman looked at Val appraisingly. She did not rise but she held out her hand, which Val took hold of gently. 'How do you do?' she said. 'Samuel has told me about you. It's nice to meet you, Valerie.'

'Yes, thank you,' Val managed to utter. 'How do you do, Mrs Walker?'

Sam's mother was wearing a fine woollen dress of mid-blue which matched the colour of her shrewd, all-seeing eyes; a simple style, but obviously not one from Marks and Spencer or C&A. Her only adornment was a single row of pearls.

Val was glad that she, too was wearing a dress, the one she kept for 'best' in a small checked design of black and emerald green, rather than her usual attire of jumper and skirt.

Mr Walker came to her rescue. 'We're very

pleased to see you, Valerie,' he said, getting up from his chair and shaking her hand. 'Glad you've come to see us. And you know Jonathan, of course, don't you?'

Rather to her surprise Jonathan also came and shook her hand. He smiled at her, a little warily, she thought. He had, in fact, smiled and nodded at her once or twice when their paths had crossed in the course of their work.

'Hello, Valerie,' he said. 'Yes, indeed I know you, you're one of our valued office workers.'

The young woman who had been sitting on the settee with him then rose and came over to her. 'Hello, Val,' she said in a friendly way. 'I'm so pleased you've come. I'm Thelma.'

Val took her outstretched hand. 'Hello, Thelma,' she said. 'Pleased to meet you.' She remembered then that she had heard somewhere that it was not really the correct mode of address. You were supposed to just say, 'How do you do?'

From her appearance one might imagine Thelma to be prim and aloof. Her ash blonde hair and light blue eyes made her look like a snow princess in a fairytale, so Val thought. She wore a pale blue twin set with a row of pearls at her neck, and a Gor-ray pleated skirt; casual wear but she looked the height of sophistication.

'Come over here and talk to me,' she said warmly, leading the way to a large settee up-holstered in green velvet. Val looked towards Sam, and he nodded encouragingly at her. The three men stood by the fire talking together, and Mrs Walker seemed to be lost in her own thoughts, staring into the fire.

'I expect you're feeling rather bewildered, aren't you?' said Thelma.

'Well, yes, I suppose I am,' replied Val.

'You don't need to be. Mrs Walker's OK when you get to know her. Or when she gets to know you, I should say. I found her very intimidating at first, but I learnt not to be in awe of her. She would be the same whoever her sons chose to marry. No one would be good enough, according to Beatrice.'

They were speaking quietly, and nobody seemed to be taking any notice. Val was surprised at Thelma's friendliness. She had expected a cool, if not unfriendly, reception. But the young woman was just the opposite.

'I thought you would have been very acceptable as a daughter-in-law,' she dared to say now. 'Your father's a solicitor, isn't he? Not like my father, he's employed at the mill as I'm sure you know. Not that there's any mention of marriage with Sam and me,' she added hastily. 'We only met in August, but we get along very well.'

'Sam's a very honest and dependable young man,' said Thelma. 'He won't mess you about, you can be sure of that. Jonathan has been influenced a lot by his mother, but he's the one I fell in love with.' She smiled. 'We're getting married soon. You'll be invited to the wedding, of course.'

'Thank you,' said Val. 'That will be two weddings I'm going to very soon. My best friend, Cissie, is getting married at the end of November and I'm her bridesmaid. When ... when will yours be?'

'The second Saturday in December, at the Parish Church,' said Thelma. 'Actually, we've put

253

it forward. It should have been next spring, but ... well ... I've discovered that I'm pregnant,' she added in a whisper. 'But I expect you know that, don't you?'

'No ... no, I didn't know. Honestly, I didn't. Sam hasn't told me.' So what she had assumed was correct, but Sam had kept it to himself.

Thelma nodded. 'Yes, I said Sam was dependable. Good old Sam. He's not one to gossip. And it doesn't matter two hoots what your father does for a living, nor you neither. Beatrice worked in a mill before she married Joshua ... and it's come out recently that theirs was a hasty marriage as well.'

'I knew she had been a mill worker,' said Val. 'Sam did tell me that, and my mother remembered her from a long time ago. But I didn't know about ... the other thing.'

'Apparently she raised the roof when Jon told her about us, until Joshua let the cat out of the bag! So she hasn't said a word of reproach to me. My parents were rather shocked ... well, disappointed in me, I suppose. But they're all getting together to plan the wedding.'

'As a matter of fact, the same thing has happened to my friend, Cissie,' said Val. 'Her mother went mad at her, but she wants her to have a proper church wedding, all the same.'

'It's always a nine days' wonder,' said Thelma. 'People forget... I don't suppose I would have chosen to start a family so soon, but that's what's happened. We're looking for a house now. We've seen a nice semi that we like on the other side of the town but not too far from Jon's place of work.

I don't want to be too near to my in-laws, nor to my own parents, either.'

Sam and Jonathan had left the girls on their own as it seemed as though they were getting on well together. The two young men were deep in conversation, and Joshua had gone to talk to his wife. At exactly five o'clock by the silver carriage clock on the mantelpiece Mrs Walker rang a bell at the side of the fireplace, and Mrs Porter appeared promptly.

'Will you bring in the tea now, please, Mrs Porter?' said Beatrice. 'We are all ready, and looking forward to sampling some of your excellent baking.' She smiled graciously at the woman.

'Certainly, Mrs Walker. It's all ready.'

The party rearranged themselves, coming nearer to the fire, the focal point of the room. Sam located a nest of occasional tables which he placed in front of the settee and the easy chairs. Mrs Porter returned with a tea trolley laden with what appeared to be quite a feast. She poured the tea from the silver pot into cups of delicate bone china with a pink rose design. Val wondered if they were Shelley or Coalport – they were certainly not from the pot stall in Halifax market – but she would not dare to turn a plate over to see the name of the maker.

There were dainty sandwiches, cut in triangles without any crusts, of fresh salmon and cucumber, roast ham, and chicken; bite-sized sausage rolls and small slices of pork pie; buttered scones, almond tarts, and fruit cake, rich with sultanas, raisins and cherries.

Mrs Porter's baking, as Beatrice had said, was

delicious, as was everything else that was served. Val was tempted to have two of everything, but she did not want to appear greedy so she had only one cake. She ate several sandwiches, though, as they were scarcely more than a mouthful.

Conversation lapsed whilst they ate their tea, and Val took a surreptitious look around the elegant room. Green was the predominant colour, dark green velvet curtains, a thick-pile carpet in a paler shade of green, and what she thought was an Indian rug at the hearth, patterned in green, red and black. Water colours of Yorkshire scenes – the moors, dales and ruined abbeys – hung on the walls, and silver-framed family photographs stood on the mahogany display cabinet and bureau. She noticed a Crown Derby vase of blue, red and gold, and figurines that she thought were Royal Doulton. It was all so luxurious, but she tried not to look too openly, as though she had never seen such lovely things before.

Joshua kept a conversation going by talking about Blackpool, where Sam and Val had met. He had happy memories of the place where they had gone for family holidays when he was a lad.

'We had some grand times there,' he reminisced. 'Dancing at the Tower Ballroom, riding on the Big Dipper, and the Golden Mile... There was a carnival there – 1923, I think it was. I was on holiday with some pals. We had a rare old time... It was before I got married, of course, and settled down. Aye, there was no place like Blackpool, and I believe it's enjoying a boom time again at the moment. We'll have to give it a try, eh, Beatrice?'

'I don't think so, Joshua,' she replied with a

frosty half-smile. 'I prefer Bournemouth or Torquay, and Southport is far more genteel than Blackpool if one has to visit Lancashire.'

'Well, we enjoyed Blackpool, didn't we, Val?' said Sam. To her surprise he took hold of her hand, a gesture that his mother noticed with a slight tightening of her lips.

'Yes, I had a good holiday there ... with my friend Cissie,' Val added. 'A very nice hotel, and good weather.'

'And then you met me, didn't you?' Sam looked at her fondly as he spoke.

She nodded. 'So I did,' she said quietly. She knew that Sam was trying to show his mother that she, Val, was rather more than a casual acquaintance, but she didn't want him to aggravate the situation.

Sam changed the subject. He turned to his brother. 'So ... have you two decided where to spend your honeymoon?'

'The Lake District,' replied Jonathan. 'We intend to tour around for a few days, Windermere, Grasmere, Keswick... Thelma's parents know of some very good hotels, and it should be quiet at that time of the year. And by that time we hope we will be ready to move into our own home, don't we, Thelma?'

'Yes, we hope so,' she replied. The look they exchanged left Val in no doubt that they loved one another. She had summed Jonathan Walker up as cold and aloof, although there had been a slight thaw in his manner of late, but he clearly had a romantic and amorous side as well.

Val was relieved when the visiting time came to

an end. Beatrice Walker glanced at the clock at six thirty, then summoned Mrs Porter to remove the remnants of the meal. The social gathering was over.

Val shook hands with her hostess. 'Thank you for inviting me,' she said. 'It's been good to meet ... all of you.'

Beatrice inclined her head. 'I am pleased to have met you, Valerie.'

It was Sam's father who invited her to come again. 'It's been grand to get to know you better. And we'll be seeing you in a couple of weeks, won't we, at our Masonic do?'

'Yes, I'm looking forward to it,' she replied.

Once she was in Sam's car she breathed a sigh of relief. 'Gosh! I'm glad that's over! Did I do all right?'

'You were fine, love,' he assured her. 'Mother could have been a lot worse, believe me! And you seemed to be getting on well with Thelma.'

'Yes, she was so friendly and ... normal, not as I expected at all. She actually told me that she was ... she told me why she and Jonathan were getting married quite soon.'

'Yes, it caused quite a rumpus at first,' said Sam. 'But then Mother had to eat humble pie, I'm afraid, because a few skeletons in the cupboard were revealed. It would have been a question of the pot calling the kettle black.' He did not say any more, and Val, wisely, did not tell him that she already knew of the situation. She did tell him, however, that Cissie's wedding had been brought forward for the same reason.

'So she's marrying Walter Clarkson after all,' said

Sam. 'Didn't she get friendly with a lad called Jack when we were in Blackpool?'

'Yes, but that came to nothing,' said Val hurriedly. 'Then …. well … this happened with Walter, so they're getting married. I think she's quite pleased about it now.'

'Yes, he seems a steady sort of chap from what I know of him,' said Sam. His opinion of Cissie, though, was that she was rather a scatterbrain, not an ideal wife for Walter. He liked her though, she was a good-natured girl and she was Val's best friend, so he kept his thoughts to himself.

The Masonic Ladies' Evening was Val's first experience of what might be called a grand occasion. It was to be held at one of the high-class hotels in the town where there were the facilities that were needed, a large dining room, a room for dancing and a bar.

'Don't worry,' Sam told her. 'I shall be there at your side all the time; and I was so proud of you when you came for Sunday tea. I believe my mother was quite impressed with you.'

Beatrice, in fact, had said very little to Sam regarding his lady friend, but as she had made no derogative comments it indicated that she had been agreeably surprised. His mother had told him that Priscilla Ford, the girl she had intended to invite as Sam's partner – and whom she had earmarked as a suitable wife for her younger son – had asked if she could bring her 'gentleman friend' to the event. He was a young man who had recently joined the firm where she worked as a shorthand typist, and they had discovered that they had much in common. Sam could not tell whether his mother was relieved or disappointed, as she made no comment about the situation.

Jonathan and Thelma were already in the taxi-cab when Sam called for Val at seven o'clock on the Friday evening. She had been given the afternoon off work – a privilege that did not go unnoticed by her colleagues, although they did not make any adverse remarks – giving her time to pay a rare visit to the hairdresser and to prepare for the evening ahead.

Her dark hair had been trimmed and arranged in a modern gamine style which suited her dainty features. She had applied a little more make-up than usual; green eye-shadow and a touch of mascara, and a brighter shade of lipstick to match her dress of cherry red. When she looked at herself in the full-length mirror she was surprised at how different and elegant she looked. High-heeled black patent leather sandals and a small black satin evening bag completed her ensemble.

She smiled at her reflection. 'I think you'll do, lass,' she whispered, a remark that was reiterated by her father when he saw her in her finery. She felt that she might do Sam proud, and that Mrs Walker would not be able to find any fault with her appearance. She was sorry that she had only her winter coat to wear, rather than a fur coat or stole, but it was of woollen tweed, not at all shabby, and she would be leaving it in the cloakroom.

She made sure she was ready when Sam knocked at the door, then escorted her in a gentlemanly way to the taxi.

'Hello, Val,' said Thelma. 'Good to see you

again.' Jonathan smiled and nodded.

The hotel was just outside the town centre. They took a lift to the floor where the dining room was situated. Val was glad of Thelma's company as they stood in a queue to leave their coats.

'You look lovely,' Thelma told her. 'Red is just your colour, isn't it?'

Val returned the compliment. Thelma, again, was wearing blue, a shade darker than her eyes, a simple-styled dress in shimmering satin. Val guessed that it had not come from C&A, but she felt that her own dress was quite equal to the occasion.

Sam thought so too. 'You look beautiful,' he whispered when he met her in the crowded bar adjoining the dining room.

'Thank you, and you look very handsome,' she replied. He was wearing an evening suit, as were the majority of the men. She felt proud and honoured to be his partner.

The evening passed in a whirl of exciting experiences such as Val had never known before. Their party consisted of the Walker family, herself and Thelma, and a few invited guests, including Thelma's parents who were friends of Joshua and Beatrice. Val assumed that Priscilla, the quiet fair-haired girl, was the girl whom Mrs Walker had had in mind as a partner for Sam. She and the ginger-haired bespectacled young man who was with her seemed very well suited.

Val was glad of Sam's bolstering company throughout the meal. She had spoken briefly to his mother, who had actually said, 'You look very nice, dear.' Then Joshua and Beatrice were occupied with their other guests, leaving the young people alone.

Val was confused and astounded by the number of courses that were served at the meal, and the amount of knives, forks and spoons. She knew, though, that the correct procedure was to start with the cutlery on the outside and work inwards.

There was fruit juice to start followed by a clear soup, beef consommé; then a fish course, dainty morsels of whitebait in a creamy sauce. She was somewhat perplexed when they were served next with what looked like ice cream in little silver dishes. Sam, noticing her bewilderment, told her, in a quiet voice, that it was called a sorbet, a water ice that was eaten to clean the palate before the main course was served. It was delicious, a delicate lemon flavour which did, indeed, refresh the appetite for what was to follow.

The main course was roast beef, rarer than Val would have liked, but very moist and tender, with Yorkshire pudding, roast potatoes and a variety of vegetables. The dessert was Eve's pudding, apples with a sponge topping, served with fresh cream. There was a choice of red or white wine to accompany the meal, then coffee and chocolate mints to finish off what had been a splendid feast.

Then it was time for the speech-making. The Director of Ceremonies banged on the table with a gavel, then introduced a distinguished-looking man, whom he called the Worshipful Master. 'He's the head of this Masonic lodge,' Sam explained. 'My father was WM a few years ago.'

The WM, as he was called, welcomed the guests and said he hoped they were enjoying the evening.

He reminded them that this was the Ladies' Evening, when all their long-suffering wives were acknowledged and thanked for their loyalty and support. A man with a pleasant baritone voice stood up and sang a song to honour the ladies.

'Here's to their health in a song,' he warbled, as everyone raised their glasses.

The Worshipful Master's wife, a corpulent lady in emerald green satin, with diamonds sparkling at her throat and ears, gave a charming speech of thanks, before every lady was presented with a gift. It was a small china dish with a floral design, made by the Coalport factory. Val thought it was exquisite and knew she would always treasure it as a memento of the evening.

Following the meal and the speeches they all moved into the ballroom, seating themselves at small tables at the sides of the room. Sam and Val, Jonathan and Thelma, and Priscilla and her friend, Cedric, sat together as they were the only young people in the party.

Val and Sam had not danced together since their meeting in Blackpool, and it brought back happy memories for them. There was a variety of dances, to the accompaniment of a small band, including modern, old-time, and a progressive barn dance where one moved on to a variety of partners, young and not so young, short and tall, slender and extremely large.

Val and Sam danced together several times, then, as a gesture of courtesy, she supposed, Jonathan asked her for a dance. She was glad it was a waltz, which she found the easiest to do. 'Enjoying yourself, are you?' he asked, smiling in what she would once have thought of as a supercilious manner, but she knew now that it was the way he behaved with everyone.

'Yes, thank you, very much,' she replied, and that was the end of their conversation.

Priscilla and her partner seemed happy together and very compatible. Sam danced with her once, as it was only polite to do so, leaving Val alone with Cedric.

'This is all very new to me,' he told her confidentially. 'I didn't know what to say when Priscilla asked if I would come with her, but I'm glad I did.'

'It's new to me as well,' she told him. 'It's the first time I've been to such a posh do!'

He laughed. 'Same here! Shall we try this dance, if you don't mind me falling over your feet?'

They managed the quickstep quite well. Val decided he was a very pleasant young man, though rather bashful. She would be interested to know how his friendship with Priscilla proceeded.

The evening came to an end at midnight. 'Carriages at 12 o'clock' was the quaint wording on the invitations, harking back to Victorian times. Their taxi was waiting, but as Val was the first to be dropped off there was time only for a hasty goodnight.

Sam walked her to her door, kissing her briefly but tenderly as they stood there for a moment. 'It's been a wonderful evening,' he said, 'thanks to you, and I shall see you again tomorrow, at seven o'clock. Think about where you would like to go.'

'I don't mind,' she replied. 'Tonight has been lovely. I'm so pleased you invited me. Goodnight, Sam. See you tomorrow...'

264

She didn't care at all where they went, so long as she and Sam were together. She was starting to feel that it might be forever.

EIGHTEEN

'I've been wondering,' said Cissie, as she and Val walked home together one evening during the following week. 'I'd like to invite Janice to come to the wedding. What do you think?'

'Yes, that would be a great idea,' said Val. 'And Phil as well?'

'Yes, if they can both manage to come.'

A recent letter from Janice had told them that Phil had paid a visit to Blackpool and then stayed on to help in the hotel, as Janice had been having problems with the staffing.

'I should imagine he will have gone back home now,' said Val. 'I don't think there'll be any visitors staying there now.' It was the first week in November, and the Illuminations would have ended in Blackpool.

'I'd better get a move on then,' said Cissie. 'It's only a few weeks away. I'll send an invitation to Janice and include both of them. It'll be good to see them again, won't it?'

Janice was surprised but very pleased to receive the invitation to Cissie's wedding in Halifax. It was on the last Saturday of November at 12 o'clock at the church that she and Walter attended, followed by a reception in the church hall.

Her father insisted that she must go. 'You're ready for a break,' he said, 'after all the hard work you've done. And your mother would agree with me if she were her normal self.'

It was unusual for Janice to have told her father of the invitation before telling her mother, at least it would have been unusual at one time. But Lilian was still living in a little world of her own.

'And Phil's invited as well,' said Janice, 'so perhaps I could combine the wedding with my visit to see him in Ilkley.'

Alec agreed that this was a very good idea. Phil had returned home the previous week after helping out at the hotel for the rest of October. This had been a real godsend to Janice and her helpers. The Hotel Florabunda was now closed until the following spring, but its future was very uncertain.

'If I go over to Yorkshire to stay at Phil's place, we could both travel from there to Halifax,' said Janice. 'I don't know how far it is, but Phil will be able to sort things out. I'll phone him tonight and ask him about it.'

Phil was delighted to hear that Janice was coming to stay at his home for a few days, and pleased to hear about the wedding as well.

'It's only a short distance to Halifax,' he said, 'and I'm sure my dad will lend me the car.' They decided that Janice should travel by train to Leeds on the Friday, where he would meet her and take her on to Ilkley. She would stay there until the following Monday.

'Have you come to any decision about what you're going to do?' he asked. 'I mean about a job, or whatever?'

'No, not really,' she answered. 'It all depends on how well Mum recovers.'

'Is she still the same?'

'Yes, pretty much so. It will be up to Dad and me to decide about everything. We can't worry her with problems about the hotel or about anything else. She seems to have forgotten about it.'

'Give her my love,' said Phil. 'And try not to get too downhearted about it all. It will all sort itself out, I'm sure...'

Phil was a very sensible young man who took things in his stride, and he had a calming influence upon Janice. Since the hotel closed at the end of the season Alec had insisted that she must have a well-earned rest. She knew now, though, that it was time that she found herself a job of some sort until it was time for the hotel to open up again, probably next April. But did she still want to be actively involved in the running of the hotel? And would her mother be fit by then to return to her duties? Indeed, would Lilian ever be her normal self again? These were the crucial questions. She decided she must have a serious talk with her father that night. They waited until both Ian and Lilian had retired to bed.

'We can't see into the future,' said Alec. 'And perhaps it's as well that we can't. Who can tell how your mother will be in a month's time, or by Easter? That's when we usually open for the season.' He smiled. 'I'm saying "we", but I know I have very little to do with it. The hotel was Lilian's responsibility, and just lately it's been yours. You've done a marvellous job, Jan, but I know it wouldn't be right to expect you to go on doing it. It's messed up your plans already. You should have been settled in at university by now.'

'Don't underestimate your own contribution, Dad,' said Janice. 'You help with all the odd jobs that need doing, and carry the luggage up and down. You're there in the background, and I know Mum's very glad of your help. But ... do I want to carry on running the hotel ... with help, I mean? That is ... if Mum isn't well enough to do it.' She paused for a moment. 'Quite honestly, Dad, I just don't know.'

'It's not what we would have wanted you to do, your mum and me. She was determined that you should have the chances that we never had when we were young. Not that I would ever have thought of going to college. But your mum was clever, and if she'd been given the chance she might have done something different. But you know how it was. She had to leave school and work in the boarding house, like so many more girls at that time.'

'And she did a fantastic job as well,' said Janice. 'I was talking to Phil about it, how she managed to run the hotel with no real training, except what she had learned from her mother. When I started doing the waitress job I got quite interested in the hotel work, you know, planning menus, and getting to know the visitors. To be honest, I was never all that sure that I wanted to go to uni, but I knew it was something that you both wanted me to do, especially Mum.'

'You should have said so, Janice. We would never have made you do something you didn't want to do. But you're a clever lass, you'd have done well.'

'That's as maybe... But when Mum was taken ill I was ready to jump in with both feet and keep things going. I didn't realize what a difficult job it is. If Phil hadn't come along when he did I don't know what would have happened.'

'Yes, he's a grand lad,' said Alec. 'Let's get down to brass tacks... I'm trying to look ahead, and it's well nigh impossible. We have to assume that we're going to open again next year. We'll start getting enquiries about bookings well in advance, especially from folks who've been here before.'

'Yes, that's true. Would you believe that some people have already booked in advance for the same time next year?'

'And we don't want to let them down. We can't make a decision to close down just yet. I'm hoping it will never come to that, but the way your mother is at the moment...' He stared dejectedly into space.

'It's early days yet, Dad.' Janice was trying to take a positive view. 'It's only a couple of months since she had the operation. And it's too late now for me to go to uni, so I shall have to get a job of some sort. A temporary one, so that I can start working again here next spring, with or without Mum. We've already got Freda to help us, and Nancy and Olive. What we could really do with is someone to take over the financial side of things – until Mum is well again, I mean. Maths and book-keeping and all that have never been my forte.'

'There's plenty of time between now and Easter,' said Alec. 'And don't worry about the money side of things, about there not being enough to keep going. The hotel's been doing well recently, and the wage that I earn helps as well. We certainly won't go bankrupt.'

'But it's time I started working,' said Janice. 'I shall start looking straight away.'

She found a job a few days later as assistant in a newsagent's shop on Dickson Road, a few minutes' walk from her home. It was the shop from where they had their morning and evening papers delivered, and Janice saw the advert in the window when she went to pay the paper bill.

'Would you consider me for the job?' she asked Mrs Nelson, the co-owner of the shop. 'I'm looking for work, and this would be perfect.'

'And you'd be perfect for us an' all,' replied Mrs Nelson. 'The advert's only just gone in, but we need look no further. So you're not going off to college then, Janice? I thought you might have been starting later, with your mum being poorly.'

'No, I've had to give up on that idea ... for now,' she added. 'I might help out in the hotel again next year. It depends on how Mum goes on.'

'Yes, we were so sorry about it, Brian and me. Do give her our best wishes. And Brian will be delighted when I tell him that you're coming to work for us. Just fancy that!'

It was arranged that she should work part time, an early shift from 8 a.m. till 1 p.m. for three days, and a late shift from 2 p.m. till 6.30 p.m. for the other three, with Sundays free.

'We don't expect you to come at crack of dawn to see to the papers,' Barbara Nelson told her. 'Brian and I see to all that, but we get a lot of people calling in on their way to work, and in the evening when they're going home.'

It was a pleasant family run store where they sold sweets and tobacco, greeting cards and stationery and, in the summer, postcards and requisites for the holidaymakers. It was interesting work but not too arduous, giving Janice time to see to things at home. She cooked an evening meal for all of them each day when her dad came home from work. Lilian was well enough now to potter around in the kitchen and make a cup of tea or a sandwich. She seemed quite interested to hear about Janice's new job and said she would be quite alright whilst her daughter was at the shop.

Janice's employers agreed that she should take a long weekend at the end of November to go to her friend's wedding in Halifax.

It was good to see Phil waiting for her when she arrived at Leeds station. He gave her a friendly hug, then carried her case to where the car was parked.

'It's not far to Ilkley,' he said. 'Sit back and enjoy the ride.'

'I haven't seen much of Yorkshire,' she said, 'only Leeds when I came for my interview, but I've been very impressed by the scenery on the journey here.'

It was only twenty miles or so to Ilkley, through Wharfedale, one of the picturesque dales on the fringes of the industrial towns. The moorland was bleak, brown with bracken and heather which had bloomed and faded. Sheep grazed between the strangely shaped outcrops of rock, a wild and lonely scene which had a beauty all its own.

The town of Ilkley, though, was busy on the Fri-

271

day afternoon with shoppers on the main street, near to the River Wharfe. Phil's home, The Coach and Horses, was a mile outside the town, a long, low greystone building which opened on to the street. The car park and main entrance were at the back.

Phil parked the car in their own private garage, then took Janice through the family entrance and up the stairs to their living quarters. Phil's mother was awaiting them in the comfortable living room. She put her arms round Janice and kissed her cheek in such a friendly way that she felt at home at once.

'It's lovely to meet you at last,' she said. 'I've heard so much about you.'

'And it's good to meet you, too, Mrs Grundy,' said Janice. 'Thank you for inviting me to stay.'

'It's a pleasure, my dear... And how is your mother going on? We were so sorry to hear about her operation, but glad that Phil was able to help out.'

'She's about the same,' replied Janice. 'The operation seems to have changed her personality. She's not at all like she was before, but I suppose it's good that she's not worrying about the business.'

'Time is a great healer,' said Mrs Grundy, 'and she has a loving family to care for her. Now, Phil; you show Janice to her room, and I'll make a pot of tea. Ralph's down in the bar, but he'll be up directly. We're not too busy just now. Two couples booked for a meal tonight, and there'll be some coming on spec because it's Friday, the start of the weekend. But we've no one staying at the moment.'

Janice's small room was at the front of the building overlooking the main road which led to Skipton. There was a view of the moorland which Phil told her was the famous Ilkley Moor. It was a pretty room with floral curtains and bedspread, a small wardrobe and a frilled dressing table. There was a washbasin and pink towels, as it was a guest room, with the bathroom and toilet along the passage.

Phil gave her a hug. 'I'm glad you're here. Just sort yourself out, then come and meet my dad.'

Mr Grundy was an older edition of Phil, though plumper and shorter with greying hair. He was jolly and out-going, just as Janice had imagined a country landlord might be. Patience Grundy, whose name suited her very well, was less exuberant. It was from her that Phil had inherited his thoughtful grey eyes and more placid manner.

Phil was let off his duties that evening, so after they had dined at six o'clock on steak and ale pie – one of the dishes to be served later to the guests – they spent some quiet time together.

He showed her the downstairs rooms, the low-ceilinged dining room with oak beams and a delft rack holding old china plates and toby jugs, pewter tankards and horse brasses; and the bar area, a stone-flagged room kept warm with a log fire in the huge hearth, a well-stocked bar, round – somewhat wobbly – tables and wheel-backed chairs with chintz cushions. They enjoyed a quiet drink in a cosy corner away from the Friday night regulars. Then Mrs Grundy insisted that Janice should go to bed with a cup of hot chocolate to help her to sleep in a strange place.

After a hearty breakfast the following morning, cooked by Phil, they set off for Halifax. Janice was surprised that this town, also, was only a short distance away. They drove through Bingley and the outskirts of Bradford, then took the moorland road leading down to the town in the valley.

'This is rather a hasty wedding, isn't it?' Phil said on their journey. 'Cissie got friendly with a lad called Jack, didn't she, while they were in Blackpool?'

'Oh, I suppose that was just a holiday thing,' said Janice. 'It must have been because she went back to Walter. I got the impression that she wasn't too sure about him, or about what she wanted at all. But I suppose we mustn't ask too many questions!'

'Oh, I see,' said Phil with a grin. 'I thought she was a nice friendly girl, both she and Valerie. It'll be good to see them again.'

Halifax, in the valley bottom, was a typical mill town with a myriad of chimneys and rows of terraced houses leading up from the town centre. Phil, who had been many times before, pointed out the eighteenth-century Piece Hall where wool traders used to meet to sell their cloths. They were rather early for the church service so they had a cup of coffee in Woolworth's and made use of the facilities.

Janice powdered her nose, touched up her lipstick and adjusted her small red hat, something she rarely wore, but she considered it fitting for a wedding. It was the only new garment she had bought. It complemented her black and white checked coat and toned with the red dress she was wearing.

After asking for directions they found the church on the outskirts of the town in an area of identical streets with small houses. It was a grim-looking, soot-ingrained building with a tall steeple, and a small garden area with stunted bushes. There were already a few cars parked at the back, and they followed a few people who were entering the church.

Although the outside was bleak and uninviting the inside of the church was just the opposite. A friendly young man asked them if they were for the bride or the groom.

'Er ... the bride,' answered Janice, and he led them to a pew on the left hand side of the aisle. They knew no one else there, and when Janice had bowed her head and said a brief prayer, as she had been brought up to do, she had a surreptitious look around.

Fortunately the church was warm with heat coming through the iron grilles in the floor. The pulpit, altar and pews were a warm shade of glossy wood, the pews covered with flat red cushions which matched the needlework kneelers below the seats. There was a large display of autumn flowers – red, orange and golden yellow – on the altar, and over all, a comfortable friendly ambience.

Two young men were sitting in the front pew. She assumed that the dark-haired one was Walter; he was looking back anxiously every few moments. In a little while a middle-aged couple arrived and sat at the front; the groom's parents, she guessed. They were followed by a woman of a similar age wearing a fox fur over her tweed coat, and a large hat. Cissie's mother, thought Janice. She nodded at the people she passed, but did not look over-joyed to be there.

The organist struck up with the Bridal March, and everyone stood, casting sideways glances to see the arrival of the bride. Cissie looked pretty, and happy, as a bride should be, in a pale blue dress and a tiny matching hat with a short veil. She held on to the arm of a small man in a grey suit who was looking at her fondly.

Val looked lovely in her dress of a warm peach shade, as radiant as though she was the bride herself. She caught sight of Janice and Phil and smiled at them as she walked past.

Janice gathered, from the vicar's clothing of a simple white surplice and blue stole, with no fancy accoutrements, that this was what was termed a 'low church'. They sang the traditional hymns, 'Praise my Soul the King of Heaven' and 'O Perfect Love', and the vows were exchanged with no hesitation. From the way that Walter smiled at his new bride it was obvious that he loved her very much. Janice hoped that Cissie, too, was sure about what she was doing.

There was the usual wait whilst the register was signed in the vestry, then they all stood as a loud chord introduced the Wedding March, smiling at the happy couple as they walked down the aisle as man and wife.

There was a surge for the door, and Janice and Phil followed the crowd to a building at the rear of the church. Small tables were arranged around the room, covered with white cloths, with a vase of small chrysanthemums in the centre of each.

It was an informal occasion with no 'top table' for important guests. The vicar welcomed everyone and invited them to help themselves to 'the bountiful feast that our good ladies have prepared'. It was, indeed, a good spread, like a Sunday School tea party, but on a grander scale. There were forty or so people there, church people, family members, and friends from the mill where Walter and Cissie both worked. They stood in an orderly queue to fill their plates with sandwiches, chicken legs, sausage rolls, and slices of pork pie, followed by Black Forest gateau or strawberry cheesecake. When they were seated the ladies of the parish served them with tea from huge enamel pots.

Val and Sam came to join Janice and Phil at their table. The two girls hugged one another, and the men, who had met only briefly in Blackpool, shook hands.

'I'm so pleased you could come,' said Val, 'So you're staying with Phil? And how is your mother...?'

Conversation flowed easily, and Janice thought what a pleasant young man Sam was, and how well suited the two of them seemed to be. Cissie came over to join them later, holding on to Walter's arm. She introduced Walter to the ones he did not know.

'This is Janice. We stayed at their hotel in Blackpool, Val and me. And this is Phil. They met while we were on holiday, like Val and Sam did.'

Walter shook hands courteously. 'It seems that quite a lot went on in Blackpool, then?' he commented. 'Only you, Cissie, who didn't meet someone, eh?'

'Ah, but I was already spoken for, wasn't I?' she answered speedily, smiling up at Walter with an innocent look in her big blue eyes.

'We hope you'll be very happy,' said Janice. 'I'm sure you will be.'

'Yes, thank you... So am I,' replied Walter.

'And thank you for the present,' said Cissie.

Janice had sent their gift, a damask tablecloth with matching napkins, by post. All the wedding presents – toast racks (only two of them!), cutlery, a tea and a dinner service, a mirror, food mixer, pressure cooker, bed linen and towels – were displayed on a long table at the side of the room. On a smaller table there was a two-tiered wedding cake with figures of a bride and groom on the top.

'I think we're wanted over there,' said Walter, as the vicar beckoned them over to the table.

'Cissie and Walter said they didn't want much speech-making,' said the vicar, 'and Cissie's dad, Joe, he's a man of few words, so it's my very pleasant task to propose the health of the bride and groom. Will you all raise your glasses, please? To Cissie and Walter. We wish them health, happiness, and every blessing as they start their married life together. God bless you both.'

Everyone repeated, 'Cissie and Walter', and sipped the brown sherry. Alcohol was rarely served on church premises, but this was a special occasion. The bridal pair cut the cake, whilst the photographer, one of the church members, took their photograph.

Several more photos were taken, of Walter and Cissie, on their own and with the bridesmaid and best man, family groups, and one with all the guests. The couple left, an hour or so later, in a shower of confetti, to go to their new home to change their clothes, before leaving for their honeymoon in Scarborough.

'That was a nice friendly occasion,' Janice remarked as they made their way back to Ilkley.

'Yes, Walter seems a steady sort of chap,' said Phil, 'though maybe without a great sense of humour. But who can tell? Cissie seems happy enough, and Walter appears to think the world of her.'

'Yes ... I'm glad they've been able to get a little house of their own.' Cissie had told Janice that Walter had bought – or had put a deposit on – a small terraced house, and it was ready for them to move into straight away. The furniture that they wanted would have to be purchased bit by bit, but they had all the essentials they needed to start with. 'Walter has a good job, and I should imagine he's pretty careful with his money. I'm not so sure about Cissie...' Janice laughed. 'She's what my mum would call a flibbertigibbet. But maybe she'll settle down now she's married.'

It had been good to see Val again as well, and to see that her friendship with Sam was progressing nicely. Probably too soon, though, for them to be thinking of a more definite commitment. As for herself and Phil... Janice had been warmly welcomed by his parents and she was very happy to be with him again. But who could tell what the future might hold?

They spent an enjoyable Sunday together. Phil drove to the edge of the moor, then they climbed

279

up to the 'Cow and Calf' rocks from where there was a magnificent view of the surrounding area, with Ilkley down in the valley. Although the weather was chilly it was fine, with a sun that was doing its best to shine. They enjoyed a picnic lunch, sandwiches and hot tomato soup from a flask, then returned to a dinner of roast beef and Yorkshire pudding for their last evening together.

'Have you decided what you're going to do next year?' Phil asked, as they spent some quiet time together that evening, his parents both being occupied in the bar and restaurant.

'I'm hoping to keep the place going, to the best of my ability,' said Janice. 'Freda and myself, with Nancy and Olive, and maybe an extra pair of hands. I hate to say it, but I don't feel that Mum will be ready by then to take any active part ... if she will ever be. And then, at the end of the season, we will have to consider, Dad and I, whether we want to carry on with the hotel ... or not. It's a drastic decision, but we'll have to face facts.'

Phil nodded. 'Running a hotel is a mammoth task. I could come and help out next year – that is if you would like me to – as I did last month. Actually, I've already mentioned it to my dad, and he's agreeable.'

'Oh, Phil, would you really? I didn't like to suggest it again, but it would be such a help. But it's from April till October. Can you be spared for so long?'

'I'm quite sure I can. Dad's still very much in charge of the kitchen, and he doesn't take kindly to anyone trying to compete with him. Don't get me wrong, we get along very well, but I don't

280

intend to stay here forever.'

'I'm really pleased,' said Janice, 'and I know Dad will be. I shall enroll for night school classes after Christmas, and learn a few more tricks of the trade.'

Phil drove her to Leeds the following morning to board her train. His parents had urged her to 'Come and see us again soon.' She and Phil were hoping they might be able to meet for a short time over the Christmas period. He kissed her in more than just a friendly way as they said goodbye. 'Love to your mum, and don't get despondent,' he said. 'I'm here for you, you know that, don't you?'

As she gazed out of the window at the vast expanse of moorland Janice reflected on how she had felt so much at home in Yorkshire. Blackpool was her home town. She was a part of its lively scene, its laughter and noise and gaiety when it came to life during the summer months. But there was a solemnity and strength in these lonely hills and valleys that appealed to her quieter self. She knew that they would welcome her back again.

NINETEEN

The marriage of Jonathan and Thelma in mid-December was vastly different from that of Cissie and Walter which had taken place a few weeks earlier.

Valerie was a guest at the wedding, but as Sam

281

was to be the best man, he had explained to her that his place would be at the 'top table' with the bridal party.

'Sorry, love, but it's protocol,' he told her. 'You won't feel left out, though. I shall reserve you a place on the table with my aunt Hannah, and uncle Percy. She's my mother's sister and she's very easy to get on with, no airs and graces, if you know what I mean! I know you'll like her, and she will like you as well.'

Sam had told her that this wedding was turning out to be something of a watershed for their family, a time for mending broken relationships, and those which had been neglected over the years. He had confided to her that Thelma being 'in the family way' had brought to light some things that had been swept under the carpet.

'It appears that my parents' marriage was the same,' he said with a wry grin, 'but Mother has tried to forget it. Anyway, she's been forced off her pedestal, unwillingly at first. But now she and Thelma's mother seem determined to make this the wedding of the year!'

Sam had suggested to his brother that both lots of grandparents should be invited, not only Jacob and his wife, but Beatrice's parents, Mary and Fred Halliwell, who lived in Filey. And George, Beatrice's once ne'er do well brother – who now owned a string of small shops in Halifax – had been invited along with his wife Nellie. It remained to be seen whether or not they would accept after years of receiving the cold shoulder. But on the day they were all there, the Walker family and the Halliwells, with a goodly number of friends and colleagues of both Jonathan and Thelma.

When Val entered the church, Sam, who had been looking out for her, dashed up the aisle to greet her. He introduced her to his aunt Hannah and her husband who were seated in a pew near to the front of the church. The woman greeted her warmly, though in hushed tones as befitted the surroundings.

'We'll have a good chat later,' she said. 'I'm so pleased to meet you, my dear.' She had a look of Beatrice, but younger and plumper and full of smiles.

The parish church was in a prominent position on a hill just outside the town centre. Subdued organ music was playing as the guests arrived, ushered to their pews by groomsmen wearing morning dress, as were Jonathan and Sam. Val guessed there would be top hats as well for this grand occasion, the wedding of a mill owner's son.

The church was decorated for Christmas as the festival was only two weeks away. Garlands of holly, Christmas roses and golden chrysanthemums adorned the stone pillars and the window sills. On the altar there was a display of scarlet poinsettias, and a large Christmas tree with sparkling lights and baubles stood to one side of the chancel. There was a small Nativity scene on a table beside the tree with a few figures – shepherds and angels – in position. Val remembered from her Sunday School days that the scene was built up gradually through the Advent season, with Mary and Joseph, then the Baby Jesus being added last of all.

Beatrice and Joshua Walker arrived, she dressed in furs and a large feathery hat, and he in morning dress. Beatrice preened herself in a way reminiscent of the Queen Mother as she smiled and acknowledged the guests as she passed by.

A small choir of boy choristers and a few men took their places in the choir stalls, just before the vicar, resplendent in a richly embroidered cloak and stole came to stand on the chancel steps. The organist played the Bridal March – just the same as at Cissie's wedding, Val recalled – as Thelma came down the aisle on her father's arm. She was a truly beautiful bride. Her dress was a simple style in ivory satin with long sleeves and a high neckline. Her fine lace veil reached to her waist, held in place with a coronet of orange blossom on her pale blonde hair, which was swept up in a coil on top of her head. There were four brides-maids – Thelma's sister, her best friend, and two young cousins – all dressed in red velvet, a fitting colour for a December wedding.

The marriage service was similar to the one that Val had previously attended, with the same hymns that Walter and Cissie had chosen, traditional ones sung at weddings throughout the years. Thelma and Jonathan exchanged loving looks as they repeated their vows. Whilst the immediate family members were in the vestry the choir sang two anthems, 'Sheep May Safely Graze' and 'O, for the Wings of a Dove', a small chorister singing the solo part in a clear and pure treble voice.

Thelma looked radiant, and Jonathan very proud as they walked back down the aisle. Sam, escorting the chief bridesmaid, smiled at Val as they passed by. She thought how handsome he looked in his morning suit. There were times when she could scarcely believe that she was his girl-friend. As she had come to know him better she had realized that his position in the mill was not of supreme importance to him. He was thankful for his good job and did not take for granted the money that he earned. The mill workers knew him as Mr Samuel and were inclined to treat him with deference, but he cared little for that. He regarded himself as one of a team who all worked together for the good of the company.

Val stayed with Hannah and Percy as they stood outside the church watching the professional photographer at work. This seemed to go on for ages; the bride and groom on their own, then with bridesmaids, best man and groomsmen, and, fin-ally, family groups and one with all the guests. Just as it had been at Cissie's wedding, but this photo-grapher was more concerned about getting things exactly right – and charging the appropriate price, thought Val.

When at last the session came to an end, the bridal pair were showered with confetti as they entered the limousine to be chauffeured to the hotel where the reception was to be held. Val travelled with Hannah and Percy in their car. The venue, situated a few miles from the town, had once been a grand country mansion. It stood in spacious grounds, and despite its luxury there was a warm and friendly ambience to the place. A log fire blazed in the entrance hall and a pleasant warmth emanated through the rest of the rooms.

The guests lined up to shake hands with the

bride and groom and both sets of parents. Beatrice, to Val's surprise, smiled at her and said, 'Hello, Valerie, it's nice to see you again.' Val couldn't think of a suitable reply so she just smiled at them both. Joshua Walker gave her a sly wink.

When they took their places in the oak-panelled dining room Val found she was on a table, not only with Hannah and Percy, but also another couple. Hannah introduced them.

'This is my brother, George, and his wife, Nellie. And this is Valerie, our Sam's lady friend.'

The man had a look of both his sisters. He was corpulent and jolly, with a red face and a rather bulbous nose. His wife was of the same build – her tight-fitting dress of royal blue velvet showed off her every curve – with platinum blonde hair and prominent blue eyes highlighted with eyeshadow and mascara.

Val found that they were both very friendly. They chatted throughout the lavish meal of hors d'oeuvres (tiny morsels of meat and fish, not really to Val's liking), chicken soup, roast lamb with sauté potatoes and green vegetables, and sherry trifle followed by coffee and chocolate mints, all elegantly served from silver salvers by a team of black-suited waiters.

'So I reckon you'll be next, you and Sam,' George remarked to Val, much to her confusion. She found herself blushing, and Hannah came to her rescue.

'Give over, Georgie, you're embarrassing the lass.'

'Oh, sorry luv,' he said. 'I was thinking how well Sam had done for himself.'

286

'We haven't known one another all that long,' Val explained. 'Well, I knew Samuel but he didn't know me. I work in the office at Walker's, you see, and we met in Blackpool at the Winter Gardens, when we were both on holiday there.'

'Oh ... I see!' George chuckled. 'I'll bet that didn't go down too well with her Ladyship, her son hobnobbing with one of the plebs.'

'Now now, Georgie!' said his sister reprovingly.

'Well, I dare say the lass knows what I mean, don't you, luv? Lady Muck we call her. She started off wi' nowt, just as we all did, all us Halliwells. We were fair flummoxed when we got an invite to this 'ere wedding, weren't we, Nellie? But I said, "Let's go, eh?" Joshua's OK, he was always a decent sort of chap. He's had summat to put up with, married to her.'

'She's not so bad,' said Val. 'It's taken a little while for her to get used to the idea of Sam and me, but she's coming round to it ... I think.'

'A few skeletons have popped out of the cupboard, George,' said Hannah. 'Enough said, eh? But I think our sister is starting to look at things rather differently. It's high time we let bygones be bygones, isn't it?'

'I'll say so,' agreed George. 'I persuaded Mam and Dad to come an' all, and they seem to be getting along fine with old Jacob and his missus.'

The four grandparents were seated at a nearby table and appeared to be most compatible, with no sign of any difference in social standing.

'Jacob must be well into his eighties by now,' observed George. 'I remember him as a bit of a tyrant, but happen he's mellowed with age. Getting old's a great leveller.'

'Shut up, George!' said his wife. 'We've still got a lot of living to do. Don't forget you've promised to take me on that round the world cruise.'

'Aye, so I have, one of these days... Hey up, it's time for the speech-making.'

Wine, both red and white, had been flowing throughout the meal. Now champagne was served to accompany the speeches and the cutting of the cake. There was a toast to the bridesmaids, then the best man's speech in which Sam praised his brother for all his sterling qualities, and wished the pair every happiness.

'I thought they didn't get on,' George whispered, though quite audibly, to Val.

She whispered back. 'I think they're better now. I hope so...'

Jonathan made a speech on behalf of his wife and himself, then they cut the three-tiered wedding cake. The guests then dispersed, forming little groups then moving on to chat to someone else.

'Well, how did that go?' Sam asked Val. 'Sorry I had to neglect you, but I'm sure my aunt looked after you, didn't she?'

'Very well indeed,' said Val. 'I've had a lovely time.'

'You've got yourself a grand little lass there, Sam,' said George.

'Yes, I know that, Uncle George.' Sam smiled at Val as he took hold of her arm. 'Come along, I'll introduce you to my grandparents.'

She met both sets of grandparents and felt that she need no longer fear that she could not be a part of this family. They were a mixed bunch, such as you might find in any family gathering.

They mixed and mingled for a while until Thelma and Jonathan reappeared, ready to depart for their honeymoon in the Lake District. Thelma wore her favourite colour of blue, an autumn suit of soft woollen tweed with a tiny blue feathered hat. She threw her bouquet to the crowd. According to the old tale, whoever caught it would be the next bride. Val stood back, not reaching out for the flowers. To do so would seem too eager and presumptuous. It was caught by the bridesmaid who was Thelma's friend. She smiled up at the young man who was with her and he didn't seem to mind. It looked as though there might be another wedding before very long.

TWENTY

By Christmas time, Cissie and Walter were settled in their little home. As the two families, the Fosters and Clarksons, were friendly, Christmas Day was an occasion when they all met together, this year at the home of Walter's parents.

Cissie was feeling well, and was not yet 'showing' – as her mother called it – very much. She intended to carry on working at the mill until March as her work in the mending room was not too strenuous. She had been told that the baby was due towards the end of May. She was finding that Walter was a kind and considerate husband, and she was happy and contented enough when they were together in the evening by their own fireside.

Val and Sam's relationship was blossoming. Sam spent more time at her parents' home than she did at his. She was invited for the occasional Sunday tea and they had also visited Sam's aunt Hannah and her husband. Hannah had really taken to Val and the liking was mutual. Val and Cissie were still good friends although they no longer went out together a few times a week as they used to do. Their holiday in Blackpool would be their last jaunt together, despite their intention to visit the resort again the following year.

When the new year of 1956 arrived, Janice enrolled for night school classes in 'cordon bleu' cookery. She could cope with the basic meals, but wanted to try her hand at more adventurous dishes. She was leading a full and busy life, working at the newsagent's shop and looking after her family at meal times. She had spent a couple of days in Ilkley with Phil and his parents just after Christmas. He still intended to come and help out when the holiday season started. Lilian was a little improved but nowhere near ready to take up the reins again.

Phil arrived in Blackpool a couple of days before the Easter weekend to settle in and to plan the menus for the week ahead with Janice. They were not fully booked – they seldom were at the start of the season – but Janice was relieved this year that they could start quietly. Freda had said that she would prefer to return to her part-time duties, helping with the preparation of the meals, now that Phil was part of the regular staff.

What concerned Janice more than anything was the financial side of the business; bookkeeping and dealing with money did not come easily to her. She was amazed at how her mother had coped with it all and managed the hotel as well. Janice was relieved when her father found someone who would help with the financial side. He had been talking about their problems with a colleague at work, and learned that the man's wife who had been a bank clerk, was looking for a part-time job. She was pleased to find work that would fit in with her family commitments and agreed to come in each Saturday when the visitors settled their bills, either by cheque or bank notes. She would deal with all the receipts and the banking, and work out a more professional way of bookkeeping. Janice knew that her mother had done the job well enough, but in a casual manner, such as her own mother had done. The system would be much more efficient with ledgers and account books.

The number of visitors dwindled after Easter until the next Bank Holiday which was Whitsuntide, seven weeks later. Again, they had not had as many bookings for this week as in previous years, something that Lilian would once have been concerned about. The small number of fourteen guests did not worry Janice and, as things turned out, it was fortunate that there weren't any more.

The Saturday and Sunday passed in the usual flurry of changeover day and getting to know the new guests. Lilian had started greeting the visitors on their arrival as she had always done, although she took no active part afterwards. On Sunday she started to complain of a headache although she didn't make a great deal of fuss about it. She had never made much of her ailments and, even now, she was not depressed or dispirited.

She went to bed early on the Sunday evening and slept reasonably well. She awoke early at six o'clock and Alec knew at once that something was wrong. She was holding on to her head, shouting incoherently about the pain. Alec put his arms round her as she staggered about the room, then she gave a cry and fell to the floor. She had lost consciousness, but Alec felt that there was still a steady pulse.

He shouted to his daughter who was in the next room. Janice was already up and dressed as she liked to make an early start. Phil, also, was quickly summoned from his room on the top floor. Alec phoned for an ambulance which, fortunately arrived within ten minutes, although the wait seemed endless. The ambulance men placed an oxygen mask over Lilian's face although she seemed to be breathing quite normally.

'She'll be alright, won't she, Dad?' asked Janice, although it was a futile question.

'Let's hope so, love,' he said. 'I'll go with her to the hospital and see what they say. You'll have to carry on here, I suppose, with the breakfasts and everything. It's a good job you're here, Phil... All we can do is just hope ... and say a little prayer. Look after our Ian, won't you?'

Janice burst into tears as the ambulance drove away. Phil put his arms around her. 'I know ... it's dreadful, love, but they'll look after her. They did the last time. She's in good hands.'

'Do you think ... will she need to have another

operation? We thought it was all sorted out, whatever it was.'

'I can't say, love. All I know is that you and I have to carry on for now. We've got a houseful of visitors. Well, not full, but quite enough to cope with under the circumstances.'

Janice pulled herself together. There was breakfast to be cooked and served, and an evening meal to prepare. Nancy and Olive were soon there to help, and Janice told her brother that Mum had gone to hospital because she had a bad headache again. She was trying to play it down, although she was seriously worried. They decided not to say anything to the guests. Lilian never appeared at breakfast time so there was no point in alarming them. Not yet, thought Janice, wondering how they would manage to get through the week ahead.

Alec rang from the hospital just after breakfast had ended. Lilian was now in the theatre undergoing an emergency operation, and he would stay there for the rest of the day. Ian was not at school as it was the half-term holiday. He sat around listlessly until Janice persuaded him to go and play football with his mates.

All they could do was wait for news from Alec and try to carry on as normally as possible. After a snack lunch they started to prepare for the evening meal. They put on a simple meal on Mondays, after the customary roast that was always served on Sundays. Today it was shepherd's pie – minced lamb with a browned potato topping. This was followed by apple pie and custard. The homemade apple pies were in the freezer – Janice had baked a batch during a quiet time at the hotel – and they just needed defrosting.

She and Phil worked mechanically, saying very little as they went through the motions. Alec rang again just as the visitors were sitting down for their meal at six o'clock. Lilian was now in the recovery room and he would stay with her, waiting for her to regain consciousness.

'Do you think you could come, Janice love?' he asked. 'I know your mum will want to see you there when she comes round.'

'Yes ... of course I will, Dad,' she replied.

Phil, Nancy and Olive all agreed that she must go at once, they would see to everything that needed doing. She took a taxi to the hospital, a couple of miles from the town centre, then followed the maze of corridors to where Alec was sitting, in a private room, at Lilian's bedside. He was looking fondly at her as he held her hand. Her head was bandaged and her face was ghostly pale, but she appeared to be breathing normally.

'Oh, poor Mum,' said Janice, 'having to go through all that again.' She stooped and kissed her mother's cheek. 'It's over now, though, and she looks peaceful enough.'

After only a brief moment Lilian's eyelids started to flicker, then she opened her eyes, confusedly at first, until she caught sight of Alec and Janice. Her eyes lit up then, shining like stars.

'Oh ... it's so lovely to see you,' she said in a whisper. 'Alec and Janice.' She tried to lift her head to look around, but found she couldn't do so.

'Keep still, love,' said her husband quietly. 'Don't

try to raise your head. The nurse will help you when you want to sit up.'

'Where am I?' she asked in a puzzled voice.

'You're in hospital, love,' said Alec. 'You remember ... the bad headache? We had to bring you here again, but you're going to be fine.'

'Where's Ian?' she whispered.

'He's at home, Lilian. He sends his love. I expect you'll be in here a little while, but we'll come and see you every day, Janice and me.'

'That's nice,' she muttered. She gave them a radiant smile then, suddenly, her head fell sideways on the pillow as she lost consciousness again. Alec and Janice could see that the monitor at the side of the bed had changed its rhythm, although they didn't understand it fully.

'Quick ... get the nurse,' cried Janice. 'Dad, go and tell them... I think she's...' She took hold of her mother's hand. 'Mum ... Mum, don't go to sleep again.'

Alec was back almost at once with a doctor and a nurse. 'Could I ask you to leave us, please?' said the doctor, kindly, 'We must act quickly. We'll do what we can...'

Father and daughter stared at one another blankly as they left the room, then sat in the waiting room outside the main ward.

'She'll be alright, won't she, Dad?' said Janice fearfully. 'She survived the operation, and she's always had a strong heart.'

'As far as we know,' said Alec. 'We must just wait ... and hope.'

And pray, thought Janice to herself as she uttered silently, 'Please God, let Mum be alright.'

The doctor returned some ten minutes later. They could tell from his sombre face that the news was not good. 'Mr Butler ... Miss Butler,' he began. 'I'm very sorry. We've done all we can, but I'm afraid we couldn't save her. I'm so dreadfully sorry,' he repeated as both Alec and Janice gave a gasp of shock and dismay. 'It was a cardiac arrest; her heart just stopped beating. We tried to restart it, but it was no use.'

'But my wife has never had a bad heart,' said Alec, shaking his head.

'It's the shock of the operation,' said the doctor. 'There's always a risk with any operation, even with the strongest of patients. And the second operation on the brain, the strain was too much, but we had to try... Would you like to come and have a look at Lilian?'

They followed him silently back into the room. All the lines of stress and pain had gone from Lilian's face. It was the first time that Janice had seen a dead person. She had preferred not to look at her grandma. Yes, she mused, that was her beloved mother ... and yet it was not. Her spirit had departed and, with it, the vital spark that had made her the living and loving person that she had been. Janice gently touched her hand.

'Goodbye, Mum,' she whispered, trying to believe that her mother was at peace now, somewhere else, which was what she had been told, so many times, would happen after death.

Alec was in tears, the first time she had ever seen her father cry. They attended to the formalities then, dejectedly, took a taxi back home with Lilian's few clothes and belongings in a carrier bag.

'However are we going to tell Ian?' asked Janice. Alec was calmer by the time they arrived home.

'I'll break it to him,' he said. 'You go and tell Phil and the girls. What about the hotel? You won't feel like carrying on, will you?'

'I'm too numb to think about anything at the moment,' said Janice. 'My mind still won't take it all in.'

Phil, with Nancy and Olive, were still in the kitchen having cleared away and stacked the dishwasher. They had also set the tables ready for breakfast, as they sometimes did. Nancy and Olive would not go home until they had news about Lilian.

They were all shocked at the news. Janice's tears started again as Phil put his arms around her. 'Oh, my darling, I'm so very sorry. How dreadful, and so unexpected.'

'Her heart couldn't stand the strain, Phil... There's so much to think about, and I can't, not at the moment.'

'What about tomorrow?' asked Nancy, a little fearfully. 'We'll have to serve the breakfasts, won't we?' They were all trying to adjust to the awful news.

'Yes, I suppose so,' said Janice, sounding weary and unsure. Then she spoke again, more positively. 'Yes, we must, of course we must. But after that... I don't know, I'll ask Dad what he thinks we should do. Thanks ever so much for all you've done. You'd better get off home now ... and we'll see what tomorrow brings.'

Janice and Phil went to talk to Alec in the living room. Ian had gone to bed, too stunned, it seemed, to cry about his mum. He said he would read for a while then try to get to sleep.

The three of them attempted to look rationally at the situation. They decided it would not be possible for them to cope with the visitors for the rest of the week. Janice knew that their neighbours, also, were not fully booked and might be willing to accommodate a few more guests. It was quite late in the evening when Janice and Phil went round to ask the landladies of the next door houses if they could put up a few more visitors, starting with the evening meal on the next day. They both agreed at once, very shocked and sorry to hear the sad news of Lilian's demise.

Janice and Phil also agreed to keep the hotel running until the end of the season, rather than give back word to the people who had already booked. They would, however, accept no more bookings. Then, when the season came to an end, big decisions would have to be made.

Cissie's pregnancy continued uneventfully. She was well and active, and people said she looked radiant, as mothers-to-be were often told. She worked until six weeks before the expected date which was towards the end of May.

Both she and Val had been sad to hear about Lilian Butler's death and felt very sorry for their new friend, Janice. Lilian had been so well last August. It was hard to believe that she had gone.

It was on the last day of May, a Thursday, when Cissie's labour pains started in earnest. She had

had one or two false alarms but she knew by late afternoon that this was the real thing. Walter was due home from work quite soon so she decided to stick it out as long as possible.

He looked at her with concern, then threw his arms round her and kissed her.

'I'm going to be a daddy,' he said, 'Isn't that wonderful?'

'You wouldn't think it was all that wonderful if you were suffering like I am!' she retorted.

'Yes, I know, love, but you're going to have our baby!'

He ran to a nearby phone box and rang for a taxi, and very soon they were arriving at Halifax General Hospital on the outskirts of the town. Walter kissed her fondly as he left her in the care of the attendant nurses, then he went home to wait. They did not have a phone, but his parents did, so it was agreed that they should receive the call when there was any news.

If the wait was long for Walter it felt even longer for Cissie. She was left alone for most of the time during the first stage of labour, in a side ward so that her moans would not disturb the women in the main ward. Why did I let myself get into this state? she thought. Never again! She was given a routine enema which she found embarrassing and degrading. Then at midnight her waters broke.

The nurses were then very attentive. She breathed hard at the gas and air machine, and in her semi-conscious state she vaguely remembered Jack and their encounter at the Tower Ballroom, then their love making – if it could be so called – on Blackpool promenade. She thought of Walter, too, their coming together, then their engagement and marriage.

'Another push, Cissie, love,' said the midwife. 'Good girl! I can see the head...'

'Another one; a big push now, Cissie... There, you've done it! You have a lovely baby boy.'

One nurse dealt swiftly with the afterbirth, and Cissie watched in a daze as the other nurse picked up the crying infant and cleaned him, then wrapped him in a towel.

'Here you are, Cissie, love,' she said, 'Sit up and then you can hold him.'

As she looked dazedly at the baby boy in her arms Cissie knew at once who the father of the child was.

On Friday morning Val was surprised to see Walter coming into the office. He was beaming from ear to ear. 'I'm a dad!' he shouted. 'I thought you'd like to know. Cissie's had a little boy.'

'That's wonderful news,' said Val. 'So how is she? No complications? They're both OK?'

'Yes, mother and baby doing well, as they say. She went in yesterday when I got home from work, and the baby was born in the early hours this morning. So his birthday's the first of June. He was seven and a half pounds. I believe that's quite a good weight, though I don't know much about such things.'

Val had never seen Walter look so pleased with himself, like a dog with two tails.

'So what are you going to call him?' she asked. 'I don't suppose you know yet, do you?'

'We've been thinking about it for a while. Cissie's father's called Joseph – that's OK I suppose

– but my dad's Archibald! So that's out. We thought we'd better steer clear of family names, then we don't offend anybody.'

'May I go and see her?' asked Val.

'Yes, of course, you're her best friend. She'll be pleased to see you. I think she'll be in for about a week. Perhaps you could leave it till after the weekend? The parents will be visiting in force on Saturday and Sunday, and I'll be there, of course. What about Monday? Visiting hours are afternoon and evening, so it'll be evening, won't it?'

'Yes, that's fine,' agreed Val. 'Give her my love ... and congratulations to you both.'

'Thank you. I didn't realize I'd be so thrilled,' said Walter.

'Well, he's on top of the world,' said one of Val's colleagues as he left the room. 'I always thought he was a po-faced sort of chap.'

'He's OK,' replied Val. 'He's a good husband to Cissie, and they seem to be happy together.'

She was dying to see Cissie, and the baby, of course. She could not help wondering as her thoughts returned to the week they had spent in Blackpool.

'Would you like to come with me to see Cissie and her new son?' she asked Sam.

'I think you should go on your own,' he replied. 'Not that I don't want to see her – I think Cissie's a great girl – but she's your friend. I don't want to intrude on girl's talk! I'm sure you'll have a lot to talk about.'

Val had been busy knitting. She wasn't an expert by any means, but it was what one did for a new baby. She had chosen lemon wool which would do

301

for either sex, and had painstakingly knitted a tiny matinee jacket and a pair of bootees. She took a bus to the hospital on Monday evening with the gift for the baby, a bunch of miniature roses and a box of Milk Tray, Cissie's favourite chocolates.

TWENTY-ONE

Cissie was in a ward with several other women, beds on either side of the long room. She was sitting up in bed looking very pretty in a pale pink bed-jacket and nylon nightdress. She had applied some bright pink lipstick and her blonde hair was combed in a halo around her head. Cissie made the most of her appearance, whatever the circumstances.

At the end of each bed there was a cot in which the babies were sleeping peacefully. Cissie threw out her arms and embraced her friend.

'Oh, how lovely to see you. I've been dying for you to come.' Then she drew back, cringing a little. 'Sorry, I'm a bit sore here.' She touched her breasts. 'I'm breast feeding...' She grimaced. 'It's no joke, I can tell you. Anyway, do you want to have a peep at him, my baby boy?'

Val bent over the cot. It was a fallacy that all babies were red and wrinkled and that they all looked alike. This little baby was plump and round-cheeked, and although he was tiny he had a nose that was unmistakable, and a mop of dark, almost black, hair. Cissie was as fair as could be, and, Val remembered, so was ... Jack.

She stood up and stared at her friend. 'Cissie, he's the image of...'

'Yes, of Walter,' replied Cissie. 'Isn't he just? Walter can't get over it. He says to everyone, "Look, he's the image of his daddy!"'

'Well, that must be a relief,' said Val quietly. 'You see, it's turned out alright after all.' But ... had it? she wondered.

'Yes, I suppose so,' said Cissie. 'Well, what's done is done, and I've got my lovely baby boy.'

She was delighted with the gifts that Val had brought, then she told her about the daily routine in the hospital. 'They wake you up at an unearthly hour,' she said. 'That is if you're not already awake with a screaming baby.'

'And ... do you have to see to him?'

'Of course. They make you breast feed. They say it's best for the baby, and some mothers seem to love it, but it hurts like hell, I can tell you! I dread it coming round every four hours, and I've so much milk I'm wet through all the time.'

'But that's a good thing, to breast feed, isn't it?' asked Val.

'I suppose so,' said Cissie again. 'I shall put him on a bottle as soon as I can. They don't like you to, the midwives, I mean. But when I'm at home I shall please myself. Anyway, that's enough about me... How's your Sam? Still going strong, is it?' Val nodded happily. 'Who'd have thought it, eh? You and the boss's son. I was wrong, wasn't I, saying that it wouldn't work? You make a lovely couple, and he's such a nice chap.'

'Yes, I think so, too,' said Val.

Cissie went home after eight days in hospital. Walter was with her over the weekend, but when he went to work on Monday she was on her own. She could not believe the difference a tiny baby could make to the household. His equipment; pram, carrycot, nappies, baby bath, talcum powder, baby wipes, safety pins, seemed to be all over every room. Her life was controlled by feeding times, every four hours, and this went on through the night as well. The aim, she had been told, was to get the child to sleep right through the night, but this was not happening yet. In fact he was worse at night. The moment he was laid in his cot he started to yell, even if he had just been fed.

Walter was able to escape to work after a sleepless night – although he usually slept right through the noise – whereas Cissie was left on her own until teatime to cope with the endless changing and washing of nappies, feeding the baby and trying, somehow, to prepare an evening meal. The amount of nappies he used was incredible. They were everywhere. Soaking in buckets, revolving round in the washing machine – at least that was a blessing – or drying on a clothes horse round the fire. On sunny days they dried outside on the washing line, but at the moment they were getting more than their fair share of rain, which only served to make Cissie feel even more alone and dispirited.

One gloomy afternoon when she had been home for almost two weeks Cissie sat by the fireside holding her baby son. They hadn't given him a name yet because they couldn't reach a decision.

She had fed and changed him but he would not settle. Her breasts were sore and uncomfortable. Even a towel wrapped round her was not enough to soak up the excess milk. When she looked in the mirror she knew she looked a sight. Her hair was straggly and needed washing, then cutting and styling. She was pale and her eyes had lost their usual brightness through lack of sleep.

She looked down at her child. He opened his eyes and looked back at her, at least he seemed to do so although she knew that he couldn't focus properly yet. They were Walter's eyes, though, just as he had Walter's nose and his dark hair. She was growing fond of this little baby, but the thought suddenly occurred to her that there had been no need for any of it – her pretense of finally giving in to Walter's persuasion, their engagement and their marriage – because she had not been pregnant after all. Her brief sexual encounter with Jack had not left her pregnant as she had feared. She hadn't needed to rush into an early marriage. She could still be single and fancy free, waiting for the right man to come along.

She looked again at the little innocent child and, despite herself, her feelings towards him started to change. She loved him but she knew that she was also angry and resentful about the trick that Fate had played on her.

It was a couple of weeks later, towards the end of June, when Walter came into the office to see Valerie.

'I'm afraid Cissie is very down in the dumps,' he told her. 'Do you think you could come round and see her? I'm sure a chat with you would help to cheer her up as much as anything would.'

'Yes, of course,' said Val. 'What's the matter with Cissie? Is it sleepless nights? That would make anyone feel out of sorts.'

'Partly,' said Walter, 'although that's been rather better since she put him on a bottle. But that's caused another problem with … er … with her milk. She'll tell you about it.' He looked a little embarrassed. 'I just know she's irritable and not herself at all. We'd been getting along so well, Valerie,' he said in a confidential tone, and she felt sorry for him.

She nodded. 'They call it the "baby blues". Apparently this can happen after the birth of a baby. It's post-natal depression. Yes, my half-day is on Thursday, so I'll come round and do my best to cheer her up.'

Val set off for her friend's house two days later with a little blue teddy bear for the baby and a box of chocolates for Cissie. Their small terraced house was about ten minutes' walk away from Val's home. Cissie had told Val that they intended to move to a semi with a garden when they were able to afford it.

She had obviously made some effort with her appearance, knowing that her friend was coming. Her hair was freshly washed and she had put on some make-up. Her eyes had lost their former sparkle, but she managed a smile as she flung her arms around Val.

'It's so good to see you, it's been ages,' she said.

'Not all that long,' replied Val, although she realized it had been more than a fortnight. 'I knew you were busy and had quite enough to cope with.

Anyway, I'm here now.'

She followed Cissie into the living room at the back of the house. A small fire was burning in the grate although the day was sunny, and several nappies were airing on a clothes horse on the hearth.

'Oh ... let's have a look at him!' Val went across to where a carrycot rested on two dining chairs. 'He's grown a lot since I last saw him. Look at his chubby cheeks and those dear little hands! He's gorgeous, Cissie. You must be so proud of him. And he's sleeping so peacefully.'

'For once,' said Cissie. 'You should hear him sometimes! It's enough to wake the dead! Although Walter manages to sleep through it, until I give him a poke. He's supposed to be helping to feed him now he's on a bottle. Anyway, sit down and we'll have a chat. I can't tell you how good it is to see you.'

She was very pleased with the teddy bear and the chocolates, but it was clear, as Walter had said, that she was depressed, though trying not to let it show.

'Have you decided on a name for him yet?' asked Val.

'Yes, he's called Paul,' replied Cissie. 'It's a name you can't shorten or mess about with. Not like mine ... I'm Cecelia, you know, some daft idea of me mam's, I suppose. But I've always been called Cissie. I suppose that's slightly better, but I've never been right keen on it.'

'It suits you, though,' said Val. 'I expect your mum's thrilled with the baby – with Paul – isn't she?'

'Oh, you know Mam. Yes, she made a fuss, I must admit. With me being the only one, there's

307

only me to give her grandchildren. But as far as being any real help to me, I can forget it. I know what she thinks – I've made my own bed and now I must lie on it.' Cissie suddenly burst into tears. 'Oh, Val, I'm so fed up and tired. Here I am, stuck at home day after day with a crying baby, and it need never have been. I didn't need to get married!'

The same thought had occurred to Val, but she knew she must try to help her friend to make the best of what had happened. 'You've got a lovely baby,' she said, 'and there's no doubt that he's Walter's child. Just imagine if he was fair, like you and … Jack. You'd have felt guilty about it forever, having to deceive Walter. As Paul grew up it might have become more obvious that there was some doubt about the father.'

'But I did deceive Walter, can't you see? I tricked him into doing what I'd always refused to do. And I didn't need to, because I wasn't pregnant. After that ... thing ... with Jack, nothing had happened. I needn't have got married, don't you see?'

'Yes, I do see,' said Val. 'But it's too late now, isn't it? You've got a beautiful baby, and Walter's a good husband, isn't he?'

'Yes, I suppose he is,' said Cissie grudgingly. 'He knows there's something wrong with me, and he's trying to do his best. I was determined to stop breast feeding, and the midwife and doctor agreed, although they weren't all that keen about it. Anyway, I had to take some pills to stop the milk, and that made me ill for a few days, all hot and feverish. So Paul's on a bottle now.'

'And that's what you wanted. Isn't it easier?'

'In some ways, I suppose. He's still not sleeping through the night, though. Walter agreed that we should take it in turns in the night. I make the bottle ready for when he wakes up, but it's gone cold by then and I have to warm it up again. And it's usually me that has to do it because Walter's asleep.'

'He does have to go to work the next day...'

'While I stay at home and do nothing, I suppose?'

'I didn't say that, Cissie.' Val was aware that her friend was very disgruntled, and possibly with good reason? 'Oh, come on, love. I know it seems awful now but it's sure to get better. You've got all the summer ahead of you. It's better than having a winter baby, surely?'

'Don't tell me to count my blessings, or I'll scream! That's more or less what Walter's mother said, and I felt like scratching her eyes out.'

'Oh, Cissie, I'm so sorry, really I am. I don't know what to say, except that I'm always there for you. Perhaps I could babysit sometime, then you and Walter could go out?'

'It's all changed so much, Val. This time last year we were looking forward to going to Blackpool. We said we'd go again this year, didn't we? But look what's happened. I'm married and I've got a baby, Mrs Butler's died, and Janice didn't go to her fancy college. And you're going out with Sam Walker. At least one of us is happy... I'm sorry, Val,' she said when Val didn't answer. 'I'm glad you're getting on so well with Sam, honest I am. I'm not jealous, you know. Come on, tell me what you have been up to? You don't need to tell me everything,' she added with a sly grin, which was more like the old Cissie.

Baby Paul woke up then and screamed until he felt the teat in his mouth, then his cries stopped and he gulped noisily at the milk.

'D'you want to hold him for a bit?' said Cissie. Val took hold of the little bundle very warily. 'He might be a bit smelly,' Cissie told her. 'I change him after his feed.'

'No, he's adorable,' said Val, looking down at the misty brownish-grey eyes that seemed to be staring up at her. She had never really thought ahead to the time when she might have a child of her own. Cissie had been catapulted into this situation. Val hoped it would be different for her when it happened. Surely a baby was a precious gift, though, whatever the circumstances? She hoped that Cissie would soon get over her present feeling of resentment over what had happened.

By the time she left an hour later her friend had cheered up a lot. Val had promised to babysit one evening soon. She was still concerned, though, about Cissie's state of mind.

Val was still seeing Sam regularly. They were growing closer, enjoying one another's company more and more each time they met. Sam was tender and loving, but he kept within what Val considered to be the correct limits. She was very aware of what had happened to Cissie. Both she and her friend had been brought up to believe that you should wait until you were married before 'going the whole way', which was what girls usually called it. But Val understood now how easy it might be to overstep the boundaries.

It was in early July, whilst they were enjoying a meal at their favourite country inn, that Sam asked her if she would consider going away with him in August when the mill closed for their annual week's holiday. She agreed that she would love to, although she was wondering what her parents would say.

'Where are you thinking of going?' she asked. 'Blackpool?' she added with a grin.

'Er … no. I thought we could go touring in the car. Maybe up to Scotland. Have you ever been there?'

Val said she hadn't but she would love to do so. She was also wondering about what he had in mind. What about the sleeping arrangements? Two single rooms? She guessed that Sam would be just as concerned as she was about the propriety of it all.

'I shall have to ask my parents,' she said. 'I know that might sound silly and old-fashioned, but it's what I must do.'

He smiled. 'Of course, but I think they know me well enough now to feel that they can trust me. And you can trust me, too, Val. You know that I love you.' He looked at her tenderly, reaching out his hand across the table to take hold of hers. 'But it must be right for both of us.'

Her heart gave a surge of joy at his words. It was the first time that he had actually said that he loved her, and she knew she could not be the one to say it until he did so.

'Yes … I know, and I love you, too,' she whispered, feeling herself blush a little. 'I shall tell my parents tonight about the holiday. Oh, Sam, it will be so exciting, won't it? I've always wanted to visit Scotland...'

The summer season at the Florabunda was continuing successfully through June and July, as far as bookings were concerned. It was difficult to think of the hotel, though, without Lilian Butler at the helm. Janice went on resolutely from week to week, with Phil as her co-worker, and assistance from Freda, Nancy and Olive. They maintained the high standard that Lilian had always insisted on, but for all of them it seemed that the heart had gone out of the place.

Janice and her father had decided they would take no more bookings, and it became clear as the season drew on that the number of visitors was dwindling. They estimated that the hotel would be only half full in August, and by September the number would have decreased even more.

It was Alec who raised the question of whether they should continue to the end of the season, or try to find accommodation nearby for the guests who had booked, and close down the business. Janice had intimated that she could not run the hotel indefinitely no matter how much assistance she had. It was just not the same without her mother there.

Alec, Janice and Phil got together for a serious talk one evening. 'It's decision time,' Alec began. 'I know I've never had a great deal to do with the business, but the hotel is our home as well. Obviously we can't stay here unless we keep the place running. And you don't want to, do you, Janice?'

'I can't, not without Mum,' she replied. 'I started by helping out as a waitress last summer, and then ... well ... we know what happened. Mum was ill, and I said I'd try to keep it going.'

'And you've done a grand job, you and Phil,' said Alec. 'It's marvellous the way you've pulled together. But now there's no need for you to carry on being involved in the hotel business at all, if you don't want to, Janice.'

'No, I don't,' she answered, 'at least, not here. Like I said, it's not the same without Mum.'

'So I was wondering,' Alec went on, 'whether you could go to university, like you intended doing. I've been very concerned that you gave up your place to help out here, and I know your mum – God bless her – would be as well. You know how keen she was for you to go to university, and it isn't too late. You could reapply, and go and get your degree, like you planned to do.'

Janice smiled at her father. 'Thanks, Dad. I know what you mean, and I realize it's what Mum wanted for me. But it's too late. I would need to have applied much earlier than this. Anyway, I've given up on that idea. I would have gone and got a degree, but I had no idea what I wanted to do as a career, only vague notions about being a librarian or something to do with books.'

'So what have you got in mind now?' asked Phil.

He was wondering, too, about his own plans for the future. He had been happy working here in Blackpool because he was with Janice, and he enjoyed anything to do with catering. It had been a sad time, though, as well, as they had all been conscious that Lilian was no longer with them.

Phil knew that his time here was soon coming to an end. He had grown very fond of Janice. Their friendship had progressed from just being friends to something more loving and tender. She had responded to his kisses and embraces, but their loving was still quite innocent. Phil had known how much she was grieving for her mother, and that he must be gentle and understanding with her. He knew, though, that he did not want their relationship to come to an end.

Phil was looking at her inquiringly and showing concern. She knew that her plans might affect him as well. They had not talked about a future together – she was not yet twenty years of age – but she felt that he would not want their friendship to end when he left Blackpool, and neither would she.

She looked from Phil to her father as she answered. 'I've become very interested in the hotel business. I was starting to feel quite involved in it even before Mum was taken ill; but I knew that would have to end because I was going to college. But I didn't, the way things worked out.'

'You mean you'd like to continue in the hotel business?' asked Phil.

'But not here?' added her father. 'You've said you don't want to carry on running this place?'

'No, there would be too many memories,' said Janice. 'This was Mum's hotel, and Gran's before her. I was thinking I might do some more training for the catering business, every part of it – cookery and baking, menu planning, keeping accounts and hotel management. And there's a college right here in Blackpool. I wouldn't need to go away. I would be here, Dad, to see to you and Ian and make your meals.'

'Don't worry about us, love,' said Alec. 'It's important that you should do what you really want to do. You mustn't feel that you have to organize your life to fit round us.'

'I'm not, Dad,' she insisted. 'It's what I really want to do. I'll make enquiries about the college course, and I'm pretty sure I'll be able to start there in September. They have students from all over, and I suppose they stay in digs, but I'd be able to come home every night.'

'It sounds good,' said Alec. 'What do you think, Phil?'

'I think it's a great idea,' he answered. 'Janice is getting really proficient at cooking, you know. Aren't you, love?' he said turning to her.

She grinned. 'If you say so, Phil. Yes, I enjoy it very much. I've been doing it because I had no choice, and it's been sad with Mum not being there. But I think I've inherited some of her skills and I feel that it's what I'd like to carry on doing... Somewhere different, maybe, sometime in the future.'

She and Phil looked at one another and smiled. Alec noticed the glances they exchanged and he felt pleased. Phil was just the sort of young man he would have chosen for his beloved daughter, and he knew that Lilian would have agreed with him. No one could tell what the future might hold, but he hoped that these two young people would plan a future together.

TWENTY-TWO

Val's parents were quite agreeable about the idea of her going away with Sam in August. Her mother had looked rather doubtful at first, which was only what Val had expected, but she had come round at her husband's persuasion.

'Sam's a grand lad,' said Bert Horrocks. 'I like him more every time I see him. Seemed odd at first, mind, to be calling him Sam, but he's like one of the family now. I reckon she'll come to no harm with Sam Walker, Sally. Anyway, she'll be twenty-one in September, won't you, Val?'

'Yes,' said her mother. 'So she will. How time flies! We know we can trust you, Valerie love. Cissie got herself into rather a pickle, didn't she? But it seems to have worked out alright for her and Walter.' Val's mother, of course, did not know the half of it.

She and her husband were full of plans for their own holiday. They had booked, this time, for a coach tour to Devon, staying at the popular resort of Torquay. It would be the first time they had ventured so far afield.

Val did not know whether Sam had told his parents of their proposed trip to Scotland. They had other things on their minds at the moment. Thelma had given birth to a baby girl during the first week in June, a few days after Cissie's baby was born. Beatrice, apparently, had forgiven

Jonathan and Thelma for their misdemeanour and was thrilled with the baby, her first grandchild. They were calling her Rosemary Jane, tactfully avoiding any family names so as not to cause offence. Val had seen her when she and Sam had been invited round to the couple's new semi-detached house. She was a beautiful baby with Thelma's fair hair and complexion.

To her surprise Val had been invited to the christening at the end of August. Sam was to be the child's godfather, which was only to be expected, and so Val was included in the invitation. She was not asked to be a godmother, however, something she had not expected or wanted.

She had been asked to act as godmother to Cissie and Walter's baby; they had finally decided on the name Paul Henry. That christening was the week before the one of Thelma and Jonathan's child. Val was delighted at the honour although, as Cissie's best friend, it was inevitable that she would be chosen.

Cissie was going through the motions, registering the birth of the child, arranging the christening, coping with the routine of changing, feeding and bathing the baby – this was becoming gradually less chaotic than it had been at first – but she knew, deep down, that she was not bonding with the child as she ought to be. She supposed she loved him and she would never want to neglect or hurt him, but there was still a feeling of resentment at the heart of her. She did her best to hide her feelings from Walter. He was very patient with her and her fits of moodiness. He guessed it was 'baby blues', the term that Valerie had used to describe the way mothers of new babies often felt.

Val, also, knew that her friend was still far from contented with her lot and she, unlike Walter, was aware of the real reason. She had no choice, however, but to tell Cissie about the holiday that she and Sam were planning.

'How very nice,' said Cissie, with a touch of sarcasm. 'It's alright for some, isn't it?'

Val didn't reply, and Cissie looked at her despairingly. 'Sorry, Val ... I didn't mean that. I'm really pleased for you, you'll have a great time... But it was you and me last year, wasn't it, planning our holiday to Blackpool? What a long time ago it seems, and who would've thought all this could happen?' She gestured towards Paul in his carrycot, the pile of baby clothes waiting to be ironed, and the bottle ready for when he woke up. He was starting to stir now, waving his little arms and making a faint noise like the mewing of a kitten.

'He's waking up,' said Cissie. 'D'you want to give him his bottle?'

'Yes, I'd love to,' said Val. 'You pick him up, then I'll take him.'

Cissie lifted the baby out of the cot and placed him on Val's lap. He was starting to cry in earnest. She put her arms round him and he looked up at her, his cries stopping at once.

'There you are, you see,' said Cissie. 'He knows his aunty Val, doesn't he?'

'He's a bonny little lad,' said Val, taking the bottle from Cissie and placing the teat in his wide open mouth. 'I'm sure you're very proud of him, aren't you, Cissie? I know that Walter is. You should see him at work. I've never known him look so pleased with himself. The other girls have noticed it as well.'

'Yes, he's OK, I suppose – Paul, I mean. I know he's a lovely baby, everybody says so. It's being stuck here with him, day after day, and night after night, though I must say he's getting a bit better at night.' She sighed. 'It's bound to get better. It can't get any worse.'

'How about me coming to babysit again?' suggested Val. She had done so once, a couple of weeks ago to give Cissie and Walter a break, and her friend had seemed better afterwards.

'OK then, thanks,' said Cissie. 'It'll make a change.'

They arranged that Val should come on the Tuesday evening in the following week. It was nearing the end of July and the nights were light until almost ten o'clock.

'There's a pub we like near Hebden Bridge,' said Cissie sounding a little more enthusiastic. 'If it's fine you can sit outside in the garden.'

'And you've got your own car now,' said Val. 'That must make things a lot easier for you.'

'Yes, I suppose it does. We don't have to rely on Walter's dad any more. Walter says I should learn to drive meself, but it's not possible at the moment. P'raps one of these days...'

Walter had managed to find enough money to buy the car. It was a Morris Minor, several years old, but Val could tell that Cissie regarded it as a symbol of affluence, and that would be a point in Walter's favour. By the time she left, her friend was sounding much more cheerful.

When she arrived at their house again the

following week Cissie was looking very pretty in a blue dress that matched the colour of her eyes. Her hair was newly washed and she had put on some blue eyeshadow and bright pink lipstick.

'You look very nice,' Val told her. 'I hope you have a lovely time, and don't worry about Paul. I'll look after him.'

'I know you will,' said Cissie. 'He's had his bath and I've fed him and put him down, but he's a bit restless. He's not crying blue murder like he used to do, but he's grizzling a bit. I hope he'll be alright...'

She looked a little anxious, and Val knew that she did care about the little boy despite her seeming indifference at times.

'He'll be fine,' said Walter. 'Give over worrying. You know he'll be OK with Val, and we won't be away all that long. Come on now.' He rattled his car keys. 'Let's get going.'

'I've left a bottle ready in the kitchen in case he's still restless,' said Cissie. 'It might need warming up, just stick it in a pan of hot water for a minute or two.'

Walter smiled. Val had found him much more amenable lately. 'Stop fussing,' he said. 'Val knows what to do. It's very good of you to come, Valerie. We'll be back about eleven or so, then I'll run you home. Bye for now...'

Val settled down in the small living room at the back of the house. It was a terraced house, similar in style to her own home and the one where Cissie's parents lived. There was a tiny kitchen opening off the back room, and two bedrooms and a small bathroom and toilet upstairs.

They had adequate furniture for their present needs, but Val knew that the front room was still unfurnished, and one of the bedrooms, which was to be Paul's nursery, still held only a cot. The Parker Knoll chair that she was sitting on – one of a pair – had been a wedding present from one set of parents, and the G-plan dining table and four chairs had been bought by the other two parents. The curtains were a bold contemporary design of black, red and orange rectangles, matching the red fabric of the chairs and the red carpet square.

Val had just started reading her Agatha Christie book, engrossed in the doings of Miss Marple, when she heard the sound of crying. When she went upstairs she found Paul was red in the face and seemed hot all over as well. He had wrestled with his bed clothes which were in a tangled pile all around him. His mop of dark hair was damp and clinging to his scalp. He was crying furiously, the tears running down his chubby little cheeks.

'Oh deary me! Whatever's the matter?' said Val. 'Come along, let's have a look at you.' She felt a surge of affection for the little lad in such distress. She realized, though, that it was a novel experience for her. Maybe it did get wearisome if you had a child who was continually crying.

She lifted him out of his carrycot which was on a small table at the end of the bed where Cissie and Walter slept. His skin felt damp and hot as though he were feverish. Val hoped that this was not the case. She knew that Cissie and Walter would not have left him if they had been at all worried.

'Come on then, you lovely boy,' she said, cradling him in her arms. He stopped crying for a moment and looked up at her. 'Let's go downstairs, shall we, and see if you'd like a little drink? That's what Mummy said, didn't she?' How easy it was to talk to the little child, although he couldn't have a clue what she was saying. The gentle tone of her voice and the comfort of her arms seemed to soothe him.

She carried him carefully down the stairs and into the kitchen. His bottle still felt warm and did not need warming up again. She sat down and put it to Paul's mouth. He took a gulp or two then turned his head away and could not be persuaded to take any more. She held him a little longer, then went upstairs and put him down again. He lay in his cot and she felt he might settle. She tiptoed out of the room.

It was only a few minutes later when she heard him crying again. She decided to leave him a little while. Surely he must be tired and would soon drop off? But his cries did not stop, so again she brought him downstairs. The bottle soothed him for a moment, then again he spit it out and would not be comforted.

'I know what we'll do, Paul,' she said. 'Aunty Val will bring your cot down, then she doesn't need to keep going up and down the stairs.' She laid him gently on the hearthrug. There was no fire in the grate as the weather was warm. 'Now, you stay there, and I'll go and fetch your cot.' She dashed up the stairs and down again with the carry-cot. Paul was still crying, seeming more distressed than ever.

It was a long evening for Val until she heard the

key turn in the lock just after eleven o'clock. Paul had slept in fits and starts, but she had spent most of the evening nursing him, which was what she was doing when his parents returned. They were both very concerned, and Cissie felt guilty that she had left him.

'Don't blame yourself,' said Val. 'You weren't to know he wouldn't settle down. And he doesn't know me, does he, not like he knows you? He'll feel better when you're holding him.'

'I hope so,' said Cissie. 'Oh dear! I wonder what's up with him?' She was holding him now, and he did seem a little calmer.

'Perhaps he's teething?' said Walter.

'What? At two months old! Don't be silly, Walter!'

'Well, I don't know do I? Do you think we should get the doctor?'

'I don't know,' said Cissie. 'He's very hot, but he's got himself into a right old paddy, haven't you, Paul?' Val noticed how lovingly she spoke to the child.

'We mustn't panic,' said Walter. 'Try to settle him down, and if he's no better in the morning we'll get the doctor... I'll run you home now, Valerie. I'm sorry he's been such a trouble to you. You won't want to come again!'

'Of course I will,' said Val. 'Bye for now, Cissie. Let me know how Paul goes on.'

'Yes... Thanks, Val,' said Cissie, sounding distracted. 'I'll change him – he's wet through – and make another bottle. Don't be long, Walter...'

When Walter returned the baby seemed to have settled. He had taken less than half his bottle, whereas he usually gulped the lot. Then he went to sleep and his parents gave a sigh of relief.

But their optimism was short-lived. Paul had a restless night, and so did they. So much so that Walter ran to the phone box at eight o'clock to ask their doctor to call as soon as possible.

Dr Matthews was there within half an hour. 'Now, let's have a look at the little lad,' he said. 'Oh yes, he's certainly feverish. And you say he doesn't want his milk? Has he been sick at all, any vomiting?'

Cissie replied that he had not been sick. 'What's the matter with him, doctor?' she asked.

'Probably it's infant flu,' he replied, 'but I can't be sure yet. I'll give you some medicine that should help to soothe him. Try him with his bottle again, and just keep him as warm and comfortable as you can. I'll come back later today and see how he is. Don't worry. If it's flu, as I think it is, then he should be as right as rain again in a few days. It's one of those infant ailments that babies succumb to, and we don't know why. I'll be back later, sometime this afternoon.'

'What does he mean?' said Cissie, looking worriedly at Walter when the doctor had gone. 'Why does he need to come back later? Why can't he tell us now what's the matter with him?'

'I don't know, Cissie,' he replied. 'I can't answer all your questions. I'm just as worried as you are. Just be thankful that he's coming back, and that he's not rushed him into hospital. Like he said, it's probably something simple. I've heard people say that babies are up and down like a yo-yo sometimes. One minute they're poorly and the next they're as right as ninepence.'

'I suppose so...' said Cissie. 'Poor little lad! I'll try him with his bottle again.'

Baby Paul was still distressed, not screaming now but whimpering and murmuring as he lay in his carrycot. She lifted him out and nursed him whilst Walter prepared a bottle. He had not gone to work today, but he had phoned at the same time as he had called the doctor, to say he would not be there.

As Cissie looked down at her little son she was filled with a sudden compassion for him. She felt guilt as well, and self-reproach. She put the bottle to his mouth and he started to suck, though nothing like as voraciously as he usually did. As a rule he enjoyed his milk and drank it to the last drop. He had already gained several pounds since his birth and looked a sturdy and strong little boy. Again, though, he took a few gulps then turned his head away. He was still very hot and clammy, his face was a feverish red rather than the rosy hue of good health.

Cissie felt tears spring to her eyes as she gazed at him. Was she being punished? she wondered. Had her little child been taken ill because she had neglected him, not physically, but mentally? In her mind she had been resentful of him and had not felt the mother love for him that she knew, deep down, that she ought to have felt. How dreadful it would be if her little boy – their little boy, hers and Walter's – were to be taken from them when they had had him for such a short time. She knew, as she had known from the moment of his birth, that he was Walter's child. For the first time she found she was glad about that, glad that together they had made this little baby.

'Please, God,' she prayed silently, 'please make him well again ... and I'm sorry that I didn't love him as I should have done.'

She started to cry audibly then, her sobs reaching Walter's ears. He came to comfort her.

'He'll be alright, I feel sure he will. The doctor would not have left him if he'd been really worried. Come along, Cissie, put him down again. He seems to have gone to sleep. Perhaps he'll sleep it off, that's what my mother always says.'

The baby settled for a little while. They waited anxiously, not moving far away from him. Suddenly the child gave a gulping sound, and when Cissie dashed to the cot she saw that he had been sick. His blankets were soiled and when she picked him up he was still vomiting. She remembered that the doctor had asked about that. Was it a sign of something more serious?

Together they changed the blankets and put a clean nightgown on him, then Cissie sat and nursed him, frightened to put him down again.

'D'you remember, Walter?' she said. 'Dr Matthews asked if he'd been sick, and he hadn't, not then, but he has now. D'you think it means that there's something more serious the matter with him?'

'Don't start worrying when there's no need, Cissie, love. It's probably something doctors always ask. We'll have to wait and see... What about a cup of tea and something to eat? I could make us a sandwich?'

'No. I couldn't eat anything, Walter. A cup of

tea, perhaps?'

Walter very rarely helped with making meals, which was fair enough. He was the one going out to work, the bread winner, as her mother would say. Offering to help in the kitchen was a sure sign that he was concerned, moreover, that they were in this together, waiting and hoping that their little boy was not seriously ill. He made a few ham sandwiches as well as the tea. Despite her insistence that she was not hungry Cissie managed to eat a few of them. Paul had dropped off to sleep again, wearied with his crying and vomiting.

The respite, however, was short-lived. When the doctor arrived in the early afternoon he was very unwell again.

Dr Matthews looked grave. 'I'm afraid it's more than infant flu,' he said. 'I wasn't sure before, but now, with the vomiting and his fever I'm pretty sure that your little boy has meningitis, and we must get him into hospital straight away.'

Cissie gave a horrified gasp. 'Meningitis! But that's... Is he going to die, doctor?'

Walter was there at her side at once. 'Don't panic, love. Just listen to what the doctor's saying.'

He still looked serious. 'It would be wrong of me not to warn you,' he said. 'I know the word meningitis frightens people, but it's not always as bad as it sounds. I think – I'm almost sure – that your little boy has what is called viral meningitis. And with constant care he should be well again quite soon. There is another sort, bacterial meningitis, which is more serious. The only way to tell is by taking a drop of spinal fluid from the child. So we must take him to hospital straight away.'

'Can we go with him?' asked Cissie tearfully.

'Yes, of course you can,' replied the doctor. 'I'll run you there in my car; it will be better than waiting for an ambulance... You don't have a phone, I suppose?'

Walter shook his head. 'No, I'm afraid not. It's very good of you, Dr Matthews.'

'No trouble at all. Just get the little lad ready, and then we'll be off.'

With the doctor's help the child was quickly admitted to the children's ward in the hospital where Cissie had given birth to him two months ago. The doctor, understandably, could not wait. Cissie and Walter stayed for a while, and were reassured by the kind concern and care of the doctor and nurses. They knew they were leaving Paul in capable hands.

'Come back and see him this evening,' said the nurse who was in charge. 'We will have some news for you by then.'

'Come along, Cissie, let's get home,' said Walter. 'We'll have to tell our parents. There's nothing they can do, but they ought to know.'

They went home by bus, then Walter drove the car to the homes of their respective parents. The men were at work as it was still only late afternoon, but both grandmothers showed great concern.

'Poor little lamb!' said Cissie's mother, with more feeling than Cissie had ever known her to express. She put an arm round her daughter. 'He'll be alright, you'll see.' She cast her eyes heavenwards. 'I'll say a little prayer for him.'

Trust my mam to think she'll get special

328

treatment from the Almighty! thought Cissie. But she knew that her mother meant well.

'Thanks, Mam,' she said, kissing her cheek. 'We'll let you know as soon as we know ourselves.'

They went home to a house that felt strangely empty.

'It feels odd, doesn't it?' said Cissie, 'with Paul not being here.'

'Yes, very strange,' agreed Walter. 'It's amazing the difference a tiny baby makes to a household. It seems as though he's always been with us, but it's only two months. I can't imagine life without him now.'

'Oh, Walter, don't say that!' cried Cissie. 'I couldn't bear to lose him now... He's going to be alright, isn't he?'

Walter was quiet for a moment. 'We've just got to hope and pray that he will be. You heard what our doctor said, and the doctor at the hospital. It's most likely the meningitis that is not too serious – viral, did they say? – not the other sort.'

'I'll never let him out of my sight again,' said Cissie. 'I feel so guilty, Walter.'

'Why, Cissie?' He put his arm round her as they stood in the kitchen, trying to put a scratch meal together before they went back to the hospital in a few hours' time. 'Why ever should you feel guilty? You've been a wonderful mother to Paul, and I know it hasn't been easy. You're the one who's got up at night, most of the time, to see to him. You've done everything you could for that little lad, so don't start blaming yourself, Cissie, love.'

I've done everything except love him as I should have done, she thought to herself, but did not say.

She remembered the bitter thoughts she had harboured about the child's conception. There had been no need for her to trick Walter the way she had done. But she could tell him none of this. It would have to remain her secret forever.

'Yes,' she replied. 'I know I've looked after him as well as I could. But I've been irritable sometimes, with the feeding, and making bottles, and the dirty nappies, and him crying all the time. Poor little lad! And it's not his fault, not any of it. He's got to get better, Walter!' she cried in desperation.

'Don't get despondent, Cissie. And trust Him up there.' He smiled a little as he pointed up to the ceiling. 'You heard what your mother said. She's put in a special word, and Hannah Foster has to be obeyed!'

Cissie gave a weak smile. 'I've put in a word meself. Let's hope He's listening... Come on now, Walter, you open that tin of beans, an' I'll make some toast. Not that I feel much like eating, but we've had nowt to eat all day except a sandwich or two.'

They worked together in a companionable silence. Cissie felt that she had never been closer to Walter. She regretted her former indifference towards him, and the way she had used him. Her lukewarm feelings had undergone a change, they had gradually grown into affection, and now, at last, into what she knew was love. They loved one another and they loved their little child. Surely that would be enough to save their precious son?

The sister who was in charge met them when they entered the children's ward later that evening.

330

When she smiled at them they knew that the news must be what they had been wanting to hear.

'Paul's doing quite well,' she said. She paused for a moment as both parents murmured, 'Thank God for that... So he's going to be alright?'

'We've done the tests, and we've found that the meningitis is not the more serious type. He's still rather poorly and he'll need constant care for a few days. But the prognosis is good, and we're hopeful that he'll be back to normal before long.'

'That's wonderful,' said Cissie. 'Isn't it, Walter?'

'I'll say it is,' he agreed. 'Thank you ever so much for all you've done. Now, can we see him?'

'Of course you can. He's asleep at the moment.' The nurse led them into the ward where there were several cots and small beds. Paul was in the end cot, lying on his back with his eyes closed.

Cissie bent over and took hold of his tiny hand. He opened his eyes at once and stared sleepily up at the two faces leaning over him. Then he blinked, and a smile of recognition spread over his face.

'He knows us,' cried Cissie in delight. 'Look, Walter. He's smiling at us.' It was the first time since his birth that the baby had smiled or really shown any sign that he knew them.

'Yes, babies know who loves them,' said the nurse. 'You'll have to trust him to our care for a few days. We want to make sure that all is well before we let him go home. He's due for his last bottle now. Would you like to give it to him?'

Cissie was overjoyed to feel the child in her arms again. 'Aren't we lucky, Walter?' she said.

'We're the luckiest couple in the world,' he replied.

TWENTY-THREE

'The bonny, bonny banks of Loch Lomond...We used to sing that song at school when we were about eight years old,' said Val.

'Yes, so did we,' agreed Sam. He burst into song.

*'You tack the high road, an' I'll tack the low road,
An' I'll be in Scotland afore ye...*

We didn't have a clue what we were singing about but it was one of our favourites. It was in a little red book, *Songs of the British Isles*.'

'And to think that we're actually here!' said Val contentedly.

She and Sam were strolling along the lakeside path by the shores of Loch Lomond, on the second stage of their holiday north of the border. They had stayed in Edinburgh for the first two days, seeing all the sights of the capital city. The castle, the Royal Mile, Holyrood House, Princes Street with its enticing shops and colourful gardens, and taking in the magnificent view of the city from the hill called Arthur's Seat. Then they had travelled north to Loch Lomond where they were staying for two days before driving to Inverness for the final days of their holiday.

'And there's Ben Lomond,' said Sam, pointing to the mountain in the distance. He started to sing again, as there was no one else near enough to hear him.

"'Twas there that we parted in yon shady glen
On the steep steep side of Ben Lomond...'

'You've a very tuneful voice,' Val told him. 'You've been hiding your light under a bushel. What are you? A tenor?'

'I've no idea. I used to sing in the school choir until my voice broke, then I never bothered after that. But I like a nice tuneful song... Scotland certainly lives up to its reputation, doesn't it? The scenery, and the food – those Scottish breakfasts are quite something! And the Scottish welcome they're so proud of, they really are very friendly... And we're having a wonderful time, aren't we?' They stopped for a moment and he kissed her gently.

'This time last year we were in Blackpool,' said Val. 'Exactly a year since I met you... Since I got to know you, I should say, because I already knew you, sort of, didn't I?'

'What an amazing coincidence it was that we were both in the Winter Gardens that night,' said Sam. 'But we'd have got together sometime, I'm sure we would, you and me. There you were, right under my nose all the time, and I didn't realize.'

'Well, we're together now, aren't we? And that's all that matters,' said Val happily. 'What a lot has happened since last August! Cissie's married to Walter, and they've got a baby...'

'Paul's quite well again now, is he?'

'Yes, he seems to have made a good recovery. I was worried sick when Cissie told me he'd gone into hospital with meningitis. I'd been looking after him, and I wondered if I should have got the doctor myself. But they've no phone, and I couldn't have left him. But he's fine again now, thank goodness. Cissie's planning a grand christening party to follow the service in church. She's thrilled to bits with her little boy now, I'm glad to say, but it took a while.'

'Yes, I suppose it was a shock to her, having to get married in a hurry like that. It was the same with Jonathan and Thelma, although she's more level-headed than Cissie, and they've no financial worries, not so far. I could never have imagined Jonathan as a father, but he's really over the moon with little Rosemary. He's a different person since she was born, well, since they were married, I suppose. And Mother's a lot easier to get on with these days.'

'So it's all "Happy Families", is it?' said Val. 'I'm certainly relieved that she's got used to me being around. I was really worried when we got back from Blackpool. I thought ... well, it was good while it lasted, but it's never going to work.'

'And I was determined that it would... You've no worries about us now, have you, darling? I'm so sure, you see.'

'No, none at all.' She turned to smile at him, and he kissed her again.

'So it's all ended happily,' said Sam.

'Yes, it has, for us. But it's not been such a good year for Janice in Blackpool, losing her mother so suddenly. A year ago Mrs Butler was very healthy and energetic. I still can't believe she's gone. Janice must be devastated, and her father and brother

334

as well.'

'She's still with that RAF lad that she met, isn't she?'

'Yes. Phil's been helping out at the hotel, but they're closing down very soon, before the end of the season. They didn't have many bookings for September and October, so they've found accommodation for the guests at nearby hotels, and they're closing at the end of August. The hotel's already up for sale, so Janice said in her letter, and her dad's looking for a little house for the three of them.'

'And Phil will go back home to Yorkshire, I suppose?'

'Yes, I think that's the idea. Janice is going to a catering college in Blackpool in September, to learn about hotel management as well as the cookery side of it. It's a daytime course, for a year, and she'll be living at home with her father and brother. But I'm sure she'll see Phil whenever she can. They've been working together for several months, so it will be hard for them to be apart. I hope I'll be able to keep in touch with them.'

'Well, Ilkley's not so far away, is it? That was another lucky meeting in the Winter Gardens, wasn't it, for Janice and Phil? I remember poor Cissie being down in the dumps that night because both of you had "struck lucky", as you might say!'

Val laughed. 'Yes, I think that was why she cottoned on to that Jack ... whatever he's called. Jack Broadbent, I think that's his name. He was a real shifty character, but she wouldn't listen. You couldn't blame her, I suppose... He let her down badly, but the good thing to come out of it is that she got together with Walter. He's a good husband, and she's realized that now.'

They headed back towards the country inn at the side of the lake, where they were staying. It had come up to all their expectations for food, comfort and friendliness. They had separate rooms, next door to one another, with a view across the lake to the distant mountains.

They dined sumptuously again that evening on freshly caught salmon, with new potatoes and a variety of salads, followed by a cream gateau, rich with fruit and flavoured with liqueur. After they had drunk the coffee that ended the meal Val suggested that they should take a stroll, as they had done the previous evening.

'We need to walk off that enormous meal,' she suggested. But Sam had other ideas.

'Perhaps not tonight,' he said, 'although I know what you mean. We'll certainly have put on a few pounds by the time we go home. No ... I think it's time for a celebration.'

They went upstairs, and he led her into his room. There, on the dressing table, was an ice bucket containing a bottle, which Val guessed might be champagne and, at the side, two glasses which she had learnt were called champagne flutes. Val sat down on the easy chair and Sam perched on the edge of the bed opposite to her. He leaned forward.

'Valerie ... you've reminded me, although I could hardly forget, that it's exactly a year since we met. It's been a wonderful year, getting to know you and growing closer to you every day. And I know

now that I want this to be forever. I love you, Val ... and I think you feel the same way about me?'

'You know I do, Sam,' she replied. 'I love you too, so very much.'

He stood and went to the dressing table where he opened a drawer and took out a tiny leather box. He knelt down in front of her and took hold of her hands, then he leaned forward and kissed her gently.

'Valerie, my darling,' he said, 'will you marry me? That's all I want to know. It's as simple as that.' She stared at him for a moment. This had come right out of the blue. He had not even hinted at what was in his mind. There was a tiny frown on his face as he regarded her anxiously.

Then she answered him. 'Of course I will, Sam. But ... it's rather unexpected. I'd no idea.'

'Oh, come on now, you must have had an idea. That's why I asked you to come away with me, to be completely on our own.' He opened the box and took out a ring in the shape of a dainty flower, a central sapphire surrounded by small diamonds. 'I hope it fits,' he said, taking hold of her left hand and placing it on her third finger.

'It's beautiful,' she said, 'and it's a perfect fit.' She laughed. 'I sound like Cinderella, but it's not a slipper. Oh, Sam, this is all so amazing!'

'And you are amazing, too,' he said as their lips met in a kiss full of tenderness and longing.

'Get up off your knees,' she said with a giggle, 'and let's have a taste of that champagne.'

'It's from the bar downstairs,' he said. 'I didn't tell them what we were celebrating, but they probably had a good idea.'

Sam drew out the cork slowly and carefully, but was unable to prevent a fountain spraying across the room, although probably not as much as it appeared to be. He poured the sparkling pink champagne into the glasses and handed one to Val. He sat on the bed and she sat next to him.

'Here's to us,' he said. 'To you and me. May we always be as happy as we are today.'

'To us...' she repeated as they touched their glasses then took a sip of the fizzy drink. To Val champagne never tasted much different from lemonade, but of course she did not say so.

'This is the happiest day of my life,' she said. 'But you do know, don't you, that I'm not twenty-one yet?'

'But you will be next month...'

'Yes, but I'm still – officially – under age. I'm sure my parents will be delighted, but perhaps you should have a word with them before we tell anyone else?'

Sam smiled. 'Yes, maybe I should do it the old-fashioned way and ask your father for your hand in marriage. He isn't likely to refuse, is he?'

'No, I'm sure he will be pleased, and so will Mum, although they might not have expected it quite so soon.'

'But I'm sure, and so are you, so there's no point in waiting any longer ... to become engaged, I mean. And also...' he said with a questioning smile, 'to move our relationship on a stage further? I've held back, Valerie, darling. I've tried to curb my feelings for you until I was sure that you loved me, too. I know that I love you in every possible way, and I hope, so much, that you feel the same?'

Val felt a slight blush colour her cheeks as she answered, 'Yes, I do, Sam. I've never felt surer about anything.' She looked down at the sparkling ring on her finger. 'I love the ring, it's so beautiful. Just what I would have chosen myself. How very clever you are, and just the right size as well.'

'Yes, I bought it in Leeds a couple of weeks ago, with the understanding that they could make it larger or smaller. I felt sure you would like the design, and I was almost sure that you would say yes. All the same, my heart was in my mouth until you gave me an answer.'

'I shall wear it with pride while we're away,' she said. 'But when we get home perhaps I'd better keep it hidden until you've seen my parents. Then we can tell everybody, can't we?' A sudden thought struck her. 'Do your parents know about this?' she asked. It was his mother that she was really thinking about.

'No, not yet. I've told Jonathan and Thelma. They were very pleased, and not at all surprised.'

Val reflected how Sam's brother had changed over the past year. She knew that his change of heart had been brought about by the support he had had from Sam about his hasty marriage, and also by Thelma's attitude towards her, Val, and her relationship with Sam. She had found the young woman to be an unexpected ally and she looked forward to furthering their friendship.

'I don't think my parents will be surprised either,' said Sam. 'We will see your parents first, of course, then you must be with me when I tell mine that we are engaged and will soon be married. It will be soon, won't it, darling?'

'I hope so,' she replied. 'When do you think it should be? Next spring, or summer?'

'A spring wedding would be perfect. Maytime, perhaps? I'd really like it to be as soon as possible, but I suppose there will be all sorts of preparations to be made. You can be sure when my mother has got used to the idea – and I think she already has – there will be no stopping her. It will have to be the wedding of the year, like Jonathan and Thelma's.'

Val looked thoughtful as she answered. 'I would really prefer it to be … just a nice friendly occasion, nothing too flashy. My parents will be involved as well, you know – the parents of the bride – and they're not used to "a lot of palaver", as my dad might say.'

'Let's not worry about it now,' said Sam. 'To-night is just about us, you and me.' He raised his glass again, and Val did the same. 'To you and me,' he said, and Val repeated the words. They put their glasses down, and he took her in his arms in a passionate embrace.

Their love making was tender as well as ardent. Sam made sure that she would not find herself in the predicament that Thelma and Cissie had done. He was gentle and considerate, and Val felt that she was truly loved and cherished.

She returned to her own room at midnight, but lay awake for a while recalling with delight and wonder the happenings of the day. And looking forward to a future that was full of promise.

The publishers hope that this book has given you enjoyable reading. Large Print Books are especially designed to be as easy to see and hold as possible. If you wish a complete list of our books please ask at your local library or write directly to:

Magna Large Print Books
Magna House, Long Preston,
Skipton, North Yorkshire.
BD23 4ND

This Large Print Book for the partially sighted, who cannot read normal print, is published under the auspices of

THE ULVERSCROFT FOUNDATION